"A LARGE CAST, SWIFT PACING, AND GOOD LOCAL COLOR . . . A GRIPPING YARN."
—*Publishers Weekly*

Soldier. Cop. Lawyer. Dismas Hardy's done the tough jobs and had some tough luck. Now he's kicking back and tending bar at the Shamrock in San Francisco. But the past returns in the form of Rusty Ingraham—a former fellow prosecutor who drops by to warn Hardy that a perp they put away nearly ten years ago just got released . . . and might still be looking for revenge. Next thing Hardy knows, Ingraham's houseboat becomes a murder scene, with a dead woman aboard and Ingraham, presumably, at the bottom of the bay. To save himself, Hardy's got to solve the case. But there's more than one kind of payback, and it's not just the ex-con who might have wanted it. Now, as Hardy tangles with a mob enforcer, a rejected lover, and a renegade cop, he is haunted by the knowledge that the later you pay, the steeper the price. . . .

"[Lescroart has a] sensitive touch with psychologically complex characters . . . a tense, tough, page-turning plot."
—*Playboy*

continued . . .

Praise for the novels
of John Lescroart

The Motive

"Surpasses anything Grisham ever wrote and bears comparison with Turow."　　*—The Washington Post*

"Unfolds like a classic *Law & Order*."
—Entertainment Weekly

The Second Chair

"Lescroart gives his ever-growing readership another spellbinder to savor."　　*—Library Journal*

"Great characters and a wonderful sense of place."
—Chicago Tribune

The First Law

"With his latest, Lescroart again lands in the top tier of crime fiction."　　*—Publishers Weekly*

The Oath
A *People* Page-Turner

"A terrific crime story."　　　　　　　　*—People*

"Hardy and Glitsky are like good wine, improving with time."　　*—The Orlando Sentinel*

The Hearing

"A spine-tingling legal thriller."
—Larry King, USA Today

Nothing But the Truth

"Riveting . . . one of Lescroart's best tales yet."
—*Chicago Tribune*

The Mercy Rule

"Well-written, well-plotted, well-done."
—Nelson DeMille

Guilt

"Begin *Guilt* over a weekend. . . . If you start during the workweek, you will be up very, very late, and your pleasure will be tainted with, well, guilt."
—*The Philadelphia Inquirer*

A Certain Justice

"A gifted writer . . . I read him with great pleasure."
—Richard North Patterson

"Engrossing." —*The San Francisco Examiner*

"A West Coast take on *The Bonfire of the Vanities* . . . richly satisfying." —*Kirkus Reviews*

The 13th Juror

"Fast-paced . . . sustains interest to the very end."
—*The Wall Street Journal*

Hard Evidence

"Engrossing . . . compulsively readable, a dense and involving saga of big-city crime and punishment."
—*San Francisco Chronicle*

Dead Irish

"Full of all the things I like. Lescroart's a pro."
—Jonathan Kellerman

ALSO BY JOHN LESCROART

THE
VIG

JOHN LESCROART

A SIGNET BOOK

SIGNET
Published by New American Library, a division of
Penguin Group (USA) Inc., 375 Hudson Street,
New York, New York 10014, USA
Penguin Group (Canada), 90 Eglinton Avenue East, Suite 700, Toronto,
Ontario M4P 2Y3, Canada (a division of Pearson Penguin Canada Inc.)
Penguin Books Ltd., 80 Strand, London WC2R 0RL, England
Penguin Ireland, 25 St. Stephen's Green, Dublin 2,
Ireland (a division of Penguin Books Ltd.)
Penguin Group (Australia), 250 Camberwell Road, Camberwell, Victoria 3124,
Australia (a division of Pearson Australia Group Pty. Ltd.)
Penguin Books India Pvt. Ltd., 11 Community Centre, Panchsheel Park,
New Delhi - 110 017, India
Penguin Group (NZ), cnr Airborne and Rosedale Roads, Albany,
Auckland 1310, New Zealand (a division of Pearson New Zealand Ltd.)
Penguin Books (South Africa) (Pty.) Ltd., 24 Sturdee Avenue,
Rosebank, Johannesburg 2196, South Africa

Penguin Books Ltd., Registered Offices:
80 Strand, London WC2R 0RL, England

Published by Signet, an imprint of New American Library, a division of Penguin Group (USA) Inc. Published by arrangement with the author. Previously published in Donald I. Fine, Inc., and Island editions.

First Signet Printing, August 2006
10 9 8 7 6 5 4 3 2 1

Copyright © John Lescroart, 1990
Excerpt from *The Hunt Club* copyright © The Lescroart Corporation, 2006

All rights reserved

Ⓟ REGISTERED TRADEMARK—MARCA REGISTRADA

Printed in the United States of America

Without limiting the rights under copyright reserved above, no part of this publication may be reproduced, stored in or introduced into a retrieval system, or transmitted, in any form, or by any means (electronic, mechanical, photocopying, recording, or otherwise), without the prior written permission of both the copyright owner and the above publisher of this book.

PUBLISHER'S NOTE
This is a work of fiction. Names, characters, places, and incidents either are the product of the author's imagination or are used fictitiously, and any resemblance to actual persons, living or dead, business establishments, events, or locales is entirely coincidental.

The publisher does not have any control over and does not assume any responsibility for author or third-party Web sites or their content.

If you purchased this book without a cover you should be aware that this book is stolen property. It was reported as "unsold and destroyed" to the publisher and neither the author nor the publisher has received any payment for this "stripped book."

The scanning, uploading, and distribution of this book via the Internet or via any other means without the permission of the publisher is illegal and punishable by law. Please purchase only authorized electronic editions, and do not participate in or encourage electronic piracy of copyrighted materials. Your support of the author's rights is appreciated.

To Al Giannini

1

At 2:15 on a Wednesday afternoon in late September, Dismas Hardy sat on the customer side of the bar at the Little Shamrock and worked the corners of his dart flights with a very fine emery board. A pint of Guinness, pulled a quarter of an hour ago, had lost its head and rested untouched in the bar's gutter. Hardy whistled tonelessly, as happy as he'd been in ten years.

He'd opened the bar at 1:00 P.M. sharp and had served a bottle of Miller Draft to Tommy, a regular who'd retired from schoolteaching some years back and who now spent most afternoons by the large picture window, talking to whoever would listen. But today Tommy told Hardy he had an appointment and left after one beer. Tommy was all right, but being left alone didn't break Hardy's heart.

Hardy finished one flight and raised his head. He took the Guinness and sipped at it. Through the window over Tommy's table, light traffic passed on Lincoln Blvd. Across the street, the evergreens and eucalyptus that bordered Golden Gate Park shimmered in a light breeze. There had been no fog that morning, and Hardy guessed the breeze would still be warm. If you want summer in San Francisco, plan your vacation for the fall.

A bus pulled up across the street and stopped. When it pulled away, it left a man standing, lost looking, at the corner.

A minute later, the double doors swung open;

Hardy scooped up his flights and swung himself around the end of the bar. He stood behind the porcelain beer taps and nodded at the customer.

If it was a customer. At first glance, the man didn't bring to mind visions of bankrolls and limousines. Whether he had sufficient money for a beer seemed questionable. His shirt was open at the collar and frayed badly. His baggy pants needed pressing. Under a forehead that went all the way back, eyes squinted adjusting to the relative darkness of the bar, although the Shamrock was no cave. He needed a shave.

"Help you?" Hardy asked, then as he looked more closely, the pieces began to fall into place. "Rusty?"

The man let loose a low-watt smile that seemed to require an effort. He stepped closer to the bar. "Ten points." He stuck his hand over the bar and Hardy took it. "How you doin', Diz?" The voice was quiet and assured, cultured.

Hardy asked what he was drinking and said it was on him.

"Same as always."

Hardy closed his eyes, trying to remember, then turned and reached up to the top shelf, grabbed a bottle of Wild Turkey, and snuck a glance at the man who'd shared his office back in the days when they'd both worked for the district attorney.

Rusty Ingraham had aged. There was, of course, the hair, or lack of it. At twenty-five, Rusty had sported a shock of orange-red hair and a handlebar mustache. Now, with no facial hair except the stubble, bald on top and gray on the sides, he looked old—handsome still, but old.

Hardy poured him a double.

"Prodigious," Rusty Ingraham said, nodding at his glass.

Hardy shrugged. "You know somebody at all, you know what they drink."

"Well, you found your calling." He lifted the glass, Hardy raised his pint, and they both said "Skol."

"So"—Hardy put down his glass—"you still a lawyer?"

Ingraham's lips turned up, yet there was a gentleness Hardy hadn't seen before. Before he'd left the D.A.'s, Ingraham might have had some sensitivity but it didn't ever come out gentle. Now his half-smile was that of a man looking back only. The good times, whatever they'd been, would never—could never—return. He sipped slowly at his whiskey. "You must have been out of the field awhile yourself if you still call them lawyers."

Hardy grinned. It was an old joke. "Attorney then—you still an attorney?"

Like a flame trying to catch on a wick, the smile flickered back. Hardy was getting the feeling Ingraham hadn't spoken to a soul in a long while. "I still have that distinction." He paused. "Though I rarely stand upon the 'Esquire' in correspondence, and as you can see"—he gestured at his clothing—"my practice is in a hiatus." He drank again, like a drinking man but not hungrily, not like an alcoholic. There was a difference, and Hardy was keyed to it.

"You do this full-time?"

Hardy's eyes swept the room, proprietary. "Nine years now. I own a quarter of the place."

"That's great. And you're still with Jane?"

"Well, we got divorced once, but we're going at it again." He shrugged. "I'm confident but cautious."

"Yep. You always were."

"So what about you? I noticed you came by on the bus."

Their eyes met a moment, then the flame of Rusty's smile went out. "I got my car stolen a month ago. It's still gone. A major hassle. So I spend a lot of time waiting for the N-Godot."

Hardy liked that. The N-Judah, which ran behind the Shamrock, was a notoriously slow line.

"Otherwise, you pretty much see it, Diz. I hang out. I live in a barge down at China Basin. Chase an ambulance every month or two, hit a good nag now and then. I've still got one good suit. I get my shoes shined and for a day or two I can get by."

He tipped up his glass and asked Hardy if he could buy him one. He put a ten-dollar bill in the gutter. Hardy refilled them both but didn't grab the bill.

"Actually, Diz, I came by here today for a reason. You remember Louis Baker?"

Hardy frowned. He remembered Louis Baker. "Eight aggravated to thirteen?"

"Nine and a half, it turns out."

"Nine and a half," Hardy repeated. "Hardly worth the effort."

"Not even hardly."

Hardy took a belt of his stout, set the glass down, and swore. "I must've sent down a hundred guys. You too," he said.

Ingraham nodded. "All told, I put away two hundred and fourteen assholes."

Hardy whistled. "You were red-hot, weren't you?"

"Yeah, but there was only one Louis Baker."

Baker had been a cancer in Hunter's Point for the first twenty years of his life. He had a huge head, a well-trimmed Afro, and the body of a defensive safety. In spite of having a sheet ranging from the petty—vandalism and car theft, burglary and muggings—when he was in his teens to the heinous as he matured, he was convinced he would never do hard time, and not without reason.

The D.A. had been forced to drop charges on him twice for murder and four times for rape. He was good at not leaving evidence, or at making witnesses reluctant to testify.

The one time Baker went to trial for attempted murder and mayhem on a man who had talked too long to his girlfriend in a 7-Eleven, the man had finally refused to identify him when the crunch came. He got all the way to the stand, then looked at Baker at the defendant's table and evidently decided that if he pointed the finger at him, he would not live to see his grandchildren. So he suddenly couldn't say for sure that Baker had been the man who'd cut off his ears before stabbing him in the stomach in the middle of the afternoon.

Hardy had been the prosecutor in that case.

The D.A.'s office—Rusty Ingraham this time—had finally gotten him for armed robbery of four victims, one of whom he'd wounded, but as it was only Baker's first conviction, meaning that in the court's eyes he wasn't yet a hardened criminal and hence a candidate for rehabilitation, the judge had been inclined to be lenient and had given him eight years.

When the verdict came down, Baker had quietly hung his head for a short time, then looked over at the prosecution table. Hardy had wanted to come down for the verdict, see this guy finally get put away, and he was sitting next to Ingraham. Baker looked in their direction, directly at Ingraham, seemingly memorizing him.

"You, motherfucker," he said, "are a dead man."

The judge slammed his gavel. Ingraham made a motion to aggravate Baker's sentence in view of the threat, and the judge slapped on another five right then and there.

The bailiff got the huge man to his feet, got some help from two deputies, and started pulling him across the courtroom while he glared at Ingraham.

Then Hardy did a stupid thing.

Baker's glaring, his posing, his tough-guy bullshit struck Hardy funny for a second—for just a second. But it was enough.

Here was this twenty-one-year-old punk, going down for a long time, who thought his ghetto glare was going to put the fear of God or something into the man who'd sent him there. So when Baker, struggling in his chains, fixed Hardy with the Eye, Hardy pursed his lips and blew him a good-bye kiss.

At which point Baker had really gone birdshit, pulling loose from the bailiff and two deputies and nearly getting to the prosecution table before he was quieted down with nightsticks.

The scene replayed itself in Hardy's dreams for months; it wasn't helped by the letter Hardy received during Baker's first week in prison. He'd found out who Hardy was from his own lawyer, and when he got out, the letter said, he was going to kill Hardy too.

Hardy sent copies of the letter to the warden and the judge who'd sentenced Baker, but the parole board ruled on these matters, and since the judge had already bumped his time for threats, they didn't feel compelled to do it again. The letter Hardy received back from the warden explained that although many inmates were bitter just after sentencing, most came around to serving good time and concentrating on getting an early parole.

Most, maybe.

Baker? Hardy wasn't so sure.

"So he's out?"

Ingraham pulled his cuff back and checked his watch. Hardy wasn't positive, but it looked to be a hell of a Rolex. "If they're on time, in about two hours."

"How'd you hear about it?"

"I got a friend in Paroles. He called me. And I checked with the warden at the House. Nobody's meeting him at the gate. Who would? Supposedly taking the bus back to town."

Hardy whistled. "You *have* checked."

"The guy got my attention."

"So what are you going to do?"

His old office mate sipped at his drink. "What can you do? Something's gonna get us all. Maybe lock up more carefully."

"Did you ever pack?"

Ingraham shook his head. "That's for you cops. We gentlemen who believe in the rule of law are supposed to have no need for that hardware."

Hardy had come up to the D.A.'s office after a tour in Vietnam and several years on the police force. Ingraham had come up through Stanford, then Hastings Law School.

"You planning to debate with Louis Baker?"

"I'm not planning on seeing the man."

"What if he comes to see you?"

"I called the warden after I got the word. He says Louis has been a model inmate, has found the Lord, gets max time off for good behavior. I've got nothing to worry about. Neither of us do. Evidently."

Hardy leaned across the bar. "Then why are you here?"

Ingraham's smile finally caught. "Because it sounds like a heap of bullshit to me." He leaned back on the barstool. "I thought it might not be a bad idea to stay in touch for a couple of weeks, you and me."

Hardy waited, not getting it.

"I mean, call each other every day at the same time, something like that."

"What would that do?"

"Well, hell, Diz, we're not going to get police protection. Nobody's gonna put a tail on Louis to see if he heads for our neighborhoods. This way, if one of us doesn't call, at least we have some clue. One of us bites it, maybe, but the other one is warned."

Hardy picked up his Guinness and downed the last two inches. "You think he really might do it, don't you."

"Yep. I'm afraid I do."

"Jesus . . ."

"One other thing . . ."

"Yeah?"

"I thought you might recommend what kind of gun."

Jane was in Hong Kong buying clothes for I. Magnin. She would be back this weekend.

They hadn't quite formalized living together again, although some of Jane's clothes hung in the closet in Hardy's bedroom. She still had her house—their old house—on Jackson, and would stay there once in a while, on nights she worked late downtown. But three or four nights a week for the past three months she'd slept here, out in the Avenues, with her ex-husband.

Padding now from room to room, he realized how much he had come to need her again. Well, not need. You didn't really need anybody to survive. But once you got beyond survival, you needed somebody if you wanted to feel whole, or alive, or whatever it was that made getting up something to look forward to rather than dread.

After he'd finished his shift and Moses McGuire had come in to spell him at the Shamrock, he shot five or six games of 301 to keep his hand-eye sharp. The newly formed flights worked well, and he held his place at the line until he was ready to quit, leaving unbeaten.

He drove home in darkness, parking his Suzuki Samurai, which he called his Seppuku, on the street in front of the only white picket fence on the block. Inside, he cooked a steak in a black cast-iron pan and ate it with a can of peas. He fed the tropical fish in the tank in the bedroom, read a hundred pages of Barbara Tuchman and realized anew that the world had probably always been very much like the wonderful place it was today; he went into his office to open his safe and look at his guns.

He'd recommended to Rusty that he consider buying a regulation .38 police Special. It was a no-frills firearm that, using hollow-point slugs, you nicked a guy on the pinkie and he'd spin around like a ballerina and hit the ground.

Hardy lifted his own Special from the safe. The Colt .44 was more of a show gun, and heavy, and the .22 target pistol might stop a charging tree rat, but that was about it. The Special was the one.

He pulled a box of bullets from the back of the safe and carefully loaded the weapon. Immediately he was nervous and walked into his bedroom, opened a drawer in his night table and deposited the Special there.

It was 9:48. He figured he would sit at his desk and wait for Rusty's call at 10:00, then watch some *L.A. Law* and turn in—a quiet night.

He picked the three darts out of the board across from his desk and starting throwing, easy and loose, trying not to think about Louis Baker, or Jane, or Rusty Ingraham.

Someone had once told him that the way to turn water into gold is to go to the middle of a jungle and light a fire and put a pot of water on to boil. Now, you ready? Here's the trick. For a half hour, don't think of a lion. Pick up your pot of gold and go home.

Hardy checked the clock on his desk. It was 10:12. Maybe he'd gotten it mixed up and they weren't starting until tomorrow morning at 10:00. Still.

He took the piece of paper that Rusty had given him and dialed the number. The phone rang eight times and Hardy hung up. Anyway, Rusty was supposed to call him at night, and Hardy call Rusty in the morning, unless one of them was not going to be home. Then they'd change the schedule on those days. It was only going to be for two weeks.

At 10:35 he tried again. They must have said they'd start the next morning.

Hardy wasn't tired. None of this seemed very real, but he did lie down on his bed and take the Special out of the drawer next to him. He flipped off the light and pulled a comforter over him, his clothes still on, the gun in his hand. He looked at the clock by his bed. It was 11:01.

No call.

2

It was dark when the telephone rang in the kitchen. Hardy, gun in hand, woke up from another of his fitful dozes, flicked on the kitchen light and got to it before the second ring.

"Rusty?"

"Who's Rusty?"

A woman's voice, far away, crackled on the wire after a short delay.

Hardy's head was clearing. "God, it's good to hear your voice."

"Were you asleep?"

The clock on the stove read 3:10. "It's three o'clock in the morning here," he said. "I was just jogging around the neighborhood and happened to hear the phone."

"In the morning? I can't get this straight at all."

"It's okay."

"I don't even know what day it is. There, I mean."

"That's all right. I'm right here and I don't know what day it is."

"And who's Rusty?"

Jane was halfway around the world and there was no need to worry her. "My old office mate. I was just having a dream, I guess."

He held the telephone's mouthpiece in one hand and became aware of the gun in the other. He almost thought of telling her then. Look, sweetie, I'm standing in my kitchen holding a loaded .38 Special and

I am considering the possibility that someone, who's probably good at it, is trying to kill me. But don't worry. Have a good time in Hong Kong. Don't think about lions.

What he did was ask her how her trip was going.

"Good, except it looks like I've got to stay another week, maybe ten days."

"Peachy."

Silence.

"Dismas?"

"I'm here. I was just doing a few cartwheels."

"This happens, you know."

"I know. I'm sorry. I'd just like to see you."

"Me, too." She went on to explain about the vagaries of supply in the East. Ships carrying thousands of bolts of material from the labor-cheap factories in the Philippines, Thailand and Korea coming in to Hong Kong to be made into designer clothes by the—relatively—labor-cheap tailors there.

"But we can't commit, really, I mean buy, unless we see the colors, feel the quality of the material."

"I know," Hardy said. "Feel the quality . . ."

"And two of the ships are running late. They could come in earlier but even so, it'll take a few days to go through the bolts."

"I got it, really." Hardy put the gun on the counter. "It doesn't thrill me, but I'll live." Poor Dismas. "Otherwise, how's the trip going?"

"Well, people are starting to get nervous about ninety-seven. You can feel it already. Nobody wants to talk long-range, like by next year some plans may evolve and the Brits will be gone. It's weird."

"It's better," Hardy said. "People ought to remember they might be gone by next year."

Jane paused. "My cheerful ex-husband."

"Hey, not so ex-."

"Not so cheerful either. Gone by next year! You can't live thinking like that."

Hardy wanted to tell her you'd better, that even a year was pretty optimistic. He was tempted to remind her that their son hadn't even made it that year, but he let it pass. She didn't need to be reminded of that. "You're right," he said. "You can't live like that."

"Dismas, are you all right?" she asked. "Are you doing anything for fun?"

"I am tearing up the town. I'd just rather be doing it with you." He realized he was being a pain in the ass. "Look, I'm sorry. It's three A.M. and you tell me you'll be gone another week. I'm a little disoriented, is all. A little case of vu zjahday."

"Vu zjahday?"

"Yeah. It's the opposite of déjà vu. The sense that you've never been somewhere before."

Jane laughed. "Okay, you're all right."

"I'm all right."

"I love you," she said.

"Maybe when you get home we talk some long-range, huh?"

A beat, or it might have been the delay on the line. "It could happen," she said.

Frank Batiste wasn't sure anymore that he was happy to have made lieutenant. It was more money and that was all right, but sitting here in the office all day, the conduit for gripes going up and edicts coming down, was wearing him down.

In ancient times they killed the bearer of bad news, and he was starting to understand why. Maybe, somehow, the news would go away, or wouldn't have to be thought about.

He couldn't just hide in here all day. He forced himself up from his chair, feeling the beginning of back pain, and opened the door.

The homicide department was commencing to take

on the feel of a country-club locker room. Several golf bags leaned against desks.

He walked back through the room, nodding at the guys and getting ice for his troubles. Hell, it wasn't his doing. He even sided with the men. Maybe he should step down as looie, let someone else deal with this crap. But what would that do? Just put someone else in, someone who wouldn't be as sympathetic to the team.

If only the City That Once Knew How had a god-damn clue, he thought. Now it didn't know how to wipe its own ass. And nowhere was it more clear than here in Homicide. These fourteen guys—it sounded funny, but was true anyway—were the shock troops against the worst elements in the city. No one got to Homicide without nearly a decade of solid police work, without a lot of pride, and without some special mix of killer instinct, stubbornness and brains. These guys were the elite, and if you cut their morale you had a problem.

But last week, for the first time in seven years, the department had brought charges against two men on the squad. A month before, the two officers—Clarence Raines and Mario Valenti—had gone to arrest a telephone-company executive named Fred Treadwell for murdering his lover and his lover's new boyfriend. Treadwell had resisted arrest—kicking out a window of his second-story apartment, cutting his head upon his exit, falling to the alley below, breaking an ankle, smashing his head again as he pitched into some gar-bage cans and escaping on foot to his attorney's office.

Treadwell and all the other principals in this triangle being gay, his attorney immediately called a press con-ference and trotted poor Fred out with his cuts, breaks and bruises, charging police brutality.

Valenti and Raines, two of the elite with perfect records, had, it seemed, suddenly not been able to contain their prejudice against gays (probably as a re-

sult of their own latent homosexuality), and had
beaten Fred to within an inch of his life, leaving him
for dead in the alley behind his apartment.

Somebody took Fred's lame story—or the righteous
outrage of the gay community—seriously enough to
bust Raines and Valenti and begin a formal
investigation.

As if that weren't enough, at about the same time
as the charges came down, the latest budget cuts were
announced. Effective immediately, no overtime was
to be approved for "routine procedural work," which
meant writing reports and serving subpoenas.

A significant number of murder cases now were
what they called NHI cases. It stood for "No Humans
Involved," and a kind interpretation meant that the
victim, the suspect and all the witnesses were at best
petty criminals.

These people were not fond of policemen and
tended to be hard to find during normal business
hours. So the service of subpoenas would most often
take place in the early morning or late at night, and
the cops going out after their witnesses would put in
the overtime knowing this was their best chance of
doing their job. Now the city had decided it wasn't
going to pay for that.

Which led to the golf clubs. The guys went out at
eight or nine o'clock, knocked at doors, found no one
home, played a round of golf, went back to the same
doors and tried again, still found no one home, came
back to the office, and wrote reports on their day in
the field.

It sucked and everybody knew it.

Jess Mendez nodded at the lieutenant and called
over his shoulder. "Hey, Lanier! What time you tee
off?"

Batiste didn't turn around. He heard Lanier behind
him. "I got three subpoenas first. Say nine-thirty."

Abe Glitsky's desk was near the back window with

a view of the freeway and, beyond it, downtown.
Today, however, at 7:50, there was no view but gray.

Glitsky did not have a bag of clubs leaning against
his desk. He was also one of only two men in the
squad who worked without a partner. He and Batiste
had come up to Homicide the same year, and neither
of them had given a shit about their minority status—
Glitsky was half Jewish and half black, Batiste a
"Spanish-surname"—so there was a bond of sorts between them.

Batiste pulled up a chair. "Forget your clubs, Abe?"

Glitsky looked up from something he was writing.
"I was just going to come see you."

"Complete a foursome?"

Abe moved his face into what he might have
thought was a smile. He had a hawk nose and a scar
through his lips, top to bottom. His smile had induced
confessions from some bad people. He might be a nice
person somewhere in there, but he didn't look like
one. "I'm glad you think it's funny," he said.

"I don't think it's funny."

Abe put his pen down. "Flo and I, we're thinking
we might make a move."

"What are you talking about?" This was worse than
golf clubs.

"L.A.'s recruiting. I'd have to go back to Burglary
maybe for a while, but that'd be all right."

Batiste leaned forward. "What are you talking
about? You've got, what, nineteen years?"

"Close, but they'll transfer most of 'em." He motioned down at his desk. "I was just working on the
wording here on this application. See where it says
'Reason for leaving last job?' Should I say 'incredible
horseshit' or keep it clean with 'bureaucratic non-
sense'?"

Batiste pulled up to the desk. "Abe, wait a minute."
He wasn't about to say Abe couldn't quit—of course
he could quit—but he had to say something. He put

his hand on the paper. "Can you just *wait* a god-damn minute."

Abe's stare was flat. "Sure," he said. "I can wait all day."

"You know it'll turn around."

Abe shook his head. "No, I don't, Frank. Not any-more. It's the whole city. It doesn't need us, and I don't need it."

"But it does need us—"

"No argument there. Give me a call when it finds out." Abe took the paper back and glanced at it again. " 'Incredible horseshit,' " he said. "It's a stronger statement, don't you think?"

Hardy parked at the end of the alley and turned up the heater. His Samurai was not airtight and the wind hissed at the canvas roof. On both sides, buildings rose to four stories, and in front of him fog obscured the canal and the shipyards beyond.

It was not yet 8:30. The gun—still loaded—was in his glove compartment. It was a registered weapon. It was probably one of the few legally concealable fire-arms in San Francisco. Hardy's ex-father-in-law was Judge Andy Fowler, and when Hardy left the force, he'd applied for a CCW (Carry a Concealed Weapon) license, which was never, in the normal course of San Francisco events, approved.

But Judge Fowler was not without influence, and he did not fancy his daughter becoming a widow. Not that being allowed to pack a weapon would necessarily make any difference. But he had talked Hardy into it, and this was the first time Hardy had had occasion to carry the thing around.

Okay, he would legally carry it then, even concealed if he wanted to.

He turned off the ignition. He slowly spun the cylin-der on the .38, making sure again that it was loaded.

Stepping out into the swirling fog, he lifted the collar of the Windbreaker with his left hand. In his right hand, the gun felt like it weighed fifty pounds.

He hesitated. "Stupid," he said out loud.

But he moved forward.

The alley ended in a walkway that bounded the China Basin canal. To Hardy's left an industrial warehouse hugged the walkway, seeming—from Hardy's perspective—to lean over the canal further and further before it disappeared into the fog. The canal, at full tide, lapped at the piling somewhere under Hardy. There was no visible current. The water was greenish brown, mercury-tinged by the oil on its surface.

Behind Hardy the Third Street Bridge rumbled as traffic passed. Somewhere ahead of him was another bridge. Ingraham had told him that his was the fourth mooring down from Third, between the bridges.

Hardy walked into the wind, his head tucked, the gun pointing at the ground.

The first mooring—little more than some tires on a pontoon against the canal's edge and a box for connecting electricity—was empty. A Chinese couple approached, walking quickly, hand in hand. They nodded as they came abreast of Hardy. If they noticed the gun they didn't show it.

The second mooring, perhaps sixty feet along, held a tug, which looked deserted. Next was a blue-water cruiser, a beauty which Hardy guessed was a thirty-two-footer, named *Atlantis*.

He wasn't sure he'd want to name a boat after something that had gone down into the ocean.

Ingraham had called his home a barge. It was a fair description—a large, flat, covered box that squatted against the pontoon's tires, its roof at about the height of Hardy's knees.

Getting there finally, seeing that the electrical wires were hooked up, suddenly the whole thing seemed crazy again. He was just being paranoid. He looked at his watch. 8:40.

Rusty should be up by now anyway.

Hardy leaned down. "Rusty?"

A foghorn bellowed from somewhere.

"Hey, Rusty!"

Hardy put the gun in his pocket and vaulted onto the barge's deck. Three weathered director's chairs were arranged in the area in front of the doorway. Green plants and a tomato bush that needed picking livened up the foredeck.

A two-pound salmon sinker nailed to the center of the door was a knocker. Hardy picked it up and let it drop, and the door swung open. There was no movement from inside, no sound but the lapping canal and the traffic, now invisible back through the fog. The wood was splintered at the jamb.

Hardy put his hands in his pocket, feeling the gun there, taking it back out. He ducked his head going through the door, descending three wooden steps to the floor-level inside.

A line of narrow windows high on the walls probably provided light normally, but curtains had been pulled across them on both sides. The room was cold, colder than it was outside.

In the dim light from the open doorway, nothing seemed out of place. There was a telephone on a low table in front of a stylish low couch. Hardy picked up the receiver, heard a dial tone, put it back down.

Then he saw the pole lamp lying on the floor on the other side of the room. He reached up and pulled back the curtain for a little more light. The lamp's globe was broken into five or six pieces scattered around the floor.

At the junction of the rear and side walls a swinging half-door led to the galley. Another door in the center of the rear wall was ajar. Hardy kicked at it gently. It opened halfway, then caught on something. A wide line of black something ran from under the door to the wall.

Hardy stepped over it, pushing his way through. His stomach rose as though he were seasick, and he leaned against the wall.

What was blocking the door was a woman's arm. Naked, she was stretched out as though reaching for something, as though she'd been crawling—trying to get out? There was something around her neck— something strange, metallic—holding her head up at an unnatural angle. Hardy realized it was a neck brace. Hardy looked back to the stateroom.

It was painted in blood.

There was a sound like something dropping on the front deck and he dropped to one knee, steadying the gun with both hands and aiming for the hall doorway.

"This is the police," he heard. "Throw out your weapon and come out with your hands up."

3

Like the other housing projects in San Francisco, Holly Park had at one time been a nice place to live. The two-story units were light and airy. The paint and trim had been fresh. Residents who did not keep their yards up to neighborhood standards could, in theory, be fined, although such infractions were rare due to the pride people took in their homes.

In 1951 seedlings had been planted to shade and gentrify the place—eucalyptus, cypress, magnolia. Within the square block that bounded Holly Park there were three communal gardens and a children's playground with swing sets and monkey bars and slides. Curtains hung behind shining windows. In the four grassy spaces between buildings, now each a barren no-man's-land called a cut and "owned" by a crack dealer, people had hung laundry and fixed bicycles.

One hundred eighty-six people over eighteen claimed residence in Holly Park. There were one hundred seventeen children and juveniles. Every known resident was black. One hundred fifty-nine of the adults had police records. Of the juveniles between twelve and eighteen, sixty-eight percent had acquired rap sheets, most for vandalism, shoplifting, possession of dope, several for mugging, burglary and rape, and three for murder.

There were four nuclear families—a man, his legal

wife and their children—in Holly Park. The rest was a fluid mass of women with children.

Because Holly Park was provided by the city and county for indigent relief, by definition every resident was on welfare, but twenty-two women and thirty men held "regular" jobs. The official reported per capita income of all the adults in Holly Park was $2,953.13, far below the poverty level.

Income from the sale of rock cocaine was estimated by the San Francisco Police Department to be between $1.5 and $3 million per year, broken down to about $50 to $75 per hour per cut, twenty-four hours a day, seven days a week.

So far this year—and it was September—ninety-six percent of the residents of Holly Park over the age of seven had been victims, perpetrators or eyewitnesses to a violent crime.

Police response time to an emergency in Holly Park averaged twenty-one minutes. By contrast, in the posh neighborhood of St. Francis Wood, it averaged three and a half minutes, and Police Chief Rigby was upset about how long it took.

Some people believed that the solution to the drug and crime problems in the projects was to put a wall around them and let the residents kill each other off.

There are all kinds of walls.

Louis Baker was cold.

He opened his eyes, awake now, unsure of where he was. It was dark in the room, but a slice of gray light made its way through where the plywood sagged off the window. The box spring he had slept on had a familiar smell. He sat up, pulling the old army blanket around his massive bare shoulders.

At least it not be the joint, he thought. Praise God.

He stood up, shivering in his bare feet, and put on the suit pants they had given him when they let him out the day before. He crossed to the crack at the window and looked down into one of the cuts.

Pretty much the same. Gray building, gray fog, the constant wind. No trees, no grass, nowhere to run, nowhere to hide. Martha Reeves and the Vandellas. Now it was Rap, already coming up from three, four places. That was cool. Faces changed, music changed, even people sometimes. But it was the same turf, his old turf. Territory, turf. You controlled it you could be happy. The constant.

He pulled the blanket up closer and put his eye to the crack, checking down the cut. Kids standing around. Some business maybe going down.

His Mama called out from down below. "You movin', child? You up?"

She was not his mother but he called her Mama. He was not even sure they were related. She had just always been around, always been Mama.

"Comin' down," he said.

Mama dressed exactly the same. There was no fashion here in Holly Park. There were no politics. Nothing external was going to change things here. Louis knew that. It was all inside, as it had been for him.

Mama was large. She sat sipping instant coffee at her Formica table. Her hair was held by pins and covered, mostly, with a bandanna. She wore a plaid flannel shirt, untucked, over a pair of faded blue jeans that was tearing at the seams by her generous hips.

Louis kissed her, spooned some coffee crystals into a mug, poured boiling water over it and sat down across from her.

"It's good to be home."

"What you be doing now?"

Louis shrugged, blowing on his cup. "Get a job. Something. Got to work."

"An' be careful, right?"

He reached over and touched her face. "Don't you worry, Mama. Nothin' else, I learned careful."

But he wondered then, for a second, if it was true. When they let him out, he had not given a thought to careful. But seeing Ingraham just when he got out had brought it all back. Back on the streets, he best be careful every minute.

He saw Ingraham again—taking care of business before he had even come down here to Mama's—and his blood ran hot. The rage was still there. Beatin' it was the thing.

He gripped at his mug with both hands, bringing it to his mouth.

But that had been old business. Finished now, he hoped. He wouldn't have any cause to think about it again. It was settled.

" 'Cause out there, you know . . ." Mama motioned to the back door.

Louis followed her glance, then scanned the kitchen. Over the stove the paint was peeling in wide sheets. A poster of Muhammad Ali was taped up next to a religious calendar—he noted the suffering Christ.

Mama kept the place pretty clean, but she was old. What was the point of putting in a window over the sink? The plywood wouldn't break—it kept out the wind. It made the kitchen dark, but dark was safer. The whole house was dark.

"I know 'bout out there, Mama. Here's what I do, so you don't worry. I go see the man, he set me up or not. Come back here and start setting up."

"Set up what?"

He stood up, leaning over to kiss her. "The house, Mama. We gonna clean house."

"Hardy in chains," Glitsky said. "I like it."

"It is a good time," Hardy agreed. He had stood up when Glitsky entered the living room, and now one of the patrolmen was unlocking the cuffs. "Damn,

those things work good." He opened and closed his
fingers, rubbing his wrists, trying to get the circulation
going. "If this affects my dart game, I'm suing the
city."

Glitsky, ignoring Hardy, asked Patrolman Thomas
if he could stand outside and direct the homicide-
scene team below as it arrived.

When he went outside the other patrolman, Ling,
said, "The body's in there."

Glitsky nodded. "What are you doing here?" he
asked Hardy.

"Long story."

"With a loaded gun?"

"Makes it longer." He shrugged. "It's registered.
I've got a permit."

Ling spoke up. Glitsky realized he was the shortest
cop he'd ever seen. When he had come up there'd
been a minimum height requirement of 5'8", but some
court had ruled that since many Asians were under
this height, the rule unfairly discriminated against a
class of people and therefore had to go.

Ling was about 5'5", but since he had been the one
left below to handle Hardy if he got feisty, Glitsky
assumed he could take care of himself.

"Can I see the gun?" he asked.

Ling handed over Hardy's weapon. He checked the
cylinder and clucked disapprovingly. "It's loaded," he
said to Hardy.

"It works better when it's loaded."

Glitsky flipped open the cylinder and let the bullets
fall, one by one, into the palm of his hand. He put
them into the pocket of his blue parka and smelled
the weapon. "It hasn't been fired."

"No, sir," Ling said. "I realize that."

"Come on, Abe," Hardy said. "I didn't shoot
anybody."

"My friend here has a rich fantasy life," Glitsky

said. He handed the gun back to Ling. "You think this is Dodge City or what? You can pick it up back at the Hall."

"Abe, it's a legal weapon."

"And this is a murder scene, Diz. It can't hurt to check the paper on it."

Hardy turned to Ling. "And what brought you guys out here?"

"The couple who lives on the next boat over were going out for a jog and passed you walking around with a gun in your hand. They saw you come in here, and they went back to their boat and reported it."

"The only two good citizens in San Francisco and I run into them on their morning jog."

"Good citizens abound in our fair city," Glitsky said.

"They are Chinese," Ling said, as if that explained it.

"All right. Let's go see the body."

"I hope you've had your breakfast," Hardy said.

From identification found in the purse by the bedside, the woman was tentatively identified as Maxine Weir, thirty-three years old. Her address was 964 Bush Street.

From the trail of blood, she had been shot the first time as she exited the bathroom after taking a shower. That first shot went through the towel that had been wrapped around her.

There was a splatter of blood on the wall by the door to the bathroom, as though she had either been spun around by the shot or had put her hand to the wound and then to the wall to steady herself.

It was impossible to determine the order of the remaining shots. One had entered high on the right breast and did not appear to exit, probably hitting the clavicle and ricocheting downward. A second had passed through the side of her abdomen and out her back. Another had hit her in the right thigh. She had clearly gone down by the bathroom and lay still—perhaps pretending to be dead—for a few minutes. A pool had formed there. Then she had crawled across the room and into the hallway, where she had died and where Hardy had found her.

Glitsky came away from the body with a glazed, guarded look. He had told Ling to wait in the living room to send in the techs. Hardy sat on an upholstered chair in the corner, elbows on knees, his hands folded.

"What about the bed?" he asked.

"I'm getting there."

A second trail of blood began on the bed, which was still made up. Someone had been lying on top of its covers when they'd been shot. The trail crossed the room like a thin strip of syrup to the back door. Glitsky opened the door.

There was a walkway about four feet wide that must have been used mostly for storage. Paint cans, cardboard boxes, a bicycle, other garage stuff filled the space on Glitsky's left, by the piling. The right side had been AstroTurfed. A large pot-style barbecue squatted by the other back door, which led to the galley. Paraphernalia for outdoor cooking hung on the wall by that door.

The blood drew a line in the middle of this area, swerved over the AstroTurf, paused and pooled at the railing, disappearing over the side of the barge.

Glitsky came back inside, shivering even in his parka. Hardy was standing now by the bed.

"The walking dead," Glitsky said.

"Look at this." Hardy knew enough not to touch anything. He had been a good cop once.

There was a small hole in the center of a splotch of blood on the bed, at about shoulder level if the victim's head had been on the pillow.

"Rusty was first, I guess," Hardy said. "He was sleeping, maybe. Lying down. She was in the shower, heard the shot, came out and got hers."

Glitsky jammed his hands further into his pockets. "What the hell are you talking about? Rusty who?"

"You don't know?"

"No."

Hardy let out a breath. "Ingraham. Rusty Ingraham. He lives, lived here. Louis Baker shot him."

Glitsky was looking somewhere over Hardy's shoulder, not focusing, putting it together. "Louis Baker."

"And I'm next."

"I'll have a cheeseburger with everything, to go."

The young man punched his register. "Would you like onions and pickles?"

Glitsky nodded. "Everything please."

"Will that be here or to go?"

"To go, please."

"That'll be one cheeseburger to go." He pushed some more buttons, waited until the machine stopped whirring, then looked up with relief. "That's two-sixty-seven."

Hardy, having just endured the same litany over a much more difficult order of two fish sandwiches, fries and a Diet Coke, rolled his eyes. "Do you want that here or to go, Abe?" he asked when the boy went to retrieve the order.

Glitsky kept his face straight.

They sat at a tiny yellow table on a stretch of sidewalk midway between the Third Street Bridge and the Southern Pacific Station. Every few minutes a train's whistle would sound, shrill and distant.

It was early afternoon. The fog had burned off completely and it was getting warm. They had stayed at Rusty Ingraham's barge through the morning, waiting while the techs photographed and collected and dusted, while the deputy M.E. had examined and moved Maxine Weir's body, while they had begun preparations to drag the canal.

Hardy opened his bag. "After all that, I get onion rings. Did I say fries or what?"

Glitsky chomped into his burger. "Twice, I think, maybe three times."

"Rocket scientist," Hardy said.

"No dumber than walking around with a loaded weapon out in the open. You should've called me first."

"And you would've come, right?" He had already told Abe why he was at the barge, about his telephone arrangement with Rusty.

Abe chewed some more. "Probably not."

"No probably about it."

Glitsky reached over and grabbed Hardy's drink. "You mind?" He sipped through the straw. "Louis Baker, huh?"

Hardy grabbed the cup back. "Louis Baker scares me, Abe. No kidding."

"Yeah, that makes sense. I think I'd be nervous myself. Baker know where you live? You moved since you were a D.A., right?"

"So did Rusty."

Glitsky chewed and swallowed. "So how'd he find him?"

"Maybe he's listed. He's a working—he was a working attorney."

"Quit talking about him in the past tense, would you?"

"He's dead, Abe. You know it and I know it."

"I don't know it. Maxine Weir is dead. Otherwise, we're dragging the canal, checking the blood type on the bed, see if we can match it to Rusty, see if we can find him. I'll let you know when I think he's dead."

"He's dead," Hardy said.

Glitsky shrugged. "Suit yourself."

"So what am I gonna do?"

"I don't know. About what?"

"About Louis fucking Baker, is what."

"Don't get all excited, Diz. We finish our lunch here and I locate Louis and drive down and have a talk with him."

"And what if he's sitting outside my house, or even in it, with a gun?"

Glitsky said, straight-faced, "That'd be in violation of his parole." The inspector finished his burger, took Hardy's cup back and had a last loud slurp of Hardy's drink through the straw. "Just don't you do anything, Diz. We frown on private citizens shooting one another."

"Yeah. Well, I frown on being shot at. I see him around my house, I'm going to shoot first."

Glitsky leaned across the table. "Do me a favor. Let him get a shot off. Make sure he's armed."

"The rules, huh?"

Glitsky nodded. "The rules, that's right." He stood up.

"I don't think Louis told Maxine about the rules," Hardy said. "Or Rusty either."

Glitsky picked up Hardy's cup and dumped some ice in his mouth. He chewed a minute. "Guess he forgot," he said. "Other things on his mind."

"When can I get my gun back?" Hardy said.

4

"You have to remember, Sergeant, that everyone we deal with is a convicted felon. Not some, not most—all."

The supervisor was a plain woman with a no-nonsense attitude that somehow managed to convey warmth. Perhaps it was the Oliver Peoples glasses—tiny little lenses magnifying robin's-egg eyes. The name on the little strip by her door said Ms. Hammond, and Glitsky liked her right away. She had the back-corner office in the Ferry Building, with a view over the water to Treasure Island, up to the Bay Bridge, out to Alcatraz. People paid three grand a month for one-room apartments with that view. It might be one of the perks of the job—he knew she didn't make that much.

Her office was clean and functional, brightened by the view and a small forest scattered in pots. Twenty-one parole officers reported to her.

"Well, what I meant was—"

"No. It's all right. It's just helpful to remember where these people are coming from. What they face outside."

"Well, it's possible our man—Louis Baker—was outside about an hour before he killed somebody."

Ms. Hammond sighed heavily, nodding. "Yes. That happens, too, I'm afraid." She scooted her chair across the floor from her pitted green desk to a battered

green file cabinet. After a minute looking at something, she sighed again. "You want to see Al Nolan."

"Is that bad news?"

She looked at her watch. "It's two-thirty. If he took
a normal lunch at noon, he might be back."

Glitsky wondered if the entire bureaucracy was
sinking, every department bogged down in bad faith
and bullshit. But Ms. Hammond faced him, shrugging.
Shrugs and sighs. She probably didn't know she did
it. "Some of them need more supervising than others.
Let me show you the way."

She led him down a long corridor that reminded
him of the Hall, into a large room that was subdivided
into cubicles.

Al Nolan, a white male in his late twenties, was
opening a Wendy's bag and putting the contents on
his desk. He wore a bowling shirt with the name Ralph
stitched over the right pocket. His long brown hair
didn't look too clean and was pulled back into a ponytail. "Al," Ms. Hammond said, "this is Inspector Sergeant Abe Glitsky . . ."

Nolan held up a hand. "Hey, it's my lunch hour.
You mind?"

Glitsky heard Ms. Hammond's intake of breath.
"Lunch is supposed to start from twelve to one-thirty,
somewhere in there, Al."

"Well, at noon I had to take my car down to the
garage, and the guy didn't have a clue what was
wrong, so I had to leave it and take the bus back.
You know the buses." He, too, shrugged.

"You know, Al, that sounds to me like two and a
half hours of your own time."

"Yeah, but I didn't get to eat yet."

Glitsky butted in. "They paying you for this?"
Turning to Ms. Hammond. "Excuse me."

"Hey, what? I'm not supposed to eat? We're enti-
tled to lunch."

Ms. Hammond, getting impatient, said, "And what

do you suppose the state of California gets to ask of you in exchange?"

Nolan chewed a few fries. "In exchange for what?"

"In exchange for your lunch break?"

"Hey, I do as much work as anybody here. More than some."

Glitsky just waited.

Ms. Hammond smiled. The warmth was gone. "You know, Al, that's just not true." She laid a hand on Glitsky's arm. "Mr. Nolan is on the state's time now, Sergeant. If his eating bothers you, he'll throw his"—she paused—"afternoon snack away." She turned and was gone.

Nolan rolled his eyes. "Her time of the month," he said, and gestured for Glitsky to pull up a chair. "Who we talking about now?"

Glitsky was tempted to get into it. This attitude was making him crazy. He wondered if Ms. Hammond's sweet grandmother nature wasn't really to blame, and everyone on the top ought to start right now being a hard-ass of the first order, whip things back into shape. Kick ass and take names. Fire people like Al Nolan. Then he remembered—nobody ever got fired from a government job. Kill your neighbors, come to work drunk, miss thirty days in a row calling in sick . . . hey, it robbed a person of dignity to take their job away.

Glitsky found himself sighing. "Louis Baker," he said. "We're talking about Louis Baker."

"Yeah, I just saw him this morning. Seemed okay, a pretty nice guy."

"Well, we think maybe he killed somebody last night."

Nolan took a bite of burger. "No shit? Well, these guys can be very cool about things."

"About killing people, you mean."

"Whatever. You know, they don't talk to us. They just check in, lie about having a job or an offer, then split."

"Did Louis Baker say he had a job?"

"Now you mention it, no." He seemed to ponder that a moment. "Well, he's only been out a day. Hasn't learned the ropes yet."

Glitsky leaned forward. "So what did you talk about?"

"Mostly the Giants, I guess."

Glitsky could have guessed, too. The Giants were in the thick of the pennant race.

"I think they'll stay in the city."

"Who?"

"Who we talking about, man? The Giants. I mean, a pennant is what we need. No way are they gonna let 'em go to San Jose if we get another pennant. The team is happening. Who'd Baker kill?"

"We don't know if he killed anybody. He's a suspect is all."

"He probably did."

"Why do you say that? You just said he was a nice guy."

Nolan shrugged. Glitsky wondered if people here all had shoulder and back problems from the shrugging. "So he's a nice guy. That just means he's got manners. I mean, everybody says Ted Bundy was the nicest guy you'd ever want to meet, and how many people did he ace, twenty, thirty?"

"So you figure Baker killed somebody. Why? Did he say anything to you about last night?"

"These guys kill each other."

"The victim wasn't black, Mr. Nolan."

"No shit. I just assumed."

"Caucasian woman."

"Well, maybe he was just unloading after all that time in." Nolan looked at Glitsky man-to-man. "You know." He pointed at his crotch. "No conjugal visits at the Q. Lot of guys get out and that's the first thing they do."

Glitsky, suddenly very weary, shook his head. "No, it wasn't that."

Nolan, thoughtful, chewing. "Well, they kill white guys too."

It was still early afternoon, balmy with a light breeze. Glitsky had the windows down on both sides of the Plymouth. Driving down Mission, he had intended to get on the freeway and head south to Holly Park and see if he could get a few words with Louis Baker.

But Al Nolan had gotten inside of him—young, hip, pony-tailed Al Nolan with his "Ralph" fifties-style bowling shirt, probably seriously thought he did a real job. And real clever to boot. Above it all with that glib shit that all these cons were just passing time before they went back. Jive about the Giants. For a minute Glitsky thought about bringing Al to the Hall and booking him for obstructing a homicide investigation. See how funny he thought that was.

He drummed his fingers on the dash. Then there was Marcel Lanier and the other cops in homicide with their damn golf clubs. What was the use?

He tried to get his mind kick-started back on Louis Baker. About why was he going down now to see Louis Baker. Sure, Hardy had *his* reasons. But for him, wasn't it the same reason Al Nolan had for assuming Baker was guilty—because he was a black ex-con?

There wasn't any hard evidence making him a suspect. There was Hardy's suspicion, and Hardy's fear. But Hardy, all white, points the finger at Baker, all black, and Abe Glitsky—half and half—jumps on the white wagon with both feet. Well, shit, why is that, Abe?

Look at the facts. Okay, so Hardy is your friend, and an ex-cop. Ex-cops also kill people. And Hardy was apprehended—let's not forget that, apprehended—there at the scene with a loaded weapon. Sure, he had his stated reasons, but why didn't Glitsky suspect him? Well, he knew Hardy. Also, Hardy's gun hadn't been fired. Still . . .

He pulled over and glanced at the yellow pad full of notes next to him on the seat.

Start at the beginning, Abe. Like you've done a hundred times before. Look at the victim. There aren't two victims, not yet. In spite of what Hardy might think, or say . . . There is one known victim. Her name is Maxine Weir and *she* lived at 964 Bush Street.

Louis Baker and Holly Park could wait. Let's see who the facts point to.

He put the car back in gear, passed the freeway entrance and turned up Van Ness toward Bush Street.

Hardy didn't even feel safe at the Hall of Justice.

He'd been there since before noon, trying to get his gun back. He had called Moses McGuire at home and asked him to trade shifts at the Shamrock. He had looked in at Judge Andy Fowler's—Jane's father—courtroom, but they had been in recess and the judge was not in his chambers.

They were being pissy about the gun. Glitsky was not above giving his friend a little object lesson in the letter of the law, and he had taken the weapon downtown so that Hardy could sign for its proper return, so the registration could be validated. Thank you, Abe.

But the gun had not even been logged in yet, and no one seemed in a hurry to get it done so Hardy could retrieve it.

Finally, realizing he probably wasn't going to have much luck, he took the elevator upstairs to the third floor, where the assistant D.A.s had their offices.

He found himself breathing more easily as he walked the long halls, hoping to recognize someone and give himself an excuse to stay inside and off the street. Up here, almost everyone wore a coat and tie or a uniform and most were white. Hardy did not suppose Louis Baker would get up in costume to blow him away. Downstairs, every black man Hardy saw had been turning before his eyes into Louis Baker, walking around free as a breeze, carrying a bullet with Hardy's name on it. If he felt that way in the Hall of Justice, where they had metal detectors at all entrances, Hardy did not want to think about what he would feel like outside.

There were about one hundred assistant district attorneys in San Francisco. Almost all of them—except a few political appointees who worked for the man himself, District Attorney Christopher Locke—plied their trade, two to a room, in ten-by-twelve offices equipped with two desks and whatever files, bookcases, posters, plants, mementos, and bits of evidence might have accumulated in the course of two busy people working on too many cases with not enough time.

There were no names on doors, no indication of rank or personality. Most of the doors into the hallway were closed, and a significant number of rooms with open doors were empty. Hardy did not remember if it had been like that when he had worked here. Probably, since nothing else seemed to have changed very much.

He passed the case-file library and leaned across the counter, looking in at the banks of color-tagged folders.

"What you want, Hardy?"

It was still Touva—a tiny round woman with Brillo hair who had already been an institution when Hardy started out. She forgot nothing and filed with a fanatical precision—if nothing else went right in a case, you could at least always get your files when you needed them. She looked at Hardy impatiently, by all signs unaware that he had not worked there in almost a decade.

"How you been, Touva?"

"I been busy, of course. You got a case number, Hardy? I got no time to chat."

"No case."

"Okay, then. Later."

Dismissed, he kept walking. A couple of faces looked familiar to him, but he was surprised that he saw no one he actually knew to talk to. Had it been that long? He felt like he'd gone back to his old high school.

Finally he stopped near a doorway where a studious young man was sitting in a chair studying blowups of photographs that Hardy did not want to look at too carefully. He had seen enough of that stuff firsthand this morning. He had already decided who he had to talk to.

"I'm trying to find Art Drysdale's office," he said.

The kid tore himself away. "Probably a good idea anyway," he said.

"Pardon?"

"Oh, sorry. Talking to myself. Probably a good idea to get away from this for a minute. Drysdale, you said?"

They walked back past the file library. Drysdale's office was two doors beyond it on the other side of the hall. As Hardy knocked, the kid, into his work, was already halfway back to his room.

"It's open."

Drysdale was turned away from the door, his feet propped up on the windowsill, talking on the telephone. There was no one at the other desk. Hardy moved some folders from a chair to the floor and sat to wait.

"No," he was saying. "No, we don't know that."

He listened. Hardy noticed his knuckles white on the receiver.

"You want my opinion, it's not even likely. I think it's a big mistake."

He said "uh huh" and "right" a few times, loosening his collar with one hand, the knuckles on the other one staying white. "All right. It's your decision." A beat, then loudly. " *'Course* I'll do it. It's what we do, isn't it? But it sucks, Chris. Sir. It really sucks." He slammed the phone down. "Son of a bitch."

He swiveled in his chair. "Yeah?" he began. Then, recognizing Hardy, "Hey!" He stood up, extended a hand. "Here's a sight for sore eyes. What brings you downtown?"

Pushing sixty, Drysdale still looked like he could put on a uniform and be right at home on the ballfield. Before turning to law he had been a star for USC and then played three years of pro ball, including forty-two games as a utility infielder in 1964 for the San Francisco Giants. A framed newspaper article on the wall of his office was headlined "Drysdale No Relation to Dodger Don," which was an important point to make in a town that hated the Bums. Don Drysdale, the Dodger pitcher, had a last name in common with Art, but no genes.

Art had been with the D.A.'s office for over thirty years. At one time or another he'd been in charge of Misdemeanors, Vice, White Collar and Homicide, and now served as a kind of minister without portfolio, unofficially doing much of the work that the citizens elected Christopher Locke to do.

Drysdale himself wasn't the District Attorney because his pragmatic view of life was out of sync with the political structure in San Francisco. He did not favor affirmative action in the District Attorney's office, and he had once been foolish enough to make the point to a group of reporters and editors who had been doing profiles on potential candidates for public office.

"If you were elected D.A.—"

"But I'm not running for D.A., or anything else."

The early denial being part of every campaign, that didn't slow anybody down. "If you were the D.A., what percentage of new hires would be—substitute one—gay, Black, Hispanic, female?"

Drysdale's answer, now famous in the lore of the city, was "If they could do the job, I'd hire chimpanzees. If they can't, they're worthless to me."

Of course, the media played this to mean that Drysdale thought women, gays, and other minorities of all stripes were worthless. He had followed his aphorism with the more balanced statement that some jobs—airline pilot, brain surgeon, prosecuting attorney—ought to be filled by qualified candidates, not by quota, but San Francisco reporters know news when they hear it, and calling chimpanzees smarter than minorities was good copy, even if that wasn't what he said, much less meant.

Now it was old news either way. Art Drysdale didn't worry about it. He coached his inner-city baseball team that had finished second the previous year in the city's Police Athletic League playoffs, went home to his wife, who had her own design firm, and otherwise counseled the young female, gay, Black, Hispanic, Caucasian, or (he sometimes felt) simian attorneys who weren't succeeding in putting bad people behind bars, which was their job. He was the most popular man in the office.

"So to what do we owe this surprise, Diz?"

"I think the big surprise is hearing you yell at someone."

Drysdale waved it off. "Aw, that's just Locke. Sometimes the old seniority isn't the blessing it's cracked up to be."

"What's he doing?"

"Somebody's got to investigate a couple of cops."

"That's ugly."

"Yeah. Plus it's nothing we'd ever charge on our own. But we're showing our continued sensitivity to the plight of harassed gays by the fascist police force. Subtle stuff like that."

"Why'd you draw it?"

Drysdale grinned. " 'Cause it's such a lemon. Locke gives it to a rookie here and bingo, end of career, or at least end of cooperation for a year or two with the department. Me, I'm immune I guess. Seniority. I've offended everybody at least once anyway. Can't do any more harm."

"Who are the guys?"

"Clarence Raines and Mario Valenti. Homicide. You know 'em?"

"No. But Homicide guys?"

"I know." Drysdale picked up an autographed baseball and tossed it back and forth. "Plus there's my well-known discretion." He flipped the ball across to Hardy. "But you, sir? Coming back to the trade?"

Hardy laughed, said no and ran down his last twenty-four hours.

Drysdale was thoughtful for a moment. "Ingraham left here after you, right?" He shut his eyes, remembering. "Something went wrong."

"What was that?"

"Gimme the ball."

Hardy tossed it back to him. It flashed from hand to hand, faster than Hardy could follow it. Drysdale closed his eyes again, a juggler in a trance. Finally he stopped. "Nope, it's not there."

Hardy lifted his shoulders. "Well, he's dead anyway. I guess it can't matter too much anymore."

"I know a guy, though, hates his guts. You might want to talk to him. Tony Feeney."

"He should've died a long time ago."

Feeney was Hardy's vintage but a different grape. Dark hair, pressed three-piece suit, trim body, shined shoes. No hint of mellowing out.

"Well, he did die this morning."

Feeney seemed to gather something inside himself. Then he astounded Hardy by giving himself a thumbs-up and saying, "Fuckin' A," like he'd just won a big one.

Then, realizing what he had done, he came back to Hardy. "If he was your friend I'm sorry, but—"

Hardy stopped him. "Before yesterday I hadn't seen him in half a dozen years."

"How'd it go down?"

"Looks like somebody shot him."

"I hope he walks, whoever did it."

"Well, whoever did it shot his girlfriend too."

"You know who it was?"

"Yeah, they think so. I think so."

Feeney opened his desk drawer and popped a Life Saver. He offered one to Hardy. "Fuckin' Ingraham. Always gotta be a woman around. Girl should've known better."

Hardy didn't know what that meant, but he'd come back to it. "What'd he do to you?"

Feeney had an unlined angular face with a small mole on the same spot of each cheek. Hardy thought he could be a model—not so much handsome but a definite "look." "There was a cop named Hector Medina," he began. "Used to be in Homicide. Now he runs security over at the Sir Francis Drake."

Feeney went on to explain that about seven years before, over a casual dinner with some D.A. friends, Rusty Ingraham had told the gang that "everybody knew" Hector Medina had killed Raul Guerrero instead of arresting him. Guerrero had been a lowlife who'd been hassling women for years in the lower Mission and had come under suspicion for rape and murder. When Hector had gone out to question him, the official story was that Guerrero pulled a gun and Medina had to shoot him.

As with any incident of this type, there had been an investigation and Medina had been cleared.

Now, though, at this dinner, Ingraham had gotten into it. He was showing off for the woman he was seeing, impressing her, Feeney guessed, with his inside knowledge, and he'd said everybody knew that Medina had planted a gun on Guerrero and simply blown him away.

Okay, people are allowed to bullshit each other. But then the story got to the D.A., and Ingraham got called in and he didn't retract it. It was the truth, he said. Everybody knew it.

And so they'd started another formal investigation on Hector Medina, and Feeney had drawn the assignment.

"You know what it's like coming down on a cop?"

Hardy nodded. "Drysdale was just talking about it."

"He pulled Valenti and Raines, didn't he? Poor bastard. I hope he doesn't need any investigating done for the next two or three years."

"They lock you out, huh?"

"What do you think?"

Hardy the ex-cop knew. Nobody closed ranks tighter than policemen. "So Ingraham testified, or what?"

Feeney shook his head. "No. It never came to that. There just wasn't any evidence. I couldn't get it to trial. But you know how these things are. Medina was suspended for the second time during my investigation. The word got around. Soon enough everybody believed he'd purposely killed Guerrero, who, of course, was a scum. They reinstated Medina, gave him his back pay, but he only lasted about three months before he quit. Nobody feels too good about a killer cop, even if—"

"But he wasn't."

"Well, there was no evidence. But sometimes two accusations are enough to put a man down."

"So what about Rusty?"

"The only thing Ingraham did was screw up my career for the next few years. I mean, whatever Medina
was or wasn't, *I* was the guy digging up dirt on this
inspector sergeant of Homicide. So testifying cops get
sick on the day I go to trial, evidence isn't tagged right
or gets lost, reports get filed in the wrong folders,
witnesses don't live where they're supposed to.
They're a real creative bunch, homicide cops, when
they put their minds to it. And I had Ingraham to
thank for it."

Hardy sat back, his ankle on his knee, and looked
at the city behind Feeney's back. All this was interesting, but didn't seem to have much to do with Louis
Baker, or Rusty being dead. "So that was it?" he
asked.

Feeney laced his fingers behind his head, arching
his back. Hardy heard a few pops. "No. The good part
is that old Rusty lost his credibility with Locke. The
assignments just dried up. He only lasted maybe four
months longer than Medina."

"He got fired?"

"What he got was the message. He sought, as we
say, other meaningful work."

"So you haven't seen him in . . . ?"

Feeney straightened up in his chair. "Many years,"
he said. "And when did you say he was killed?"

"Last night."

He nodded. "Good. For the record, I was playing
poker with four other guys from this office all last
night. I can give you their names if you want."

It was like a thing, man. If you ran with Dido, you
did something with your shoes.

Lace was checking it out. It was like a sign in the
cut that you were part of it. Lace looked down at his

feet, at the high-top Adidas, the shoelaces curling like skinny snakes around his feet.

He pushed off the building, hands in his pockets, and looked out through the cut. Dido doing some business. Couple of honkies waiting in the shiny black car. One guy out talking with his man.

Dido looked bad. Dido always looked bad, but today, hot and still, you could see him. He wore the Adidas, like always, yeah, but that's why he had his name. With the black tank shirt you could see the power—the dark skin looking oiled, shining in the sun. Arms like Lace's legs. Couple of years ago, when Lace still a boy, he and Jumpup used to ride around, one each on Dido's shoulders.

The only man around bigger than Dido was just got back from the big house. He was out doing something now with his shack. It was in Dido's cut, so it was Lace's business.

He kicked his way slowly down the cut, his long shoelaces trailing in the dust behind him. With a nod of his head, he drew in Jumpup, a year younger than himself, but bigger. At thirteen, Jumpup could nearly jam a basketball already.

Lace didn't know if the man planned to be on the street, if he had a name. Dido told them—the Mama told him—the dude was Louis Baker, but that wouldn't be their name for him if he was going to be here. Like, Lace was Luther F. Washington. But he was Lace. Jumpup, same thing. Been called Jumpup since he could walk. Lace didn't know his other name. Those names didn't matter.

The man was working without a shirt, setting out a few cans of white spray paint. He wore some baggy pants with a thin black belt and hard shoes without socks. There was a long scar from the top of his shoulder swinging across his back and under his arm. It was old, blacker and shinier than the rest of him. His chest reminded Lace of a horse—maybe three times as broad as his own, covered with curly black hairs that here and there glistened with drops of sweat.

Jumpup said, "Too buffed." Impressed.

His arms. Just moving easy, you could see the cords rippling under the skin. The man was humming.

They stood across the cut in the shade of the building opposite him, watching as he shook one of the cans and began spraying white paint over the graffiti that covered the side of the Mama's place.

Lace checked far down to his right. Dido still doing that business. He nudged Jumpup on the arm, and together they moved out into the sun and across the cut.

The man was covering a lot of Lace's work. Dido favored a dark blue in his cut. 'Course there were older colors too, from before—words, symbols, dicks, some magic stuff. Red and green mostly before the blue.

The man was being careful. Starting at the corner, he was already halfway down the side of the building. Not doing the whole thing, just spraying white over the marks so there was new white and old white, but no colors. No sign it was Dido's cut. It got Lace a little worried, but there might be nothing in it. The man had done his hard time—he got Lace's respect.

Lace and Jumpup were close enough now. He turned to face them and nodded. "How you boys?"

Lace felt Jumpup go back a step, but the man went back to spraying. Maybe he didn't know.

"You stayin' here?" Lace asked.

The man stopped long enough to nod again. "That's right." Spray spray spray. Nothin' to think about.

"You back in from the big house?"

He stopped again, straightened up. Way up. "You readin' my mail?" he asked.

"You ain't be covering Dido's name?" Jumpup, getting right to it.

"The blue," Lace explained.

The man stepped back, halfway across the cut, looked at his work. "This be my home, now, with Mama. I like a nice white place." He showed some teeth and stepped back up to the wall.

Lace had to say something. "Jumpup and me, we do the color in the cut here."

He lowered the spray can. "No, I don't s'pose. Gotta be just so."

"We been doin' it." Jumpup sounding tougher, but, Lace noticed, still standing behind him.

The man shook his head. "I only got so much paint. Takes some skill with the can." He stepped to the wall and sprayed, covering over a red circle. "Like that," he said. "No waste. You learn that at the House. The Lord don't like it much neither. Waste."

"I can do that," Lace said.

The man squatted down now, even with them. "If you could, it would be some help. I got some glass I want to put in. But I don't know . . ."

"Lace and me can do it," Jumpup said.

"We paint the cut," Lace repeated.

The man handed them each a can. "All right. Slow, though. Let me see you do a little."

Louis Baker positioned them about five feet apart and they started spraying over the graffiti while he took the plywood off the side window.

"What's happening here?"

The boys, startled, stopped spraying and turned around. Louis Baker, about to put the glass into the window where the plywood had been, lowered the plate to the ground. Dido had his arms folded in front of him.

"That's a white wall," he said. "These homeboys helping you out?"

Louis Baker nodded. "That's right. Cleaning up the new house."

Dido stood dead still, squinting into the sun. Without his saying a word, Lace and Jumpup put their cans down and began sauntering back down the cut.

The two big men—one twenty-one, one mid-thirties—stood about two yards apart. Louis Baker straightened up, folded his arms across his bare chest the way Dido's were. Lace and Jumpup were off a ways, looking on.

A car honked out in the street. Dido took a last look at the wall, shrugged and began trotting back down the cut. Business was business.

Louis Baker, humming again, opened a can of putty.

5

Johnny LaGuardia couldn't understand why people didn't seem to get it. The concept was so simple, and these hockey pucks—now it looked like two in the last two days—either kept getting it wrong or just blew it off altogether.

Here's the deal—you got a situation where you need some money. Gambling, women, speculation in municipal bonds—it didn't matter to Angelo "the Angel" Tortoni. The banks, for one reason or another, would not help you out. Maybe they didn't see the wisdom of your borrowing money to go put it on the nose of Betsy's Delight in the fourth at Bay Meadows. Maybe you had defaulted on past loans. Maybe your collateral was already hocked. Whatever.

Mr. Tortoni—the Angel—he'd help you out. Johnny LaGuardia had seen grown men go down on their knees with tears in their eyes, thanking the Angel for money that appeared when there wasn't any cash to be found anywhere. He knew for a fact that the Angel's money had paid for college tuitions, covered a guy's "lost weekend," helped out some married lady who didn't want a fourth baby. This man—the Angel—took care of his people.

And most of those Mr. Tortoni helped showed him respect. They paid the vig, the vigorish—a reasonable ten points a week—until they could repay the principal. Then most of them came in, not just with the money but often with a gift to show their gratitude

that Mr. Tortoni had believed in them when no one
else would, had fronted them some of his own hard-
earned money to help them out in their difficult
time.

And most of them understood that the reason Mr.
Tortoni could do this important community work was
because he remained a good businessman. He didn't
lose out on his loans. The vigorish kept him liquid.

That was most of 'em.

The other ones were why Johnny LaGuardia had
a job.

He stood at the entrance to the lobby of Ghirardelli
Towers and looked back over his shoulder at the deep
purple sky. Over the Golden Gate Bridge a high
cloud-cover glowed deep orange, the kind of clouds
he used to think, when he was a boy, had been raked
by the angels.

Someone was playing congas pretty well on the
steps by the Maritime Museum and the lights above
Ghirardelli Square had just been turned on. It was
still warm from the day, with a light breeze off
the bay—the smell of crabs cooking down at the
Wharf.

This was Johnny's favorite time of year, of day and
of his life so far. He was meeting Doreen for dinner
at Little Joe's in an hour. He'd have the cacciuco and
a bottle of Lambrusco and then they'd go back to
her place.

He should feel great.

But last night was Rusty Ingraham, and now he had
a bad feeling about Bram Smyth, who was supposed
to have met him at the bar at Senor Pico's at 4:30,
nearly three hours ago.

He ought to have a talk with Mr. Tortoni, he
thought. About these guys who do the ponies. Well,
maybe he wouldn't, now he thought about it. Mr. Tor-

toni didn't need two cents from Johnny LaGuardia about how he ran his business, but the fact was these guys were unreliable.

He pushed open the lobby door and crossed the marble to the bank of mailboxes with buttons under them. Bram and Sally Smyth lived in number 320.

He pushed the button, waited ten seconds, pushed it again. He looked at his watch, knowing that his impatience might make him hurry things. He counted off thirty seconds.

Okay.

One-twelve, the third button he pushed, answered. He had a delivery for Mr.—he looked at the mailbox of one of the other two that hadn't answered—Ortega in 110. Could he leave it with her?

He stood at the inner door until it buzzed. Then he quickly pushed it open and was inside. Taking the stairs up to the third floor, he couldn't get over what a joke these security buildings were.

The third-floor hallway was wide, carpeted, quiet. The Smyths' door was immediately to Johnny's right as he came out of the stairwell. He put his ear to the door and listened for a moment. Somebody was in there talking. He knocked.

The talking stopped. He could imagine Smyth holding a finger up to his lips.

Come on, come on. Don't make it so hard on everybody.

Johnny LaGuardia had several weapons that he used for various jobs, but the silenced Uzi was probably his favorite. Like the Secret Service guys, he carried it in a swivel-up holster under his arm. The thing was really small for so much firepower, easily concealed under a sports jacket.

He moved the jacket out of the way and swung the Uzi up. There was some more movement inside the apartment.

He could just wait. He knew that after about five

minutes Smyth would creep to the door and listen, then—with the chain on—he'd open the door a crack. But Johnny had a date with Doreen, and it was getting late. He'd given Smyth every opportunity to be civil.

He crossed to the far side of the hallway and aimed at the deadbolt. This part was fun—the way the gun made a little zipping sound and the door exploded inward. As far as the chain.

He took a few steps, shoulder down, across the hallway and hit the door with his shoulder; the chain gave way like so much tinsel.

Bram Smyth and, he guessed, Sally were halfway out of their dinner seats, staring at the doorway, at him. He realized he still had the gun in his hand. "Bram, goddammit," he said. He started unscrewing the silencer.

Smyth looked like what he was—a Yuppie stockbroker. He still had his tie on, his tasseled moccasins.

"Did we have an appointment or what?"

Bram looked at the woman, put on a sick smile. "Hey, was that today? I thought it was tomorrow. I'm sorry, I got the—"

Johnny shook his head. "You didn't hear the doorbell? I come up here and knock?"

Bram motioned ambiguously. "Johnny. We're having a romantic dinner here. Were."

Another smile at his wife. Everything was under control, he was telling her, the fucking wimp, except somebody just shot my door off.

"Sometimes you don't let yourself get interrupted." He held his hands up. "Bad timing, I guess. Right?"

Johnny glanced at the woman, who had sat back down and was sipping white wine with her legs crossed.

She was doing okay, trying to go with it, but her hands were shaking.

Elaborately, Johnny put the gun back in his holster.

He nodded at Sally, smiled at Bram. "Excuse us, would you? Bram, you mind we talk a second in the hallway?"

They were on the rug, the shattered door pulled behind them.

"I'll have it tomorrow," Smyth said. "I thought it was tomorrow, Johnny, swear to God."

"Eight hundred tomorrow."

Smyth's eyes widened. "Johnny, it's four."

Johnny shook his head. "How long you been paying on Thursdays now? Four months? Five? You're into next week's vig."

The guy was going to pee on his nice suit in about two minutes. "Look, the stock business, Johnny, it's up and down. I mean one week I'm golden and the next I'm flat. You know?"

Johnny held up a hand. "You needed money. Mr. Tortoni, out of the goodness of his heart, helped you out and the deal was you pay him back anytime you want, but until you do, you go the vig, *capisce?*"

Smyth hung his head. "Yeah. Tell him I'm sorry. Tomorrow, okay."

"Okay." Johnny stuck out his hand. "Your door's broken," he said. "You might want to call the maintenance people."

Smyth looked at Johnny's extended hand.

Johnny smiled. "What? I'm gonna break your arm?"

Smyth let out a breath and smiled, taking Johnny's hand.

Johnny gripped tight and brought his left hand down across the arm at the elbow, hearing the crack as Bram Smyth crumpled to the ground. He looked up at Johnny, holding his broken wing, tears streaming down his face.

"Eight hundred," Johnny said. "Tomorrow."

*   *   *

Glitsky kept telling himself that he wasn't doing this for the money. Still, the fact that he wasn't going to get any overtime made a difference.

Ray Weir, the murdered woman's husband, hadn't been home in the afternoon. Many working men weren't. So Abe killed the rest of the day at the Youth Guidance Center, interviewing a potential witness to another killing. The boy, a seventeen-year-old Puerto Rican kid, improbably named Guadalupe Watson, was not a big talker. A friend of Guadalupe had put him at the curb in front of Rita Salcedo's house when her husband Jose chased her outside and shot her in the back as she ran from him.

But if Guadalupe had been there, he didn't remember it.

The lack of cooperation didn't exactly roll off Glitsky's back, in spite of the fact that it happened all the time. Some people didn't want to talk to cops— ever, about anything. It could only come back and get you.

So Abe had talked and talked and waited and listened to a seemingly endless succession of yes and no, Guadalupe answering only what was asked, volunteering nothing, and in all probability lying when he did manage to mumble out a syllable.

Then it was five o'clock, or close enough to it, so he'd gone home, had dinner with Flo and the kids and now was walking up the steps leading to Ray Weir's house, thinking about overtime, more or less. Or none.

The front door opened on a small lobby. To Abe's left a stairway led to the upper flat of the duplex. On the wall by the stairs was a logo of an old-fashioned tripod motion-picture camera with the name Weir inside. He climbed the stairs and stood at the small landing for a moment, waiting again, listening again. Sometimes you heard things.

This wasn't one of those times. He pushed the button by the door, didn't hear a bell ring, then knocked.

The door opened on a man who looked like nobody, or anybody. As Glitsky introduced himself and produced his identification, he tried to get a physical handle on him.

Ray Weir was the guy you opened your checking account with at the bank, the mid-level manager in a cheap gray suit who rode in the elevator with you, your buddy's cousin from, say, Nebraska. He had light brown hair, regular features. Neither skinny nor fat, short nor tall. A quiet, nice-guy loner type who one day might find himself walking into a tower carrying an automatic weapon.

"Is this an official call?" he asked.

Glitsky wasn't sure what that meant. "Well, I'm officially investigating your wife's murder, if that's what you mean."

"You might as well come in," he said.

Glitsky, checking in after dinner, had found out that they had located Ray from some information that had been in Maxine Weir's wallet. A couple of blues had caught up with him at work and informed him of Maxine's death. Now he seemed resigned, lost, and immediately asked Glitsky if he was a suspect.

"Why?" Glitsky, crossing the living room, thought he might as well go for it. "Did you kill her?"

He sat on a floral couch, motioned Abe to an easy chair. "No, but I mean, you know, with being separated . . ."

"Did you want to kill her?"

He looked someplace over Glitsky's shoulder, focusing on something so intently that Abe turned around. The wall behind him was nearly covered with eight-by-ten glossies of a beautiful woman. Glitsky stood up and walked over for a better look. Some of the pictures had the name Maxine Weir on them, and Abe tried to reconcile this stunning face with the woman he had found in a neck brace on Ingraham's barge that morning. He could not do it.

Ray had come up behind him.

"I wanted her to come back. I didn't want her dead."

"How about her boyfriend?"

"Him I wanted dead."

"But you didn't kill him?"

Ray's eyes went back to the pictures. "Seven years." He shook his head. "You know what it's like to be with someone that beautiful when she's in love with you? It's like nothing else. You walk in a room and you're the proudest man there. It doesn't really make too much difference what else is going on in your life. I mean, my scripts. So nobody wants them. At least I've got Maxine, I'm worth something. You know?"

Glitsky didn't much buy the line. His wife, Flo, was a fine-looking woman, but he sure didn't define himself by what other people thought of her. He also noticed that Ray didn't deny killing Rusty Ingraham. On the other hand, Rusty wasn't officially dead yet, so he said, "Were you separated a long time?"

"Five months, eleven days today."

Glitsky kept coming back to the pictures. There were several nudes, tasteful, also erotic. She hadn't looked the same this morning with bullet holes in her.

"How did she get with Ingraham?"

He tried to laugh, but it didn't come out right. "That was pathetic. You had to know her."

"I'm trying to," Glitsky said.

They were back sitting down. Ray was smoking an unfiltered Camel. Glitsky saw another cigarette butt with lipstick on it in the ashtray. "Pathetic, how?" he asked.

"It was the way Maxine was. There always had to

be a dream. I guess it comes with being an actress. Maybe we writers have it, too. I think it's what kept us together so long, that shared dream."

"What was the dream?"

"Oh, the usual, I guess. Fame and fortune. She becomes a star and I write the Great American Screenplay." He drew on his cigarette and blew out a long stream of smoke. He leaned back on the couch. "Then she had the accident and met Ingraham and the dream just changed."

"To what?"

"All of a sudden it was just the money. For some reason, Ingraham made her feel like she was too old to be a star. At thirty-three. Look at her, she's not too old."

Glitsky didn't have to turn around to remember what she looked like. "But Ingraham told her she was?"

Ray shook his head. "Not so much told her as made her see that the dream—our dream—just didn't work. It wasn't realistic, like a dream has to be realistic. Jesus."

"So what happened?"

"She finally saw she had a chance to make some money right away, without the rejection, without having to keep herself ready for the break."

"How was that?"

Ray looked at Glitsky for a moment in surprise, as though he didn't understand why this wasn't common knowledge already. "Well, the insurance."

"What insurance?"

"She got badly rear-ended and sprained her neck something awful. Ingraham was literally hanging around the emergency room when she came in. What a sleaze the guy is."

Is, not was. Glitsky made a mental note.

"Anyway, Ingraham told her he could get a settlement for like a hundred grand, maybe more, and she bought that. Then she started thinking if she got that much money, she'd just invest it and retire for a couple of years. And then I became no fun because I didn't want to do that. I'd still want to write even if I was already rich." He stubbed out his cigarette. "But it wasn't her dream anymore. I guess Ingraham played make-believe with her better than me." He stared down at the floor.

Well, motive is pretty solid, Abe thought. "What do you do during the day, Ray?"

Ray looked up, the question taking him off guard. "I'm a courier downtown. Bicycle demon."

"You mind telling me where you were last night?"

The eyes looked down and up. "I was here all night."

"By yourself?"

Again a pause. "I'm afraid so. Does that make me a suspect?"

Glitsky gave him his best man-to-man. "You were a suspect before I got here. I'm trying to eliminate you because I don't have the feeling you killed somebody you loved that much. Do you own a gun, Ray?"

"No. I mean, yes. Well, I did."

Glitsky waited.

"After the accident, Maxine got—" He stopped. "It was after she moved out, actually. Living alone, she wanted the protection, she said. She got really paranoid, in fact, and finally asked if she could take it and I said yes."

"So she had it?"

He nodded.

"And what kind was it? Maybe we'll find it in her apartment."

"It was just a popgun, really. A twenty-two."

Glitsky knew the kind of wound created by that type of gun. He'd seen several of them that morning. "You know, Ray," he said. Then he stopped himself. He'd been about to tell him he was starting to look like a pretty good suspect. In fact, if there was any physical evidence tying him to Ingraham's barge last night, Glitsky would bring him in right now.

Ray waited.

"When was the last time you saw Maxine?"

He thought about it. "Three weeks ago, maybe. She needed some money for rent and came by here. She said, you know, when the insurance came in, we'd both have a ton anyway."

"You were going to split that?"

He lit another cigarette. "Well, it was community property. Even if we got divorced. One of those weird times when California law helps the husband."

"And you helped her out?"

Ray looked down at the floor again. "She softened me up first."

"How's that?"

Ray Weir lifted his shoulders, an embarrassed kid.

"You made love? Three weeks ago?"

Ray was nervous now. "I know it doesn't look very good, but we are, were, still married. And she came up, looking so beautiful. Radiant, really."

Glitsky had to ask. "With a neck brace she looked radiant?"

He shook his head. "She didn't have the brace. She stopped needing that a couple of months ago."

"But—" Glitsky said, remembering that Maxine had had the brace on when found dead. "Never mind, go on."

"Well, there's nothing more. We made love. I gave her the money. She left." He stubbed out the newly lit cigarette. "I thought . . . anyway, that's the last time I saw her."

Glitsky let the silence build for a minute before he stood up. "Ray," he said, "if I were you I'd get myself a good lawyer."

"But I was here all last night. I didn't leave the flat."

"That's what you said."

"You don't believe me?"

"I'd believe you better if you'd made some phone calls or ordered out for pizza or something."

Ray started to say something but stopped himself again. "Well, I guess that's about it, then."

Glitsky stood by the door for an extra beat while Weir held it open for him. "That's about it," he said.

Normally, Hardy worked from around 12:30 to 7:30 P.M. and Moses McGuire picked up at 6:00 until 2:00 A.M. So for an hour and a half almost every day they shared duties behind the rail.

"Who ordered that?" Moses was a purist. Hardy was squeezing a lime wedge over a Manhattan. Moses whispered. "Whoever ordered that, cut him off."

Hardy looked down at the drink, seeing it for the first time. He swore and dumped it into the sink. He tapped the side of his head, grabbed a fresh glass and the sweet vermouth, and started another one. "Good catch," he said.

"Cherry," Moses said, "is the proper garnish for a Manhattan. You need your Mr. Boston?" Referring to the bartender's guidebook.

Hardy finished making the drink, put it in front of the customer and came back down to the front of the bar, where Moses was now sitting on his stool, talking to his sister Frannie.

"He's like a thermos," Hardy said.

Frannie sipped at her club soda. Hardy thought she looked fantastic—highlights in her red hair, green eyes almost laughing again. "A thermos?"

"You know how a thermos keeps hot things hot and cold things cold?"

"Yeah?"

"Well"—Hardy paused—"how do it know?"

Frannie smiled, impossibly attractive—sexy. Impossible because this was Moses' little sister, about five months' pregnant. Impossible because Hardy had known her since she was in high school. Impossible she had come so far—Hardy had not seen her since a couple of weeks after Eddie died. Eddie, her husband.

Hardy's eyes left her, went to Moses, who leaned back on his stool. "A guy puts a lime in a Manhattan, I feel it down to my toes."

"Hey, I'm a little distracted, all right?"

"Maybe it's the gun." Moses did not like having a loaded weapon in the bar, but Hardy had come straight from downtown and was not about to leave it outside in his topless Samurai.

"What gun?" Frannie said.

"Nothing," Hardy said.

But Moses explained. A little.

"This morning?" Frannie asked, suddenly worry all over her.

"It's no big deal," Hardy said.

"Some guy's trying to kill you and it's no big deal?"

"He puts a lime in a Manhattan . . ."

"Yes, okay, it's entered my mind, all right?" His eyes went from Moses to Frannie. "Anyway, it's not definite anybody's trying to kill me."

"But you're walking around with a gun?"

Hardy leaned over the bar. He smelled jasmine. "Frannie, I took the gun with me this morning. I haven't gotten around to getting home yet. End of story."

"But you're not going home?"

He straightened up. "I've considered it, living there and all like I do."

"But what if this man tries to get you? What if he goes to your house?"

"Tell the truth, I'm more worried about me having to, or being tempted to, kill him if I see him, which my friend Abe tells me would be a problem."

"Well, I don't think you should go home. I think it's too dangerous."

Hardy patted Frannie's hand on the bar. "Okay," he said, closing the subject.

Moses had gotten up and was pulling a Bass Ale at the spigot. "How about you think about tending some bar."

"I'm talking to your sister."

"And she is my date tonight. I am off work and I am pouring beer. Something is wrong here."

Surprisingly, Frannie covered Hardy's hand and squeezed it. "I mean it," she said. A look passed between them. Hardy had been telling himself he wasn't all that worried. Naturally, he'd been a little concerned, but the earlier adrenaline fear he'd felt in Rusty's blood-soaked bedroom had passed.

Now, Frannie hearing about it fresh, she was passing some of it back to him. And it was a fact that he had garnished the Manhattan with lime. He tried to tell himself that it was just the way women were, especially Frannie, who'd so recently lost her husband. Nervous. But suddenly he wasn't sure that was all it was.

"Two margaritas, no salt," Moses called over, and Hardy started pouring into the blender. Moses sidled up next to him. "No sugar, either," he said.

Hardy couldn't get the till to balance, and he had continued to pour some pretty shabby drinks. Gin and Coke. Rum and ginger ale. Thinking about it made him shudder. He'd started three Black and Tans backward, forgetting that while Guinness floats on Bass Ale, the opposite wasn't true.

It was just after midnight and he had closed down the bar early. No sense continuing the charade longer than he had to. The clientele would get over it. After all, this was the Little Shamrock, Established in 1893. It wasn't going to go out of business over closing early one time. Moses might bitch a little, but Hardy would explain it later.

He found he just couldn't pay attention thinking that someone was going to come in and shoot him just as he was reaching up to the top shelf or wiping down a section of the bar with his rag or ringing up a drink tab.

After talking to Tony Feeney, Hardy had at last been able to get his gun back, and now it was stuck in his belt behind him as he counted the money for the sixth time. It was no use. He had $597 in cash and the register showed he'd rung up $613. It wasn't going to balance.

He went to his tip jar and made up the difference, then crossed to the dartboards with a last Guinness, trying to decide what he was going to do.

He had talked to Glitsky and found out that he hadn't gone down to talk to Louis Baker, that the ex-con was still on the streets.

Glitsky had started to explain something about other suspects, but Hardy, working the bar, was busy and didn't have time for police procedural bullshit. Suspects be damned. Louis Baker had threatened Hardy's life and was free as a bird. Thanks for all your help, Abe.

What Hardy was not going to do now, he was sure, was go home. Rusty Ingraham had gone home.

He kept all his dart paraphernalia in a well-worn leather holder that he carried with him at all times, most often in the inside pocket of whatever jacket he happened to be wearing. Now he took it out and began fitting the pale blue plastic flights into the twenty-gram tungsten darts.

There was one Tiffany lamp on over the bar and two in the dart area. Hardy had dimmed them down as low as they would go. He looked up at the clock on the mantel across from the bar, which hadn't ticked since the Great Earthquake in 1906 and didn't look like it was about to start now. Standing up, preparing to throw a round of darts, he first went back and checked for the third time that the front door was locked.

Since he was up anyway he went into the bathrooms, both of which had barred back windows, but you couldn't be too sure. The place seemed secure.

He stepped up to the dart line and flung his first dart. It missed the whole board. Hardy stared at the dart, stuck in the wall next to the board, as though it were a vision. There was no way he could miss the whole board. That was like Nicklaus whiffing a tee shot. Even warming up, you didn't miss the board.

Well, at least no one else was around to see it. He went and retrieved the dart, then took the .38 from under his belt and put in on the table next to his Guinness.

It wasn't only going home, he realized. He shouldn't even be here at work. Baker could ask anyone and find out where Hardy spent his days, and Dismas wasn't going to tend bar with his loaded police special on his hip. Or even on a shelf under the bar.

He started throwing again, more naturally now. Not really aiming. The round all fell within the "20."

His first thought was to go to Jane's, but not only didn't he have a key to her place, it was where he used to live when he was a D.A.

Moses? Everybody here knew Moses was his good buddy, knew where Moses lived.

Abe? Screw Abe.

Pico and Angela Morales? They had kids and little if any extra space.

He thought about a hotel, but since San Francisco's main industry had become tourism, you couldn't get a room here anymore for under $150 night, and Hardy, doing okay, still did not have that kind of money. And who knew how long it would be?

Well, it couldn't be too long. If Glitsky didn't do something, then Hardy would. Flush Baker, make him commit.

Then what? Blow him away? He shied from the thought, but there was something there.

He finished his Guinness and pulled the darts from his last round out of the board. He picked up his gun, took his empty pint glass to the sink and turned off the lights at the switch by the mantel. Letting himself out the front door, Hardy stood in the recess off the sidewalk, his hand on the gun's butt, scanning the shadows, listening.

There was a high, patchy cloud cover and it was not very cold. Traffic on Lincoln was very light. Hardy stepped onto the sidewalk, turned right and walked quickly back around the corner to Tenth, where he had parked.

Distracted when he'd come to work, he had left the top down on his Samurai, and as he slid onto the damp driver's seat he saw that somebody had opened his glove compartment. Papers were strewn on the passenger seat, on the floor.

Looking around again, he saw nothing move. Behind him, beyond the near buildings, the Sutro Tower rose in front of a crescent moon, a skeleton clawing at the scudding clouds.

Hardy put the car in gear and turned onto Lincoln, up toward Stanyan and the tower. It wasn't a skeleton. It was just a bunch of metal and bolts and wire—an idol to the great god television. Maybe seeing it close-up would help. No sense in getting worked up over imaginings, letting the mind play tricks.

But Rusty Ingraham was missing, dead. *That* wasn't a trick. He had been at home, forewarned even, and Louis Baker had found a way to get to him.

Hardy was sure Louis would also find a way to get to him.

He kept driving, not knowing where he was going.

6

"Why are you still working?"

The coffee was beyond good—Graffeo's best made in an espresso machine. Hardy, still pretty tired after a rough night on Frannie's couch, was dressed in the clothes he'd arrived in a little after 2:00 A.M. He looked over the steaming mug at Frannie Cochran.

The last time he had seen her, her husband's death was still strangling her.

Four months ago it had been strangling everybody. Especially because it had looked at first as though Eddie Cochran—twenty-five, idealistic, happily married with a just-pregnant wife, on his way to Stanford Business School in the fall—had killed himself.

But neither Moses nor Hardy had been able to believe it, and they wanted to make sure Frannie got her quarter million dollars in insurance if Eddie had been killed. Moses had offered Hardy twenty-five percent of the Shamrock if he could pretend he was a cop again and prove Eddie had not killed himself. Which Hardy had done.

And getting involved with Eddie's death had done something for Hardy, too. His original life goal had not been to bartend at an Irish place in San Francisco. He, like Eddie Cochran, had once burned with idealism, with notions of good works. But the flame had died down, along with his law career and his marriage to Jane, in the aftermath of his son's death. When Michael was seven months old Hardy had left the

sides of his crib halfway down on the first night the
child was able to pull himself up. The fall to the floor
was about four feet. Michael landed on his head.

Afterward, Hardy had dropped out, damned if he
was going to care about things if they were going to
hurt that bad. Moses McGuire, whose life Hardy had
saved in Vietnam, had taken him on as a bartender
at the Shamrock, and years had passed, one after another, all pretty much the same.

Until, that is, Eddie died. Until Eddie had been
killed. And finding out about it, having to care, had
jump-started something in Hardy. Even as it had killed
something in Frannie.

But now she was looking alive again, blooming. Literally. The baby she was carrying barely showed in
her belly. She wasn't wearing maternity clothes yet,
though Hardy knew she was nearly five months along.
First pregnancies could be like that. Jane had been
the same way with Michael. There had been no obvious body change except bigger breasts for almost six
months and then whammo, the stomach popped out
and everything became more real right away.

Hardy took Frannie in, her red hair washed and
gleaming, green eyes squinting as she sipped her own
decaf. She had taken to using light makeup around
her eyes, some lipstick. Her cheeks had filled out from
the hollow carved by her grief, and now she appeared
to laugh easily again, as she had before. She laughed
now.

"And what would I do if I didn't work, then?"

"Eat bonbons. Watch soap operas. Go shopping. Be
a woman of leisure."

"Nice view of womanhood."

"Okay, how about become an astronaut, run for
Congress, conduct Mahler's Fifth."

"Better."

"But you're pregnant. You should take it a little
easy until after the baby's born."

"If I take it too easy I'll get fat."

"Well, you're gonna anyway."

She pouted at him. "I will not be fat. I will be pregnant. There is a difference, Mr. Hardy, and I'll thank you to remember it."

Hardy looked at her nonexistent stomach. "Sorry, baby," he said to it, reaching over and patting.

She put her hand over his and held it there a second. "I almost don't believe it still," she said. "If it would kick or something. There's no other sign . . ."

Hardy took his hand away and his eyes rested for a second on her breasts. "Yes there is," he said.

She laughed, embarrassed, sipped at her coffee. "I don't know. I guess I just decided to keep working until it's born. It's nice not to need the money, but I want to keep busy. If I get too much time to think . . ."

Hardy knew what too much time to think could do. Frannie had gotten nearly a quarter million dollars from Eddie's life insurance. She was twenty-five years old. There would be time not to work if she wanted that.

Hardy reached out and patted her hand again. "And now a houseguest to boot."

"I'm sorry about the couch," she said.

"The couch is fine."

"And you're really in trouble, aren't you?"

Hardy shook his head. "Not trouble. Maybe a little danger. It's why I need a place nobody would think to look for me."

"And it's also why you have a gun with you."

"That too."

Frannie put down her mug. "It's still hard for me to believe people just get up in the morning intending to go and shoot somebody."

Hardy nodded.

"And you're sure this man . . . ?"

"Louis Baker."

"Louis Baker. You're sure he killed your friend?"

Hardy worked it around for the time it took him to swallow his coffee, nodded again. "Yep."

"Then why didn't Abe Glitsky go arrest him yesterday?"

Hardy had thought about that a lot last night. Why hadn't Abe just gone down and taken him off the streets? It worried him, but he said only that Abe had told him that there were other suspects.

"But couldn't he arrest more than one person and question them all?"

Hardy shook his head. "They don't like to arrest people unless they charge them. Abe said my suspicions weren't evidence."

"Well, isn't there any? Evidence I mean."

"I don't know. It'll turn up."

"And you're sure he did it?"

They were sitting at a teak table in a round breakfast nook off the kitchen. Hardy looked past Frannie, down the hill, to a school-bus stop at the corner. A dozen or so students were milling around—mostly black kids. For a moment, Hardy wondered if his certainty about Baker might possibly have to do with his color. There *were* other possibilities, things that might've happened there on Rusty's barge. But the probability, the overwhelming probability, was Baker. Hardy didn't base his suspicions on Baker's race. Hell, Glitsky was half-black, and Abe was one of his best friends. He had to smile at that—"Some of my best friends . . ."

"Dismas?"

She saw the smile lines fade around his eyes. He came back to her, refocusing. "Sorry. Went away for a minute."

"You see something?"

"Yeah, I saw a bunch of kids down there and wondered if I was getting to be a racist. But then I thought about Baker, who is nothing like you or me *or* them."

Frannie had been raised by her brother Moses and

had known Hardy since Moses had gotten back from Vietnam. Hardy had saved Moses' life over there. She had sat on his lap when she was twelve and thirteen, fantasizing about her brother's friend, Dismas the hero, now a policeman, handsome in his pressed blue uniform. Then Hardy had gone on to law school and become an assistant district attorney. He'd gotten married and had a child with Jane Fowler, then the boy had died and Hardy had gotten divorced, quit his job and had been around more, first drinking at Moses' place, the Little Shamrock, then becoming a bartender there.

That's when she had gotten to know him again, stopping in for a beer at the Shamrock to visit Moses. And had it not been for the "keep off" sign he had worn like a badge, she might have started fantasizing again. But instead she turned him into a litmus test. She would not date a guy twice unless he was "at least as good a man as Dismas Hardy," she told her college girlfriends. And she'd found one—Eddie Cochran— and she had married him. And lost him . . .

She stared across the table at the worried face, so different than Eddie's had been. Hardy's face had lines and creases and whole chapters of his life on it. She thought now it was more interesting than handsome. But he was like Eddie—or Eddie had been like him—both worried so much about doing the right thing, about good motives. Dismas would never put it that way, but Frannie knew him, and that's what it was.

Now someone was trying to kill him, and he didn't want to suspect him for the wrong reasons. She got up and went around behind him, putting her hands on his shoulders. "You and I both know you're not a racist," she said. "Not even close."

Hardy shrugged. "I don't know. I don't think of it as an issue anymore. Maybe that means I don't care about it. All I know is that Baker was an animal ten years ago, and we put him in a cage and he swore when he got out he'd kill me and Rusty, and Rusty is dead and gone the day he gets out. What would you think? How much more evidence would you need?"

She thought a moment, then leaned over and kissed him on the top of the head. "I don't think much."

"That's the right answer," Hardy said.

Abe Glitsky, running a little late for work, parked in a space behind the Hall of Justice and went in through the back door, nodding to the pair of uniformed officers who stood by the metal detectors. He turned left by the booking station and went around to the elevators, stopping to pick up an early morning candy bar.

There were six elevators in the bank, and he waited, by his watch, three and a half minutes for the first door to open. During this time he spoke to no one and munched his candy bar, thinking about Hardy's problem, deciding he probably had one. He owed it to his friend to talk to Louis Baker—at least talk to him, see where he had been two nights ago.

It was dead quiet on the floor. For a moment he thought there must have been a sick-out or some other protest a little more formal than golf clubs. He stuck his head in Investigations and found no one around. No one.

He had been around when Dan White killed Mayor Moscone and Supervisor Harvey Milk, and the Hall had the same feel it had this morning. He opened the door to Homicide, passed through the small reception cubicle, which was empty, and opened the door.

The wide-open room was jammed with what looked like every investigator—homicide, robbery, white collar, vice—in the department. The chief himself, Dan Rigby, was talking in front of Lieutenant Frank Batiste's office.

No one even acknowledged Glitsky's arrival. He leaned back against the doorpost he had come through and folded his arms, listening. Rigby was speaking very quietly.

". . . persons responsible for this will be let go. You got a message to give me, any of you, you come deliver it in person, or you want to memo it, that's fine, too. But this, this . . ." He paused and Glitsky saw the vein standing out on the side of his neck. "These insulting, demeaning, unprofessional acts not only won't be tolerated, they will be investigated with the whole weight of the department, and the perps here will be charged with criminal trespass, criminal contempt"—he was hammering the word *criminal*— "destruction of city property, vandalism and anything else me and anyone on my staff can think of."

Rigby stopped talking. A couple of guys had come in behind Abe, catching only the last words. One of them said "What's up?" which everyone ignored. Several people were smoking in the room, and even through the smoke Abe could detect a locker-room smell beginning to rise. People were nervous, moving in the few seats, shifting from foot to foot.

Rigby looked around the room, making eye contact with everyone who had the guts to meet it. It took a long time, and nobody else said a word.

"So," he said finally, "I'm giving you perps—and I know you're in this room—one chance this morning to own up. You come to me, to my office . . . ," and at this a couple of people snickered. "You think it's funny?" Rigby bellowed. Even Glitsky jumped. The snickering stopped.

Rigby went back to his near whisper. "You come up to see me, wherever I am, by noon. Save the department the time and expense of finding out who you are and you'll get to keep your pension. If we're forced to launch a full-scale investigation to find you,

you're out of the department, you lose your pension and if I have any clout at all with the D.A., and I do, you'll do time."

The guy behind Glitsky whispered again. "Somebody get killed? What'd I miss?"

Rigby was coming through the massed bodies in the room, following one of his aides. Glitsky moved from the doorway to let him pass. Others started streaming out behind him.

Frank Batiste had been standing next to Rigby and now motioned to Abe. He threaded his way around the outer wall, overhearing snatches of people's remarks: "Guy can't much take a joke, can he?"

Impersonating Rigby's whispered voice: "Criminal trespass, criminal criminal . . ."

"At least he'll get out of his office for a while, maybe see what's going on around here."

". . . my office by noon. Right. Like noon someday next month."

Laughter. And some people making noises under their breath as they left the room, sounding like *cluck cluck cluck.*

"Jesus. What happened, Frank?"

Batiste motioned Abe inside his office and closed the door behind them. "Just tell me you didn't do this, Abe. Please tell me that."

"Do what?"

"Come on, Abe."

"Swear to God, Frank. I just walked in this morning to this. I have no clue what's going on."

Batiste searched Glitsky's face for some sign that he was lying. Perhaps satisfied, he went around his desk and sat down wearily. "Last night somebody let themselves in Rigby's office with about four chickens."

Glitsky had been to Rigby's office a couple of times. There was a rug on the floor that had been a gift to the city from the Shah of Iran; a heavy, stunning mahogany desk; several pieces of leather furniture that, Glitsky guessed, cost about what a patrolman made in a year. It took a moment for the significance of the chickens to sink in, and when it did, he smiled. "Pretty clear message," he said.

"It isn't funny," Batiste said. "The room is floating in chicken shit."

"You don't think it's funny?" Abe said. Then, at Frank's scowl. "No, sir, me neither. That sure isn't funny."

"Rigby doesn't think it's funny."

Glitsky bobbed his head. "I picked that up. I'm a trained investigator."

"Abe, your ass is in a major sling if you did this. I mean it."

Glitsky rolled his eyes and came back to his lieutenant. "Frank, what in the world makes you think I had anything to do with this? There's a hundred-odd people in this department."

"Yeah, how many of them are applying to L.A.—?"

"Thinking of applying—"

"Okay. But who just happened to use the phrase 'chicken shit' the day before this—this fiasco?"

"I think I used 'horse shit,' Frank."

"Horse shit, chicken shit, same difference."

Abe was fighting back his laughter now, wanting to get into the difference with Frank, but feeling it wasn't really a good time, maybe never would be a good time. Instead he said, "If somebody'd trotted a horse in there—"

But Batiste had had enough. "Get the fuck out of here."

Back at Glitsky's desk, Marcel Lanier was waiting. "So the judge says 'Farmer Brown, you are charged with the most heinous of crimes, the crime of bestiality, of having sexual intercourse with animals . . .'"

"Not now, Marcel," Abe said.

But Lanier continued. "'Specifically, you are charged with carnal knowledge of horses, cows, sheep, dogs, cats, chickens.' Just then Farmer Brown holds up his hand and says, 'What kind of pervert do you think I am, Your Honor? Chickens? Yuck.'"

Glitsky found the paper he'd been looking for, making sure of what he had written under "Reason for Leaving Present Employment." He wondered if it was strong enough.

Hardy had fond feelings for the Sir Francis Drake Hotel. When his father returned from the Pacific Theater after World War II he had spent his first night back in the States in a VIP room the hotel had reserved for returning POWs. Later he and Hardy's mother had the honeymoon suite; it was possible that Hardy had been conceived there.

But the great hotel, a block north of Union Square in the heart of downtown, had not so much fallen upon hard times as it has been victimized by the boom times.

The San Francisco Hardy's father had returned to had been The City That Knew How. It had a vital port, a refreshing year-round climate, great food, neighborhoods, a tiny downtown with an accessible feel. In fact, it had much of what corporate America wanted. Men who had been in the war and passed through the city on their way home were now running businesses and did not see why they had to slave away, freeze in the winter, sweat the summers out in Cleveland or Detroit or Omaha when they could have a corner building on Russian Hill.

And these men, the first generation, knew what they had and did not much want to mess with it. San Francisco's lack of a skyline was part of its charm. The city did not need big buildings to make a big statement. If you wanted to take a moment to look around at this twinkling clear gem of a city spreading before you, you could go to the Redwood Room high atop the

Fairmont Hotel. You could hit the Top of the Mark, or Coit Tower. Or, downtown, you could go to the Starlight Room of the Sir Francis Drake Hotel. Forty years ago.

Hardy sat there now, at the bar. It was just after eleven in the morning, and he looked through the streaked windows to the other Francis across the way—the Saint Francis Hotel, which dwarfed the Drake. A few blocks further north, the BankAmerica building threw its fifty-six stories' worth of shade around the surrounding ten blocks of downtown; the Transamerica Pyramid, the Embarcadero Center Towers—in their fashion as symbolic, Hardy thought, as the spires of medieval cathedrals. Just a different god.

Hardy took his coffee and walked across the faded rug of the nearly empty Starlight Room. Except for due south, which afforded a view of the shipyards and Hunters Point, every direction was blocked by high-rises.

Hardy had danced up here with Jane, had stood with his arm around her at the floor-to-ceiling windows, looking down all around them at their city. It had been a genteel place, a spot to touch base or regroup, out of step with the hipness of the rest of the city. Even then it had been, from Hardy's and Jane's perspective, where "old people" of forty or fifty drank Happy Hour doubles and danced to a combo, not a rock band.

Now Hardy felt like one of the old people himself. A voice behind him said, "They gotta get to these windows."

Hardy spun around, jittery. For a moment he had almost forgotten he was being hunted. "It doesn't really matter," he said, "there's not much to see anymore."

Hector Medina was a short, squat man with a square face and thinning hair. He wore a brown business suit and black shoes, which were not shined. He showed Hardy his security-cop's badge and they went back to the bar, where Hardy had his coffee refilled and Medina ordered a glass of plain water, no ice, no lime.

"This must be my week for cops," he said. "Memory lane."

"I'm not on the force anymore," Hardy said. "The message I left . . ."

"Yeah I got it. Ex-cop, cop. I'm an ex-cop. I still feel like a cop."

"You're chief of security here, aren't you?"

Medina coughed. "Yeah. Some Japanese tour lady loses her purse and I get to investigate and find it under her bed. A farmer from Kansas finds out the hooker he picked up is a guy and has a fit. Tough cases." He sipped at his water. "Shit, what am I talking about? It's a good job. But don't mistake it for real police work." He wiped his mouth with the back of his hand. "So how can I help you?"

Hardy wasn't sure how Medina could help him. It wasn't entirely clear to him why he'd even come down here, but it was better than sitting at Frannie's with a loaded gun and a head full of questions. He'd thought he might as well get some of them answered. "It's about Rusty Ingraham."

Medina picked up his glass again, then put it down. "You know, I had a feeling."

"Why's that?"

"You know Clarence Raines?"

The name sounded familiar but Hardy shook his head.

"The department is fucking him over. Him and his partner."

"Is he one of the guys they're bringing up—"

"Yeah, yeah. Those guys. So Clarence came to see me to ask about . . ."

". . . because something like this happened to you?"

"Something exactly like this. Except they didn't wind

up killing their suspect, what's his name, Treadwell. They should have. At least my guy couldn't talk."

"So what'd you tell Clarence?"

"My advice? I told him, him and his partner both, to go into business."

Hardy didn't get that.

"Business, you know. Sporting goods, insurance, something out of the line, 'cause their police careers are over right now. Once you're charged . . ." He finished his water.

"That's what happened to you?"

"Ingraham," Medina said.

"He brought the charges?"

"No, no. He's too clean for that. Too hands-off. He just pointed the finger and sicced the dogs on me."

"But you got off."

" 'Cause the D.A. knew a good cop when he saw one. He knew the asshole I killed was a dirtbag. Scum of the earth."

"Who'd tried to kill you anyway, right?"

Medina looked over Hardy's shoulder, silent. Then, "There was a gun in his hand. It never went to trial."

Hardy fiddled with his coffee cup. A man could say a lot saying nothing, admitting nothing. Hardy might never know the story, but it was becoming clear to him that maybe Ingraham had been onto something with Medina—the accusation might not have been all air.

"So you wouldn't say Ingraham and you were close?"

Medina grunted, smiled. "You could say I'd like to kill the son of a bitch, frankly."

"You won't have to."

Medina blinked, his look going over Hardy's shoulder, then back. He seemed to settle back on his stool, as though some tension he had been holding in a long time was finally releasing its grip. "My luck keeps holding," he said.

"What does that mean?"

"It means I haven't seen Ingraham or talked to him in maybe five years, and last week I called him up and this week he's killed. Somebody will probably check his phone records, put it together and want to talk to me about it."

"You called him up?"

Medina sighed. "Clarence coming to see me, talking about his situation, it got me stirred up."

"So what did you say to him?"

Again that gutteral grunt. "That's what's funny. I didn't say a damn thing. I heard his voice and realized I didn't want to prove it, that's all. It was over. If I want to do something, I'll work with Clarence's hand. Mine's folded."

Medina lifted the glass to his mouth, saw it was empty and still tried to suck the last drops from it. "I gotta get back to work. Nice talking to you."

He got to the elevator button, pushed it, then walked back to Hardy. "If I wanted to kill Ingraham, and believe me, I thought about it, I would've done it seven years ago when it would've done some good, and there wouldn't have been any evidence there, either."

The elevator door opened and Medina turned a half-step toward it.

"Nobody says you killed Ingraham," Hardy said.

"Somebody will," Medina said. "You watch. You get accused once, you're in the loop."

Medina made it to the elevator as the doors were closing. If he was putting on an act, it was damn convincing.

Hardy, checking in with Glitsky from the pay phone by the men's room, heard, "No body yet, Diz."

"It's out in the bay somewhere, Abe. He must have

fallen or been thrown overboard and the tide took him out."

"I don't know if it's that strong. The tide, I mean."

"How about if you guys check that?" Hardy heard a crunching in the phone. Glitsky was chewing ice again. "You know, your teeth are all going to crack and fall out."

"We dragged the canal, Diz. We can't drag the whole bay."

"Isn't the blood type enough?"

Glitsky had told him that the second bloodstain, from the bed out the door to the pool by the rail, was B negative, fairly rare. Ingraham's old records confirmed that had been his type.

Ice crunched in the phone's earpiece. "Means somebody with B negative bled. Doesn't mean Ingraham died." Crunch crunch. "Necessarily."

"Sure, Abe. Probably somebody just had a nosebleed. The bullet hole in the bed must have been there before."

"Hey, we're going on somebody was shot, probably Ingraham. But we have a real live dead person, Diz. Maxine Weir. And her husband's got means, motive and no alibi for opportunity."

Hardy was losing his patience. "I'm telling you, Abe, Louis Baker did this. He killed them both—"

"Why would he kill the girl?"

"She was there. I don't know."

"You just said it. You don't know. Look, to make you happy I'll go see Baker today."

"Thank you."

"But no promises. The man is out on parole. He checked in with his parole officer. He is following the rules. I have no reason to think he even saw Rusty Ingraham, much less killed him. I'm sorry if you're paranoid about it—"

"This is not paranoia, Abe. Don't you think Rusty

getting it the day Baker gets loose is a pretty big coincidence?"

"Coincidences happen, and I hate to keep reminding you, but Rusty isn't officially dead." Glitsky's voice changed. It was starting to get him wound up. "And dig it, Diz, I do have a murder victim here—Maxine—who you don't care about but I'm supposed to. Plus I got a full caseload, like four other current homicides, to say nothing about a file full of oldies but goodies still outstanding. I'm doing you a favor—a favor, you understand?—to even see Louis Baker. Technically, it's a pure hassle of a guy on parole, but I'm gonna do it 'cause you're not always as full of it as you are right now."

Hardy figured he'd pushed hard enough. "Okay, Abe, okay."

"You want to do something worthwhile with your time, find me a body, or give me a reason we haven't found one, something to make me believe Rusty's dead. Then you've got me on your side."

"All right, I'll do that."

He could hear Glitsky's breathing slow down. "All right," his friend said, "you do that."

7

The dreams had been bad, and Louis Baker hadn't slept until nearly dawn.

In the dreams there was a bright light beckoning to him, but then there was always the yard bell waking him just before he could get to the light. Sometimes, though, before the bell, there would be some other people close around him, pushing up against him, not exactly going for the light themselves, really unaware of it, but getting in his way enough so he'd have to break through them, smashing faces, stomping on their bodies if he had to.

A couple of times he had woken up on the floor, drenched in sweat, still flailing at the people in his way.

The Mama wasn't around as he came down the stairs. The house looked different, and it took him a while to realize it was the windows. There were things he still had to do, but he was glad he'd done the windows up first. Where you lived had to be right. Especially now, after those cell years. Now it was Mama's place still, but he could feel it starting to be his turf. He didn't want to sink into it yet. There was a lot to get straight, but the light through the windows felt like it gave him a start.

He stood at the kitchen sink, barefoot and bare-chested, his prison pants tied with a rope around his waist. He let the water run until it got hot. His hands rested on the cracked tile of the drain, and the porcelain was streaked brown and red with rust. He stared out through the window at the warm day. It must be late morning already, early afternoon, no bell to get you up whether you slept or not.

He arched his back, rotating his stiff neck to get the kinks out. Steam rose and clouded the window in front of him as he filled a juice glass with the hot water and went to sit down at Mama's table. He dropped two teaspoons of Nescafé into the glass and stirred it with the handle of the spoon.

He had not yet done any inside painting, but he had pulled down the wallpaper where it had been peeling loose. Just came in yesterday after the boys had gone back to working the cut. He'd been pissed off, trying to decide how to handle Dido, and the hanging strips of dirty paper had pissed him off more and he'd ripped them down. Now the kitchen's walls looked unfinished, but that was all right. Unfinished was all right. Unfinished meant you had started something, not let it go on its own.

A knock at the front door. Louis Baker got up with his juice glass and went to answer it. The front room, too, was lighter with the glass in the windows, although Mama kept the blinds drawn in here all day anyway.

The Man, he come in a lot of styles, Baker thought. This one, he be some kind of man of color, knows who he is. Something in Baker knew immediately what version of the Man he was dealing with—turnkeys got you good at that. The mean ones who wait 'til you were turned and sap the back of your legs. The others, doing their jobs. Some, scared all the time, having to keep the upper hand, dangerous. Most on the take one way or the other.

This one here, Baker sensed was doing his job. Street clothes, but Baker knew who he was. He didn't have to look at the badge the Man held out. Man could've said he was reading the meter, Baker knew the Man when he saw him.

Baker brought him back in the kitchen, sat at his chair with his back to the wall, motioned the Man to sit. He waited.

"We got a problem, Louis."

He waited.

"A dead man over at China Basin."

Baker felt his legs go mushy. He was glad he was sitting down. How could they have put him there already?

"I don't know nobody in China Basin."

The Man smiled. Not a smile that made you like him, with the scar running through his lips top to bottom. Baker thought about his bad dreams. The people around him, keeping him from the light. They, some of 'em, smiled like this Man.

"You do, Louis, or you did."

"No, man, I don't. I been, you know, in the joint. I'm just out now two days. I don't see nobody. I just been livin' here, cleanin' it up."

"Cleanin' it up?"

Louis pointed around. "The place, you know. Put up windows. Some paint."

The Man half turned on his chair, came back to him. "You remember your trial, Louis? When you swore you'd kill the two guys who were putting you away?"

"Yeah, I did that. A mistake."

"It was more a mistake actually to do it." Digging.

"What you sayin'?" He almost said, out of habit, I didn't kill Ingraham, but then the Man would say, How'd you know I was talking about Ingraham? It could have been Hardy. Better find out what the Man knows before you open your mouth, tell him something else. To the Man, denying and admitting were two sides to the same coin—both told him you knew something, did something.

"I'm saying it looks like Rusty Ingraham got shot dead two nights ago."

"I'm sorry to hear that."

"So where were you?"

"I just tole you, I got off the bus. I came home."

"Anybody see you?"

Louis scratched at his bare chest. "Why don't you ask around?"

The Man slammed his hand on the table, some coffee spilling over the sides of the glass onto Baker's hands. The time it took to recover and look up, the Man had his piece out on the table, leveled at his chest. "You want to play games with me, I'm good at games."

"I ain't playing no games."

"Let's play who killed Rusty Ingraham."

He let his eyes rest on the gun a minute. "I ain't playing no games," Baker repeated. "You taking me in or we talking here?" Might as well get to it, he thought. They either made him there or they didn't. If they did, thought they did, he was going back in.

He kept staring at the gun. People got shot resisting arrest. "You got another piece on you?" he asked. "Gonna plant me?"

It surprised him, the reaction. The Man straightened up a little, smiled that smile again, slowly pulled at the flap of his jacket and holstered the weapon.

"Here's the message," the Man said. "If I find even one of your hairs at Ingraham's place, some cloth we can't match in his closet, a fingerprint, anything, you're on the bus. You hear me?"

What Baker heard was *we got nothing on you.*

His legs started firming up again.

But the Man kept talking. "And the other thing is this. The other D.A., Hardy. You remember Hardy?"

Baker nodded.

"Hardy is a friend of mine. If Hardy winds up dead

for any reason, I'm not going to care about evidence.
I'm talking you and me, and I'm hoping you hear me."

This Man was good, Baker thought. Scary. "You
hear me?" A whisper.

Baker nodded. "I hear you."

The Man stood up, did a full circle in the kitchen.
"Nice wallpaper," he said, and walked back through
the living room and let himself out the front door,
leaving it open.

Louis Baker gave it a while, finishing his coffee. The
street outside was empty, the Man gone. He stretched
in the doorway, then walked up the sidewalk to where
the cut started.

The side of the place, whitened over yesterday by
the time he had gone in, was sprayed over in swirls
and designs of dark blue.

He walked up the cut, shirtless, his nostrils flaring.
Dido's name was written in six places along his wall.

Further up the cut he saw the brother talking to two
white boys near the sidewalk. Passing something back
and forth. The younger bloods, Lace and the other,
were not in sight, though he knew they must be around.

Probably saw him coming and moved aside.

Glitsky had told him to find a reason to believe Rusty
was dead, but Hardy had no ideas at the moment so
he thought he would take care of business first.

He had left his car at the Union Square Garage,
and after talking to Hector Medina had thought he
would walk around to clear his head. He stopped for
another cup of coffee, this one an espresso, in Maiden
Lane and ate two cheese croissants. He was due at
the Shamrock to start his shift in about an hour, and
had to call Moses with the news that he wasn't going
to work at the Shamrock until his problem with Louis
Baker was settled.

"What do you mean?"

"If I bartended another day there, the integrity of our bar would be badly compromised." Hardy told him about his continuing creative drinkmaking the previous night.

"So pay more attention."

"Not that easy, Moses. Somebody's trying to kill me." Hardy realized it sounded unreal, melodramatic. "Look," he said, "I'm out of my house. Wouldn't make much sense to go to my regular job. The guy finds out where I work, walks in and good-bye, Diz."

"You know who it is?"

"Yeah."

"You know where he is?"

"Generally."

"Well?"

Hardy paused, again working that idea out. "It's a possibility," he said. "But the police have a good opportunity to get him first, and that would make it easier."

"I don't know if I'd give 'em too much time. The cops, I mean."

Hardy didn't feel like getting into whether or not he was going to shoot down Louis Baker on sight. "We'll see," he said. "In any case I hate to stick you, but I'm not coming in."

"So how do I reach you?"

Something stopped Hardy from just saying, Oh, I'm at Frannie's. He didn't want her brother thinking she was being put in danger. He didn't want Moses to let it slip at the bar—Oh, Hardy's staying at my sister's place.

He was also, in some way, reluctant to acknowledge to Moses his closeness to Frannie, to get into why he had decided to go to her place. Moses was her older brother. He had raised her. It would take too much needless explaining. So Hardy just said, "You don't reach me. I'll be in touch." And hung up.

Since he was right around the corner anyway, he then walked into I. Magnin's, where Jane worked, and left a brief message for her to receive in Hong Kong. He wasn't home. He'd explain later.

And all the while the idea had been brewing that if he could prove the genuineness of Rusty's fear to Glitsky, then Abe would get on it with Louis Baker.

The afternoon yawned open before him. He couldn't go home, wouldn't go to work, and didn't want to sit in hiding. He figured that the reason Abe was having trouble believing him was the way he'd come upon him—handcuffed—on the barge. It was coloring Abe's view of his explanation of things—the undeniable involvement of Louis Baker. So Hardy needed some corroborating evidence that his story about Rusty was true, and the best bet for starters seemed to be to find out if Rusty had gone out to buy a gun, right from the Shamrock, as he had said he was going to. Since there was a mandatory three-day wait between sale and delivery on handguns, Ingraham's weapon and the papers for it should be sitting in a store someplace on the bus line between the Shamrock and the China Basin Canal.

Officer William Ling was off duty, but he was in for the long haul in police work, so regular hours were not something he concerned himself with. He knew and accepted the life of a beat cop, and for now it was all right that it was mostly tedium. Walking and walking some more, moving the bums along, orienting the tourists, directing traffic when called for—if he lived and worked in a small town he'd probably rescue a lot of kittens stuck up in trees. His area in the First Precinct—Market Street south to the China Basin Canal, the bay west to 7th Street—did not have a lot of trees.

He wasn't even in a squad car yet. The street beat

was the initial weed-out. Every rookie cop had done it for a time—how long usually a function, like everything else, of who you knew, and Ling didn't know anybody.

Well, that wasn't true. Now he knew Inspector Sergeant Glitsky of Homicide. Whether Glitsky knew or remembered him was another question.

He figured he had already put in somewhere between ten and fourteen miles today, and it had been a hot one. Now, going on five o'clock, it was still warm with no wind or fog. There was even a rare trace of smog.

He came abreast of the *Atlantis* and nodded at the Wangs, who were sitting having tea on their aft deck. The Wangs had turned in the call on the armed man— the friend of Glitsky—who had been on Ingraham's barge.

He stopped walking, taking in the sight before him. Previously his reasons for coming back to the scene of his first murder had been nebulous—a mixture of professional interest and private curiosity. Suddenly now, the area itself seemed full of opportunity—the yellow tape still surrounding Ingraham's barge, the city dredge in the middle of the canal slowly crabbing its way out toward the bay. At least a half dozen persons were active in and around the barge—people to help, get to know, connections to make.

Ling let himself under the tape and presented himself to a man in shirtsleeves who looked to be in charge. Of course, he towered over Ling. Everyone was taller than Ling, but this man was well over six feet.

He shook Ling's hand, checking something on the clipboard he held in his hand. "They call you Bill?" he asked.

"Just don't call me late for dinner," Ling said.

Ling was used to it. A double take, then the realization that, damn, this little Chink is a person under there. He smiled. The tall man stuck out his hand again. "Jamie Bourke. I'm running this drag line. You want to just watch or do something?"

"Doing something would be fine."

"Not authorized, you understand, no overtime."

Ling nodded. "I understand."

"You wouldn't believe the guys come around, offer to help, and suddenly you're tagged for like ten hours o.t. and no budget for it."

"It's my first murder scene," Ling said. "I'm interested in the process. I'd pay you to see it."

"Yeah, well, that won't be necessary either." Bourke checked his clipboard again. "Problem is we're just about done."

"You find anything?"

"No body, which is the main thing we were looking for. Hard to believe this current would take it out to the bay. We did find a gun, though. Small caliber. Probably the murder weapon."

Ling wanted to do something. Hell, he was here, wasn't he? You don't get remembered for standing around. "What about inside?" he asked.

"What about it?"

"Don't they run all kinds of tests? Fingerprints, like that?"

Bourke smiled. "I don't know the figures exactly, but fingerprints catch about as many people a year as footprints do." Then, noticing Ling's disappointment, he said, "Sure, go on down. The place has been dusted, but you see anything that looks interesting, bag it and bring it on up." He gave Ling a Ziploc evidence bag from his jacket pocket.

The living room of the barge looked about as it had the previous morning, but the slanting rays of the sun coming through the door behind him gave the place the look of an old daguerreotype. Plus, it was hot. There was a sweet smell coming from somewhere that caught Ling unawares and almost made him gag, but

after a couple of breaths he realized it was not really
so strong—it might be the bilge, something in the
canal or blood that had seeped into the floorboards.

The door to the hallway was open and the chalk
figure where Maxine had died struck him. He could
almost see her there again, the naked body contorted
in that grotesque, stretched-out, reaching pose, the
metal neck brace like some bad joke.

But the bedroom itself told him nothing. There was
a thin film of black dust covering everything he looked
at. In here, in spite of what Bourke might say about
the usefulness of fingerprints, the Homicide team had
been thorough.

He realized he shouldn't have been surprised. That
was, after all, what the job was—check out everything
in the hopes that something would tell a story.

Still, that left him, again, with no role.

The heat was really something, and he opened the
back door, stepping out to the deck. He saw Bourke
had moved down the canal, opposite the dredge, and
was talking to a couple of people in yellow slickers
who were combing through the goop brought up from
the bottom of the canal. Those people, he thought,
were earning their pay.

Taking a breath, he reentered the barge. Now the
sun was lower, coming straight in through the front
door, but he would rather have the light in his eyes
than the stifling dead heat. The lamp that had been
knocked over had not been righted. He knelt by it
and saw that it, too, had been dusted for prints. The
pieces of glass that had been there were gone—
probably taken to the lab. Disappointed, he sat in the
chair by the lamp and surveyed the rest of the room.

Nothing.

The galley was left, and it, at least, didn't look like
it had received the full treatment. Unfortunately, it
was also a very small area that was very clean. The

only sign that anyone had been there at all was a water glass sitting on the drain next to the sink, and that had probably been one of the techs having something to beat this heat. The sink itself was empty—no dirty coffee mugs, no dishes, pots or pans. Whoever had lived here kept the place neat.

Ling leaned against the galley door. Well, what did he expect? This was routine to the guys that did it. They wouldn't likely miss much.

Then something struck him. He walked back into the galley and ran a finger along the windowsill. No dusting powder. He had noticed it had been all over the windows in the bedroom and again in the living room. The metal spigot on the galley sink looked like a new fixture, its chrome bright and shiny. There was no dust on it. They hadn't dusted this room!

In a way it made some sense. The line of action had clearly been from living room, through hallway, to bedroom and out the back. The team had no doubt looked into the galley and seen that nothing to do with the murder had happened in there.

But it was his only opportunity and he had to take it. They might laugh at him when the prints on the glass turned out to be a member of the Homicide squad, but he didn't care. He'd been laughed at before. And he wasn't going back up to Bourke empty-handed.

He took a clean handkerchief from his back pocket and carefully picked up the drinking glass, dropping it into the Ziploc bag.

Moses McGuire was behind the bar at the Little Shamrock, serving drinks to a five-thirty crowd and talking on the telephone. "I don't know," he said. "A black guy."

"What'd he look like?"

"He looked black, Diz. Big, black and mean."

Hardy, from Taylor's gun shop on Eddy St., felt his head go light. "Did he say anything?"

"Yeah, he said something. What do you think, he just stood around? He asked for you and I said you wouldn't be in for a while and could I give you a message and he said 'No, I'll find him.' Him meaning you."

"Yeah, I got that."

"So what should I have done?"

"How'd he know about the Shamrock already? Who's telling him this stuff?"

"Diz, we're jamming here. He comes again, what do you want me to do? Then I gotta go."

What could Moses do? Hardy knew the bar at this time on Friday nights, and if it was normal, Moses was right—it was jamming. Two deep the length of the bar.

Hardy couldn't believe Glitsky still hadn't arrested Baker. And now the guy shows up at Hardy's work.

"Diz?"

"I'm thinking, Mose."

"Think faster, okay."

Hardy heard Moses tell people he was coming. Just a second. Be right there.

"Go tend bar," he said.

"What about—?"

"I don't know," Hardy said. "Later.'

It was something Louis Baker had done in the yard. He didn't much think about whether it did any good, or what its function was at all. But he had done it, day in and out, for the last six or seven years, and the habit wasn't going to get broken. It was also probably what had kept him in shape.

Now he took the basketball and began dribbling back and forth at the public court just up the hill from

Holly Park. Except for the trees surrounding it, the court was about like the one in the yard. There were no nets on the baskets—you ran on pitted asphalt with no key, half-court or foul lines.

Mama had come back home sometime midafternoon with a load of clothes and some high-top sneakers that fit. Maybe she'd gone down to the Goodwill—you picked the right one, they could have better stuff than Kmart.

Full dusk now, the park lights came on enough to continue. Louis hoped somebody would come by and try to get him off the court for their own game. He felt like kicking a little more ass. An hour before, he had had it out with Dido and his blood was still hot.

Warming up, he dribbled down the court, pounding the ball into the ground, laying it up to the hoop soft as patting a baby's butt (that was for the control) and then slamming the pole coming around, getting the ball on the first bounce and doing it again, full court.

What he would do then in the yard was stand at about the free-throw line and forget about the basket. There was only the backboard, and he would stare at it, visualizing faces—other guys at the House, Ingraham, Hardy.

And he would slam the ball—two-handed shots or overhand—up against the backboard hard enough so it would come back to him at the free-throw line on one bounce max, sometimes even on the fly. Smashing the ball up against the faces he saw, grunting with the exertion, getting it out that way so the hatred and anger didn't overtake him—so he was in control.

Dido had been strong but didn't know how to fight, and Louis had hit him in the throat and put him down. Then, standing over him as he struggled for breath, he told him he wanted his house white again by the morning. He knew he might have to finish things with Dido, and he had come out here pumped up. But now it wasn't Dido's face he kept seeing on the backboard—

it was the other D.A., Hardy—the one who had blown him the kiss.

He slammed the ball, barely hearing its boom against the backboard or its echo against the Project houses down the hill.

Hardy's face, smiling at him, taunting. He threw again and again until he was covered with sweat. He was in the courtroom, struggling to get at Hardy, fighting against the restraints of the guards, then later against the bars, until his arms hung down heavy as lead, useless.

He stood in the pool of artificial light, unable to lift the ball anymore, Hardy's face still up there, smiling down at him.

8

Fred Treadwell had his broken ankle propped up on his coffee table. He was listening to some old Lou Reed and feeding Poppy, next to him on the couch, bits of the pâté and crackers he was munching with his Chardonnay. Poppy ate almost everything he did daintily, hardly spilling any crumbs from the crackers. And he waited until Fred put the morsel right up to his mouth, then slowly took it right from his fingers. A poodle was the pet to have—neat, well-trained, smart.

Fred scratched at Poppy's head behind the ears and was rewarded with a sweet dry lick at his clipped mustache. He kissed the dog back lightly.

Fred Treadwell was beginning to realize that he was going to walk on the murder charge and it made him very happy. Not many people could kill their ex-lover and his new boyfriend and get away with it, but Fred knew that he was going to pull it off. He had already pretty well pulled it off.

Whoever had said the best defense was a good offense certainly was right. These straights—especially the good cops Valenti and Raines—just didn't understand the city's politics the way he did. Or the way his attorney did. His attorney, Manny Gubicza, was the best.

Brian had told him he just needed to get some space, to think things over. He hadn't said he had someone else, so when Fred had caught them both there together, in the act, he had just lost his head. Brian couldn't do that to him. Brian had been nothing, a mailroom clerk, where he was division manager. He had brought Brian up, finally made him his assistant, and then Brian hadn't needed him anymore.

Well, no, it didn't work that way.

Fred had known where Brian kept his 9mm Beretta and had gone to that drawer while they fumbled and fussed, and shot them both. Wham bam.

But then Valenti and Raines kept coming around with questions, and finally with a warrant. There had been that moment of panic, especially when he hit the ground after jumping out the window and the ankle had broken. But not five minutes after showing up at Gubicza's office, it had all turned around.

Two weeks before, he had been the subject of an investigation for a second-degree murder he had righteously committed. Now that investigation had gone south and his accusers were themselves the accused. It was beautiful. Gubicza was a genius.

The doorbell rang, Poppy yipped the way he did, and Treadwell slowly put the stemmed glass down on the table, grabbed his crutches, and moved to the door.

"Yes?" Through the wood.

"Mr. Treadwell, please."

"Who is it?" You couldn't be too careful, especially lately.

"My name is Hector Medina." A pause. "I represent Clarence Raines."

"I represent Clarence Raines." Which wasn't strictly true—he hadn't been retained or anything. But let Treadwell think he was an attorney if he wanted. Attorneys were no threat. He'd get inside if he was an attorney. "I'd like a few words with you if you would open the door."

He waited, heard "Just a moment," then some movement inside, a drawer sliding open and closed. After a moment the door opened.

Treadwell was tall, thin, but not skinny. He looked like he had spent a lot of time working out when he was younger. Now Hector's age, give or take five, he had a full head of black hair and a trim and solid physique, shown off well in a pair of shorts and a Gold's Gym tank top. A goddamn little poodle yipped continually up at Hector.

"Poppy, be quiet."

Hector looked around the apartment. White on white. Animal heads looking like they'd been bought at Cost Plus on the walls. A couple of paintings of pretty obvious phallic imagery. Some kind of music—he didn't know how to describe it—playing softly in the background. Leather and chrome, white tile, high tech.

The dog stopped barking. Hector stuck out his hand and Treadwell took it, his grip firm and dry.

"Can I offer you something? Some wine. Stag's Leap Chardonnay. Quite nice, the eighty-three."

"Sure."

Maybe the guy was nervous, the way he babbled getting a glass out of the cabinet across the room by the kitchen. Under the cabinet was a counter, some drawers, one of which Treadwell opened, then quickly closed. He opened the one next to it, searched a moment, came out with a coaster. Nervous would be good, Hector thought. It sounded right.

"I can't understand people who say you shouldn't age your whites. Or that vintage is irrelevant in California wines. Especially the Cabernets and Chardonnays. It's just reverse snobbery, really, if you ask me. An older Chardonnay, like this one, simply overwhelms its younger siblings . . ."

Definitely nervous, Hector thought. But he took the wine and sat down on one of the white leather chairs, the coffee table in front of him.

The wineglass was tinted smoky gray and was top heavy, the stem no thicker than a pipe cleaner. Hector thought it might snap off between his fingers, so he cupped his hand under the bowl and drank a little. It tasted like wine, all right.

Treadwell made his way around and settled onto the couch, the coffee table between them. The poodle jumped up on his lap, and he petted it while he sipped. "Help yourself to the pâté," he said.

"Actually"—Medina leaned forward—"I'm here to talk about Clarence Raines." Clarence had not really sent him, of course. Clarence was a good guy who played by the rules, and he was going to lose, maybe had already lost, because of it. Clarence had a wife and two children. He was going to get himself an attorney to defend this bullshit charge and maybe even beat it, as Hector had done seven years before.

And lost for winning. You beat it and you still lost. You became a security cop or worse. You no longer hung out with people who cared about what they did. Everything became gray. At least it had for Hector.

Until Clarence had come by for his advice. That had, for the first time in years, gotten him going again. Remembering what Ingraham had done to him. *Ingraham.*

Then that guy this morning, Hardy, poking around. Funny how things just didn't die sometimes until you put them to sleep yourself. Made sure.

So that's why he was here now. Increase the odds. Make sure. Suddenly the gray, like some internal fog, had lifted. He saw that he could do something. Clarence hadn't hired him, but he sure as hell was representing him, his best interests.

Treadwell sipped at his balloon glass. "I don't know if I should say something about Mr. Raines. There'll be a trial, I presume, and—"

"You're a fucking liar." Treadwell reacted as though he'd been slapped, so Hector kept up the press. "You know good and well that nothing you said about these two guys is true."

Treadwell recovered. "Are these insults part of your legal repertoire? I can't see them doing much good with a jury."

"I'm talking to you one on one."

"And calling me a liar. A fucking liar, actually."

Hector took a second, put his glass down, pulled himself back together a little. "Look, Mr. Treadwell. Clarence Raines has been a good cop for fifteen years. He's got a wife and family and pension to consider."

"He should have thought of those things when he attacked me. Is he asking to settle?"

"No. I'm asking. I want you to drop the charges."

Treadwell sat back, comfortable again. "You must be joking." He leaned forward and spread himself some pâté on a cracker. "Perhaps you don't understand. These men are gay bashers. They were about to have me charged with the murder of two people, one of whom I cared about very much. Very much."

"It's the classic, isn't it?" Hector said. "You charge them to get the heat off you."

"I don't think it's impossible that they killed Brian and his friend."

Hector drank some more of the wine. This wasn't working. He never really believed talking would do any good, but he thought it might be worth an effort. Okay, he'd made the effort. "You know," he said, "you could get hurt a lot worse than you are right now."

Treadwell cocked his head, surprised, almost amused. He glanced behind Hector, to the cabinets in back. "That sounds very much like a threat."

"A statement," Hector said.

"I should warn you that on the advice of my attorney I have a voice-activated recorder in the apartment here."

Treadwell smiled, and Hector thought it looked very

much like the smile Raul Guerrero had given him when he thought he had beaten another rap and was going to walk. The smile Raul Guerrero had been wearing as Hector shot him through the heart.

Hector hung his head a moment, then looked back up, now wearing a smile of his own. He took another sip of wine, spread some pâté on a cracker. He held it out for the poodle, who obediently jumped off Treadwell's lap and skirted across to Hector.

The dog ate the cracker and Hector rubbed around its ears. It came a couple of steps closer and yipped cutely, begging. Hector moved his hand back from the ears, caught the poodle by the neck and flipped it by the head, breaking it over his knee.

Treadwell screamed.

Hector stood up, and while Treadwell struggled out of the couch in his cast, almost falling across the table trying to reach his dead pet, he went over to the drawers under the cabinet and lifted the tape from the cassette player.

"You're an animal!" Treadwell, looking up, tears on his face.

Turning around, Hector clucked once. "I asked you nice first." He started for the door. "Oh, and thanks for the tip on the tape," he said.

"I'll get you for this. I'll call the police."

"You do that. That'd be good. Your good friends the police will certainly believe another far-out accusation. It'll do wonders for your credibility."

Treadwell lunged for him, but the cast made the effort ludicrous. Hector moved back a step, now at the door. "There's hardball," he said, "which is a game. And then there's the life-and-death one. Think about it."

Then he was out walking down the hallway, Treadwell's sobs echoing through the closed door behind him.

*   *   *

The lap of the water.

The moon out over the bay, its reflection like a long yellow aisle up the canal.

Early on a balmy evening, a salt breeze carrying on it the soothing susurrus of the Friday night traffic on the Bay Bridge.

On a bed, all the lights out, with a beautiful woman.

"This is romantic," Flo Glitsky said.

Abe tightened his hand in his wife's.

"I mean, this is much better than all the dates our friends have. They do boring old things like go out to dinner or a movie. Get together with friends. Concerts, the opera, dancing. Not me and my man, though. Uh uh. The romance has not faded from our lives. We go to murder scenes and hang out."

"We'll be going to dinner soon enough," Abe said.

"I'm serious, who needs dinner." She moved her hand on his leg. "I've got hors d'oeuvres here anyway."

"Flo . . ."

"I know," she said. "All right."

"I'm just trying to see it," Abe said. "This was about the time, maybe a little later."

"Didn't you say like ten o'clock?"

"Between eight and midnight is the best guess. I figure after it was dark. Like now."

"The moon—" she began.

"It wouldn't have mattered. Fog, remember?"

"Would the fog have muffled the shots?"

"Well, nobody heard any. But the people at the next boat up were out 'til about ten-thirty, eleven."

"So it was before then?"

Glitsky nodded in the dark bedroom. "Likely."

Flo turned sideways and rested her head on the pillow that remained at the head of the bed. She wore designer-style jeans and wrapped her legs around her husband's waist and closed her eyes.

"I'm just trying to picture it," he said.

"I know." She leaned forward a little and rubbed his back. "Take your time. I was kidding about dinner."

The high tide was running a little stronger and the barge bumped lightly against the tires on the walk. Abe let out a long breath. "You think I take this too seriously, don't you?"

"Not really."

"But sometimes?"

Flo turned on her side, resting on her elbow. Her blond hair gleamed in the moon's light that came in through the open back door. "I find a time like this a little difficult to understand, yes."

"Why is that?"

She thought about it a minute. "Because of the hassles with your work lately, I guess. Applying down to L.A. One side of you pulling away from all this, and the other here at the scene with sexy old me on our night out."

"It's habit maybe."

"No. It's not habit. I know your habits and this isn't one of them." She paused. "Thank God."

They were both comfortable. Her legs were still wrapped around him and he rubbed the one across his lap with both his hands.

"So what does being here tell you?" she asked.

"Nothing I didn't know. Consciously, anyway."

"They found the gun—the murder weapon—in the canal?"

"Yeah, they found a gun, but I had a hunch she wasn't poisoned anyway."

"Maybe it's Dismas."

"Oh, it's partly Diz, no doubt about it."

"What part, huh?"

He nodded. "That's the thing." He extricated himself from her legs, ignoring her "hey!", and walked to the door of the bedroom, flipping on the light switch.

"Diz has got Louis Baker coming in here and blowing Rusty Ingraham away. Diz is not dumb. And he is legitimately scared."

"Right."

"But the problem is, where is Rusty's body?"

"Maybe out in the bay?"

Abe walked over to the back door and leaned against the sill. "Washed out by this raging torrent, huh?"

She had gotten up and stood next to him. "Maybe."

"And the girl—excuse me, woman—Maxine Weir? Why was she killed?"

"Because she was here, Abe. That makes sense. Louis Baker killed her too."

"Okay, but why the neck brace? M.E. report says her neck was fine."

"That I don't know."

Glitsky sat down on the bed again. "Why is everybody so quick to believe it's Louis Baker?"

Flo came beside him. "Well, that's obvious, isn't it? He threatened Ingraham and Hardy both. He said he'd do it, Abe."

"It's pretty convenient. Or stupid. I'm not sure which more. The actual day he gets out of prison . . ."

Flo shrugged. "Crime of passion. Waited a long time and couldn't wait anymore."

"Then he would've done Diz too, wouldn't he? Or tried?"

"Maybe he did. Maybe he couldn't find him."

"If he found Rusty . . ."

She was silent.

"I think what bothers me, still, is that it might be because he's black and an ex-con—"

"Black ex-cons can be bad people, Abe."

"So can white ex-cons. How about whites with no records? How about a husband who's jealous as hell and comes out here and kills his wife and her lover with nothing to do with Louis Baker?"

Flo was rubbing his back again. "You said you're checking that, aren't you?"

He nodded.

"So check everything—as if you wouldn't anyway."

"And meanwhile what if Louis Baker kills Diz?"

Flo stopped rubbing. "Ah," she said. "Getting to it."

"Right. You know me, Flo. I never think of this black/white bullshit. Maybe I should've arrested Baker already. Maybe I'm just dragging my heels 'cause he's black and I'm—"

"Abe, you've arrested tons of black people."

"Yeah, but usually, I hope, with a little evidence."

"And you don't have any evidence here? Then that's it, not race."

He shook his head. "Maybe that's why I had to come here. I want to get that son of a bitch off the street and I got motive to burn, attitude like you wouldn't believe and no hard evidence at all."

Flo was silent a moment. Then, quietly, "And you're not sure he's a son of a bitch?"

"No, I'm pretty sure he's that. I'm just not certain he committed this particular murder. But I don't know if I want to risk Hardy's life on it one way or the other."

Glitsky's wife stood up again and came around in front of him, pulling his head into her chest. "Is there anybody else who worries about doing the right thing as much as you do?"

Glitsky grunted. "I should just bring him in, shouldn't I?"

She kept him hugged close. "Maybe a lot of people would."

He pulled away and looked up at her. "I can't, Flo."

"I know," she said. Stepping back now, businesslike. "So given that, what do you see here?"

"What I want to see," he corrected her, "is . . . okay, the door maybe forced, but some sign of cat and mouse, Ingraham trying to get away. I mean, look, he's sitting here thinking Baker is going to come and kill him. Then, lo and behold, Baker shows. What would you do?"

"The woman was naked. He was on the bed. Could be they weren't paying attention."

Abe shook his head. "Not if he thought someone was going to come and try to kill him. Nobody pays that little attention."

She smiled. "You have."

But he wasn't playing. "Not in a situation like that, I wouldn't."

"How about this?" Flo asked. "The whole night before, he's been up worrying about it. He lies down for a nap. The woman is in the shower. Baker knocks open the door, but it's more a bump than any big noise. Ingraham rolls over but doesn't wake up. The woman goes on with her shower, thinking the barge just moved against a piling or something."

"Okay," Abe said, "okay . . ."

"So Baker comes in and shoots Ingraham in bed. No doubt now the woman hears the shot and comes running out. Bam, bam, bam. Baker runs, knocking over the lamp on the way out in the dark. Ingraham, it turns out, isn't dead yet. He staggers out of bed and goes outside and over the side."

Abe sighed. "To be washed away by the tide?"

"Maybe."

"Why the neck brace?"

"I don't know."

"What about the gun in the canal?"

Flo had no answer. Abe put his hands in his pocket and walked back to the open door. The moon was higher, its harvest quality gone. Now it was a bright silver coin above the bridge. Flo's was a theory he at least hadn't independently arrived at, and it was as plausible, or implausible, as any of the ten he'd come up with. And what really happened might be one of the ten, or Flo's, or something else altogether. Lots of people were good at theories. What made a good cop was finding one with evidence to back it up or—more—finding evidence and going from there.

Flo came up behind him, putting her arms around him. "How 'bout dinner?" she asked.

"It's all bass ackwards," he said. "I don't see anything I hoped to find here."

Flo turned him around and put her hands up to his face, closing his eyes with her thumbs. "Just set it in that brain of yours, what you see and feel now, and it'll click in when you need it, if you need it."

He felt her up against him and closed his arms around her. "Like you do when I need you."

"Yep," she said, "just like that."

9

Sometimes when Johnny LaGuardia was pounding into her, like now, Doreen Biaggi made herself think about the way it had started between them, when she had thought he was such a nice sweet man.

She had been walking out of Molinari's with some deli instead of a real dinner because she didn't have much money, when some of the young North Beach neighborhood boys started following her, teasing her as they had always teased "the Nose." Doreen keeping her head down, trying to walk faster, crying to herself. She was always nice to people. Why did they have to pick on her?

"What you got there, Noseen, some nose slaw? Maybe some nosadella?"

Ha. Ha. Ha. Snatching at her clothes, making honking noises, grabbing at her package of deli food.

And then there was this big man, not too old, chasing them away, walking her home. Johnny.

She looked over her shoulder at him, eyes closed now, rocking back and forth, taking his time . . .

Embarrassed at her tears, at her looks, she wanted to just thank him and go upstairs to her studio apartment. But he was so caring, or seemed so then. Brushing away the tears with a gentle smudge of his thumb. Taking her out to Little Joe's—now "their" place—to cheer her up.

Opening up to him. Telling him that she hated herself, her big schnozzola, everything. And him saying (lying, but nice) it wasn't so bad, but if she hated it why didn't she just get a nose job?

But where was a clerk at City Lights bookstore going to get the money for a nose job? It had been nothing but scrape scrape since graduation from high school—three years now—and it was enough of a struggle paying rent, eating, wearing decent clothes. And so long as she looked this way she'd never be able to get out of where she was, going nowhere. It was a catch-22 . . .

He was speeding up now, and she got into it a little, leaning back into it, maybe hurry him along. She reached back between her legs and ran her fingernails along the bottom of his scrotum and he made that sound that meant it wouldn't be too long now . . .

He had made it sound so easy. His friend Mr. Tortoni could lend her the money for the surgery. With her new looks she could get hired someplace that paid better, then pay him back when she could. Until then there was only the vig to worry about, and for her it would be nothing, maybe a hundred good-faith money a week—which at the time, with Johnny Mr. Sincere LaGuardia selling her not only on the idea of the loan but on her natural beauty, her chances for coming up in the world and a glorious future, had seemed like nothing.

It started seeming like something soon afterward. The nose job had been a success and she now looked like a young Sophia Loren, but she couldn't parlay that into a job that paid any better, and after six weeks of buying nothing, not even going out to a movie, she couldn't come up with the vig.

And Johnny, who had been her friend and protector when she had been the Nose, had told her he could cover for her, just up the vig on a couple of other clients, but it was risky and he had to have some payment, some sign of good faith.

But she didn't have anything.

He'd put his hand on her, right there—the first time anybody had touched her there—and said that that was worth more than a hundred a week.

Then she was pulling away, scared, from that different Johnny—and didn't even see the hand come up so hard she thought he had broken her face—and then he was on top of her.

And she remembered listening to him explaining afterward that she didn't have a choice. Somebody had to come up with the vig. He didn't want her to be hurt and he could protect her. He hadn't hit her because he was mad at her. He wasn't mad at her, but she needed to take a little reality check. He was her friend . . .

"Oh, oh, Jesus, Mary and Joseph." Johnny LaGuardia said the litany every time he came. Collapsing, he fell against her back, his arms wrapped around her.

She felt his weight on her, and she started to cry. She would never be able to come up with the vig. This was never going to end.

At Frank's Extra Espresso Bar on Vallejo, Umberto Tozzi was on the jukebox singing "Ti Amo," sounding like an Italian John Lennon. "Ti Amo" was Angelo Tortoni's favorite song, and whenever he was in the place he played it at least once an hour. If anybody minded, they didn't say.

But the flip side was that nobody else played the song anymore. All the regulars, the owner Sal Calcagno, the waitresses, everybody, they were sick to death of "Ti Amo." It was a good song, and for a long time it had been Johnny LaGuardia's favorite, too.

Now, though, as he came up off the sidewalk behind the grilled fence, past the couples drinking their espresso or cappuccino or Peroni beer or sirops, he wasn't too thrilled to hear it because hearing it meant that the Angel was there already and he wouldn't have time to ask one of the boys why he'd been summoned down here again.

Not that he should be too worried. Mr. Tortoni was his godfather. But he was also his employer, and certainly he was no one to get on the wrong side of, and this thing last night—having to explain Ingraham's disappearance, being six hundred dollars short—had not made him happy. Which Johnny understood. Johnny wasn't happy himself. He had never been short before. But Johnny thought he had explained it.

As always, Mr. Tortoni was sitting all alone at the back of the room, back to the wall, under the poster of the Leaning Tower, at the small white table. Two of the other boys were playing pool, and Johnny nodded to them and then presented himself to Mr. Tortoni, who took a sip of espresso and then motioned for Johnny to sit next to him.

"Can I get you something, Johnny?" the Angel asked in Italian.

It was amazing how quietly the man talked, how small and frail he looked. You didn't have to talk loud to get heard; physical strength was a small part of having power. These things Mr. Tortoni had taught him.

Johnny realized his throat was dry and he said he thought a mandarin sirop would be good, and Mr. Tortoni whispered up to Sal Calcagno at the counter and in two seconds Johnny's drink was in front of him.

"You wanted to see me?"

Mr. Tortoni put his cup down and fiddled for a moment with a short cigar, which Johnny lit for him as it got to his mouth. "You've been busy, have you?" he asked through the smoke.

"Okay," Johnny said. "Trying to—"

"So maybe—no, not maybe, I'm sure it's an oversight."

Johnny waited. Mr. Tortoni smoked some more. Johnny took a drink of his sirop. Billiard balls clicked

behind him. "Ti Amo" was over and "Love Will Keep
Us Together" came on, and Mr. Tortoni made a motion to Sal Calcagno, who walked to the jukebox and
pushed the button in the back before Toni Tennille
could finish saying "You belong to me now." Bobby
Darin came on with "Volare" and Mr. Tortoni nodded, smiling, at Sal, then lost the smile and looked
at Johnny.

"Well?"

"Whatever it is, I'll fix it," Johnny said.

"You don't know? It could be you forgot. The excitement all last night, this Ingraham problem."

Johnny nodded, without a clue.

"Ingraham is five hundred dollars. I get reminded
today—bookkeepers, you know, they keep track of
things."

Johnny still didn't see it. He was thinking, Five
hundred?

Mr. Tortoni put his hand over Johnny's, soft as a
kitten. "Doreen Biaggi," he said. He went back to his
coffee. "It's a small thing, Johnny, but then again, it
isn't. Ingraham was five, Doreen Biaggi is one. Last
night you're six short. I think maybe you're nervous,
you got mixed up."

In spite of the sirop, Johnny's throat was sticking
together when he swallowed. How could he be so
dumb? He had tacked Doreen's vig onto Ingraham's,
making up a bullshit story to Rusty about Mr. Tortoni's interest rates going up to cover expenses—hell,
Johnny knew Rusty would be able to come up with
another hundred a week. So Johnny had gotten used
to thinking of Ingraham as a six.

"So you collect from this Doreen?"

"Sure, like always."

"Then you got the hundred? Her hundred?"

Johnny reached into his back pocket, praying to
every saint in Heaven that he had an even hundred
in his wallet.

"You still nervous, Johnny? Is something wrong?"

Madonna mia! A hundred-dollar bill. He took it out and put it on the table. "I don't want to disappoint you, Mr. Tortoni."

Angelo Tortoni palmed the bill and laid a hand softly against Johnny's cheek. "As I say, it's not a big thing. A hundred dollars. But the principle of it—am I right?"

"Absolutely."

"Maybe get a book," Mr. Tortoni said. "Keep track who's a six and who's a five. And who's a one." He puffed at his cigar. "That Doreen Biaggi, she's got to be a pretty girl now with the nose fixed?"

Mr. Tortoni stared now at Johnny, making sure he got the message that nothing was a secret around here.

"You know, Johnny," he said, quietly, gently, "we all got our own businesses to run. Your line of work, the temptations when you're working with cash, no records . . . I know what it can be like. You figure old man Tortoni"—he smiled, nodding—"yeah, I'm an old man, that's okay . . . you figure old man Tortoni, he just needs his five grand, whatever it is, every week, and so long as you come up with that, you're covering your end of the business. But, Johnny, that leaves out my side of the business. You might think—I'm not saying you do, I'm just saying I know the temptations and it might cross your mind—you might think you'll strong-arm somebody for more than the vig I charge 'em. Cut somebody else, maybe a girl, huh, a little slack."

Johnny couldn't say a word. Mr. Tortoni was holding his thin cigar in his right hand, the one nearest Johnny, and he put that hand over Johnny's, the wet butt end of the cigar flattening out against the back of Johnny's hand.

"I know you hear what I'm saying, Johnny."

"I wouldn't do anything like that," he managed to get out.

"I put a man like you in a position of trust. He represents my interests to the community. A man betrays that trust, I got no use for him. Lean closer to me, Johnny."

The hand still covered his, gripping lightly.

"I kiss you now and you're a dead man."

Johnny swallowed, trying to breathe. Mr. Tortoni's mouth was inches from his cheek. "If this is going on," he whispered, "it has to stop."

The strains of "Ti Amo" began again. Mr. Tortoni leaned back in his chair. He took the flattened tip of the cigar into his mouth like a nipple and drew on it. "I love this song," he said.

Frannie wasn't sure it had been a good idea, letting Dismas stay here. It was stirring things up.

Earlier, he'd almost gone back to his own house, suddenly worried that staying here was putting her in some danger. He just wasn't thinking clearly. There was no connection that could bring Louis Baker from Hardy's place to hers, and she had told him that. He was safer here and he was staying and that was final.

Now, closing in on midnight, she lay in the king-size bed, Dismas out at the kitchen table, probably staring out at the street as he'd done in every minute of his spare time since he'd been here, watching to see if Louis Baker would show up.

It wasn't like Diz. Just sitting there, brooding, with that damn gun out on the table, drinking decaffeinated coffee and waiting for Abe Glitsky to call him.

Which didn't seem like it was going to happen tonight.

Dismas had come in around six-thirty from his day of touring gun shops, excited that he'd proved something—Rusty Ingraham had indeed put in an order for a gun on Wednesday afternoon at a place called Taylor's in the Tenderloin district. He'd needed the gun as protection against Baker. Also, Louis Baker had evidently come by the Shamrock looking for Hardy. So he had placed a call to his friend Glitsky and thought with the new information, Glitsky would have enough at least to take Baker off the streets.

Frannie hadn't really understood. "So what if Ingraham ordered a gun? How does that help you?"

"Well, Abe's problem here seems to be Rusty as much as anything else. Since they haven't found his body, he is somehow not as real a victim as Maxine Weir."

"Well, maybe he's not."

Hardy had shaken his head. "You had to have seen him. The man was terrified."

"But that doesn't mean he's dead. Does it?"

He'd looked out then at the darkening street, perhaps trying to phrase it for himself. "No, not necessarily. But Abe seems to need a reason to want to go after Baker. His threat to me isn't enough, I guess, and Abe doesn't see any necessary connection between Maxine Weir and Baker."

"Maybe she was just there and got in the way."

"Right. Anyway, what I have to do is show Abe some hard evidence that Rusty's fear of Louis was legitimate. That it wasn't, say, Rusty who killed Maxine, motive unknown."

"Excuse me for being dumb, but how does the gun show that?"

"Doesn't it lead you to the conclusion that Rusty didn't own a gun? Or even have access to a gun?"

She'd thought a minute. "I guess it would."

"Of course it would. If he already had a gun, he wouldn't have had to order one."

"But why will that make your friend Glitsky do something about Louis Baker?"

"Abe is my friend, and Louis Baker is going to kill me unless Abe does something first—or I do. What I'm trying to do is get Abe to look at this with his cop's eyes. I think he sees the Baker angle now as his friend's understandable fear—without hard evidence—interfering with his real job, which is finding the killer of a known victim—Maxine Weir. I'm trying to make it clear that what Abe would call my paranoia is at least based on something real, which also improves the odds that Rusty Ingraham is a real victim too."

But the call from Abe hadn't come, and Frannie and Dismas had done the dishes and watched some television and Dismas had had a couple of beers before losing his patience altogether and beginning his vigil at the kitchen window.

Now she heard him moving out there, then a noise like the rustling of newspaper.

She turned onto her side of the bed.

Her husband Eddie had been dead for four months now. There was a hole there she would never fill, but she had been getting used to the idea of living alone, of having the baby alone, of making a new life somehow, alone.

Dismas was making her think again about Eddie. Or he reminded her of Eddie the way Eddie had reminded her of Dismas when she first met him. She told herself it was one of the hormone storms that had been so difficult in the first trimester, but she knew it wasn't just that. Dismas had inserted himself into her life, and she had welcomed it. And now even little things like doing the dishes and pouring him coffee made her shudder to think that this, too, would end. And then she would be alone again.

No, it wasn't just that. Since Eddie's death she had become acutely aware of mortality. She was trying to get over it, this feeling that everything was on its way to dying right now. And with Dismas it wasn't a theory—it was a good possibility. He believed that his life was in danger. He was no paranoid. She believed it too.

And if Dismas were gone, like Eddie already was,

all the potentiality that might be over the rest of their lives would be gone too—

When the telephone rang, she rolled over again. Dismas picked it up on the first ring, and she heard him talking too low to make out the words. It must be Abe Glitsky, she thought. The call didn't last long.

The receiver was slammed down loudly, followed by a little ring of protest. She looked at her bedside clock, glad she didn't have to get up for work tomorrow. More rustling of newspaper.

Leaning up against the doorway to the kitchen, barefoot with her flannel robe around her, her heart went out to Dismas. He sat huddled over the table, the newspaper spread out under him, his head in his hands. She crossed the kitchen and put her hands on his shoulders, rubbing.

"It was Abe," he said.

"I guessed that."

"No. Not just on the phone. It was Abe at the Shamrock today. Not Baker. He said he guessed all us black folks look the same."

"That's not fair. He should have just told Moses who he was."

"Why would he? He was looking for me. He knew I was supposed to be working there. It wasn't official business. So he asks, Moses says I'm not there, doing me a favor, and Abe leaves. Natural as can be." He breathed out heavily. "So now he really thinks I'm seeing Louis Baker in my dreams, which I am. He didn't even want to hear about the damn gun."

She pushed in at the muscles on both sides of his backbone. Dismas leaned back into the pressure. "What's the paper for?" she asked.

"Tide tables."

"You going fishing?"

"In a way." Then, "That feels good."

As he crossed his arms on the table and put his head down on them, she continued rubbing his back, kneading at his neck, knuckling the knots under his shoulder blades, the softer muscles lower down. His breathing slowed, became regular. She leaned over him and put her mouth by his ear. "Why don't you get some sleep now."

Slowly he straightened up in the chair, lifted the gun, checked the safety, stood. "Good idea," he said, then turned toward her. "You think you could spare a hug?"

She put her arms up around him and they stood there, holding one another. "You be careful, Dismas," she said into his chest. "I'm not about to lose two men I love in the same year."

It had been a warm, moonlit night, all the students back in town long enough now to know where they could go get some rock and be ready to party. Money flowing like water, early in the year when all the moms and dads send 'em off to school with their lunches packed up—money for books, for movies, for food. Money.

Dido's roll was thick in his pocket. His throat still hurt where Louis Baker had hit him. But he'd take care of that later. Now he was doing his business. He was mostly selling twenty bags—four rocks. He could do hundreds, but most of these kids tonight seemed to be into the quick-flash, onetime, try-it-out-and-party thing. Later in the year there might be fewer buyers, but those that bought would do more hundreds, so it worked out. Try the crack for a party, and pretty soon you couldn't have a party without it.

Lace or Jumpup would be there when the cars stopped, asking if there was any stuff. They were both good at sniffing the heat, but even so, you didn't let them hold any product. You never knew, some plainclothes might get clever and not drive a city-issued Pontiac.

No. How you keep control was, you held the product yourself, and the money, walking one end of the cut to the other. It wasn't smart to let a line form. Dido smiled at the image, maybe he'd open a drive-away stand.

It was late now, the night pretty much over. He stood in the shadow by Louis Baker's place and watched as the college-boy customer walked back and got into his car. He heard the girls giggling in the backseat. The car took off, spitting out tiny rocks and asphalt behind it. Lace came up beside him.

"Maybe we call it tonight," Dido said, his voice still sounding odd, croaking. He looked at Baker's wall, painted over white again. That man would have to be dealt with. It had been a good night, and would have been perfect but for the fight.

He took the roll of bills from his pocket and peeled off two for Lace, nodding in the direction of Baker's wall. "Man thinks he beat me, but who's working the cut?" he said.

Lace wasn't saying anything.

"What?" Dido asked. "I don't hear you."

"What you want me to say?"

"I asked who's working the cut." He didn't wait for Lace to respond. "You don't think I got it, you let me know."

"You got it," Lace said.

"You think that homeboy got me worried?"

Dido picked up a stray length of two-by-four and walked over to Baker's new side window, a black shining rectangle in the white wall. "Here's how much he scares me." He swung the board. The sound of the breaking window echoed down the cut and before the echo had died down, Dido was walking back to the other end to meet Jumpup.

Lace walked alongside, looking back over his shoulder toward Louis Baker's place. Waiting for the door to open and Louis Baker to come charging out.

A few cars passed on the street, but they didn't look to be more customers. None had stopped by the time they got to Jumpup, who was sitting on the curb, waiting.

"Let's take it in," Dido said, and handed Jumpup his couple of bills. The three of them started walking back where they had been, making one more pass at the cut, seeing it was secure.

As they passed the first building someone called out Dido's name. They all stopped, staring into the blackness. "You keep walking," Dido said to the two boys. He took a step or two toward the shadows, figuring it might be someone from another cut seeing them going in, wanting to buy the last of his stash.

The first booming shot took Dido in the stomach and Lace saw him back up a step. He grunted and said, "Hey!" The second shot knocked him over onto his back on the ground. He didn't say anything after that.

"Mama. Mama, get up."

There was one light on in the front room, maybe sixty watts under a yellow shade on a pitted end table next to the couch. But with the blinds pulled it shouldn't draw any attention outside. Mama was dressed but she wasn't moving. A bottle of sherry lay on its side on the floor beside the couch.

Something hurt on Louis Baker's hand and he realized that in shaking her he had picked up a piece of glass from the shards that had rained down on her. And if she hadn't even stirred when the window broke right over where she was passed out, it wasn't likely he was going to have much luck getting her up now.

But he had to get out of here, and she had a car with keys. First the breaking window, then the shots, had awakened the whole project. Now, Baker could hear people gathering outside, a few calling out, trying to do something about Dido. Nothing anybody was going to be able to do for Dido ever again.

Mama groaned and shifted on the couch. He tried shaking her, hard, one more time, but she was out. "Mama!" Pieces of glass fell from the back of the couch onto her. Louis Baker sat back on his heels and his face relaxed. He had not even glanced at the end table, and there the keys were, where they had been dropped.

Outside, he took a last look at the crowd that had now formed around where Dido lay. In the distance he heard a siren. He walked up the street, looking straight ahead. He found Mama's tiny old Dodge Colt and squeezed himself into the seat behind the wheel.

The radio came on with the motor and he heard James Brown singing "Papa's Got a Brand New Bag." He left it playing, turning up past the park where he'd been working out, leaving all of this behind for good.

10

"Okay, you've given me your phone number, now how about your address?"

"What time is it?" Hardy asked into the phone.

"Must be the crack of six-thirty, thereabouts."

Frannie came and stood, rubbing her eyes like a little kid, in the kitchen doorway. "Who is it?" she asked.

"It's Glitsky." Then into the phone, "No, I know it's you. What?"

"I need your address," Glitsky said. "I thought I'd stop by, pick you up, we go for a drive over to Holly Park where somebody who had a fight last night with Louis Baker got himself shot a little later. You interested?"

Hardy gave him the address.

Glitsky had shamed Hardy into leaving his gun back at Frannie's, saying that between him and Marcel Lanier and whatever other police personnel were on the scene they would probably have enough firepower to stop Louis Baker if he jumped out from behind some tree or crawled from under some rock and tried to blow Hardy away.

They pulled in and parked behind an ambulance. The cut was populated by a few men in uniform and a small knot of official-looking people who seemed to be just getting around to moving the body. Glitsky and Hardy walked up, and Glitsky nodded to the men pushing the gurney and lifted the covering.

A man in jeans and a Giants jacket appeared beside them.

"Hey, Abe."

Glitsky nodded, introducing Hardy to Marcel Lanier. "Something hang up the techs?" He looked at his watch. "Six hours and the body's still here?"

Lanier shrugged. "Lightning response this part of town."

"How'd you get the call? You're days."

Lanier hunched his shoulders. "Guilt got to me. All that golf last week. I just got so far behind on stuff I thought I'd hang in and pull some paper. This came in, and I remembered you'd been coming out here yesterday. Hey, did you hear about this rooster, huge fucking rooster with—"

"Not now, Marcel. What went down here?"

"Bad long night," Lanier said. "Talking to these people is like pulling teeth."

Glitsky nodded at the gurney. "Looks like this guy's night was worse."

Marcel took in Hardy. "So why are we having visiting day?"

Glitsky explained the connection.

"See, that's why I called him," Lanier said to Hardy. "I knew he'd been out here, figured it might be connected."

"I didn't think you'd talked to Baker," Hardy said to Glitsky.

"I can be a surprising guy. Following up, that's all."

"You should have brought him in, Baker I mean," Lanier said.

Glitsky pulled at where the scar ran through his bottom lip. "I would have, except there was the technicality of charging him with something."

"The word 'murder' comes to mind," Hardy said.

Glitsky just looked at Hardy, then spoke to Lanier.

"How do you know Baker killed this guy? What's his name, anyway?"

Lanier consulted a little white pad with a spiral on the top. "Jackson Jefferson Grant, street name of Dido. Wonder why his mother left out Lincoln?" He furrowed his brow. "Probably his brother," he said. "Lincoln, Washington, Roosevelt Grant."

Glitsky sighed with feeling. "Can we get back to why you think Baker did Grant?"

Lanier put his hands in his pockets and said to Hardy that Glitsky wasn't much fun lately. Then he went into it. "Baker comes back to the Project two days ago, right away gets in a beef over painting his place"—he pointed—"over there. The beef continues over the next day, and last night Baker and Dido duke it out right here in the cut, witnessed by about fifty citizens, three of whom volunteered the information. Then last night, maybe five minutes before he gets it, Dido breaks Baker's side window. I figure what happened is it woke up Baker, he said that's enough, came out, blew him away, then ran for it."

"Did anybody see him?"

"When?"

"During the shooting. Did anybody see Baker shoot this guy?"

Lanier looked at the sky. "The shots came from off the cut in the dark. People saw him a minute or two later. That's close enough for me."

"I guess that is close enough," Glitsky said. Sarcastic.

"This is one bad dude, Abe. He's out of prison three days and he's already killed two folks."

"Three," Hardy said. "This guy, Maxine, and Rusty."

Glitsky felt his patience going again. "We don't know about Rusty. We don't even know if Rusty's dead or not. And we don't know he killed Maxine either. And we don't know for sure whether he killed

Grant here, and we still don't know he's trying to kill you, Diz—"

"He killed Dido," Lanier said. "You can take that to the bank."

Hardy shook his head. "It's funny, Abe, how I know all that stuff and you don't."

"Abe's in a bad mood lately," Lanier said. "It colors his judgment."

They were walking down the cut toward Baker's place. "You find the gun?" Glitsky asked.

"Nope. What's the problem there?"

"Just that it's traditional to try and find something tying a murderer to the crime."

Lanier and Hardy exchanged glances. "Look, Abe, if you want to take this thing in another direction, I'll give you the case. But for no overtime and no support, they get what they pay for. This guy Baker is a righteous badass. He stole his own Mama's car after killing Dido and I've got plenty to bring him in on. Am I right or not?"

Glitsky stopped walking and stared around at the scarred buildings, the boarded windows, the grassless, bottle-strewn cut. He shouldn't confuse what might have happened on Rusty Ingraham's barge with the shit that had obviously gone down here between Louis Baker and the late Dido Grant. "You're right," he said.

"Fuckin'-A I am," Lanier said.

Since they were here, Glitsky thought he might as well try and find out what time Louis Baker had gotten in on Wednesday night. Cover all the bases. Maybe they were right. Maybe he was forgetting to think like a cop.

Foreign turf. It made Louis Baker nervous.

There hadn't been much sleeping. He had known where he was going when he got into the car. Up to

the Fillmore. Ain't nobody going to notice a black
man in the 'Mo. Least any particular one, one you'd
attach a name to.

He'd pulled up behind the Baptist Tabernacle
Church and let the car keep running for the heat until
the sun started to come up. It wouldn't do to leave
the car out on the street. The Man didn't really check
plates as a matter of course, but the way his luck had
been running, he didn't want to put out any invita-
tions. Just sitting in the car in the big lot was enough,
so as soon as it was light he had to leave it.

He'd been hungry, but the first thing was to get
some protection—a knife, a gun, something. A gun
would be best. He wasn't going to have the Man after
him again, taking him down without some kind of
fight. He'd waited too long to get out and he wasn't
going back. He'd take somebody with him or do himself first. 'Cause back in the House wasn't living. It
wasn't even surviving. It was just time.

There was something clean about knowing now for
sure that the Man was on his ass again. It restored
things to how they'd always been. When that one
yesterday—the colored man—had come out to the
Project, to his place, and talked to him, it was just
warming up.

He'd heard about that in the House, how they
would do that. Come at you the first day or so, keep
you off balance. Get you back in for something as
soon as they could think of it.

Well, there wasn't any doubt now with Dido dead.
They got everything they wanted handed to them on
a platter. It was just as well. What he and the warden
had talked about, maybe going straight, had gone bad
right at the bus station. Ingraham . . .

The sun was up enough now. Better get out and
moving.

Ingraham's image up in his mind before him, that
honky I-got-it-you-never-will smile. He closed the car

door quietly and made his way along the Cyclone fence up toward the brick church, allowing himself a smile now. Who was dead? Not him. Laugh that one away, counselor.

But then Hardy wasn't dead, was he? And he, Louis Baker, was on the run again, this time for killing Dido, Ingraham, whoever else they wanted to think of. No doubt about that. He was set up real good.

And Hardy's face came up and pushed Ingraham's aside. Hardy, still alive, walking around enjoying his freedom. Was that right? Was that justice?

He knew it was all the justice he was ever going to see. He turned out of the lot onto Fillmore Street, hands in his pockets.

He knew a store here, around the corner, sold guns. A gun would be the thing. He couldn't buy it, of course, but getting into places had never been a problem for Louis Baker.

They were in the car driving back to Frannie's. Glitsky had asked Hardy over to his house for a barbecue the next afternoon, their first social engagement since the old days.

At Holly Park, Glitsky had said, a badly hungover Mama hadn't seemed to understand a great deal of what Glitsky had asked her about Louis Baker, but she did say enough to leave him wide open as a suspect on Wednesday night. He had arrived at the Project sometime after dark, she couldn't be sure of the time. But after dark meant at least eight. He'd been released from San Quentin at two P.M., and it was less than an hour's bus ride from there to San Francisco. He'd told her he had stayed downtown to "take care of some business."

"What business could he have had downtown, ma'am," Abe had asked, "if he'd been locked up for about nine years?"

She hadn't known the answer to that.

Hardy, sitting in the room listening while Lanier and Glitsky talked, believed she damn well knew the answer and said so to Abe as they were driving to Frannie's.

"Yeah, well, you know," Glitsky said, squinting against the morning sun as he swung east on 280 up toward 101. "It's not as if I can't believe Baker killed these people, but it's my job to get the evidence to prove he did. There's a difference."

"Well, it's my job to stay alive, and we both know the guy's a killer. You can agree he killed at least *one* of these people."

"Maybe."

"Come on, Abe. You don't see that?"

Glitsky tightened his hands on the steering wheel. "Diz, what I see is the famous 'usual suspect.' Face it, the guy's a black ex-con and we all know the recidivism rate is like a hundred and two percent, he's got no family and no—"

"Oh, spare me."

Glitsky held up a hand. "I'm not saying I feel sorry for him. I'm looking at facts. He's a shithook, okay. No job. No chance of getting one. So he's going to go wrong again if only because that's what he does, it's how he knows to get by. If anything, if he gets accused of any other murders where he happens to be in the neighborhood, I'll be tempted to think he's less likely, just hard-core unlucky—"

"Yeah, well, if the murder happens to be me, do me a favor, check him out."

The car swung west again and they exited the freeway at Fell/Laguna. "You know, Diz, if I didn't have such a good suspect in Maxine's husband, I'd think about Baker more. I don't even have Baker at the barge."

"Was her husband there? Weir?"

"No . . . not yet."

"Pretty compelling. Next thing you'll be questioning Hector Medina."

"Who's Hector Medina?"

Hardy ran down Medina's connection to Ingraham, the recent contact. Glitsky thought about it. Turning down Divisadero, heading over to Frannie's, he shook his head. "You want to get back to basics, I got the same problem with him that I have with Baker."

Hardy knew what was coming.

"Rusty Ingraham's body. Where is it? It's only been two days, three. He might have just run away. He's not even a missing person yet.

"I think Weir may have killed her and shot Ingraham, maybe left him for dead, and now lying low—"

"So why hasn't he called me? We had this deal, remember. It's what started this whole thing."

"Have you checked your messages?"

"I've called in five or six times, most recently after you got me up this morning."

"Well, I'll give you that—I think he would have called you."

"Thank you."

"But then why don't we have a body? We dragged the canal."

"It must have floated out. Did you check for that?"

"I wouldn't even know how to. Our resources, especially lately, are a little limited. You saw how quick they got Dido off to the morgue. Anyway, the tide at China Basin doesn't seem strong enough, and I was there last night, paying attention."

"What if I show you it is strong enough?"

"Then your case for Rusty being dead gets better. It gets closer to something I can look into more officially. Anyway, Lanier's got an all-points out for Baker."

They pulled up in front of Frannie's. "I still worry about one thing, though," Hardy said.

"What's that?"

"Old Louis is still out, walking around. And I believe he's killed everybody he's wanted to in the past couple of days except for one special dude." He slammed the door and stuck his head back through the window. "Me."

11

Hardy lay on a blanket looking at the clear blue sky, his head on Frannie's lap. A friend of hers, Cindy something, was finished singing an old Jackson Browne song about just packing up your sorrows, leaving them on the curb, and the Trashman, he'd just haul them away . . .

"I wish," Hardy said.

"Oh, stop." Frannie cuffed him on the side of the head. "How many days like this do we get, and you just won't let yourself enjoy it. That was great, Cindy, in spite of old sour face here."

"Hey, I loved the song." Hardy sat up. The holster felt plain silly under his arm, but he was not about to go out to a public place like Golden Gate Park and risk running into . . .

So in spite of the warmth of the day, over his shirt he wore an old blue-and-white Yosemite windbreaker that had belonged to Frannie's late husband Eddie.

"That's all you can do with troubles," Cindy said. "Just let them go. What's gonna be is gonna be."

About as comforting as it was original.

"It shouldn't be so bad," Frannie said. "Look where we are right now."

Which was in the Shakespeare Garden in the park, the three of them sitting on a blanket littered now with the remains of the lunch Cindy had brought over for Frannie. She had friends who kept doing nice things for her. She was that kind of person, Hardy knew. He and Cindy had split a couple of sips of Chianti out of a straw bottle, but Frannie was sticking to her no-alcohol pregnancy regimen. A light breeze blew high in the trees over them.

Cindy strummed some other chords on her guitar. Hardy thought Cindy was cute. Nice. But no Frannie. Not close. Most of the other people Frannie's age struck him as way younger than he was, which of course was true, but in Frannie's case he never thought about it. Cindy, with her turned-up little nose and her guitar playing, seemed more a contemporary of the teenagers who were playing Frisbee out across the lawn than a twenty-five-year-old woman.

Hardy leaned back down on Frannie's lap. "You're right," he said. "Look where we are."

Cindy played another song, and Hardy, drowsy, closed his eyes. He felt Frannie put her hand on his chest where the Yosemite logo was, probably thinking about Eddie. He pushed that out of his mind. He was here and Cindy was right. Never mind originality. *Que sera sera,* Hardy thought, but it meant something different for him. No doubt Cindy . . . maybe Frannie too . . . thought Jackson Browne was an oldie—how about Patience and Prudence doing "Que Sera Sera" on the *Hit Parade*? Hardy had only been four or so but he remembered that . . .

When he opened his eyes, Cindy had gone. The Frisbee game had stopped. The breeze had died down.

"Hi," Frannie said.

"Did I sleep?"

"About an hour."

"Where'd Cindy go?"

"Back home. She says good-bye." She put both her hands under his head and lifted. "You want to get up? I'm a little stiff."

"You could've woken me, you know."

Frannie stood and stretched her back. "I don't think you've been getting very good sleep these past few nights. Couldn't hurt to catch up a little."

"I can't believe it. I never do that."

Frannie shrugged, gathering up the blanket. "Well, you did."

"I hope I didn't hurt Cindy's feelings."

"She liked you a lot."

"Why? What did I do? Fall asleep. Kvetch about her songs."

Frannie stopped her picking up and faced him. "Dismas. You are yourself. No games. You do what you do, not trying to make any impression. It's just who you are. And I think you're great. You should know that."

"Okay."

"And now you're embarrassed."

Hardy leaned back against a tree. Frannie's eyes were bright green under her shining red hair. Although looking at her no one would have concluded that she was pregnant, she had filled out so that Hardy could hardly see the frail girl he'd caught when she fainted at Eddie's graveside.

"You're the one," he said. "I'm very proud of you."

She knew what he was talking about. Her eyes seemed to shine with the threat of tears, but she held them back, scrunching her nose up and forcing a smile. She walked up to him, put her arms around him and hugged him hard. "You go and pack your sorrows," she said. "Trashman comes tomorrow."

He felt something turn over inside of him. He looked out through the trees, trying to decide what it was.

"A body?"

"Well, something very close to a body."

"That's dead."

"Yeah."

Pico Morales shook his head. Pico was the curator of the Steinhart Aquarium, also located in Golden Gate Park, and Hardy had dropped Frannie off at the Japanese Tea Gardens and gone over to see his friend, who worked every day but Sunday. They stood now in the glow behind the tanks in the tropical fish section. In the tanks fluorescent reds and blues and yellows and greens floated against the glass or darted from rock to rock. On the other side a steady stream of people filed by, hypnotized.

"I don't have any ideas," Pico said.

"Come on, Peek, seawater is your life."

"But bodies aren't."

They moved down a couple of tanks. "What I need is just something that would act like a human body in seawater. That would float the way a body would."

"A rubber mat, something like that?"

"I don't know. Wouldn't something like that, on the surface, catch some wind? And that would affect it."

Pico made a note on a clipboard attached to one of the tanks.

"What do you see?" Hardy asked. Both of the men were squinting into a tank.

"That angel fish, see under its eye, that little spot? It bears watching, is all. We've been getting these cancers lately, maybe fungus. I don't know what it is. We're analyzing our tropical water."

"You have different water?"

Pico straightened up. "You're the one who said it. Seawater is my life. It might be anything. Second-generation problems if we got a goddamn cyanide batch. Who knows?"

"Cyanide?"

Pico was moving to the next tanks. "The tropical hunters, Diz," he said. "A lot of them use cyanide over the reefs."

"But doesn't cyanide kill the fish?"

"It does. Breaks my heart. Another hundred years

we might not even have any reefs left. I'm not kidding.
The cyanide kills the coral too. But"—he held up a
finger—"but a few of the hardier little devils make it,
and they fetch a small fortune, which is why it keeps
getting done."

"And you buy your fish from these guys."

Pico looked at him. "You think we'd support that
shit? We are very picky about our suppliers, but some
fish get through the cracks. At least maybe they do.
We see some pink-eye in an angel fish, it makes me
wonder."

They came out to the room Hardy was most familiar
with, just off Pico's office. A huge circular concrete
tank sat four feet off the floor, three-quarters filled
with seawater. In that tank Hardy, Pico and a small
group of other volunteers had spent many hours walking around with great white sharks. A great white
shark can't breathe if it isn't moving through water,
and these giants had almost always been hauled in
traumatized near to death from being caught and
taken on fishing boats. Every one had eventually died,
but it remained Pico's dream to have the first great
white shark in captivity in his aquarium.

The two men pulled themselves up and sat on the
concrete lip of the pool. Pico took a cigarette from
his shirt pocket and lit up. "But bodies," he said, "you
know what a human body is, essentially? It's a big bag
of seawater."

"I think it's your poetic side I love the best,"
Hardy said.

"It's true. Chemically, it's like ninety-seven percent
the same thing."

"Okay."

"So a body floating in seawater would be like part
of the water. Freshwater, depending on air in the lungs
and how much the tissue had become waterlogged or
whatever, the body would move up or down, but in
salt water, the specific densities are so close it would

always float. You could spray dye on the water and
watch where it goes, and that'd tell you the same
thing."

Hardy kicked his feet against the concrete. "Nope.
Same thing as a rubber raft, where the wind or a passing boat might change the course. It's got to float, but
not on the surface."

Pico said, "Aha," and jumped down onto the floor.

"What?" Hardy followed him into his office.

Pico reached behind the door and pulled down one
of the wetsuits that hung there. They were always
there—the volunteers used them when they walked
the sharks.

"The closest thing to a body is a body. Put this on,
go and hang in the water and see where it takes you."

How did things get so complicated? Glitsky was thinking. He was driving south on 101 past Candlestick
Park, on his way out of the city and out of his jurisdiction to interview an ex-cop with only the slightest connection to any active case. He shook his head. Flo was
right—he cared too much. He had to turn over every
rock to make as sure as he could he at least didn't
get the *wrong* man . . .

One of his first cases . . . Haroun Palavi, in the
country about seven months, importing rugs from
Iran, had killed his wife and the in-laws living with
them. Neighbors had heard them all screaming at one
another for weeks. When Glitsky questioned Haroun
he had no alibi—he'd been in his warehouse working
alone. There were no other plausible suspects. Haroun's fingerprints were all over the murder weapon,
which he'd tried to explain by saying that he'd come
in and just picked up the gun he'd found near his
wife's parents. He was scared. He thought the killer
might still be around.

So Glitsky had arrested Haroun. He'd investigated

and found that one of the neighbors, another Iranian woman, had talked a lot to Haroun's wife and found out that she was miserable in this country and wanted to go home. Haroun was ruining her life and her parents' lives. At the time, Glitsky had thought that she'd probably just nagged Haroun until she pushed him over the edge. He didn't understand these Iranians anyway, but he did know, or thought he knew, that they had this eye-for-an-eye mentality, and seemed, in general, to hold life pretty cheap. Haroun hadn't done a very good job of learning English, either.

So Haroun had gone to trial and was found guilty and sentenced to fifteen-to-life second-degree murder plus two for the gun, of which he served three days before they found him with a crushed skull and a broken neck on the floor of his cell. It was an effective way to kill yourself, Glitsky thought, diving headfirst from your upper bunk onto cement, although most people lacked either the nerve or the imagination for it.

And that would have been the end of the case except that about two months later the Iranian neighbor woman turned up dead, too, and it finally transpired that Haroun's business partner, Revi Mahnis, couldn't take a woman's no for an answer. Under questioning he revealed that Haroun's wife had threatened to tell Haroun that he'd been propositioning her. So he'd had to kill her or be humiliated and out of business. Both. And, because her parents were there, he had to kill them, too.

It had been Glitsky's darkest moment on the force, knowing that his preconceptions and prejudices had killed an innocent man. He wasn't about to let it happen again . . .

He took the San Bruno turnoff and doubled back on the frontage road, looking for a street name. It was a light-industry and duplex neighborhood wedged between the freeway and El Camino Real.

He didn't want to be hasty in jumping to a conclusion about who had murdered Maxine, but it still bothered him, coming down here because the lab was backed up and Hardy had said that Hector Medina had a possible connection to Rusty Ingraham. It was a reach. Here he'd got a righteous murder victim and, if you looked at the statistics, the best suspect—an estranged husband. If he was writing a book on murders he'd start with the chapter on families. After that the book would get thin pretty quick.

But the lab still didn't have squat on the results of picking apart Ingraham's barge, so he still couldn't place Ray Weir at the scene. He was pretty sure they'd find something that did that, and when they did he'd go down and bring Ray in. Not exactly open-and-shut, but just about as close as they came.

As for Rusty Ingraham, Abe wanted to believe that he was hiding out from the jealous husband Ray Weir. But he had to admit Hardy's point that he would have at least gotten in touch made some sense. Of course, until there was either a body or some compelling reason why there wasn't one, Rusty remained officially alive, and, more to the point, not a homicide victim. And if he wasn't a homicide victim he wasn't Glitsky's business. Life was complicated enough.

He'd gotten Medina's number from the telephone book and called down for an appointment.

"So the faggot told, huh?"

Glitsky hadn't known what he was talking about. "I wanted to see you about Rusty Ingraham."

A laugh. "That, too. All the roosters home to roost. Well, come on down. I got nothing to hide."

There were cars parked on lawns all down the street, oil smears on driveways, bottle caps, beer cans and broken glass in the curbs. It was a hot, still, gas-smelling afternoon. The four trees on the street had lost their leaves; an abandoned yellow schoolbus with broken windows sat on its rims at the corner. The sky seemed to hang low, a hazy blue-white.

Medina was wearing a dirty white tank-top T-shirt over baggy khakis, washing his car in his front yard with a teenage girl. The one-story frame house had once been painted lime green with yellow trim, colors from a decade before, once perhaps brightly gay, now faded to garish.

As Glitsky got out of his car Medina began drying his hands on a chamois. The girl didn't even look up— just kept wiping at the front windshield with a soapy sponge. Medina crossed the small yard and met Glitsky near his car by the curb.

"I'd rather we didn't say anything in front of Melanie," he said. He didn't offer to shake hands.

Glitsky leaned against his car's hood. "You got me stumped," he said.

Medina, squat and flat-footed, turned the chamois over in his hands. "You don't have to play games with me. I used to be a cop."

"Sure, I remember you. I understand you got a raw deal. What kind of games might I be playing?"

"Good guy, bad guy?"

Glitsky spun around from his waist, exaggerating. "Somebody else here I don't see?"

The girl called, "Daddy, I need more soap."

He turned to her. "In the bucket, sweets. Just go to the bucket." He came back to Glitsky. "My daughter. She's not all here."

Glitsky watched her go to the bucket and squeeze out her sponge, then come back to the car. He took a breath and let it out. "Why I'm here is because you talked to a friend of mine, Dismas Hardy, and said you'd had something to do with Rusty Ingraham in the last couple of weeks. Ingraham's missing and I wondered if you might have a lead on it, if he said anything to you about where he might go."

Medina shook his head, as if clearing it. "Hardy said Ingraham was dead."

"Hardy jumps to conclusions. Something went down

where he lives. We found some blood matches his
type, but no body. He could be alive, anywhere."

"Shit," Medina said.

"Shit what?"

"Shit he's not dead, that's what."

"Well, he might be. We just don't know. But either
way, if you talked to him—"

"I didn't. I told your friend I didn't."

"He said you'd called him."

Medina shifted on his feet, stared out over Glitsky's
shoulder. Abe waited him out.

Medina turned around and said his daughter's
name. "Melanie." She stopped cleaning the windshield, obedient. "You wanna get us a couple beers?"

He motioned with his head and went to sit in the
shade of the cement steps by the front door. Glitsky
followed, glad to get out of the heat. When Melanie
came out, Medina patted next to him and she sat
down. He popped the tab on a can of Lucky Lager
and handed one to Glitsky, did one for himself, giving
Melanie a little sip first.

"I never talked to him. You can believe me or not,
I don't care."

Glitsky drank beer.

"I did call him, but I just hung up. What was the
point? What was I gonna say that would make any
difference after all this time?"

"Okay . . ." Glitsky didn't know where he was
going.

"I mean, Ingraham was the wrong target. If I
wanted to do something, not feel so goddamn"—he
stopped, searching for the right word—"impotent,
there's better fish to fry."

At Abe's lack of response, he said, "I'm talking
about Treadwell."

"Who's Treadwell?"

"Treadwell. The faggot who's trying to set up Valenti and Raines."

"Treadwell," Glitsky repeated. "Is there a connection here I'm missing?"

Medina wiped some sweat off his forehead with the chamois. "The thing with Ingraham, what he did to me, that's done now. I do my job, take care of Melanie best I can. I mean since Joan left after the . . . the trouble, it's been all me. And this, this anger is in me all the time." The aluminum can made a cracking sound in his hand. "So for a minute there I had a notion to go settle things with Ingraham. That's all it was. The call."

"So what about Treadwell?"

Medina's eyes narrowed to a squint as he brought the beer can up to his mouth. Stalling. "Nothing," he said. "Treadwell was nothing too."

"Hector," Abe said. "You brought up Treadwell. I didn't."

Medina squeezed the can again, studied it. "I figured if I talked to Treadwell it might do some good for those cops Valenti and Raines. Ingraham, it was long past the time it could mean anything."

"So you talked to Treadwell?"

"Yeah."

"About Raines and Valenti?"

He nodded. "Tried to talk him out of it. Of his charges of police brutality, gay bashing."

"And?"

"And nothing," Medina said. "Nothing. He listened to me, about what it's like being accused of something crazy, how you never get out from under it. Then he said fuck you, good-bye."

Glitsky looked at Melanie, watched a kid ride by on a skateboard, tried to figure what he was missing here. "So why were you afraid Treadwell had talked? When I called you, you said, 'So the faggot talked.' Remember? What did that mean?"

"I don't know. I guess I been afraid he'd accuse me of something again—trespass, I don't know. Something. It's his style. And I'm the right guy to do it to. People are lined up to believe bad shit about me."

Glitsky gave it a moment, finishing his beer. "But nothing about Ingraham?"

"I never said a word to him and that's God's truth."

Glitsky stood up, stretched out his back. "You know, Hector," he said, "you've been in this business so you know. There's a feeling you get when people aren't telling you everything. They may not be lying exactly, but there's something else happening."

"I never talked to him!"

Melanie jumped next to her father. He patted her leg and she leaned into him, staring now at Glitsky.

"That's what you said. For the record, though, do you remember where you were Wednesday night, three days ago?"

Medina didn't even have to think. Knew right off. "I worked a double shift that day, eight to four, four to midnight. It's in the log."

Glitsky nodded. "I'm sure it is."

Medina patted his daughter again, this time on the head. "Let's do the tires next, honey," he said. She jumped up and ran over to the bucket. "Look, I got this kid to raise. That's what I do. I lead a quiet life, keep out of trouble."

"But you went to Treadwell's."

Medina looked up at the white sky and drained his beer. "Hey, sometimes you gotta do something for your soul." He gestured around the hopeless plot. "You think this is enough?"

Abe took it in, nodded, and thanked Hector for his time.

Back on the freeway Glitsky opened his car windows and let the wind blow over him. Hector Medina talking about the good of his soul rang as true as ex–Interior Secretary Watt claiming a deep and abiding

concern for the environment. And if talking to
Treadwell was good for his soul, worth threatening
the quiet life he had with his daughter, how much
more satisfying would it be to have aced Rusty Ingraham? Now that would have been real good for the
soul.

Of course the log said he had worked a double shift
on Wednesday, so he had an alibi, but alibis were
made to be broken. His name might be in the log, but
Glitsky wondered if anybody had actually seen him.
And even if they had, it wasn't a far stretch to imagine
that a guy like Medina knew people who did bad
things—either returning favors or for cash up front.

So now he had two out of three suspects with a
reason to dust Ingraham. If only he could count on
the fact of Rusty's death. And maybe Hardy would
find something . . .

He guessed it all came down to the lab. If there
were prints or hairs or fibers on the barge that belonged to Ray Weir, he'd have probable cause and go
get the guy. On the other hand, what if they found
evidence that Baker or Medina had been there? Then,
even without a body, Glitsky had to admit that things
started to look bad for Rusty Ingraham. And maybe
for Hardy too.

When he had been released from prison, Louis Baker
was given his two hundred dollars gate money. Buying
the paint for Mama's place, the windows, some food,
had run him $161.19 all told. And he'd given the
Mama a ten for the tennis shoes. The bus ride home,
this and that, had come to another ten, give or take
some change, and breakfast this morning had been
three and a half.

So he was down to twelve bucks. And no place to
stay, and still no gun.

It was different than it had been before he was sent

down. Every pawnshop had bars on the windows now. He could see the thin tape around all the doors and windows with the alarm trip-wires, and although he'd always been able to pick a lock, he had never really been much of a B and E man. The technology made him cautious.

But the fact was he needed money, and he needed a weapon. He was not about to be brought back in, even for questioning. If they tried to take him back down, he'd take some of them with him. He was thinking about the wardens, about Ingraham, about Hardy, about all the people who'd done it to him. There might even be something fun about shooting it out, going out in a blaze. Quick and easy. And it sure wasn't shaping up that he was going to have much of a life on the outside.

It was a small liquor store. He'd been watching the traffic for about two hours, a small steady trickle of people in and out. There had been bars up across the windows before it opened, but now they were tucked back accordion-style on both sides of the front door.

Louis walked in out of the afternoon sunshine. He was pretty sure when he'd been outside, but once he was inside he was positive. The location was right. A white guy running a liquor store in this neighborhood ought to have a gun under the counter, but you couldn't always bet on it. But when you saw the National Rifle Association calendar over the cold cabinets you could start putting your money down.

He came in the door, saw the counter ran along the wall to his right about fifteen feet. The man was in his mid-fifties. He sat on a stool behind the register, and Louis nodded at him, friendly as you please, as he came in. He'd made sure the place was empty, but he hadn't gotten five feet inside the door when a police car pulled up out front and a guy in blue got out.

Shit.

Louis walked casually to the back left corner of the

store. What he wanted was something long and relatively heavy. The cop went to the back, opened one of the cold shelves and stood looking at soft drinks.

You didn't want to start with the cop, especially with his partner out in the car. A lone guy, you could maybe get him from behind, put him down, but if he did that here the proprietor would probably shoot him, and if he didn't the partner would.

Louis kept scanning the shelves as though he were looking for something, thinking c'mon, c'mon, c'mon. Finally, the cop found his 7-Up or whatever cops drank and was at the counter.

He had to stall a minute or two, but he couldn't take very much longer without getting somebody suspicious. He reached into his pocket and made a pretense of counting his money. Showing he already had money, that was a good idea. Counting to see if he had enough to buy that special bottle of something.

He heard the register ring. Okay, it was time. He reached up to the top shelf and took down a bottle of Galliano. It was made for this kind of work.

But the cops were still there, parked right at the curb. Louis looked right at them. "Bright out there," he said.

The man turned his head and squinted a little. The cop in the passenger seat was lifting the can to his mouth. Louis saw a display of sunglasses at the other end of the counter. Come on, he kept thinking. *Drive.*

The man behind the counter had taken the bottle and was ringing it up. Louis put on a pair of shades, looking at himself in the mirror above the display. The cop was saying something to his partner, laughing. Goddamn, *move.*

"That all?" the proprietor said.

Louis left the pair of glasses on, reaching into his pocket for his money. The car outside made a clunk noise, dropping into gear, and Louis smiled. "I think the shades, too."

The man had put the bottle into a paper bag and Louis threw some bills on the counter, picking up the bottle.

He leaned forward to pick up the money. "I don't think this is . . ." was as far as the man got before Louis swung, hitting him over the left ear.

Before the man hit the ground Louis had vaulted over the counter. A snub-nose revolver hung by its trigger guard from a nail under the counter. There was a box of cartridges next to it on the shelf. Louis put the gun and the cartridges into his pants pocket, jabbed at the register until it opened and took out all the bills. He lifted the tray and found two hundreds and five fifties. He put a foot against the man's head on the floor and gave it a nudge. He was out cold and would not be waking up in the next thirty seconds, which was all Louis needed.

He jumped back over the counter and stood at the door, looking both ways. There was no one within fifty yards so he walked outside, hands in his pockets, and turned right. At the corner he turned again, heading back up toward Fillmore and Mama's car.

If they were going to nail him for a couple of murders, a little candy-ass liquor-store boost wasn't going to have much effect on his sentencing either way. And it evened out the odds, which was what you needed to survive—a little edge. That and knowing who to take out next.

"Are you kidding me?" Abe Glitsky was saying. "Are you *kidding* me?"

The tech, a young Filipino, maybe twenty-six, seemed to shrivel back into himself. "These were my orders, sir."

Abe put his hand to his head and pulled at his hair-line. He took a step backward, spun around in a full circle, trying to get a grip, and came back to the counter.

"Look, son, I'm sorry, I don't mean to take it out on you, but I have a murder investigation I'm running my ass all over town trying to complete and I need your reports."

"Yes, but we're told to . . . we have an inventory of nearly eighty objects from the chief's office that we are to give first priority."

"Over a murder scene? The chief wants the chicken-shitters apprehended over a murderer? I don't *believe* it."

"Yes, sir," the boy said.

"Does Rigby think whoever did this was dumb enough to leave prints around? You think cops might think of that?"

"Yes, sir."

Abe put both hands on the counter and pressed down. On the wall behind the boy was a poster of a laughing man saying, "You want it when??!!" Another one, next to the first, said, "What part of NO don't you understand?" Ha ha.

Suddenly he let up his pressure on his hands, un-tensed his shoulders and, without another word, turned and walked through the door, slapping the wall on his way out.

It was clear what he had to do. He had to stop fighting the system here. It was what it was, and you were either a part of it or you weren't. For a long time he'd been a part of it. Now he'd just spent a Saturday trying to do things right. Because he cared about doing his job. He could accept not getting paid for his time, could accept Lanier's easy-out attitude with Louis Baker. Might have even accepted a lab refusing to work overtime and having him wait until Monday.

But what he couldn't handle was that the chief of police was using the crime lab on a priority basis to catch a couple of pranksters who'd put some chickens in his office.

Downstairs at his desk Glitsky opened his top drawer and took out the application he'd filled out for the LAPD. He sat down, read it over, signed it and addressed an envelope. On his way out he dropped it in the mailbox by the back door of the Hall.

Hanging in the water, motionless, the tide pushing him where it would, Hardy thought he'd give it a couple of tankfuls' worth of air—maybe forty-five minutes—and see where he was when he came up.

Still reluctant to go back to his house and not wanting to overstay his welcome at Frannie's—was that really it?—he had borrowed one of Pico's wetsuits, rented the tanks, bought a mask and dropped into the water off Ingraham's barge at a little after six o'clock when the tide was already running out. It was a feeble current at this point, but it was moving him and Hardy thought it would be strong enough.

If Rusty had been in bed when he was shot it was reasonable to think he hadn't been wearing much that would weigh him down, so he would simply float out, just under the surface, as Hardy was doing now.

He started immediately moving out toward the bay, which was good for his theory about what had happened to Rusty. He had thought there was some chance, hard by the barge, that the tide would create an eddy and he would go around in circles. But he had swum to the point he thought Rusty had gone over and then let himself hang in the water, and after a couple of false starts when he was nudged back into the barge, he found himself out in the channel.

Even with the face mask, visibility was very poor, perhaps two feet. Under the water there was only the sound of his breathing. He wore gloves and foot pockets without fins, the same material as his wetsuit. The China Basin Canal was a rarely used waterway, but he kept half an ear out for the sound of an engine—he didn't favor the idea of being rammed by a boat coming in to tie up.

Otherwise, he hung in the water, warm, insulated, invisible—and safe. In some ways it was comparable to a night drop in a parachute, an experience Hardy had had more times than he cared to remember. For the first time in four days Louis Baker left his consciousness.

But he also felt Frannie's arms around him as he'd held her in the park. He saw her eyes boring into his, her smile working its way under his fears and defenses. There was her body pressed against him, full breasts and belly, not any kind of little girl, not anybody's little sister . . . a grown woman in full flower waiting for her baby's birth.

Hardy remembered, was forced to remember, the time with Jane when she was carrying Michael. The beginning of nesting. The changes in the house, painting the baby's room, buying the things that had seemed so impossible—tiny sets of clothes, rattles, stuff.

He shook himself out of that. When Michael died, it had nearly killed him. Jane too. Even now he wasn't sure how far over it he had gotten. He tried never to let himself think of him, of that time with Jane, and he thought there was no way he'd allow that to happen to him again. Sometimes you learned your lesson—he wasn't meant to be a father. It got into him too deep, that sense of hope, where there was meaning to things that even his well-practiced cynicism couldn't deny . . . And the baby Frannie was carrying wasn't even his.

And what about Jane?

Jane had been through it with him, all of it, finally getting back to him, reaching through whatever dark tunnel he'd constructed to let him see some light, to realize that life wasn't all black. There were good times. There was love. Sex. Whatever it was, it was more than sex. He'd gotten along well without that for enough years to know. So call it love, Diz. You tell Jane you love her. You feel like it's love.

But, admit it, not like it used to be. Not the bells ringing and heart pounding and choked up with happiness, unable-to-talk kind of love.

So what do you want? Be real, Diz. That's puppy love, and sure, you don't have that with Jane. How could you, after you lost your baby together, after the divorce, after another intervening marriage for her?

And come on, be fair. There are good things with Jane but she just has much more of her own life, doesn't need you as much as Frannie seems to.

No commitment, though, right? He, once in a while, trying to talk about the long term, and Jane not ready, always not ready yet . . .

He yanked himself away from such thoughts. The water had, by degrees, become clearer. He could easily see his hand at the end of his extended arm. A shadow—perhaps a striped bass—flashed in his peripheral vision.

After surfacing he saw he was within fifty yards of the mouth of the canal. He looked at his watch. It had only taken twenty-two minutes and the tide wasn't even running at full ebb yet. The last rays of the sun still lit the top of the skyline and the towers on the Bay Bridge, but the canal and its banks were in shade. He struck out for the shore, feeling he'd accomplished something.

12

Manny Gubicza had his manicurist in the office. He had set up a small table to the right of Gubicza's desk with a couple of bowls of lotion, a little cushion on a towel to rest his hand, some emery boards and files. Manny didn't look at the manicurist at all. He sat back, eyes closed, his massive desk between himself and Fred Treadwell.

Out the window behind Gubicza's head the sky was still light. Although it was a Saturday, Manny Gubicza was in full lawyer regalia. The coat of his three-piece suit was hung onto a wooden valet just behind and to the left of his chair. There were the purple suspenders and matching purple tie, the light lavender silk hand-made shirt with the monogram MAG stitched in slightly darker color over the breast pocket. The shirt was French-cuffed, of course, and now with the cuffs pulled back for the manicure, the ruby cufflinks sat a couple of inches apart on the desk, staring at Treadwell like the eyes of a drunk bulldog.

"All in all, I think it's worth the risk," Gubicza was saying. "We can't just do nothing."

Treadwell was still in shock and mourning. After Hector Medina had left the night before, he had cried himself out, then finally called Manny and made this appointment to discuss their strategy. This morning he had made the arrangements to bury Poppy and left him off at the vet's. It had been the longest, saddest day of his life.

"Is there any way we can kill him?" Treadwell asked. "I'd rather kill him than anything else."

Gubizca shook his head. "Fred, we're trying to get you off on a double murder. I don't think, strategically, it'd be wise to kill someone else right now."

"I don't care."

Gubizca glanced at the manicurist, who didn't look up. "I know you're hurting. It's natural." He started playing with one of the cufflinks. "But it's my job to keep you out of jail. I am the first to admit I find this behavior atrocious. Unbelievable, really. I've never heard of anything like it. I can't believe the police would be so stupid."

"He wasn't the police. I don't believe he was the police."

Gubizca flicked his right hand dismissively. "Of course, he is. Officially or not, he represented them, and it seems to me this is a death threat against you."

"But he killed Poppy!"

"Yes, I know. That's horrible, it is, Fred. But I think what we must concern ourselves with is how to respond to this threat against you."

Treadwell was leaning forward in the brocaded loveseat. "I want to punish him."

"Of course you do. And that's the right approach. I suggest we just continue with our original strategy. In a sense, our case is stronger, since this Medina fellow really was there and did damage, whereas in the other charge . . . well, you know, the evidence with them is rather slim."

"My ankle is really broken. That's *real.*"

Gubizca smiled, warm as a toad. "Yes, and we know how that really happened, don't we? I'm not sure we want to get into that."

Treadwell sat back and pulled his cast up to rest on the loveseat. Outside it had darkened, it seemed, all at once. The manicurist finished Gubizca's right hand and was moving to the other side of his chair, bringing his table with him. The lawyer pushed a panel on his desk and the lights in the room became brighter. He reached out and pulled the chain on a small Tiffany-style lamp on his desk, holding his palm under it, admiring the manicurist's completed handiwork. "Very nice," he said.

"But what about what Medina said, about no one believing me this time?"

"Why would you lie about it? Why would you kill your own beloved pet?" He laid his left hand on the table now, and the manicurist began. "No. Don't forget that the community is our strength. They will believe you. You are being harassed by the bigotry of the straight cops. And incidentally," he said, "if we don't present a pretty convincing case, you get charged with a couple of killings you did . . ." He covered the manicurist's hand with his own and squeezed. "You didn't hear that, David." The lawyer came back to Treadwell. "Honestly, Fred. This could be a very good thing for our case." He almost said, "I wish I'd thought of doing it myself."

When he got back to the parking lot Louis Baker stood on the side of the court and watched six boys playing basketball. The court was between his car—Mama's car—and where he now stood, and after nearly an hour he decided no one was watching it.

He could be wrong, but he had a hand on the gun in his pocket as he crossed the no-man's-land in case it came to something.

He looked different. With his stolen money he had gone into the St. Vincent de Paul store and bought himself some clothes that fit, traded in the tennis shoes for hiking boots, picked up a Forty-Niners jacket, some sunglasses and a mock leather driving cap. He shaved in the bathroom of a gas station on Geary before walking back to his car.

He knew the address—he had burned it into his mind nine years ago. Turning left out of the lot on Fillmore, he headed up to Jackson Street, where Hardy had lived, might still live—you never knew. Either way he'd find him soon enough.

It was funny with Rusty Ingraham dead now, and Dido, and how the unexpected sometimes just put things in your hands. You left the joint, you maybe got intentions to go a certain way, but things happened around you and pretty soon you're sailing along like you never gave a thought to direction. The wind blew, you'd be a fool to fight it.

And now they wanted him for murder again, like they'd always done. There's trouble, first they looked to him. This time he hadn't even gotten the smell of the prison soap off him before the hassling began. Okay. Just so he knew.

It wasn't like they said it would be, but then he hadn't really believed them anyway. But he wondered why they spent so much time trying to convince the cons with the lie. In the House, see, they kept telling you that things would be different on the outside. There're all kinds of agencies and people set up to get you going straight. Which, you know, the first year you just roll your eyes and figure they got to tell you something—might as well be a fairy tale. You're in the joint a while, though, and it starts sounding possible. Like, maybe there really are jobs out there.

But none of the guys who'd been out and came back seemed to get those jobs. Which was natural . . . who was going to hire an ex-con when he can get somebody he might need to trust?

In the end you believed what you wanted to believe. And the proof was here. Louis Baker, out about three days, doesn't need no good intentions no more. Hard to live up to anyway. Now, since he's going down for it anyway, he's going to do something to make himself feel good.

He pulled into the curb under a streetlamp across from the old Victorian. There was one light in the front window, the kind people left on when they weren't home.

Louis got out of the car, put his hands in his jacket pocket, where the gun was, and walked over, up the steps, rang the doorbell. He took a couple of deep breaths and squeezed the grip on the gun.

After no one answered he tried the door, but a glance had already told him that would be a tough way in. There was a new, heavy-looking deadbolt set into the door just above the knob.

But going in the front door wasn't his style anyway. He descended the stoop and walked along the side of the house, where a cement strip drained the area between this Victorian and the building nearly flush up against it. There were three windows in that wall, all of them locked.

Coming around the back corner, he kicked the metal lid of a garbage can and it skidded for what seemed like ten seconds, sounding like a small army passing through. Several dogs started barking and Louis pressed himself deep into the shadows up against the house.

The dogs were good, he thought. Dogs were always knocking over garbage cans. Cats, too. Even raccoons. He'd wait. Prison had made him good at waiting. It would get quiet again.

He craned his neck up around him. It was maybe fifteen feet to what looked in the darkness to be a tall back fence on the other side of which an apartment building rose five or six stories. Each story had about six windows facing him, some lit, but he saw no silhouette that came to look down at the noise. On either side there wasn't even a fence—the buildings started at the property line. This would be a bad place to get trapped. There was no way out except back down the shoulder-width alley he had just come down.

He made out the wooden porch a **couple** of steps up off a back doorway. Stepping away **from the** house, avoiding the garbage can lid, he saw **some stairs** going down under the porch. There were two **windows** side-by-side down there in a little well under the porch, and one of them was open an inch at **the top.**

Louis wasn't going to throw the **house.** He was going to find out if Hardy still lived **there,** then if so, wait until he came home. He let himself **into a** laundry room and felt his way in the dark to **the doorway,** then up a couple of steps to what felt **like a** kitchen.

His eyes were adjusting. There was also a little light seeping down the hallway from the living room. On the floor by the front door he saw a pile of mail that had been dropped through the mail slot. It appeared whoever lived here now was someone named Jane Fowler, and she'd been gone for at least a week already.

He dropped the envelopes back on the floor and returned to the kitchen. He opened the refrigerator, but the pickings were slim. A couple of bottles of white wine, one of them half empty. A loaf of bread. Some plastic containers wouldn't hold enough food for a child. Four bottles of dark beer.

He took out one of the beers, the bread and a jar of peanut butter and went over to rummage through some drawers near the sink for a knife. The light from the refrigerator cut an arc through the darkness of the kitchen, falling on the wall by the door to the hallway.

Chewing on his sandwich, he took a hit of the beer and nearly gagged. The stuff was dark and thick and tasted like liquid sen-sen. He looked at the bottle—he had thought it was beer but it was called stout and the only thing it had in common with beer was its bottle. He poured it out into the sink.

He took one of the half-bottles of wine from the refrigerator and washed out his mouth. With the light he could now make out things in the kitchen. He walked over to where the light fell near the door and looked at the calendar—and stopped everything.

The name Dismas—not very common—appeared about five places in September. He smiled, swallowed his sandwich in a gulp and went back to work.

The telephone was in an alcove in the hallway, and he risked now turning on the hall light. He would only be here a few more minutes. The phone sat on an answering unit on a built-in shelf under which were a couple of phone books. Next to the phone was a Rolodex. Louis Baker flipped to H and there it was. Out in the Avenues, maybe two miles west. Take him fifteen minutes.

Flo was doing the dishes. Glitsky sat at the table, playing Monopoly with the three kids. The boys were named Isaac, Jacob, and O.J.—Flo had drawn the line at Esau. O.J. was only eight, but he already had a hotel on the boardwalk and Glitsky was hanging out in jail, waiting for doubles. The boys always got a kick out of their father the cop being in jail, but Abe didn't want to get out and land on anything, and this way the other boys could eliminate each other and he might have a chance to buy some cheap property and get back in the game.

The telephone rang, and Abe was in the middle of yelling "Let it go!" when Flo picked it up on the first ring. He heard her say, "Just a minute, he's right here," then appear in the doorway. "It's work," she said.

"It always is."

"But it's your turn," O.J. whined.

"Let Jake roll for me." He shook a finger at his oldest son. "Don't get doubles."

He walked into the kitchen. "Glitsky," he said into the receiver.

"Sergeant," the voice said, "this is Paul Ghattas." There was a pause. "From the lab."

He pictured the Filipino boy he had chewed out earlier in the day. There was a scream from the other room as one of his sons landed on a bad property. Flo disappeared, and he heard her telling them to keep it down. Ghattas was saying something, but Glitsky couldn't get his mind on it. He had told himself he was leaving the force as soon as he could and relocating to Los Angeles, and these cases that no one else seemed to care about could take care of themselves. "I'm sorry," he said, "what did you say?"

He grabbed the pencil and pad of paper from their spot stuck to the side of his refrigerator and started taking notes. Ghattas had evidently cajoled someone he knew at ballistics into doing some work, and they had definitely identified Ray Weir's gun as the murder weapon. Of course, in the barge itself they had found prints from the female victim and from Rusty Ingraham, but on the lamp they had picked up prints from a small-time local enforcer named Johnny LaGuardia. There was a last print that kind of confused Ghattas.

"There was a drinking glass, tagged 'Galley,' with as clear a print as you'd want of a guy named Louis Baker."

Glitsky felt a chill in his back.

"Problem is, we ran Baker and he's in San Quentin."

"The computer hasn't caught up," Abe said. "Baker got out on Wednesday."

"Looks like he went right back to work."

"Yes it does."

Flo had come back into the kitchen and saw Abe staring at what he had written down. She heard him thank the man on the phone, saying he appreciated someone who still cared about getting his job done.

When he hung up he didn't move for a minute, and

Flo came over behind him and rubbed her hand up and down his back.

"Hardy's in big trouble," he said. "Baker was on the barge."

Hardy felt Frannie's hand in his back pocket. He felt the gun in its holster in the small of his back.

The fog had descended once again on the city. They were walking in zero visibility, three blocks straight uphill from where they had had dinner on Noe, three blocks to go before they got to Frannie's place. Hardy had his arm around her—she walked leaning into him.

He looked up the hill. He knew there were street-lights all along, but he could only see the next one perhaps twenty feet ahead of them. Sometime during dinner, after the euphoria of proving that Rusty Ingraham could indeed have floated out into the bay had passed, he had come up against what that might mean in his here and now. But he had already had most of a bottle of wine by that time, and now he was explaining to Frannie that he felt unprepared if Louis Baker took this moment to attack.

"But he doesn't even know where you are," Frannie said.

"He found Rusty."

"Rusty happened to be where he lived. You're here."

Hardy kept walking. Baker had had four days to locate him, and it was getting to the time where it was reasonable to think he'd have made some progress. It couldn't be that hard to find someone you wanted to kill real bad.

They were coming into Frannie's block now, the buildings tight up against each other, blue light from front-room television sets showing through a few windows. The wind blew straight downhill at them and they leaned into it and each other. Up ahead of them,

Hardy heard a car door open and close. He tried to make out a shape in the dark fog, but there was nothing. Then, faintly, he heard footsteps echoing on the asphalt. He tightened his arm around Frannie.

"Hold it a second," he said. He stopped them both, pulled them back into a building entrance a few doors down from Frannie's. He took off his jacket and helped put it on Frannie. "You start walking back and wait around the corner," he said. "If you hear anything sounds like shooting, get into a building somehow. You hear me?"

Taking his gun from the holster behind him, he squinted into the fog up the hill.

"Dismas, what are you—?"

He put a finger to his lips. *"Go!"* He watched her for a few steps, then he ran across the sidewalk. The curb was lined with cars. Hardy stepped between a couple out into the street, then turned uphill.

Okay, he said to himself, the guy's big enough to be Baker. The man wore a heavy coat and a cap pulled low on his forehead. Hardy, crouching behind the wall of cars, did not take his eyes off him. It wasn't just somebody taking a walk. He came down the street slowly, taking his time, looking into doorways, perhaps looking for a street address. He kept his hands in his coat pockets.

Hardy worked his way uphill. Frannie had disappeared around the corner. He was maybe five cars down from Frannie's doorway when the guy turned into it. Hardy caught a glimpse of a face in the light from Frannie's foyer—enough to see it was a black man.

Hardy gripped the gun, moving uphill. The man stood in the doorway, waiting for Hardy to open the door so he could blow him away. Hardy leveled his gun at his back, resting his arm on the hood of one of the cars. The man knocked on the door.

Hardy cocked the hammer. He wondered if this

would classify as self-defense, or if he should call out and have Baker turn with a weapon in his hand. Hardy had seen some action in Vietnam, but he had never even considered killing anyone since, at least before this Baker madness started.

He should just pull the trigger and the problem would be over. Baker was wanted for murder. He had killed Ingraham and threatened to kill Dismas Hardy. Now he was here and no jury in the world would believe he was here for an Amway meeting. Shoot first, Diz, and live.

He took in a deep breath and began tightening his finger on the trigger as Abe Glitsky turned around in the doorway and peered into the gloom down the street.

"Jesus Christ," Hardy said to himself. Not again. He uncocked his weapon and put it in the holster, then stood up and came onto the sidewalk.

"Hey, Abe," he said. "Fancy meeting you here."

The three of them sat drinking hot chocolate at the table in the kitchen nook.

"That's Jane's house!" Hardy said.

"Is it?" Glitsky asked.

"It used to be ours together, back when Baker went down."

Frannie still wore Hardy's jacket, and she pulled herself down into it. "So he was looking for you."

Hardy nodded.

Even Glitsky seemed to buy it, finally. "If that used to be Jane's house . . ."

Hardy repeated the address, and Glitsky said that was it. Hardy sipped some chocolate. "Calling it coincidence gets a little thin about now, don't you think, Abe?"

"So is he dead?" Frannie asked. "Louis Baker?"

Glitsky shook his head. "Not yet." He turned to

Hardy. "He took two slugs. They got him in the County General."

"How'd they get him?"

"He made some noise, turned some lights on—I guess he was out of practice on burglaries, or just overconfident. Anyway, one of the neighbors knew the house was supposed to be empty and called in. Our guys caught him strolling out. When he got cornered he opened up."

Hardy leaned back in his chair. "So it's over," he said. He told Abe about his experiment with the tide.

"Well, not to be picky," Abe said, "but that still doesn't make Rusty dead."

Hardy sighed. "All right, but like you said, it sure strengthens the argument."

Glitsky held up a hand. "If you had somebody wants to argue. Me, I'm happy enough now it was Baker. He was on the barge with a motive and a handy weapon—ought to be good enough."

"So you came around to tell me that?"

Glitsky shook his head. "I got the details on the way over on the squawk box. The reason I started over here was I found Louis had been at Rusty's and I wanted to advise you to keep an eye out."

"I've been doing that."

"I know," Abe said. "I'm not blind." Glitsky wasn't comfortable with private citizens walking around armed, even if it was his best friend, even if he had a permit. "So how close did you come to doing me?"

"Miles," Hardy said.

Frannie refilled Glitsky's mug. "He's just been worried, Abe. You would be, too."

"There, see?" Hardy tried to smile, but still felt like someone had kicked him in the stomach. He hadn't made up his mind whether or not he was going to pull the trigger, but he'd come close enough.

It didn't need it, but Glitsky blew on his chocolate. "Before I found out about Baker tonight, I thought

I'd bring you my file, ease your mind with some light reading."

Hardy fingered the manila folder. "What's to read?"

"This was before we had placed Baker on the barge, remember. To let you know that there were people involved here, good suspects, who didn't know you from Ezechiel. I thought it might relax you a little, get Louis Baker off your brain."

"But don't you need your files?" Frannie asked.

Abe stood up. "I don't think so, not anymore."

"What's the matter, Abe?"

Glitsky's face hung like a bloodhound's. His eyes were shot with red. "I figure I'm finished with it, Diz. Nobody cares anymore. You know what I mean . . . So, it sure looks like Baker, probably is Baker, why don't we just gas him now and be done with it?

"It reminds me of the movie *Casablanca*, rounding up the 'usual suspects.' Well, that's not police work. It's not what I do, so fuck it." He nodded to Frannie. "Excuse the French," he said.

Outside the wind came up and whistled against the windows. Glitsky pushed his chair forward and said he had to be going home. Hardy and Frannie walked him to the door.

"So what now?" Hardy asked.

"Like I said, I'm going home. We'll see you guys tomorrow, right?"

They watched him walk, hunched over into his coat, until he disappeared into the fog, and then Frannie closed the door. She turned to Hardy. "Ezechiel?" she said.

Hardy sat on the couch. The manila folder with Glitsky's notes lay open on the coffee table in front of him. Somewhere back behind him he was vaguely aware of the shower Frannie was taking. His shirt was off and he had pulled the comforter up over his shoulders and leaned forward, his elbows on his knees, reading, and maybe starting to see something for the first time.

He hated to admit it, but with Louis Baker no longer threatening him, the facts of the matter didn't point all that more strongly to him than to, say, Ray Weir, the jealous husband, or even to Hector Medina, who had had a hard-on for Rusty for years.

Also, Abe had written "Johnny LaGuardia" with three exclamation points after his name, with a notation about *his* prints being on the fallen lamp. Hardy had never heard the name Johnny LaGuardia, even from Abe, and he wondered what he had to do with anything three exclamation points' worth.

But then he reminded himself that Louis Baker's prints were also found on the barge, in the galley, and if Baker was there, then he did it.

Didn't he?

He stood up, wrapping the comforter around him, and paced from the window to the hallway door and back. The fog seemed to glow in the streetlights, eddying gently now before him as it drifted down the hill.

It came back to him, then, the feeling of seeing Abe loom out of that same fog. Of almost shooting him in the back. Or not almost. Already his memory was getting selective about it. He hadn't really been going to shoot if it had turned out to be Baker—had he?

Abe kept getting mistaken for Baker, didn't he? Maybe, on some level, even for Hardy, they all did look alike.

Well, he wasn't going to lose any sleep worrying over the fate of Louis Baker, who'd been at Rusty's, had broken into Jane's house, who for sure was the same badass he'd always been.

"What are you thinking?"

Frannie was wrapped in a white terrycloth robe. She had dried her hair and it gleamed like a red halo around her face.

Hardy walked back to the couch, avoiding her eyes. "Just pondering what Abe would call the moral ambiguities—"

"Of what?"

He motioned to the table. "This stuff."

But that wasn't all and he knew it. He sat down. Frannie leaned, arms crossed, against the doorjamb.

"Dismas?" she said.

He knew if he looked up he was in trouble, so he reached out and started arranging papers in the folder. Frannie came and stood next to him. He raised his head and she put her hands in his hair and pulled him into her. She opened the robe and his face was against her belly, the smell of powder and woman, her skin warm and tight, her heart pounding under it.

"Come on," she said, and he followed her into the bedroom.

13

Lace was at the Mama's putting up some plywood over the hole where Dido had broken the window.

The fog, which had come in late the night before, was already lifting. A light breeze fluffed at Lace's flannel shirt. As far as Lace knew, no one in the cut had seen or heard anything about Louis Baker since two nights before, and Lace was figuring Louis ought to show up soon if he had any notion at all of claiming the cut, because it was slipping away fast.

Last night, Dido not yet in the ground, and Samson who ran the next cut over was seeing that no one worked out of this one. Lace and Jumpup, they'd laid low, letting things shake out.

He felt bad about Dido. Dido had been like his big brother, his protector. Lace wasn't sure how he was going to handle Louis Baker when he came back, but the first thing was to get his confidence, make him think he'd change allegiances like the wind blew. He didn't want Louis Baker feeling like he had to kill him the way Louis had had to kill Dido to secure the cut. So he'd make up to Mama, keep close and informed, fix the window and bide his time. Then when Louis came back and wasn't looking, something bad would happen to him.

The Mama stuck herself out around the back of the building, a mountain of a woman in a multicolored caftan. She had cooked up a pan of cornbread inside and had butter and honey to go on it. Lace drove in another nail and let himself into the kitchen.

The Mama sat at the table, cutting into the pan. The cornbread smell filled the room.

"Sit down, child," she said. "Eat up."

Lace obeyed her, savoring the flavors, the butter melted into the bread, a little honey over the top. Mama poured him a glass of milk.

"Police brought back my car," the Mama finally said. "Louis didn't do it no harm."

"They find him?"

"He got shot," she said. "Everybody always wants to be shooting."

Lace just nodded.

"Probably now he go back to the House. Police say it might be better if he don't live now, what they might fix to do to him." She cut another square of cornbread and put it on Lace's plate. "They're saying he killed Dido, you hear that?"

"He did kill Dido," Lace said.

The Mama nearly exploded. "Why you say that?" Then, more quietly. "What make you think that trash, boy?"

Lace had to chew a minute before he could swallow. His mouth was dry and he took a gulp of milk. "Dido's shot and he runs," he mumbled out.

"You thinking like the police now," she said. "Running don't make you guilty. Running keep you out of the way, that's all. First thing the Man do is look for somebody like Louis, maybe done some bad things before. Easy to lay it off on Louis, then."

"Maybe."

"Okay. Why Louis want to kill Dido?"

It was so obvious he had trouble saying it. "He want the cut, Mama."

"You think Louis that dumb? He shoot Dido and run away from the cut he wants?"

"He didn't do it, he shouldn't have run."

The Mama shook her head. "Child, child, child. Where you comin' from? He gotta run. He got no choice."

Lace went back to his cornbread, thinking that the Mama maybe made some sense . . . Louis had fought with Dido and the war was still going on with Dido breaking the window, but it would have been plain stupid to kill Dido, especially to get at the cut. Be like putting up a flag saying you did it.

Be more like it if somebody used the fighting between Dido and Louis to get rid of one and set up the other. Free up the cut, too. Lace needed to think on that.

Hardy ran his hand along Frannie's side before he slipped out of bed. She stirred, made a noise in her throat and settled back into sleep. Hardy pulled the blanket up over her, moving her hair away from her face.

They had been awake most of the night, talking and loving one another. Like old friends in one way, but in the other—Hardy was amazed at what had gone on. Now, showering, the images of Frannie over him, under him, things they'd done the second and then third time, he found himself getting excited again and turned up the cold water so he could get on with the day, with his real life.

His real life.

He put on a pot of coffee, wondering what his real life had become lately, ever since Rusty Ingraham had walked into the Shamrock. Until then he'd been doing okay—in some ways, he thought, better than okay. Certainly better than the sleepwalk he'd been in before he got back with Jane. And things with Jane were at least steady. He worked bartending with easy hours doing something he mostly enjoyed.

And then—it was like the question you sometimes

heard at parties—what if somebody told you that you were going to die in three days, or six months? What would you do differently?

And of course the "right" answer was "I'd just keep doing what I'm doing."

Well, somebody had made Hardy believe that he might die in the very near future, and he hadn't done anything like what he'd been doing. What did that mean? That he hadn't been happy with what he was doing? And how did he feel about what he was doing now? If he had one day left, would he choose to spend it with Frannie or Jane? Or alone?

Well, if he was lucky he had more than one day left, and didn't have to make that decision. The sun was high. The fog was mostly burned off. Hardy thought that when he moved back into his house—whenever that happened—he'd start going down to Graffeo's for coffee. It really was better than his canned espresso.

He went to the front door and found the Sunday paper on the stoop. He looked out at the line of cars parked along the curb, trying to imagine himself last night, huddled behind one, a gun trained on Abe Glitsky's back. It looked so different in the sunlight. Had he really done that?

Had he and Frannie really done all that, too? And what would that look like in the daytime?

He opened the paper in the nook and a front-page story got his attention right away. Hector Medina was back in the news. Fred Treadwell, it seemed, had now accused Medina of killing his dog and threatening his own life. There were two sidebars on Hector. One outlined the seven-year-old accusation that he had been a killer cop. Case closed. Hardy was still an ex-cop and ex-D.A., and that sort of reporting bothered him, never mind that he had been suspicious of Medina's self-serving protest of innocence to him. The other sidebar was an interview with Medina—evidently some reporter had called him at home the night before the paper went to press. All Hardy read there was a refrain of Medina's complaint to him—once you'd been accused, you might as well have done it, since everyone treated you like you had anyway. Of course he hadn't killed any dog, but everyone would believe he had, although he said it was the dumbest accusation he'd ever heard. Why would he kill the man's dog? And so forth.

For a second it crossed Hardy's mind that maybe he'd done the same thing with Louis Baker. He was a bad man. Therefore he was guilty of bad things that happened. And it followed—once you got accused of doing bad things, you might as well go ahead and do them. In for a penny, in for a dollar.

No. Not in Baker's case. He'd been at Rusty's. He'd gotten shot after breaking into Jane's, for God's sake, looking for him . . .

Hardy put the paper down and was staring out the windows. He felt hands on his shoulders, massaging, coming around to rest on his chest. Frannie kissed the top of his head, and he leaned back into her.

"Hi," he said.

She patted his chest and straightened up. "I love you," she said, sliding into the chair next to him, looking in his eyes, "and you're confused."

Hardy smiled. "Not so confused."

"Good."

"Not that I have any idea what I'm doing, what we're doing, what any of this means."

"That's okay. I don't either."

Hardy took her hand. "It's not casual, though, you know?"

"I know."

"I'm just trying to figure out what's my so-called real life."

"Me or Jane?"

He shook his head. "Not just that. That's part of it."

"I'm not staking any claim, you know. But I do want you to know that I love you."

Hardy looked down at the hand he held. Eddie's wedding ring was still on her finger. He wanted to say a lot of things—that saying you loved somebody was staking a claim, that he didn't know where to put his own infatuation, that he didn't trust what he called "love, the feeling"—he trusted "love, the attitude." The problem was that he had the feeling with Frannie. With Jane, he was starting to think he had the attitude and was trying to manufacture the feeling, often with decent success. But it wasn't the same as the racing he felt in his veins now.

He did, however, know that he wasn't going to just say "I love you" right now. That was too open to misinterpretation.

Instead he lifted her hand and kissed it. "You know when I said I wasn't so confused?" he said.

She nodded.

"I lied."

Frannie laughed her wonderful laugh, fixing him with dancing eyes. "Oh Dismas. Let's just enjoy this. Eddie's gone and I miss him horribly and Jane's not in the picture right now and we're two grown-ups who've known and cared about each other forever and now are attracted to each other." She squeezed his hand. "Okay, very attracted. We've got a little window in time we can have just for ourselves, so let's take it. I'm not trying to find a father for the baby and you don't have to decide between me and Jane, at least until what you call your real life starts again."

"I've never thought of the 'love as a window in time' theory."

"How about if there isn't any theory?"

"Then something can happen you're not ready for."

Frannie laughed again, shaking her head. "You ever think that life is something that happens and that you're not ever completely prepared for?"

"Yeah, and it makes me uncomfortable."

"I know. So you want to control everything, but things can't be controlled. Eddie being killed. Michael dying. Louis Baker putting you and me together like this. It's just out of our control."

"How about last night?"

Now a slow smile. "Last night was a freight train without brakes going downhill and you know it."

"But something had to get it started."

"It started when you rang my bell here. It started before I married Eddie. It started when I met you. And in our, as you say, real lives, we had it under control. Then this funny thing happened with your life being threatened. Just like funny things happen all the time."

"Well, your window of time is closing. Jane is coming back. I should move back home. Louis Baker's in custody. Why don't I feel like things are over? Settled?"

Frannie leaned over and shut him up with a kiss. "Because some things are just starting."

Hardy got up and went out to the living room, where last night's comforter lay heaped on the couch. Glitsky's file was still open on the coffee table.

Frannie came up behind him and put her arms around his waist, her face against his back. "Okay, here's the thing," he said. "Everything seems connected somehow—you, me, this Baker situation. And my instincts are telling me it's not over. There's too much unresolved—"

"You mean with Baker?"

"I mean with Rusty Ingraham. But I'm also wondering if that instinct is really me just wanting to prolong things here with you, put off my return to real life."

She rubbed her hands up and down the front of his shirt. "What's unresolved?"

He crossed over to the table, picked up the file. "This stuff here. Also, in the paper this morning another guy involved in all this shows up around another violent crime."

"But didn't they get Baker at Jane's? And doesn't that mean he was after you?"

"Absolutely."

She folded her arms across her chest. "Well?"

"It doesn't mean he killed Rusty, or Maxine, or the guy in the projects. It only means he was after me."

"Okay, but you can infer—"

"Sure you can. It's what I've been doing all along." He sat down on the couch and Frannie came over. "Last night I almost shot Abe. No, listen. I was one-hundred-percent certain it was Louis Baker on your porch, here to kill me. But I couldn't take him out without making sure, thank God. Something stopped me from pulling the trigger."

Frannie sat back, not knowing where he was going.

"If I couldn't kill Baker last night, how can I do it now?"

"How would you be doing that?"

"Multiple murder rap, he'll get the gas chamber . . ."

"But Abe even said—"

"Sure. But Abe's instincts aren't always wrong. Often, in fact, they're right. I mean, I was so scared the last few days I wasn't interested in anything but saving my ass. And that meant pointing to Baker."

"And now?"

"Now, I think I can see for the first time that Abe might have had a point, back there when this whole thing started. In his shoes, knowing what he knew, and didn't know, I'm not sure I would have arrested Baker right away either—"

"But Abe, knowing what he did, finally did arrest Baker, didn't he?"

"Not exactly. Baker got shot outside Jane's house, where we suppose he was looking for me to kill me."

"But didn't Abe say he was going to charge him?"

"No. It sounded like he said he was going to quit. Maybe let the Ingraham case slide and be happy to have Baker go down for the woman's murder, or the burglary, or even breaking his parole. He's fed up, is all."

"But Baker was coming to kill you!"

"Don't get me wrong, Frannie. I don't care too much about what happens to one Louis Baker. But he ought to go down for what he's actually done."

"So let a jury decide that. Or Abe."

"Juries can be wrong, and Abe's not interested in his current mood." Hardy flipped some pages in Abe's file, leaning over the coffee table. "There's another thing," he said.

She sat forward, a hand on his back. "What's that?"

"One way or the other I'm deeply involved in all this, right? So let's, for argument, let's say Baker didn't kill Rusty. Let's even, just for fun, say Rusty isn't dead. If either or both of those are true, then why am I, Dismas Hardy, part of this at all . . . unless I'm being set up."

"But set up for what?"

Hardy closed the file and leaned back against the couch. "Exactly."

Hardy was thinking that maybe Frannie's infatuation had ended, since she was already pissed off at him for going to see Louis Baker in the hospital. He should just leave it alone, she said. But he still felt some danger. If he was being set up . . . Or maybe he wanted to stay at Frannie's a little longer and needed an excuse. Or maybe he felt less than a paragon and wanted to soothe his conscience now that his life wasn't, so far as he knew, directly threatened. It was all jumbled, but also somehow connected.

He and Frannie had had their first fight. She said

that compulsive need to find out, to do the right thing, had killed her husband. She wasn't about to have it happen to Hardy too.

But Hardy knew that idealism hadn't killed Eddie Cochran four months ago. A bullet in the brain had killed him, and Eddie had had no more control over who had put it there than he did over the wind. Eddie had been going along, living his life, trying to make it a good one, and someone had ended it—abruptly, senselessly. If something in Frannie needed to believe that Eddie's idealism had gotten him involved in things that had led to that lonely parking lot in the middle of the night, Hardy could accept that. He knew it had been someone else's agenda, not Eddie's, that had ended his life.

He put it out of his mind as the guard let him into the hospital room. He had called Abe from Frannie's and Abe had cleared an interview with Baker, even if he didn't approve of it. He had made Hardy promise not to take his gun.

Even with tubes in his arms and a hose running into his nose, Baker looked intimidating. Hardy backed away from the bed and glanced at the door to the room, making sure the guard was still just outside.

He couldn't place him. Hardy had no distinctive memory of what Baker had looked like nine years before. A big black man. He'd sent away a lot of them.

"Yo, Louis," he said.

Baker opened his eyes. He was still heavy-lidded, perhaps sedated, but there was recognition there. Baker's eyes had a yellowish tint, both the white and the brown iris. "Well, if the mountain ain't come . . ." After the one phrase he closed his eyes again.

Hardy pulled up a chair so he could be close to Baker's face. "I hope you got a better lawyer than last time," he said. He watched Baker for a reaction but there wasn't any. He might have gone back to sleep.

" 'Cause when you get better from this tragic accident that's put you in the hospital, then you're going to go sit in a small green room and breathe some real bad air. But, you know, the good part is you won't breathe it for too long."

Baker opened his eyes. "Talk about bad air."

"They say the gas is painless, but you hear stories. Guys who get the first whiff and their heads jerk back and eyes bug out, like they're gagging on fire. It's gotta be agony, don't you think? But again, I guess it doesn't last too long."

"I ain't going to no gas chamber on a B and E."

"Fuck the B and E. I'm talking the murders."

"I didn't do no murders."

"You didn't do Rusty Ingraham? You better have a good lawyer."

"I didn't even see no Rusty Ingraham. I tole the cop that."

"And you know, he wanted to believe you, but finding your prints over at Rusty's place made him skeptical. You know that word, Louis, skeptical? It means he thinks you're full of shit."

Baker closed his eyes again.

"You sleepy, Louis? You want me to go away? 'Cause we got you on Rusty's barge, we got you in the cut. We got three dead people with your name all over 'em." Hardy saw movement under Baker's eyelids—he was thinking about things.

Hardy hadn't formally interrogated anyone since he'd left the D.A.'s office, but you didn't lose the knack. It was kind of fun, in fact, realizing that Louis probably thought he was still a prosecutor.

"Three?" Baker opened his eyes, pulled himself up. "What three? You trying to tag me for every murder in the county last week? What's a matter, you got nobody else on parole?"

The effort of talking cost Louis, and he had to lie back down, breathing out through his mouth.

"I ain't do a thing, you all decide I'm going back down."

"How'd you get a gun, Louis? Shooting at cops. Breaking and entering. You call that not doing a thing?"

Louis picked up his hand, waving all of that off. "It ain't killing."

Hardy sat back in his chair. It was not rare for a killer to deny killing anybody. But he had Louis arguing, talking. You had to use what you had and keep 'em talking.

"No, killing was Rusty Ingraham, killing was the woman at his place, killing was the homeboy in the cut."

"What woman at Ingraham's?"

"Her name was Maxine Weir."

"There wasn't no woman—" Louis stopped abruptly, retreating again behind his closed eyes, lying back.

Hardy leaned forward, smiling now. "Oops," he said.

"I want my lawyer here."

Hardy leaned over closer and whispered in Baker's ear. "Fuck you, Louis. Fuck your lawyer. This is me and you."

"I'll get a mistrial."

"I'll deny it, and who's going to believe you?"

Louis tried to lift himself on the bed, which brought on a coughing fit. The oxygen hose came out of his nose. Hardy stood and pulled his chair back while the guard came over and pushed a button by the bed. In another minute a nurse was there. The coughing fit had passed and Louis lay still, looking dead.

The nurse replaced the oxygen tubes and checked the bandages on Baker's chest and thigh. Hardy could see the blood through the gauze—a line of blood and drool had run from Baker's mouth. There was a low gurgling sound, and Hardy realized it was Baker's breathing.

The nurse turned. "He shouldn't really talk."

Hardy decided to keep pretending to be official until someone called him on it. "I'll only be another five minutes. This is a murder suspect."

"Do you want him alive to go to trial?"

Hardy glanced at Baker, then back at the nurse. "Not particularly, but I'll keep it short anyway."

Hardy pulled his chair back up and noticed the nurse saying something to the guard at the door.

"Now where were we?" Hardy said. "Oh yeah. You were on Ingraham's barge."

Baker was still struggling with his breath, as though he'd been running. "There wasn't no woman there," he said.

"You told Sergeant Glitsky *you* weren't there."

"He puts me there, he thinks I did the man."

"Correct."

"The man brung me there."

"Who did?"

"Ingraham."

"Ingraham brought you where he lives? You want me to believe that?"

"You believe what you want anyway. I'm telling you what happen."

"Okay. What happened?"

"I get off the bus an' the man is there waitin'. He goes, 'Come take a ride with me,' and I pass on it. But he's packing."

"You're telling me Rusty Ingraham pulled a gun on you?"

Baker nodded. "I told you. He shows me a piece and we go to his car. I figure he's going to shoot me, but we drive about two mile and next I know we're on this boat.

"He says he hears I'm tryin' to be a citizen now,

good behavior up the House, like that. We sit drinking water on his couch and he say he hope all that's true, but in case it isn't, he wants me to know where he lives so by mistake I don't ever come near the place, which if I do he's gonna shoot first, self-defense, do I get the message?"

The gurgling sound came again deep in his throat, and Baker swallowed a couple of times, making a face.

"Then what?" Hardy asked.

"Then I up and leave. I walk around, getting away from there. I'm a free man."

The guard came walking up. "The nurse said two minutes."

Hardy stood, looking down at Baker. He was still swallowing, a light sheen of sweat across his brow. He opened his eyes. "I didn't kill nobody," he said.

The guard rolled his eyes at Hardy. "They never do, do they?" he said.

14

A cane in one hand, Angelo Tortoni walked out of Saints Peter and Paul church at Washington Square. His wife, Carmen, held him in the crook of her elbow on the other side, and their two sons, Matteo and Franco, walked in front of and behind him as he turned left off the steps.

He walked slowly, enjoying the beautiful morning, enjoying his wife's chatter. Carmen was nearly twice the size of Angelo, but was not at all fat. He liked to think of her as sturdy—good solid legs, a hard round *culo*, a wide waist and melon breasts. She was twenty years younger than he was, originally from Italy and, because of that, well-trained but with a passionate nature and a seemingly innate knowledge of what kept your husband happy, even after a couple of decades.

Several times the Angel had thought his wife would kill him with her energy, but he was beginning now to realize that her enthusiasm was probably keeping him young. She could be tireless in the pursuit of his pleasure, as she had been last night, and then demanding that she got hers, too. Tortoni thought that was fair—he didn't think there were many woman who could bring him to life so often as Carmen did. Even when he thought he didn't want it.

The little procession crossed the square, then turned up Powell at the Fior D'Italia. Sunday was God's day. Carmen was happy. Angelo wouldn't leave the house after lunch—a few neighbors would stop by to pay their respects, perhaps ask a favor or two. Today they would find Angelo Tortoni a soft touch. He turned his head and nodded, smiling, at something his wife said. She looked down almost shyly, squeezing his arm. They slowed even more, turning uphill off Grant.

Angelo's legs were as good as any man's, but he enjoyed putting out the message that he was somehow getting frail. It might keep his enemies off guard should he ever need that. But he had found it also served to slow down all his rhythms—to give his words a weight, his judgments a finality that they had lacked when he was young and fast. A quiet voice, whispering, helped, too. When you didn't raise your voice, people had to come to you, to concentrate on every syllable. It was power.

Franco ran ahead and opened the gate in the white wall in front of his house. They turned into the small front yard, waiting on the walk for Franco to bound up the nine steps and open the front door.

It pleased Angelo that his boys took care of this security, without any supervision, to the steady hum of Carmen's voice. She was not a gossip, a scold or a shrew, but she liked to take her after-Mass Sunday walk and feel she was catching up on all the news with her husband, who didn't respond much except to nod or pat her hand. Yet it made her feel they were sharing things in their daily life, although Tortoni knew that nothing could be further from the truth. Carmen knew almost nothing about his daily life, other than that he was a counselor to troubled people, a philanthropist to those in need, an elder in the Knights of Columbus.

The foyer basked in sunlight colored by the stained glass above the doorway. Angelo breathed in the smell of lamb roasting in the kitchen. Garlic and rosemary. He helped Carmen with her coat, kissing the back of her neck before he handed the coat to one of the men. Only then did he notice Pia, the maid, standing by the entrance to the living room, wringing her hands. Carmen patted Angelo's arm and crossed over to talk to her quietly in Italian. It was probably something about lunch, something they'd burned or forgotten to buy. Well, it was all right, whatever it was.

"There is a woman to see you," Carmen said, "in the study."

Tortoni made a face. "Now?" He turned a hard glance on Pia. He didn't know any women, certainly none who would dare come to his own house on a Sunday before noon. "Do we know her?"

Carmen spoke in Italian. "Pia could not send her away. Don't be angry with her. The woman looks as though she's been beaten. She begged for your help."

Tortoni told Pia she had done the right thing. He would see the woman, find out what this was about.

He nodded to Matteo. He would go into the study and see that the woman was not carrying a gun or a knife in her purse or anywhere else. Tortoni asked Pia if she would bring him his bottle and two glasses of Lachryma Christi, the sweet yellow wine he drank after Mass every Sunday. He took off his coat, placed his cane in the umbrella stand by the door, turned around and gave Carmen a kiss on both cheeks. *"Ti amo,"* he said. Then, back to English, "I won't be long."

The study was dark, but even in the dimness he could tell at a glance that this was a stunning woman. Makeup had tried to cover the welt on her cheek, but an eye was swollen and her full red lips looked bruised. They made you want to kiss them and make them better.

She wore a light tan skirt that now, as she was sitting, came to just over her knees. Her hair was pulled back, held to one side with a mother-of-pearl comb. She reminded Angelo Tortoni of his wife on the day he married her. He dismissed Matteo and the door closed on the two of them.

He walked in his regular gait to the couch. He had planned to sit behind his desk, but after seeing her, he did not want any artificial separation between himself and this woman.

The room was kept dark by slatted wooden shades over all the windows. He reached up and opened one column of slats, and horizontal shafts of light painted the rug on the floor like some luminous ladder. Motes of dust twinkled through the rays. He raised his hand and motioned for the woman to approach.

She got up and knelt on one knee before him, picking up his hand and kissing the back of it. She had clearly been well brought up.

They spoke in Italian.

"What is your name?"

"Doreen Biaggi."

He patted the couch next to him and she sat and arranged herself, half-turned to him. The light missed her, slicing the air between them. Tortoni reached up a hand and ran a finger along her face from her chin to her eyebrow.

"Who did this to you?"

There was a knock on the study door. Angelo sat back. *"Vieni."*

Pia entered with a bottle and two glasses. He let her set the bottle onto a silver-ridged coaster on his desk. She, correctly, poured only one glass, offering it to him, but he gestured with his left hand and she handed the glass to Doreen. After pouring his, she was gone, closing the door quietly behind her.

Angelo held his glass out between them, and she raised hers to touch his. Prisms from the cut crystal danced around the room. They each took a small sip. He noticed the way she held the glass on her lap, one hand on the stem, the other on the bowl. She did not look down at it.

"I ask you to forgive me for bothering you on the Lord's day."

Angelo waved that away. "How can I help you?"

"I owe you money, and I owe you my gratitude."

He nodded. It was a good start. She wasn't just coming here to whine about her vig.

"I am also very afraid."

Angelo sipped his wine. He saw her lower lip begin to tremble, but she got control of herself quickly, taking a deep breath.

"There is nothing to be afraid of here," he said.

She looked down at her lap. As though surprised to find the wineglass there, she raised it to her lips. "I want to pay you"—she hesitated—"but I must ask for, for arrangements to be different."

Angelo was confused. After he had spoken to Johnny he had been confident things would get straightened out. "The vig is too much?"

She shook her head, sitting now in silence. A tear formed in her swollen eye. "It is not the vig. I could pay a hundred a week for a few weeks. After that"— she paused, collecting herself—"I haven't paid any vig. Johnny LaGuardia"—she looked up, her large brown eyes now liquid—"Johnny . . ." She broke, crying aloud.

Angelo took a spotless white cotton handkerchief from his shirt pocket and touched it to her face. As he watched her try to collect herself, he was putting it together, feeling his rage. Johnny had been scamming other clients to cover Doreen's short. When she couldn't make the hundred he upped somebody else on his own—maybe the mysteriously disappeared Rusty Ingraham—and started taking Doreen's vig out of her ass.

Doreen was sniffling now, wiping away the tears. "*Mi scusa*, Don Tortoni."

Worst of all, Johnny had been keeping Doreen Biaggi a secret. A woman like this, in her situation, she could be priceless to Angelo. Not directly, perhaps, she might be too classy for that. But certainly a

woman of her grace and breeding, her looks and substance, could be used somewhere—to bind an alliance,
to weaken an enemy, to blind a competitor in legitimate business. Perhaps even to marry a son.

Angelo moved closer to her on the couch. He knew
the sunlight was now falling across his face. Doreen,
embarrassed, looked down into her lap, his handkerchief clutched around the stem of the wineglass.
Closer, he inspected the face, which now, even
bruised, could, he thought, make the angels sing. The
loyalty and love of a woman such as this was a gift
from God. And he knew he could get it for nothing.
Johnny had already paid enough of her vig to cover
her principal—he would hardly even lose any money.

He lifted her chin and drew her face to his. He
kissed both sides of her bruised lips, then both cheeks.
Gently, with his thumb, he rubbed a trace of a tear
away from under her eye.

"Look at me," he said.

She raised her eyes. Johnny had nearly broken her.
Angelo smiled. "Will you eat with my family today?"
He moved his hand down over her neck, her shoulder,
coming to rest under her arm, feeling the full curve
of the side of her breast as he moved her back away
from him as though trying to get her into focus. "As
of this moment," he said, "you owe me nothing except
a smile from your beautiful face."

He touched the corner of her mouth with a finger,
lifting it as he would do to a baby. "A little smile,"
he repeated.

She tried, and he pushed again at her lip, playfully.
The smile, when it came, nearly broke his heart.

He would have to deal with Johnny LaGuardia.

Flo Glitsky and Frannie Cochran were doing dishes
together. They watched Dismas and Abe walking in

the small playground that bordered the backyard the Glitskys shared with their neighbors downstairs. They had moved into the duplex when O.J. was born, unable then, as they still were, to afford their own house on Abe's salary in San Francisco.

Now, of course, there was no chance at all, but the duplex was rent-controlled and they paid less than most everybody else they knew. Her own house was one of the dreams Flo wasn't going to get, but she had her three healthy boys and her man who loved her, and if that was the trade, she'd take it any day.

"Are you really leaving?" Frannie asked her.

It was all that had been on Flo's mind for the last two days. She had never seen Abe this down. He had actually applied to the Los Angeles Police Department and was talking about moving there as if it were settled. All Flo knew about L.A. was that if Abe thought housing was high here, they wouldn't stand a chance there. And she'd heard the public schools there were in bad shape—the teachers mere truant officers whose jobs were to keep kids off drugs and off the street until three o'clock. And not only didn't Flo believe in private schools, she knew they wouldn't be able to afford one anyway. And her boys were all smart.

Flo shook her head. "I'll let Abe work out what he has to, and then I guess we'll make some decision."

"That's how you do it, isn't it?" Frannie said. "That was always it with me and Eddie. What he wanted and what I wanted, back and forth, until we got somewhere together." She wiped at a soapy plate. "I've gotten out of that habit. I miss it, I think."

Flo took the plate from her, starting to dry it. "How long has it been now?"

"Four and a half months."

Flo, like the other cops' wives Frannie knew, didn't let herself think too often about losing her husband.

It was a possibility that came with the territory, and you accepted it and went on if you wanted to stay together.

"You're holding up better than I would," Flo said.

Abe kicked at the tanbark under the swing he and Hardy were on. His arms were looped around the chains and as he kicked he rotated from side to side, facing Hardy then turning away.

"How are you gonna be a good cop anywhere if you don't care?"

"How many guys care?"

Hardy waited on the rotation, until Abe was faced back toward him. "I think about four, but you were always one of them."

Glitsky, spinning now on the swing, shook his head. "Now I'm a professional policeperson. I go where they pay me to. Enforce the law."

"And the brass decide?"

"Correcto."

Hardy did a pull-up on the A-frame of the swing. He did another one, the two big guys playing on the monkey bars.

"Besides," Abe said, "Lanier is handling it. They'll pass off my cases to McFadden 'cause he's the other solo, and Baker will go down like he should. Order will be restored to the cosmos."

Hardy was hanging full-length from the frame. "You reading Shakespeare again?"

Glitsky stood out of the swing. "Criticism. *The Tragic Fallacy* by Krutch. You ought to check it out. Says there can't be any tragedy unless there's a Zeit-geist of ultimate order that can be destroyed and then restored."

"Zeitgeist," Hardy said.

"Kraut word. Means the general intellectual, moral,

and cultural climate of an era, such as our very own,
for example."

"I know what it means, Abe. I'm a college gradu-
ate."

"So that's why we don't have any modern tragedy.
We don't believe in the importance of any one individual anymore. Since nobody screwing up can destroy
the order of the cosmos, then nobody getting enlight-
ened can restore it, see?"

"I was just thinking about this yesterday."

Glitsky cast a sideways glance at his friend. "So
how'd we get on this anyway?"

"You said Louis Baker going down will restore
order to the cosmos."

Glitsky nodded. "Yeah, right. Let's go get another
couple of beers."

They headed back to the house, but Hardy still
couldn't let it go. "But my problem is the blindside
thing—it was like 'what girl?' "

"Maybe he was concentrating on Rusty so hard he
didn't even notice Maxine."

"You don't notice a naked woman you have to
shoot three times?"

Glitsky stopped again by the back door. They stood
on a square of porch, hands in their pockets. The boys
were playing somewhere within earshot, maybe
around the front of the house. Hardy blew out, surprised to see a vapor trail. The chill had come in fast—
a high-pressure cold that had wiped the sky almost
purple.

"Okay, so he noticed her."

"But, Abe, that's my point. Baker said he had no
idea what I was talking about when I said a woman
had been killed at Rusty's. And he sounded convincing, even to these ears."

Glitsky shrugged. "He was lying."

"I don't think so."

"Well, that's your problem."

"And if he wasn't, it means he wasn't there when Rusty got shot."

"Diz. Listen up now. His prints were there."

"Jesus, Abe, my prints were there, too."

"A-ha!" Abe raised a forefinger. "Another hot lead in the case."

"You can laugh."

"I do laugh, Diz. Dig it. Yesterday you were the personification of outraged public crying for the head of Louis Baker. I, modestly, represented the re-straining force of law in our society—"

"You got a pair of boots?"

"What?"

"It gets any deeper, I'm gonna need boots."

Glitsky put an arm around his friend's shoulder. "I am making a point. And the point is that we, the police, aren't supposed to go flip-flopping according to the whims of the public we're supposed to protect. That, old buddy, includes you. Yesterday you thought Louis Baker was guilty of everything you could think of. Today, what? You're trying to have me check out other suspects just after I find out—and for the first time—that Louis is finally in fact a righteous suspect? Prints at Rusty's. Puts him there. Now he's got a mo-tive. He's got opportunity. Now he's a suspect, and now you want me to drop him? There is some irony here."

"I *don't* want you to drop him. I just thought in your thirst for justice you might want to be completely thorough—"

Glitsky blew out through tight lips. "I'm the one who has been thorough here all along. I continue to be. But several things have changed since just yester-day. One, Louis got himself a gun and did some B and E. This makes his rehabilitation in prison somewhat suspect—at least to me. Second, he was in fact at Rusty's. We knew neither of these things yesterday, and knowing them now moves old Louis up several rungs on the maybe-he's-guilty ladder. I really would like a beer."

But Hardy didn't move when Abe pushed at the door. Glitsky sighed. "Okay, what?"

"You've looked at Medina already. Who is Johnny LaGuardia? Where does Ray Weir fit into all this? There's just things you as a cop can do that I can't."

"Thousands."

"Well, shit, Abe. Do a few of them."

Abe shook his head. "No."

"Why not?"

"Because I am out of here, Diz. Gone. Los Angeles may need me and that is another jurisdiction. These aren't going to be my cases and I don't need the aggravation. Plus, I think there's a good chance that our Louis Baker in fact did all this, and there's enough to bring him in on it, and after that it's up to the D.A. and twelve of Louis's peers, if they can find them." He pushed at the door again. "It's no longer police business and certainly not mine. Now, you want a beer or what?" But he stopped again. "Besides, why do you care? Baker is off the street. Go back to work. Let the wheels of justice grind fine, why the hell don't you?"

Hardy looked at the sky, stuffing his hands further into his pockets. " 'Cause if he didn't do it—I'm not saying he didn't, but if . . . He doesn't deserve to die for it and I'd be killing him if I let it go—"

"You bleeding your heart for Louis Baker?"

"I'd love to ace him in a fair fight and that's a fact."

"You know your odds of getting a fair fight out of him?"

"Slim, I would guess."

"And none."

"Well, at least it would be just me and him."

"Mano a mano?"

Hardy shrugged. "I can't back into what would amount

to me killing him. I've just developed a case of reasonable doubt, is all."

"You don't think he was coming after you?"

Hardy nodded. "Yeah, I guess I do think that."

"Well?"

"We're gonna hang the bastard because he's mad at me?"

Glitsky shook his head, pushed again at the door.

Hardy followed him up the stairs. At the top of the steps they stopped one last time. "I've got no great hots to save Baker, you know," Hardy said. "But something else has got to be going on here. It's just too convenient."

"You think somebody paid him to bust into Jane's house?"

"No. I think he did that on his own."

"So what else?"

"So me is what else. I've been part of this since the beginning, and now suddenly Baker's on ice and somehow it's over. But I'm still involved. Especially if I'm being used to patsy up Baker when maybe he didn't do it. Anything capital, anyway."

Glitsky, his hand on the kitchen door, ran a finger across the scar that went through his lips. "So you want me to help?"

"A little look around is all."

"Let me think about it," Abe said. He turned the knob. "Okay, I've thought about it. No."

He opened the door and said hi to Flo and Frannie.

15

It didn't feel like he'd thought it would—seeing your own images up there on the screen, your words being spoken by people who pretended to care about them. In his imaginings, the scene always had him sitting next to Maxine, both of them puffed with accomplishment, she up there filling the screen with her beauty and talent, he for the idea, the words, the artistic vision behind it all.

But now the reality was so different. As it always seemed to be lately. He was slumped in his easy chair, smoke curling from a cigarette in his left hand. Courtenay and Warren sat on the couch, the room rearranged for the screening. And Maxine? The only place Maxine lived—on the screen—didn't seem real anymore. And yet that was all that was real.

It was his first movie. This was the final cut with sound before the music was added. There was beer and champagne in the kitchen sink for afterward. Other acquaintances, friends, reclined or sat Indian-style on the floor, watching Maxine say his words, do his bidding, live the part he'd created for her.

The doorbell sounded and he half turned to see someone he didn't recognize, a man, enter and sit on the floor. Ray Weir put him out of his mind. This film, unreal though it might be, was all that was now left of Maxine. He should pay attention.

He wanted to stop the reel and just look at her. God, she was . . . had been . . . beautiful. He supposed he still loved her. No. He knew he still loved her, always would. She had been his friend and his muse. She had been what had separated him from the other drones cranking out words and scenes and treatments.

Okay, so the movie wasn't exactly an "A" feature. You made compromises when you started out, when you needed a credit or two for credibility. Everybody in the business understood that.

Those earlier scenes, nearly doing it with Bryan—their friend who played the stepfather—they were pretty tasteful, Ray thought, although Warren had done a good job of making it seem they were really screwing. But Maxine had told him about it after they'd shot that day, about the angles they'd had to use to look real and still avoid—she'd said, "You know, penetration."

But this was to be only the first step in a long career. They were going to do it again—an entire work, an oeuvre of films by Ray Weir, starring Maxine . . .

They weren't too old, in spite of Maxine's giving up on it. That was all Rusty Ingraham's doing, that negative stuff, the change in her.

He squirmed in his chair. In the room's flickering light, he saw the film still had everyone's attention. Bryan was there. No girlfriend with him of course. Warren had his arm around Courtenay, who had done a fine editing job. The print was good and clean. This was a professional effort—screenplay by Ray Weir.

They couldn't take their eyes off Maxine. But it was *his* story that was holding them. Don't forget that.

He turned a little more. The guy who'd come in halfway through was walking along the back wall, hands in pockets, checking out the glossies of Maxine on the back wall. Maybe he was another cop come back to talk to him.

Man, Ray, he thought, what are you going to do about Wednesday night?

He glanced across at Courtenay again, saw she was leaning into Warren, whispering something. The frame on the wall froze on Maxine's perfect body midair in a dive into the water. Without any music it was eerie. Gradually, he became aware of the sound of the projector.

Then someone flicked the room lights on and suddenly there was applause. Courtenay was next to him, hugging him, pulling him over next to Warren. Bryan took a bow. Ray found himself applauding.

Courtenay Moran was nearly six feet tall. She wore her blond hair cropped to within an inch of her scalp all over except at the nape of her neck, where a longer strand was held in a ponytail by a hot pink ribbon.

"It just seems pretty soon to be partying after his wife's death, is what I mean," Hardy was saying.

He watched her blow some smoke toward the ceiling. They stood on the landing at the top of the stairway outside the open front door to Ray's duplex. Hardy held a can of beer and leaned against the doorpost. In the living room, where they'd watched the movie, people were still mingling, binding into little groups, then quickly splitting off. He didn't know what this kind of schmoozing was called, or what its purpose was, where the longest you talked to anybody was forty seconds, but it wasn't getting him anywhere, so he'd walked up to Courtenay in the kitchen because she was beautiful and because he'd seen her talking to Ray.

She wore a leather flight jacket that made her broad shoulders seem broader. Her eyes were surrounded with a very dark blue-black makeup that seemed to

set them more deeply into her milk-white face. Hardy
thought that in a photograph, Courtenay's face might
appear jutting, bony. But here now, the bones were
in the right places.

"Who's partying?" she asked. "You call this
partying?"

Hardy looked back into the living room. A record
was playing a heavy Latin beat and some dancing had
started. "It's not exactly a wake," he said. Several of
the dancers appeared to him to be trying to copulate
with their clothes on.

"That's just the Lambada," Courtenay said. "It's
harmless."

Hardy tipped up his beer. Sometimes hunches could
be a waste of time, and it was beginning to look as
though this whole trip to Ray Weir's would turn out
to be one of them.

He stared at the dancers another minute. "Looks
like foreplay," he said.

"Depends on how good you are." She smiled, looking right in his eyes.

He pulled the door closed, leaving them alone on
the landing, the music thumping low and insistent.
Courtenay stepped up to Hardy and kissed him, her
hand behind his neck. She was just his height, and the
angle felt strange, but it was a good kiss that he didn't
fight as much as he might have thought he should if
he'd thought about it. She stepped back.

"I just wanted to do that," she said.

"Okay. Worse things have happened to me."

"Want to try it again?"

She wasn't really coming on to him. Well, maybe a
little. But he flashed on Frannie, from there to Jane,
and then to the Lambada going on through the door,
and he realized that it simply wasn't him. "I think it
would be better if we didn't," he said.

"All right," she said. She took a final drag on her

cigarette, dropped and stepped on it. "I always guess wrong," she said.

It was the pro forma San Francisco woman's first reaction to rejection, Hardy knew—the assumption that the man was gay.

"For the record," he said, "my sexual preference is more or less as it appears."

She looked straight across at him, her height still a little disconcerting. Her face softened. "You're married."

"Involved."

"And you're faithful?"

That stung a little, but Hardy let it go.

"As long as they don't find out," she said, "what's the problem? I don't tell Warren. He'd leave me and there goes not only him but my career, and I do love him. But love and sex—don't confuse 'em or you'll screw them both up."

A few days before, Hardy could have said he didn't confuse them, they went together. Maybe they still did with him, but he had some figuring out to do. "I'm here about Maxine and Ray."

"Are you with the police?"

"No."

"Were you involved with Maxine?"

This time Hardy laughed. "Not how you might interpret it, but it was with Rusty Ingraham."

"Was he a friend of yours?"

"Why do you ask it like that? Is it so unlikely?"

Courtenay looked Hardy up and down. "Uh huh. Very."

Hardy thought on that a minute. "He's dead."

"What?" Clearly shocked.

Hardy told her about it. He let some silence hang. Then, "The wrong guy might be getting blamed. And I could be mixed up in that."

"A friend of yours?"

"Not exactly. The police have this guy in custody. He'd threatened to kill me, too." Hardy told her why, but also said he no longer had anything to do with the police or the law.

"So what's the problem if he's in jail?"

Hardy lifted his beer can to his lips, found it empty and sat down on the steps. Courtenay sat next to him. "I guess I want to be sure I believe it. I saw the guy today and got the feeling he didn't know what I was talking about." He paused. "He didn't know Maxine was there."

"So why are you here?"

"Because if the guy they got didn't do it, somebody killed a friend of mine and nobody's looking for him."

"Or her."

Hardy picked up his empty can again, shook it, found it empty. He looked far up at her. "You want to tell me about Ray?"

She dug out another cigarette and lit it up. "What's to tell?"

"If he's the jealous type, for example."

She blew smoke at the ceiling. "It broke his heart, I'll say that."

"Maxine and Rusty?"

She nodded. "He couldn't put it anywhere. Like, it's gotta be over or not, right? I mean, Maxine's practically living with this new guy, she's moved out, what does Ray think? But he couldn't accept it. You see that shrine to her in there? All those pictures—I think every damn composite she ever had done—and even after she's dead?" She huddled into herself. "It's kind of freaky, isn't it?"

Hardy didn't know if that was freaky or not. What he wanted to know was whether Ray had ever said he was going to do anything about it. Go get her back. Like that.

Courtenay shook her head. "He had to acknowledge it first, and he wouldn't do that." She blew out smoke, remembering. "Every day, he'd come by while Warren and I were editing. Always started out in control, how's the film going, blah blah, and then he'd see some shots of Maxine and get stupid."

"Stupid?"

"Like talk to her as if she were there. Argue with her, try to talk her into coming back, ask her on dates. Weird. So finally it just got too much. I mean, we're trying to get a film cut here and it's pretty intense, and Ray comes in—I don't know, last week sometime—and Warren just cuts loose on him. Tells him to get the fuck out until he gets it settled. Go see her, figure out what's happening and deal with it." She stubbed out the butt on the landing.

"So then?"

"So he left, and next thing you know Maxine is dead."

"Killed with Ray's gun."

She turned her eyes on him. "Is that true?"

"He says he'd given it to her when she moved out—for protection."

She seemed to be wrestling with something. "Well, I don't know about that . . . And the police haven't arrested him?"

"They think they have a better suspect. I told you."

She took that in. "Wow. He must be a good one."

"A black guy on parole who'd threatened to kill Rusty, and whose fingerprints were at Rusty's place."

She digested that. "Yeah, that's pretty good all right. I didn't think Rusty could kill Maxine. Warren thinks he did but I just . . . I don't know . . ."

"Let's go see if we can find out," Hardy said.

It reminded Hardy of college, sitting on the floor after midnight. Van Morrison was playing softly on the stereo. The Lambada people had gone home. Now it was just Courtenay and Warren, him and Ray. The other three were smoking marijuana, which Hardy hadn't seen much of in recent years. He told them he had a lung condition.

They were all in a corner in candlelight, Warren and Courtenay nestled together into a beanbag chair, Ray and Hardy on the floor. Hardy had switched to water after his fourth beer, filling up the Silver Bullet can about half a dozen times.

The talk was about the movie business, minor league. Warren had gotten four or five investors together and raised close to $200,000, which by Hollywood standards, Warren said, wouldn't make a decent short but got the forty minutes of soft porn, featuring Maxine, they'd watched earlier. Ray's script was at least a credit and could help him get pitch-meetings with "real" studios down in L.A. Warren gave Courtenay and himself a salary for directing and editing, and Warren got producer points, which probably explained his new clothes, the Movado watch and, Hardy surmised, his arm around Courtenay.

It was, Hardy saw, the entire world for these people. Everything was about could it work or not in a *film*.

Hardy stretched out on the floor. Courtenay put her foot on his, careful to make it seem casual. "Why's it always a 'film'? What ever happened to the good old movies?" Hardy asked. "I thought film was the stuff inside the camera."

Warren looked wounded. "No. Film is videotape, television. Jesus."

"Sorry."

"It's an important distinction," Ray said.

"Sure," Hardy agreed. "I get it. Film is for videotape. But tape is the film used to make a film. A real film. Like a movie." Courtenay pressed his foot. "In the camera, I mean." Hardy figured he might be getting a little contact-high. He wiggled his toes.

"By Jove, I think he's got it," Courtenay said, playing Henry Higgins in *My Fair Lady*.

There was silence between songs, then a low, soulful saxophone began wailing.

"Sounds like somebody crying," Ray said.

"Can you blame her?"

Ray sat up. "Who?"

Warren snorted. "Who else?"

"Hey, come on!"

"You killed her, Ray," Warren said. "You come on."

"She's not here!" Ray was pretty stoned. "What the hell are you talking about?"

"Look around," Warren said. "She's more here than we are."

The saxophone crescendoed. Hardy found himself, like the others, staring at the many faces, bodies and poses of Maxine Weir. It was eerie. In the candlelight, occasionally a flicker would make an eye appear to blink, a cheek seem to twitch.

"I didn't," Ray said.

Courtenay rearranged herself. "He didn't," she said to Warren.

Warren shifted to stoke up another joint. "Come on. The brace was so obvious. I wouldn't ever let that go in a film."

"What's obvious?" Ray asked.

"You might as well have told everybody it was you."

Hardy was now carefully watching them both. Ray just shook his head. Warren passed him the joint, continuing, "Everybody knew she didn't need the brace anymore. Putting it on her . . ." He spoke now to Hardy, explaining. "The whole thing started with the other guy, Rusty, because of the insurance, the accident, you know?" Then back to Weir. "It's too obvious, Ray. You need to be more subtle."

Hardy wondered if Warren thought Maxine's death was some kind of joke, some rehearsal for a scene.

He'd seen her, dead and naked, neck brace and all, and there hadn't been anything sexy or funny about it. But he kept quiet.

"He didn't do it," Courtenay insisted. "Leave him alone, Warren."

"I was here all night," Ray said.

"You were not. I know because I was here all night. Sitting on the steps drinking a six-pack, waiting for you to come home."

Even in the dimness, Hardy could almost feel Weir's eyes shift. "Maybe I was asleep. I don't remember."

"How many people, you think, don't remember what they were doing the night their wife died?"

"Leave him alone, Warren."

"Well, I'm one of them," Ray said. "I just know I was here. I didn't go out. I told the police that."

"The police have got somebody else," Courtenay told Warren.

"They're dreaming, then," Warren said.

All this, almost friendly, casual in tone. Low-key, the joint going back and forth, Hardy listening, watching the three of them toss it around as though it were hypothetical. What got to Hardy, though, was the fact that Ray's wife, whom he supposedly loved even unto death, was hardly cold, was being cremated the next day, and Ray wasn't sad. Not at all.

He finally spoke up. "I know the guy they got, and they're not exactly dreaming."

Warren exhaled, into his theory now. "Yeah, well, Maxine dies, Ray isn't where he says he is, he puts a neck brace on her to tell his friends—"

"That's just bullshit, Warren." Warren waved it right off.

"—to tell his friends what he's done, what a *mensch* he is, for God's sake, so the message is out you don't fuck around with Ray Weir. Especially if you're his property."

Ray stood up, a little wobbly. "Everybody's going home," he said. The casual tone was gone.

Warren ignored him. "And to top things off, Ray now gets eighty-five grand insurance money all to himself to start financing his next film, which he already talked to me about."

"What are you trying to do, Warren? Get Ray arrested?"

"What?" Genuinely startled. "Who's going to arrest him?"

Hardy, on his feet, found himself suddenly the center of attention. "Not me, gang. I'm a private citizen. Scout's honor."

"Shit," Ray said, "I've had enough of this. I'm tired."

"But you're getting eighty-five thousand dollars?" Hardy asked.

Ray shrugged. "It's no secret. Maxine's insurance."

Warren and Courtenay were also up now. Hardy backed up a step and took in the trio. "If you're so sure," he said to Warren, "why don't you turn him in?"

Warren crossed over to Ray and draped an arm over his shoulders. He smiled. "One doesn't turn in one's friends. And Ray and I are friends. Now we're doing business too. You just like to have your partners be straight with you, that's all."

"I am being straight." It came out like a whine.

Warren looked at Ray. "I love you, man, but you are not being straight with me."

Ray cast a pleading glance at Courtenay, who put her hands deep into her pockets and tossed her head. "Come on, Warren," she said. "Whatever it is, it's not Maxine. He's allowed to have some secrets."

"Yes, can't I have a little private life? A little love life?"

"Sure. If that's it. Why don't you just tell me?"

He looked at his shoes. "I'm not exactly proud of this, Warren, but okay, maybe you ought to know. We are partners . . . I heard you knocking out there. I, uh, I had someone with me. A woman."

Warren backed up a step. "So what's the problem? You couldn't tell me about having a woman over here? I know her?"

Ray shook his head. "She was like—" he stopped. "I paid for it."

Courtenay stepped in. "Ray felt guilty about it, Warren. Can't you understand that?"

"But he told you?"

"He got it off his chest."

Warren draped an arm over Ray. "What's to feel guilty about, man? We're friends. You can tell me."

Ray shrugged. "You know, with Maxine and all . . ."

Warren was matter of fact. "Hey, *she* left *you,* remember? You didn't know she was going to get killed that night."

"I know. But I'd been such a pain in the ass with you and Court about my broken heart and all. I just needed somebody."

"Hey, we all do, right? It's better than me thinking you killed somebody. I couldn't believe the police hadn't already picked you up."

"Well, I told the police. And Court. I just didn't want it spread around. Now I've really got to get some sleep, okay. Tomorrow's going to be a long day."

Hardy still couldn't detect any warm air coming from the car's heater, and he only had another five blocks until he got to Frannie's. He wondered if luxury cars had heaters that came on hot. Then he supposed most people who bought convertible canvas-roofed four-wheel-drive vehicles, as he had done, didn't have heat on the top of their priority list.

Ray Weir was lying. He hadn't told the police he

had an alibi. To the contrary, in fact. So much so that if Louis Baker should somehow get himself clear, Ray Weir would pop up next on the Who Killed Rusty Ingraham hit parade. Especially with this new money angle. He had jealousy going for him as well as some significant monetary gain, to say nothing of his gun being the murder weapon. Warren had been right about his friend. Absent the alibi, Ray was a good call for the trigger.

And every bone in Hardy's body felt that the alibi was bogus. So Courtenay seemed to believe him. People tended to believe things that were confided to them, especially when, on the surface at least, those things didn't speak too well for the confider. But for just that reason clever people—and Ray Weir was starting to look solid for that category—had been known to confide intimate lies.

An effective technique—and in this case it had gotten Courtenay to back up Ray. She was also predisposed, which helped. Hardy wondered if she'd pressed Ray at all about who he'd been with, where they had gone. He figured not. The fact that he had "opened up" to her about it would have been enough for her. The details wouldn't have been important. Ray was feeling guilty about sleeping with someone else, betraying the object of his adoration, and on the very night of Maxine's death, as it turned out. He just *had* to bare his soul to someone, to his close friend Courtenay. It was haunting him, tearing him up. Oh yes.

Hardy parked across the street from Frannie's door and turned his front wheels into the hill to prevent runaway. He sat shivering, hands tucked under his armpits, wondering if Glitsky might start to care again if he found out about the $85,000 insurance money. It sure couldn't hurt to bring it to his attention . . .

But why? Why not be happy about Louis Baker being off the streets again? Wasn't that the goal?

Shouldn't he just move back home and go back to bartending at the Shamrock on Tuesday and pick up his life where he'd left off and be grateful he'd survived?

Except what was he going to pick up? Frannie might have called this a "window in time," and maybe for her things could go back to being the same—he didn't really believe that. Frannie was in his life now in a far different way than she'd been before. And, of course, that had changed the space where Jane had been so carefully placed.

And what about old Diz himself? He'd always thought of himself as a pretty good citizen, a man of some principle, if not part of the solution then at least not part of the problem either.

But now, a little shake of the cart, and Diz the white knight is ready to give up Louis 'cause he's done some bad shit sometime? Maybe not what they're getting him for, but something. He wondered, not for the first time, how he'd feel if Baker hadn't been black.

But, shivering in his Suzuki Seppuku, since he was being honest with himself, he knew absolutely how he'd feel—he'd feel outraged that Louis Baker was being denied due process, that Louis Baker was being railroaded because of his background and color. Not that he might not have done it, but whether or not he did, they weren't checking it out the way they should.

So why wasn't he outraged?

Is it, Diz, because maybe this black/white thing here in the liberated '90s was really only a matter of degree? Turn the fear up a notch and take a look at your true stripes. Hardy perceives his life threatened by Baker—whether or not that's reality—and to protect himself, Hardy is delighted to lock Baker away forever or sit him in the gas chamber.

But wasn't that always the reason? You perceive that your way of life, your neighborhood, whatever, is threatened, and your instinct is to protect yourself. You don't worry about justice, the right thing. You just want the damn threat to go away. The fear to go away.

And you don't really care, finally, if the fear is baseless. You just don't want to be confronted by it. You don't want to live with it or even see it. So you don't let them on your bus. Or in your neighborhood. Or date your daughter.

Hardy rubbed his eyes, feeling defenses rise against this vision of himself. That wasn't him. Some of his best friends, etc., etc. Look at Abe Glitsky, for Christ's sake.

And remember that just last night Louis Baker had, in fact, shot at the police while breaking and entering Jane's house. This wasn't some poor lamb he was dealing with here.

Fine. Grant that. But is he a murderer? More particularly, did he kill Rusty and Maxine? What happened out at Holly Park doesn't have shit all to do with Dismas Hardy, does it, Diz?

Yeah, but here's what it *does* have to do with. If Baker hadn't killed Rusty—and okay, maybe that was still a big "if"—then the guy (or woman, thank you, Courtenay) that did it . . . Ray Weir, for instance . . . was sure getting helped out by Dismas Hardy pointing at Louis Baker and saying, "Trust me, I'm an ex-cop and that's your man." Which Hardy had in fact done.

If any of this was so, and if Baker, admittedly no saint, had not killed Rusty, then Hardy found himself in a position that pissed him off. Because somebody had put him in this thing, maybe even helped him set up Baker for a fall. He thought he'd like to find out who, and kick some ass.

Hardy opened his car door and stepped out into the street. He had no desire to go back to his house, or to start bartending in two days. He owed it to himself to find out what was really going on here.

He looked up at the stars. Louis Baker could personally rot for all he cared. He knew that. But the situation surrounding him was tying Hardy in knots, and until he could get some of them untied he wouldn't be free to get on with his life.

16

"It's a fantastic opportunity!"

Manny Gubicza was afraid of this reaction. Tread-well was excited and didn't seem to understand his lawyer's reluctance. Manny should have asked him to come down at lunchtime to discuss this in person, but he had another appointment at lunch, and with his powers of persuasion all he would have to do to Treadwell was pass along the D.A.'s offer and explain how stupid it was—that is, if Treadwell listened to him.

"It's a trap," Gubicza said.

"How can it be a trap? I didn't make this up, remember. The bastard did kill my Poppy!"

"I know."

"Well?"

Fred was really hot for this. The lawyer spoke in a measured voice. "I think we can assume, Fred, that the D.A. isn't suggesting a polygraph because they want to help your case."

"But it doesn't matter! Once I—"

"Please, let me finish. The offer is that you come down and go over the statement you've already made, and if the polygraph checks, they'll proceed on the Medina angle."

"Right. That's what I want."

"No, it's not what you want."

"Manny . . ."

"Fred, listen. They're going to have to come up with

at least a hearing anyway, and eventually an indict-
ment. They've already got your statement. Medina did
it and he'll be punished for it."

"But they said they weren't going to. I know they
didn't believe me. They were going to interview Medina and he'll deny everything and they won't have
any evidence and they'll drop it."

"They might try, but haven't we been using the
media to tell this story as much as anything else?
Hasn't that been working?"

He heard the change in his ear; Treadwell had
switched him from the speakerphone. "Look, Manny,
this whole thing hinges on my credibility." Treadwell
was whispering insistently. "You think I'll let them get
me on Raines and Valenti. No way! If you know it's
a trap, you use it for your own ends. I know you think
only a lawyer can be any good under questioning—"

"That's not true, Fred," Manny lied.

"—but all I do is tell them what happened again,
and they'll see it's the truth. Think what the media
could do with that! It's perfect for us!"

Manny punched his own speakerphone, putting
Treadwell on it, and stood up. He paced behind his
desk. "Fred, here's a hard truth. In the legal world,
to the extent that something is not completely controlled by you, it's the enemy. This is not a friendly
little parlor game. Lives are at stake. Yours, for example. Valenti, Raines, Medina. People cheat in these
situations."

Manny didn't think he had to point out that he and
Fred were cheating from the git-go. That wasn't the
point. The point was to build your case from what you
decide are the facts you're going to use. They were
doing that very well. He didn't want Fred anywhere
near a polygraph. Though the results of a lie-detector
test were not admissible at trial, it could be a damag-
ing tool, especially at the pre-hearing stage. He
stopped at his window, looked down the street, across

at the Pyramid. He walked over to his desk again. "I can't let you do it, Fred."

"So we're just going to pack it in, admit that we lied."

"It's not that!"

"It even seems like it's that to me. Think what the D.A. will do with it."

"The D.A. will just continue plodding along."

"And drop Medina."

Gubicza hung his head, putting his weight on the back of his chair. "They will probably not pursue it with much vigor," he admitted.

"But Medina has to be punished."

"Fred, compare that good—Medina being punished—with the much greater good of you not going to jail for murder." He hated to raise his voice, but it was happening. "If they trip you up on Raines and Valenti, not only do those two guys walk, it's likely you go down. And once they've got you seated and hooked up to a polygraph, they might just ask you anything. And it might not be about Hector Medina and Poppy."

"So just make them promise they won't."

Gubicza cleared his throat. "Make them promise they won't," he repeated.

"Sure. Make that a condition."

"Don't you think that request might be showing our hand just a little bit?"

"How?" Warming to it now, Treadwell was making his case. "Look, they want to talk about Hector Medina, we say okay, but that's all. They'll understand that. I mean, we don't want to muck around with the murder investigation. This is a separate issue. Tied in, maybe, but separate. We build my credibility, we get Hector, it's perfect."

"Quit saying that, Fred. Nothing's perfect." He sat back down in his leather chair. "God, I hate this kind of Monday," he said.

*   *   *

Fifteen blocks downtown Art Drysdale hung up his telephone and walked down to his boss's office. He nodded to Dorothy, Locke's secretary, and just kept going. Christopher Locke, the elected District Attorney of the City and County of San Francisco, was on the telephone himself, seated at his desk, and waved his old friend to sit down. Instead, Drysdale went back outside and helped himself to a cup of coffee.

"How's business?" he asked Dorothy, planting himself on a corner of her desk.

Before she could answer, Locke called from the other room. "Art!"

Drysdale shrugged. "We've got to do this more often," he said to Dorothy, then whispered, "Do me a favor, love, and keep the phone quiet for about two minutes." He went back through the doors, closing them behind him.

"What?" Locke said. He was studying a file on his desk and didn't look up.

"That's why they keep electing you," Drysdale said. "The warm, charming exterior. The man behind the office."

Locke sighed, shaking his head, keeping it down. "What?" he repeated.

"You owe me a buck," Drysdale said.

It took a second, but then Locke stopped reading and brought his eyes up to meet Drysdale's. "Get out of here," he said.

"Swear to God."

"Gubicza agreed to it?"

"With conditions."

"What? That we don't ask any questions?"

"Nothing about Raines and Valenti."

"So what'd you do?"

"I agreed, of course."

"So what are you gonna do?"

"I said, and I quote, 'On my mother's grave I will never mention those names or anything about those cases.' "

"So how are you going to bring them up."

Drysdale sipped at his coffee. "Well, I thought I'd have the polygraph set up downtown here. That way I'll avoid the temptation to go stand on my mother's grave, may she rest in peace. Which is where I said I wouldn't bring up the murder raps."

Samson wasn't really in Dido's class, or Louis Baker's. He had this sloppy way, heavy, not tight, with long dreadlocks none too clean, and didn't put out the kind of vibe Dido had done, where when it wasn't business he was okay. Dido could laugh and shoot a hoop or two. He bought Lace his shoes. Like that.

And even Baker, you could talk to him. Stuff about the cut, this an' that, the paint, the Mama. If Dido had to go, Lace could have maybe gone in with Louis—at least until Louis killed Dido. Then maybe not. But if Dido had just died, or moved on, 'stead of Louis having done it . . .

Yeah, but that hadn't gone down at all. Now they was both of 'em clear of the cut, and Samson was a whole different breed of badness moving in.

Like here Monday not yet noon, cold as the landlord, Lace and Jumpup only sitting at the curb and he come by just to show 'em and kick 'em into the street. Now what's that shit?

"This my cut now," he say, and they watch him walk, one end to the other, couple of his troops tagging.

Where they—he and Jumpup—s'pose to go now?

Nat Glitsky was seventy-two years old and spent most of his time now (since Emma had died) in the synagogue at Fulton and Arguello, which was where his son Abe had picked him up.

They drove north up Park Presidio through the city and took Lombard over to Van Ness, then to Broadway through the tunnel and into North Beach. Nat had a fondness for big Italian lunches, and if his son was paying you couldn't do better than Capp's, which had been serving the same meals since he was dating Emma. It had been one of the few good restaurants he could take her to that didn't mind having a black woman eating with the whites. Hard to remember those times, especially now when there was every kind of humanity seated at the tables.

Nat kept his yarmulke on but hung his jacket on the back of his chair. The waiter came and he said he'd have a Negroni—Campari, bitters and gin.

"How can you drink that medicine?" Abe asked after he'd ordered his iced tea.

Nat patted the hand of his only child. There certainly was a lot of Emma in him—she hadn't much cared for Negronis either. He wondered if maybe it was something about being part or all black. Negroni. Would he try to develop a taste for a drink called a Hymonie or a Kiker?

But his son was thrashing in deeper waters. All during the ride over here they'd been talking about Abe's projected move to Los Angeles. Nat wasn't for it. What was he going to do without his family around? But he didn't bring that up yet. No sense in getting all riled up about a maybe. And Abe was still just talking—he hadn't made up his mind. At least Nat didn't think so. Not yet . . .

And if Nat knew Abe, it wasn't so much even the move to L.A. that he needed to talk about. That was just a decision and Abe had never had a problem with decisions. At least, not to talk to his father about. What Abe had trouble with sometimes was lining up the crosshairs so he could get his bead on the real issue. Well, everybody had that problem, Nat thought. Decisions tended to make themselves once you had everything else lined up. Most people just didn't take the time, acted impulsively, made the wrong moves.

Not Abe, though, not usually, anyway. Which was why they were sitting here now.

Their drinks arrived and they clinked their glasses. *"L'chaim."*

Nat sipped, put the glass down and made a kissing sound two or three times, savoring the taste in his mouth. At least Abe looked well rested. And why not? He had Flo, the great kids, the important stuff worked out. But he listened while Abe kept repeating himself about his job this, the job that, nobody cared, some friend of his—Hardy—with a problem. Finally he held his hand up.

"So what are you saying here?" he asked, then shrugged. "The job isn't good? So change the job. You don't have to do the same job somewhere else."

"But I'm a cop, Dad. It's what I do."

"You do something else. You're a man first. Am I right?"

"Yes, but . . ."

"Of course I am. Now you listen to me. How old are you? Not a child, okay? So. You know a job. A job is the same I don't care where you are. You telling me a cop in New York or Tel Aviv is different than a cop in San Francisco? Or Los Angeles? No. I don't believe it. More, I know it. Look at me. I am—before I retire—by the grace of God I have a trade. I can fix things. First I'm a kid in Delaware—Delaware! I know you know this but listen. I'm fixing bicycles and sewing machines in Delaware. I go to school. I can do things with engines and now they start calling me an engineer and I get a job in California in a little shop. So the shop gets bigger and they sell it to somebody else. I don't like how they do business. I move on. Another shop. Two, three. All the while I'm raising you and trying to keep your mother happy, which you and I know is some kind of full-time endeavor. And you know what I find? The job is a job. I don't care if it's old Mr. Levine's shop on DuPont Street or Lockheed down in San Carlos. You do your job and you get paid so you can live your life. But your job is not your life."

Nat lifted his glass again, puckered, shook his finger at his son. "You should know this, Abraham. This is not nuclear physics we're discussing here."

Abe grinned, tightening the scar through his lips. "Okay. What else am I gonna do?"

"What do you wanna do?"

"I want to be a cop."

"You can't be a cop here in San Francisco?"

"What have I been telling you?"

"Tell the truth, I don't know. Some people are making gold bricks. Some others taking the easy way. So what? What does that have to do with you?"

"It affects how I do my job."

"Why is that? You tell me why that is."

"Come on, Dad. There's all kinds of cooperation needed to finish a case, any case."

"Baloney. Excuse me, Abraham, but kosher baloney."

Abe shook his head. "You don't know."

"I don't know? You telling me I don't know?" He reached over the small table and rested his hand over his son's. "Look, twenty years ago, you're in school, your mother's starting to get sick, they hire a new supervisor they call a vice-president at the Ford Plant over to Fremont, you remember the place. So the new man tells me—I am quality control manager at this time—he tells me we have to cut costs, don't spend so much time checking everything. I tell him cut costs doesn't mean cut corners. He looks at me like I'm from Mars. We got to cut costs, he says. Bottom line. So. It's my job. I can't quit. I mean, I can, but is it worth it for the trouble to you and your mother? No, it's not."

"And the moral is?"

"The moral is, this man makes it hard to do my job. He cuts staff, hours, ups production schedules. Damn near impossible. We having the special?"

The waiter was standing over them, taking their orders. The special started with soup and bread and proceeded through pasta, salad, a main course (baked fish today), ice cream (spumoni), and coffee.

"So what happened?" Abe asked.

"So eventually they shut down the plant."

Abe chewed bread for a minute. "Did I miss something?"

"The point is, while there was a job to do, I kept doing it right. But there's always something, everywhere you go." He buttered some bread of his own. "All I'm saying is this . . . you want to be a cop, don't kid yourself it'll be different in L.A. You're either supported or you're not, but what does it matter? You're raising your family, you're doing something worthwhile."

"But—"

"But what you don't do," Nat interrupted, "is you don't do it half-assed." He looked up at the waiter, who had brought the soup and a carafe of red wine. "Bring a glass for my son here, would you?" he said. "He's taking a day off."

"Now see?" Abe said, his spoonful of spumoni halfway to his mouth. "The very case I've been talking about." He indicated a young burly man who was nodding his way across the room. Nat always said it could be a very small world sometimes.

"You eat your ice cream. Have another cup of coffee. I think I'll just go have a word with him."

Nat shrugged. "How could it hurt?"

The man was talking to the waiter as Abe pulled out a chair and sat himself backward on it. "Don't mind me," he said. Then, to the waiter, "I'd like an herb tea, please. His tab. That right, Johnny?"

"Sure, Sergeant."

Glitsky put on a smile and asked Johnny LaGuardia how he was doing. He was doing fine. He tucked his napkin in over his tie and rearranged the silverware a little in front of him. He kept his sports coat on, probably for the same reason Abe hadn't taken his off. It was awkward, showing your piece in a public place.

He'd been a very sweet-faced teenager, Abe supposed, but now, in his late twenties, there was starting to be a fleshiness under his cheeks and just a hint, a premonition, of jowls. His eyebrows were starting to meet over his fighter's nose, and his thin forehead, under the still thick black hair, was shiny with oil. He'd shaved very close, and Abe could see the tiny capillaries through the stretched skin on his face, could smell the overstrong cologne. Johnny fiddled with his water glass now. He wore three heavy rings on his right hand.

"I'm here with my father," Abe said, motioning over to where Nat was.

"That's nice," Johnny said. He looked over, creased his brow, came back to Abe. "He must of left."

Half-turning, Abe saw that he hadn't. "Old guy with the skullcap on. That's my dad."

He enjoyed watching Johnny having trouble doing the math. "Yeah, well, it's good to get out with the old man," he said.

The waiter brought Johnny a beer and Abe his herb tea. They both took small sips, Abe waiting it out. Finally, Johnny put the glass down. "So what's going on?" he asked.

"Your name came up the other day. Then I'm in here eating lunch and here you are and I think what a coincidence. I think maybe we can talk and it saves me two or three days of running around."

"How'd my name come up?"

Abe pulled the chair right up against the table, lowering his voice. "That's the thing, Johnny. Your name came up talking about prints we found at the scene of a murder."

Johnny shook his head. "Goddamn."

"What?"

"Rusty Ingraham, right?" Johnny drank off half his beer, put it on the table, belched politely and said, "Shit, I knew it."

"Knew what, Johnny?"

"You lose your temper, you get in trouble."

"Yeah, that happens a lot. You lose your temper with Rusty?"

"Hey, I didn't kill him."

"Nobody said you killed him."

"You think I killed him, you're wrong. The girl neither."

"Read my lips, Johnny, we don't think you killed them. We got another suspect in custody at County Hospital. We think he killed them, which is why he's under arrest. But what I was curious about was your fingerprints. And you knew the girl was there?"

"She was already dead."

"And Rusty? Was he already dead?"

Johnny shook his head. "I never saw no Rusty. The girl was in the hall blocking the back of the place. I took a look at her and didn't do, like, the inventory."

"You just took off?"

"Hey, Sergeant, what am I gonna do? Call the cops? What do you think they do they find me with a couple stiffs?"

"What am I doing now?"

"This is different. You got a guy on ice already. If it'd been me called the cops, you wouldn't even be looking for him 'cause *I'd* be your suspect."

Glitsky hated to admit it but Johnny wasn't too far off on that one. Especially lately. He sipped some tea.

"Yeah, but the fingerprints, Johnny. I could take you in on those."

"But you got a suspect!"

"So now let's say I'm just curious. An inquisitive guy like myself, I hate when I don't know how everything fits together."

"Maybe I should get a lawyer or something."

Abe cupped his hands around his tea, still close in, still whispering. "Johnny, you're not under arrest. We are talking, that's all. Loan sharks aren't my beat. If it's not homicide, I'm not busting anybody."

Johnny finished his beer. The waiter came with minestrone. Johnny ordered another beer, then tore off a bite of bread, swirling it around in the soup.

"Okay," he said. "Okay, here's the deal. Ingraham's vig was six."

Glitsky's eyebrows went up. "A week?"

Johnny nodded. "That's how we do the vig, *capisce?*"

"Six hundred dollars a week?"

Johnny popped some bread into his mouth. "Guys pay more. So anyway—"

"Wait a minute. What was Ingraham doing business with you for? He owed, what, six grand? Why didn't he get it from other sources?"

"Like where?"

"How 'bout a bank, for example. He was a lawyer. He must've had credit."

Johnny shook his head. "Banks generally don't lend money to put on the ponies."

"Ingraham played the ponies?"

A slug of beer. "The ponies owned the sucker. The guy was a mess." He put his spoon down. "One of these guys that say he hits the daily double, he stays around for the Exacta and puts the extra money down on it."

"Was he any good?"

"Guys like that are never good. There's something else pushing 'em. It's like a sickness. I been collecting vig from him on and off since I started working for Mr. Tortoni. Just keeps getting bigger and bigger."

"And he's never paid it off?"

"The principal? No way. He gets that kind of money, he plunks it on some nag's nose."

Abe had finished his tea. The waiter came by and put down a steaming plate of ravioli, taking away the soup bowl. "How's a guy get into it that deep?"

Johnny lifted his shoulders. "I told you, he can't help it. He gets a hunch, he's gotta play it, you know? That's how it all started, a couple hundred he didn't have. Twenty a week vig. Who can't make that? Then the vig's a hundred. One week he can't make the hundred, so he rolls it, borrows more to pay the vig. Between you and me, this is suicide. But he keeps paying, the vig keeps growing."

"So what happened at Rusty's?"

Johnny studied a ravioli on his fork for a minute. "I been in some heat with Mr. Tortoni lately. Couple guys stiffing me, coming in short." He shrugged, trying to make light of it, but Abe could see his worry. "It's business, you know, and Mr. Tortoni is someone who takes his business very serious."

"So?"

"So I gotta explain to Mr. Tortoni about how there's a body at Ingraham's, plus there's no money. So I'm short six hundred there on top of short"—he paused—"other places." He put his fork down without eating. Abe had the impression he was about to tell him something more personal, but the moment passed. He shrugged again, went back to his food. "So I got mad. I was in trouble here, you understand."

"And what'd you do? First you broke in." The face closed up. "Johnny, B and E is not murder either. I don't give a shit if you broke the door down."

"We had an appointment. He was supposed to be there."

"Okay."

"So I'm inside, there's this body. I know Mr. Tortoni's getting no money here. It really pissed me off. I wanted to throw something, knock something down."

"So you grabbed the lamp?"

"Yeah. Threw it down. It didn't help much."

"You ever get it worked out, the anger?"

Johnny seemed to be remembering something. He let out a breath. "I guess that's why they invented pussy," he said.

17

Hardy remembered the days when he had been so into his work at the D.A.'s office, the hours passed unheeded trying to piece together something that didn't fit, deciding on an interrogation strategy, formulating an opening or closing statement. Thinking hard. Caring so damn much.

He stood at the door to Tony Feeney's office—the dress-for-success assistant D.A. who had hated Rusty Ingraham was lost in his own musings. He was half-turned back to the window, feet up on his desk, far away from anything that was happening in his here and now. Reluctant to pull him from the reverie, Hardy knocked.

The feet came down, a hand came out over the desk. Shaking it, Hardy said, "Dismas Hardy, from the other day."

"Sure, how you doin'?"

Hardy said he was starting to feel like a cop again, doing legwork.

"You ever get over to see Hector Medina?"

Hardy kept standing. He shook his head. "He's not a happy man."

Feeney settled back a little into his chair. "No. No, I don't suppose he is. Did you read about his latest . . . ?"

"Yeah. It's interesting."

"Anything to do with him seeing you?"

"I don't know. I doubt it. He called Ingraham last

week. Then this dog thing. Something seemed to get him going."

Feeney sat up. "He called Ingraham? No shit?"

"No shit." Hardy pulled over a metal chair and sat down. "But I wanted to ask you about something else you said the other day."

"I was playing poker . . ." Feeney held up his hands, smiling, making a joke. Then, "What did I say?"

"You were telling me about how Rusty got Hector Medina into all this. There was some woman, you said. Somebody he was trying to prove something with."

Feeney didn't even have to think about it. He nodded. "Karen Moore," he said. "But she can't fit into all this. She and Rusty were years ago."

"Everybody in this got connected years ago." Hardy brought him up to date on the Baker investigation, or lack of it. "Hey, nobody else is looking. This old stuff could be related, that's all."

Feeney nodded, popping a Life Saver. "That's not an entirely unreasonable theory, but it's still a hell of a long shot. You still going on the assumption Ingraham is dead?"

"Ingraham is dead."

"That's what you said last time."

Hardy sat back. "How come nobody seems to want to believe this guy is dead?"

"Oh, I want to believe it. It would enhance my inner peace to believe it. I would very much like him to be dead, but we like bodies. Missing bodies aren't neat."

Hardy knew what he was saying. The case against Baker rested on his motive for killing Ingraham. Not Maxine. And the D.A.'s job, without an official finding that Rusty was at least dead, would be to try Maxine's murder before a jury that might have a hard time believing Baker killed Maxine when he had no motive, didn't even know her. The alleged death of Ingraham would be irrelevant and inadmissible. If he killed her because she was around and in the way when he killed

Ingraham, well, okay. But without Ingraham an official homicide, it would be a hard sell.

"I'm convinced Rusty's dead," Hardy said. "His blood was all over his barge. He fell overboard, got washed out in the Bay." Now he was going after Louis, he realized. Never mind his other doubts, he had to play this straight . . .

"Maybe he's scared. Maybe he's hiding."

"And maybe he's fish food."

Feeney smiled. "I'll grant that. It's possible, maybe even likely. And you don't think it's Baker?"

Hardy gave it a second. "That's what's funny. If I'd gotten this case when I was working here—I mean just the file on Baker, leaving out the other suspects—I'd do a number on it. As Glitsky tells me when he's being real professional, all the elements are there. Except the body, of course."

"Not exactly a detail."

"Except that a good expert witness, someone exactly like myself, should be able to convince a jury that Rusty collapsed overboard and the tide took him out."

"Which is what you believe."

Hardy chewed his cheek. "That one I'm going with."

"Well, if you buy that Baker was there, which I guess you've got to, what's the problem?"

"I just can't seem to convince myself, absolutely, that he's all of it. Problem is, I seem to be one of the players, and I don't know what game it is. It makes me nervous."

Feeney nodded.

"So I thought I'd start over at the beginning. You'd said there was a woman involved—with Ingraham there always was . . ."

"Right."

"And there was Maxine Weir dead on his barge."

"From what you've told me, I'd start with her."

"Her husband, you mean?"

Feeney nodded. "The stats don't lie. Look to the spouse. Especially this case. Money, jealousy, the works. Why didn't Glitsky take him in?"

"Well, he may have had an alibi—I'm not sure if he mentioned it to Abe—but they also had Baker."

"Ah, yes, the convenient Baker."

"Why do you say that?"

"Because Baker solves two outstanding homicides—three if you include Ingraham—and that's good for the department's numbers." He ran a finger through his thick hair. "It might not be laziness. On paper, Baker's a righteous suspect."

"But you don't think he's guilty?"

Feeney held up a hand. "I'm just playing devil's advocate. You can't have it both ways. If Ingraham's dead—and I'm not saying he's not—then Baker's a good bet. So is Maxine's husband. But if Ingraham's not dead, it opens a few other cans of worms."

"I'm sure he's dead. Maybe Baker did him, maybe Weir."

"You said Weir had an alibi."

"*Maybe* an alibi."

"So find out. Why waste your time with Karen Moore?"

"Maybe it goes all the way back to Medina. Why is he part of the action again just at this time?" Hardy saw the skeptical look, but pushed on. "Look, whatever's going on here began with Ingraham. He's the reason I'm in it. Medina, Baker, Ingraham, me. Something started nine years ago. If it leads me back to Maxine Weir, I'll get back to Ray's alibi."

"And you think Karen Moore may know something?"

Hardy shook his head. "I don't know. She might not know what she knows."

*   *   *

Karen Moore was an investigator for the district attorney's office, a jurisdiction separate from the regular police department. One of her colleagues told Hardy that she was down at Hunters Point trying to bring in a juvenile witness. She would be back sometime that afternoon, but he couldn't say when.

He was back in the corridor now, just after lunch, and people were reentering courtrooms after the recess. The halls were crowded. Hardy walked to a phone booth and called Frannie at work.

"Are you still mad at me?" she asked.

"I wasn't. I just had to go out."

"Eddie said that before he went out. He got killed."

"I'm not Eddie, Frannie. And I didn't get killed."

"And you're still out."

"I am."

She was silent. "Are you going back to your house?"

"Eventually, I suppose."

"Tonight?"

Hardy thought about it. "I don't know. What would you like? I don't want to fight you about every time I walk out the door."

"I'd like you to come back tonight."

"You know I've got to keep doing this until it's figured out?"

"Okay, I know that. Don't get hurt, will you?"

Hardy smiled. "Hurt's not in the game plan."

He got the log-on from Lanier, who had been writing up a report in the otherwise deserted Homicide room, where he had gone to see if Abe had had a change of heart and come to work. No, in fact Abe had called in sick.

Hardy, saying he was referred by Tony Feeney, left a message where he'd be for Karen Moore when she got back, got himself a Diet Coke and found the room—a regular office with a solitary terminal on a pitted desk.

This was San Francisco's incident report–suspect computer. One terminal, no full-time operators. Random, unsupervised log-ons. They had not had anything when Hardy worked here, so he supposed this was an improvement, but it was still far from state of the art.

He did not feel he was looking for anything, just killing time, but sometimes killing a few minutes could be productive. He typed in Louis Baker's name.

It was an interesting screen. According to the computer, Louis Baker—alias Lou Brock, Louis Clark, Lou Rawls (the guy had a sense of humor, all right), street name Puffer (whatever that meant)—was still doing his time in San Quentin.

Hardy wondered how far behind the computer's records were. He punched in Hector Medina, whose name did not appear at all. Well, that made some sense—he'd been cleared twice.

Ray Weir was in the database, though. Nine years ago—there it was again—he had been arrested for brawling at a 49ers' game. The arresting officer was not Medina. There was no record if Ingraham had been involved—he had pleaded *nolo contendere* and gotten off with a two-hundred-dollar fine. In '85 he got busted for misdemeanor marijuana possession—another hundred-dollar fine. He had an outstanding warrant on an unpaid parking ticket.

Hardy drank some Coke. So Ray was a brawler too, or had been. And, as Hardy already knew, a heavy user of marijuana, maybe other drugs. Emotional enough to cry in front of other people over his lost love. How emotionally unstable was he? What if he was on dope, strung out, violence prone, and had gone out, as Warren had at first suggested, to "settle things" with Maxine? Ray's alibi, Hardy was thinking, had better be verifiable. He took down a few particulars from the screen on his yellow pad.

Rusty Ingraham's car—a blue '87 Volkswagen Jetta—had indeed been reported stolen on August 29. But that was all the computer had on Rusty. So the database wasn't more than about three weeks behind, which Hardy figured wasn't so bad. He was starting to take down the information on the car when there was a knock.

"Mr. Hardy?"

Hardy stood up. "Sergeant Moore."

She laughed, perfect white teeth in a model's face. "Karen, please. Tony Feeney beckons, I jump. How can I help you."

She boosted herself up like a schoolgirl on the edge of the desk. She was dressed in what looked like some kind of uniform, though it wasn't a set of patrolman's blues. The pants were baggy and a leather jacket with her sergeant's stripes covered her blouse. She looked bulky, which Hardy guessed was a good cover. Any kind of close look revealed a toned body on a short frame. If she wore any makeup she'd stop traffic. But she didn't, and with nothing to set off the high cheekbones, the deep-set black eyes, the wide sensuous mouth, she was only pretty. Very.

"I don't know if you can. I'm looking into something that happened a long time ago."

"For Tony? Is this an active case?"

"No, not strictly for Tony. He gave me your name." She waited.

"It's a little personal," Hardy said. "Rusty Ingraham."

Warily. "Rusty Ingraham. There's a blast from the past. How is Rusty?"

"Actually, Rusty's dead, or appears to be." He explained the ambiguity.

"Well, I'm sorry to hear that," she said when he had finished.

"Are you?"

"Rusty and I were old news. We split up amicably enough."

"Tony Feeney acted like he'd just won the lottery when he heard."

She nodded. "I'd believe that. Tony hated Rusty. A lot of people hated Rusty. I didn't. I felt sorry for him, finally."

"Finally?"

"Well, at first I was attracted to him. You knew him?"

Hardy nodded.

"Then you know. He was pretty charismatic. Very charismatic. Never lost a case, star of the show. That was Rusty. And I was this black single mother of a ten-year-old daughter and—"

"Excuse me, when was this?"

"We're talking I guess nine or ten years ago."

"And you had a ten-year-old then?" Hardy had been figuring her for her late twenties.

Karen laughed, acknowledging the compliment. "I'm thirty-six, Mr. Hardy. And I'm also a grandmother, but thank you."

"You don't look like a grandmother."

"No, I know. I work at it, too. I like to think on a good day I can give my daughter a run."

"I'd bet on you. So back when she was ten you had this thing with Rusty."

"I was flattered. It was also the first white man I'd gone out with"—Hardy noted the "first"—"and at the time I saw it as a bit of a coup, you know. I didn't realize Rusty saw me—foxy young black chick—the same way. A conquest. Another victory."

He searched her eyes for some sign of pain or loss and saw none. Ingraham might have been an old schoolteacher, sometimes remembered, sometimes fondly.

"So how long did you two go out?"

She looked up at the ceiling. "I'd guess close to a year, maybe ten months. That was about his limit. A year. Then whoever he was seeing would suddenly be last year's model, you know, and there was nothing to show off there."

"And you didn't resent that?"

"Actually I saw it coming and beat him to the punch. By that time I had him pretty well figured out and was starting to feel sorry for him. And you can't love somebody you feel sorry for."

"Why'd you feel sorry for him? I thought he was this super success?"

"Well, that's why. It was a sickness. I really believe that, that he was a sick man. He couldn't lose at anything, or even have the appearance of losing. He didn't care about what was real—it was all the appearance."

"So what happened with Hector Medina?"

"Well, I think that's mostly why I broke it off. He just had to prove to me that he was right about Medina. He'd said it in front of a group of us, and he wasn't going to back down. We fought about it. I wanted him to just let it go. I mean, what did it matter? Medina might not have been a great cop, but he wasn't worse than a lot of others. He had a family, all that. Why stir it up? The original investigation had cleared him. But Rusty got on his high horse and there was no getting him off."

"But why?"

"That's the question, isn't it? At first, no doubt about it, he thought it impressed me, or would impress me. Solo prosecutor takes on the police department and district attorney's office and brings in a righteous conviction. He thought it would make him more romantic. The Serpico of San Francisco . . ."

"And that passed, the part about impressing you, I mean?"

"Well, it never really worked, but after he committed himself . . ." She shrugged. "But that was just Rusty. His ego."

"And to hell with Medina, right?"

"Oh, Medina didn't even exist to Rusty. He was just another trophy, like I was, I guess. He eventually got off again anyway."

"But lost his job."

"I know. No one believed him after the second investigation, but there wasn't enough evidence to bring him to trial, so he walked, but to everybody he was a killer cop."

"Do you think he was?"

"He had a reputation for being mean. Little things lots of guys do—maybe an extra thwack with the sap, cuffs tight enough to cut—nothing heavy, but they came out in the investigation."

"You know about now, the accusation against him?"

"Killing that dog? He might have done that."

"And how about Rusty? Killing him?"

"After all this time?"

Hardy explained about the connection through the Valenti and Raines situation. Putting Medina back into the action.

"I don't know," she said. "I guess it could've powered him up. But if he didn't do it when it was fresh, would he now?"

"Except back then he was married, had a good job, a future. Now he's divorced, raising a daughter alone, his job is nothing. Maybe it brought back all he's lost, all that Rusty made him lose. He snapped over it . . ."

Karen slipped off the desk and walked over to the window. She put her hands on her hips and did a couple of waist rolls, keeping loose, stretched like a cat, turned around. "Stranger things have happened, but you've got to believe time heals at least a little. If Rusty did something else, something new, I could see it better. You get any sign of that?"

"Nope. In fact, Medina told me he hadn't seen Rusty in years, although he'd called him recently."

"To say what?"

"Nothing. He said he changed his mind, hung up."

There was another question in her eyes but she didn't ask it. Instead she said, "It might be worth checking his alibi."

Hardy, sitting, ran his fingers over the keyboard in front of the terminal. "I'll do that," he said.

She came up behind him, looking over his shoulder at the screen, which still held the information about Rusty's car. "Back to basics, huh? He was driving an old Volkswagen?"

Hardy squinted at the glaring green terminal. "Does that mean something?"

"It means he must have had a bad streak at the track. He used to say he'd never drive less than a Lincoln. He'd rather walk."

"So what's the track have to do with it?"

"I thought you said you knew him."

To Hardy, Rusty had been another red-hot young attorney much like himself, trying cases and winning them, putting bad guys away. They got along fine in the office, once in a while had drinks and discussed work. That was it. "I guess not," he said.

"If you didn't know his gambling, you didn't know him at all." Karen came around and sat on the desk again. "The track is what broke us up, much more than Hector Medina, if you want to know the truth, although it was all part of the same thing, I suppose, the winning thing. He said the ponies were the ultimate challenge. He really believed, or wanted to believe, that you could learn enough, follow the jockeys and horses closely enough, so you'd never have to lose. He used to say it wasn't even gambling, you could make it a sure thing. Not every race, you understand, but when you were sure, you jumped."

"And he was successful?"

"He did pretty well." She glanced over at the screen again. "Except when he lost."

"Which was often?"

"No, but which tended to be big when he did." She shook her head. "An old Volkswagen . . . who would've thought it? He must've been losing. Big."

Hardy's fingers drummed some more on the desk. "And that's what broke you up?"

"Well, it just showed me who he was. It's why I eventually came to feel sorry for him. Nobody wins all the time, I don't care how good you are, what you know. But it was like a personal affront to him every time he lost. He'd go crazy. The universe was against him. Nutso."

She was lost in the memory now. "A couple of times he hit on me for my check after blowing his, losing on what he thought was a sure thing, and not believing he could go out and lose my check the same way on the next race." She met Hardy's eyes. "It was very sad really, the addiction. It was like he won at everything else, so he purposely picked something he couldn't win at so it could verify that he was really, at the bottom, a loser. Or that's how he saw himself." Abruptly, she brushed at her hair with her hand as if something of Rusty had stuck in it and she wanted it out. "That's just my two-bit psychology, but it makes sense to me."

"So you think he was a loser, deep down?"

"All the way down. There was just what he'd won and what he'd lost. He just wasn't there—no *person* holding it all together, giving any kind of focus. And I think his biggest fear was that people would find out he wasn't the fantastic winner he tried to appear to be. So he couldn't lose anything, ever."

"And yet he constantly tested that at the track?"

"I said it was a sickness. He couldn't help himself. The track was his litmus test. When he beat it, he could beat anybody. If it started to beat him, he'd nose-dive all over his life. We finally broke up in one of the down cycles."

Hardy thought of the Rusty who'd come into the Shamrock the week before—a little down and out, clothes not pressed, riding public transport because his car had been stolen. He still had the gab, the line, the presence, but he wouldn't have impressed anybody as a man who could take on the universe. Hardly a winner.

Karen pushed herself off the desk. "But the horses didn't kill him, did they?"

"No," Hardy said. "It was somebody with opposable thumbs."

18

Okay, Ray Weir was thinking, I've waited long enough.

He had gone to the service that morning, waited with Courtenay and Warren until they brought out the urn with what was left of Maxine. Then they'd all ridden out under the Golden Gate with one of Warren's money friends who owned a yacht—champagne, toasting Maxine's memory, dumping the ashes into the sea, freezing their butts off.

Now he was back home, and he'd waited long enough. It was a legitimate question, and he had all the paperwork here in front of him.

He had to wade through four receptionist types before he got someone who could talk to him.

He gave the number of the policy on Maxine's life, then the dates of both the accident and the settlement agreement. "I'm just checking the status of the payment," he said.

The woman asked him to wait and returned after most of "I Write the Songs" had finished playing in Ray's ear. Across the miles her voice was tiny. "You haven't received it?"

"That's why I'm calling."

"It must be in the mail," she said.

Ray's hands tightened on the mouthpiece. "The check's in the mail? When did you mail it?"

She cleared her throat, but didn't come back any louder. "Just another minute, please." Some Connecticut radio station was playing "Soft Hits All The Time"—soft hits for the soft brained, Ray thought as they rocked into a Muzak version of "I Am, I Said."

"Sir?"

"I'm still here."

"There must be some mistake. We sent the check for the full amount, eighty-five thousand dollars, ten days ago by registered mail, return receipt requested, overnight delivery, and it was signed for by"—she paused—"by Maxine Weir."

Ray suddenly felt light-headed and had to sit down. "What do you mean?" he said.

"Sir?"

"I mean, when was this?"

After a short silence, figuring it out, "We sent it out on Friday, so it probably, yes, here it is, it was delivered on Monday, last week. A week ago today."

"To Maxine Weir?"

"Yes, sir. The signature is very clear. Would you like me to send you a copy of the receipt?"

Ray almost had to laugh. He hung up.

Well, it was possible the check was still at her apartment. The policy was in both of their names—either of them could sign it. Maybe the police had found it and hadn't notified him yet.

Or she could have taken it down to the bank and deposited it. They still had a joint account, not that there was ever much in it. He would call customer service.

He lit up a joint and punched buttons on his telephone. No, there had been no deposit made to the account, would he like to talk to a manager?

He didn't know what he'd like to do. The world was spinning.

Though he was back in the Hall, Glitsky did not check into Homicide. If he ran into Batiste or one of the guys he would say he was feeling better and had decided to come in. Otherwise he'd keep it casual. He might do a little work. He was still thinking L.A., but there were items to tie up here and his father was right. If you're going to do it, don't do it half-assed.

The Filipino boy in the lab, Ghattas, had been a help on Saturday, and he had no trouble locating the gun again—Ray Weir's gun—and bringing out the report on it. He had stood on the other side of the counter while Abe did a quick scan of the results . . .

"You understand, sir, it was found in mud under about sixteen feet of water?"

"So you wouldn't expect any prints?"

"Prints are funny, you know. Oil-based. It's not so much you wouldn't expect them. It wouldn't be a shock either way . . ."

Abe looked up from the report. The boy had something else to say. "But?"

"Well, in fact we didn't find any."

Abe tried to hide his disappointment.

"But I got to thinking."

Abe was starting to like this guy. He grinned his scar-slashed grin.

"What'd you get to thinking?"

"Well, as I said, the gun didn't have any prints, but it didn't even have any smudges. It was like it had never been held."

"But it had been fired?"

"Oh yeah, no question about that. But still, even with the mud and salt water, you'd expect something. Some oil residue."

"So?"

"But there wasn't anything. Which is, maybe, I don't know, a little suggestive. So I did a trace test for Armor All."

"Armor All?"

"You know, the car stuff? Hell's Angels got wise

to this first. You wipe a weapon down, then spray it with Armor All and you won't leave a print."

"And there was Armor All on this gun?"

"Right."

"And so?"

"And so that means that whoever shot the weapon knew about Armor All."

"Uh huh?"

He leaned over the counter, eyes shining in his excitement. "It means the perp was a pro. Anybody else would have just wiped it down afterward, don't you think?"

Glitsky acknowledged that. "Okay."

"So your shooter is in the business. This isn't high tech, but I wouldn't say it's general knowledge either. So if you got two suspects and one is, say, a civilian, then maybe that one isn't so likely to be your guy."

"Ray Weir," Abe said, "the husband. A live one, up to now."

"It's something to think about, is all I'm saying."

Drysdale was going over the ground rules again. Outside the window, cars were starting to back up on the freeway heading toward the Bay Bridge. Gubizca leaned backward and could make out the clock on the Union 76 sign—4:38. The day had been shot to hell on this idiocy, and it wasn't over yet.

Fred, still enthusiastic and confident, was in the process of getting hooked up by the polygraph technician, a woman in uniform who with Drysdale would be the only people present when Fred was questioned. This was Manny's great concern. Polygraphs didn't work with distractions—with a trained subject, they didn't work at all—and Manny would not be in the actual room when the procedure took place. There would be no court reporter, no other attorneys, no one except

Fred, Drysdale, and this woman, who would probably sit behind Fred, out of his line of vision.

This wasn't as bad as it could be because Drysdale had already presented Manny and Fred with a complete list of the questions he would be asking, all either yes or no, and lawyer and client had gone over them for the past hour, making sure there was nothing Fred might slip on.

So Manny listened with half an ear, figuring that if Drysdale was planning on a blindside attack, there was almost no possibility he would do it now.

"So as I say," Drysdale droned on, "this isn't any formal proceeding, but the nature of your allegations"— here he smiled at Treadwell, at Gubizca—"are so . . . so unusual, that I believe you'll get more"— again searching for the right word—"more enthusiastic cooperation from this office in general . . ." Drysdale spread his hands out, smiling, everybody's friend. "This isn't me, gentlemen. I'm selling the whole package both to my boss and my staff, and there is some concern—possibly justified at this stage, I'm afraid— well, let's just say your cooperation here, Manny, will enhance your and your client's credibility."

"You don't believe me, do you?" Treadwell said.

"Fred, please." Gubizca wasn't about to have his client get into an off-the-record discussion with Art Drysdale, who beneath his benign exterior was one of the craftiest attorneys Gubizca had ever opposed.

"Me?" Drysdale acted shocked. "I totally believe you. That's why I'm doing this, we're doing this." He hiked a leg up on the table where the polygraph sat. There was no guile on his face, he wasn't trying to sell anything, just convey information. "Manny, of course, is right to treat this as though we're adversarial here. But, without mentioning names, I'm not giving anything away when I say that certain members of the staff here are skeptical. But this, today, this is just ammo to use against those people, so in a real sense, for today at least, we're on the same side. You tell me what happened with Hector Medina, the polygraph corroborates it—okay, so it's not formally admissible— it'll get the team behind this case. And that's what we both want. It makes my job easier." He spread his arms again, his wide and sincere smile.

The technician was finished now, and Manny walked up behind Fred and whispered that he should remember to stick to the questions asked and above all to try to keep calm. Then he left the room.

"You can sit back if you'd like," Drysdale said. He himself pulled up an old office chair covered with yellow leather and crossed one leg over the other. "As you know, we ask only yes and no questions, so we'll start with the easy stuff to calibrate this thing. Your name is Fred Treadwell?"

Fred nodded.

"Please say yes or no."

"I'm sorry. Yes."

"Your name is Fred Treadwell?"

"Yes."

They ran through the usual opening questions— name, address, day of the week—getting used to the slight scratch of the pencil on the lined paper, the hum of the machine.

"This isn't so bad, is it?" Drysdale said.

"No," Fred said, and Drysdale noted the skip in the pencil. So it was getting to him. Actually, the subject didn't have to say anything to get a reading. The body reacted even when the words weren't said. Drysdale knew this, was counting on it, and on Treadwell not understanding it.

"Okay, let's tell a couple of lies."

"But if I know I'm not trying to deceive by giving a false answer, the machine will register true, won't it?"

Drysdale gave him a broad grin. "You get this stuff,

don't you? You're right. So try and deceive me a little on this next set, okay." He leaned forward in his chair. "We're still in the test phase here, all right?"

Fred nodded, licking his lips. He looked to the door behind Drysdale, as though seeking assurance that Manny was out there to help him if he needed it.

"You have worked at your current job eight years, is that correct?"

"Yes." True.

"And you've lived two years in your apartment?"

"Yes." False.

"Two years?" Build on the falsehood and see what he does. "And you have painted it during that time?"

"The time I live there or the last two years?"

Very good, Fred, Drysdale thought. He said, "I'm sorry, have you painted the apartment in the past two years?"

"No." True.

"And your apartment is on the second floor?"

"No." False.

"So it's on the third floor?"

Pause. "Yes." False.

"But if you fell from the third story, wouldn't you do more than sprain your ankle?"

"That wasn't one of the questions." A light sweat had broken on Fred's forehead.

All innocence, Drysdale held up his hands. "It seemed to spring naturally from the previous answers." Not pushing it, he looked over at the polygraph. "Look, in any event, the machine seems to be working properly." He came back to Fred. "You've not lived in your apartment two years and the apartment is not on the third floor. Are both of these statements correct?"

"Yes."

Drysdale glanced at the machine again, took in a breath and held it a minute. Letting it out in a rush, he said, "All right, the test is over. Let's begin."

Drysdale had the typed questions in front of him. He also had Fred's Statement of Facts on Medina's attack, which he'd used to draw up the questions. He started at the beginning and asked the questions in order, lulling Fred into a space where his confidence was growing with the polygraph's support to the point that he seemed almost unaware that he was wired. It was just a conversation between Drysdale and himself, even if one side of it was only yes and no.

Drysdale paused in the questioning. "All right," he said, "now we're where the talk with Mr. Medina has turned to the alleged Valenti/Raines assault on you. Is that correct?"

It wasn't a question on the typed list, but it was so natural that Fred didn't seem to notice.

"Yes." True.

"And Mr. Medina said he represented Mr. Raines?"

Fred didn't answer.

"Mr. Treadwell?"

"That's not one of the questions."

Drysdale settled back in his seat, not pushing it yet. "Fred, we're corroborating the events of last Friday night, right? You want to look at your own Statement of Facts? You mention Valenti and Raines." He was all reason. "I'm not getting back to that case—I'm verifying the facts in this statement."

"But it wasn't one of the questions."

Drysdale smiled. "Come on, Fred. So I missed one. I made a mistake, but if you want, we can stop now. If you don't answer this question I don't see where we can go from here."

The sweat had come back to Treadwell's forehead. "All right," he said finally. "What was the question again?"

"Medina said he represented Raines, yes or no?"

"Yes." True.

"But he told you he had no formal connection to that case." Drysdale went from the questions to the

Statement of Facts. "He said he wanted you to know about the damage that just accusing somebody can do to their life?"

"Yes." True.

"And he wanted you to know that because he thought you were falsely accusing Valenti and Raines of beating you up?" Good, they were way off the question list now.

"Yes."

"And then he grabbed your dog, Poppy, was it?"

Treadwell swallowed, off the list himself now, remember. "Yes. He was just petting it . . ."

"And he broke its neck?"

"Yes. Yes. He just . . ." He hung his head, suffering through it again.

"He broke your dog's neck because he thought you were falsely accusing Valenti and Raines?"

"No! I mean, yes!"

"Yes, he thought it, or yes, you had falsely accused them?"

Treadwell was looking around, panic setting in. "He did it to threaten me," he said, "to threaten my life."

"If you didn't retract your story?"

"Yes." True.

"Your story? Your true story about Valenti and Raines?"

"Yes, he just—"

"Your story about Valenti and Raines is true, then, is that correct?"

"Yes! Yes, it's true. That part is true."

False. False. False.

"They did beat you?"

"Yes." False. "He killed Poppy, and they beat me." False. "Why don't you believe me? He killed my Poppy." Fred was slumped on his arms over the table. He raised his head. "He killed my Poppy."

Drysdale reached over and patted his hand. "I believe you, Fred. He killed your Poppy."

Fred put his head back down on the table. Drysdale kept patting his hand, feeling dirty and sad. "I think we're done here," he said to the technician. "You can unhook him."

A rust sky presaged an uneasy dusk.

Lace was wearing an army-surplus all-weather jacket and, collar up against the cold, walked the periphery of Holly Park alone. From time to time he'd nod at one or another of the small groups of younger men hanging on stoops or by their wheels, but no one asked him to join them, or offered much more than a cock of the head. Jumpup was over to Lorethra's house, inside, with her and her mama and the little ones. Lace, he'd looked in at Baker's Mama, but she had come back from the hospital with a bottle and it was way down already.

He passed Dido's old cut—his old cut—crossing the street away from it, making clear he understood the new territory. He stopped, hands in his pockets, and was startled by a hand on his shoulder. He turned around.

"Easy, my man."

Samson had backed three steps away. His dreadlocks hung like thick cobwebs around the obsidian, small-eyed, expressionless face. Lace's heart was pumping pretty good.

As though they'd been having a conversation all this time, Samson said, "Three ways it can go."

Lace shook his shoulders loose, the casual attitude. He knew how Samson was. Like an animal, you show any fear around him and he attacks. "What is?" Lace said.

"The man be lookin', askin' around maybe, sometimes the wrong stories get out."

"I got no stories."

"No. See? That's one way it can go. You got no

story, maybe you hang in the cut, run with me." Samson's teeth showed yellow. "Same ol'. Back to it, right?"

He stepped closer. There was a brightness in the tiny eyes as though he'd been using his product. Dido didn't go in for that when he was working. Well, Dido wasn't Samson, and Lace had better get used to that.

"Other story," Samson said, "is the con—be talkin' about taking over the cut, how Dido best be movin' on, like that. Come down to blood."

Lace was thinking that if Louis Baker had wanted the cut, and killed Dido, wouldn't he have stayed to hold the claim? But he said, "What's three?"

A cold wind from behind Lace blew some leaves and papers up the street. Samson squinted into it at Lace, his eyes even smaller, glinting. "Be no three," he said. "Only two stories. Be no one tellin' any third stories is what I'm saying."

Lace wondered if the gun that had been used on Dido, the one Lace had originally assumed had been Louis Baker's, whether that gun—Samson's—was still in the cut, if he could find it and get his hands on it. He clenched his fists inside the pockets of the jacket, released them, fighting the shivering that was threatening to rake over. "I hear you," he said. "Hey, I hear you. It's casual."

19

The picture of Eddie was still on Frannie's dresser. She got home from work and, changing into a sweatshirt and some jeans, noticed for the first time that things weren't fitting the same. She reached for a dab of perfume and saw the photograph of Eddie.

She stopped, her hand still outstretched. Something curled up inside her. Eddie had been caught climbing up into a friend's pickup down by Dune Beach. One leg was up on the tailgate and he'd just been turning around to answer as Frannie had yelled something at him. He was smiling his two-hundred-watt smile and his hair was blown every which way, his jacket collar turned up. She'd enlarged the picture to eight by ten and it hadn't been perfectly focused, so there was a graininess to it that for some reason added to its immediacy.

Forgetting the perfume, she watched her hand go to the frame, and she brought the picture back to the bed, where she sat holding it on her lap.

Eddie looked about eighteen in the picture, impossibly young. She closed her eyes.

It was hard to imagine that they'd been the same age. Eddie now stopped forever only eight months older than the photograph. Frannie felt she'd aged a lifetime.

But the pregnancy kept things in real time. The baby, Eddie's baby, growing inside her so slowly that it had hardly changed her yet.

There he was—her man—waving back to her. Daring to claim back a little space, charming her so she'd let him back in.

The grief over Eddie's death had affected her differently than she'd have thought. The only way she found she could cope without crying all the time was to put him, put their life together, out of her mind. Actively not to remember how it had been, how they'd been together. Move on. Look ahead.

Or, the few times she'd let down, allowed his memory back into her mind, the anger would overtake her. Why did he have to go meddle in things that weren't his business? She thought she'd loved his idealism. But that's what had gotten him killed, and she tried to convince herself that she even hated him for being that way, because it was what took him away from her. Why did she have to have met him in the first place? It wasn't fair.

Eddie's smile didn't fade, didn't change. It was grainy, like an old photograph, getting older every day. Smiling, charming, kidding her. I'm still here, Frannie. Can't deny it forever. I'll bet the kid winds up looking like me.

A tear fell on the glass that covered the picture.

The kid.

One hand held the frame. The other pressed itself flat against her belly, somehow had worked its way under the sweatshirt.

God, Eddie, she thought. Come on, this isn't fair.

What isn't fair? he said. That I'm in you? That all this moving ahead and looking forward and getting together with Diz . . . that's okay, I realize I'm gone . . . is just setting yourself up for the fall later. You've got to find a real place to put me. I was your husband. I'm the father of that little person in there. Don't hide me. Don't shut me out. I don't deserve that. If it's painful I'm sorry, but I miss you, too. Don't you think I wish I could be there?

"Yes, I do."
Well, then?

Hardy came and sat next to her where she lay on the top of the bed, the picture of Eddie Cochran facedown on her stomach.

Her hair was spread out behind her on the pillow, the face slightly puffed.

"What?" he said.

"It's just too soon."

"I know it is. I've been thinking the same thing."

She moved the picture of Eddie to the floor, put her hand on his thigh, curled onto her side against him. He rubbed her back inside the sweatshirt.

"You are the only male friend I have, Dismas."

"I am that."

"I don't know what to do. I don't know what I've done with Eddie."

Hardy patted her stomach. "Eddie's here."

"That's what I mean. I'm not just lonely." She revised that. "I'm not even lonely. I'm trying to find Eddie and that's not fair. To you."

"Move over," Hardy said.

She lay, one leg over him, her head in the hollow of his arm, a hand between the buttons of his shirt.

"Because something in me loves you," she said. "A lot."

"But there's the other stuff."

"There is."

He blew a breath out at the ceiling. "It's pretty natural. You're nesting. You want a man around. You trust me, and I show up needing a place to stay. It's a neat little dream."

"It's more than that, too."

Hardy turned onto his side and undid the button on her jeans, the zipper.

"They finally feel a little tight."

She bit at his lower lip, flicked her tongue against the tip of his. His hand, down inside her pants, pressed against her.

"See, this is real, too," she said. "This part."

The kiss, Frannie undoing his pants, freeing him. Another kiss, deep and slow, then more getting out of clothes and he was entering her, breathing her in, mouths together, bodies close and hard pressed, pushing but not moving, her legs wrapping him, holding him as far in as he could get.

The house was cold. Walking down the long hallway, he checked the thermostat and saw it was at 58 degrees. By the time he got to the kitchen, six steps later, he heard the creaks of the responding furnace. In his bedroom he realized he hadn't fed the fish in several days. Bad. He shook some food over the surface and they didn't wait for him to tap the glass.

"Sorry, guys."

He raised the blackout curtain in front of the one window in his office and looked back toward downtown, out at the twinkling lights. He could see the very tip of what the previous week had seemed the evil Pyramid presiding, like the triangular cyclops eye on the dollar bill, over the shadowy line of Jackson Heights. Leaning out, off to his right, the once spectral Sutro Tower, now vaguely benign, thrust its fingers toward some high clouds. The moon was up, nearly full.

He wondered at the change in his perception of things. He listened to his house creaking as the warmth spread in the pipes. The sound wasn't ominous.

After the coal fire was going well, after the heat had really kicked in, after he'd gone through all his mail (except for one postcard), sitting in the pool of light cast by the green-shaded brass lamp on his desk, he switched on the room's main lights and grabbed his darts from the board next to the fireplace.

These were his office darts, the same type of custom 20-gram tungsten beauties he carried with him at almost all times. He hadn't thrown since he'd left the house, but in his first round, shooting for the bull, he hit two and the last one thokked low in the "20."

He picked up the postcard. Hong Kong by night.

His ex-wife.

Carrying the card with him, he went back out through his bedroom to the kitchen. He kept no hard liquor in his house, but there were four bottles of Anchor Steam in the rack on the refrigerator door. He found some frozen chicken breasts and in the cupboard a can of cream of mushroom soup and a can of green beans. He put the breasts in his heavy black all-purpose cast-iron pan, poured the green beans and soup over them, added a little beer, covered the whole thing and turned the heat on low. Jane was appalled at his home cooking.

Frannie had made him every meal at her house.

At the kitchen table, bottle of beer in hand, he read the back of the postcard. Where was he? Would he be home to get this? Well, she guessed she'd find out next week. It wasn't exactly a game, but neither was it very serious.

That was Jane. Maybe it was serious, but she just wouldn't acknowledge that anymore. Maybe, with her marriage to him and then the second one—the rebound—that had lasted less than two months, she could only let things get so serious and then pull back. When their son, Michael, had died, he had to remember, she'd gone through it too. Sometimes it felt like it had only been him, but that hadn't been because Jane wasn't there. It was because he was blind to anything else.

Give her a break, Diz.

He was starting to smell the food. He got up and

made sure it wasn't burning, sticking on the bottom, and turned down the heat a little. He opened another beer.

Well, what was there to be so serious about, anyway? She was good at her job and liked it. She liked him, too. At least that. She knew who she was. He thought, with a pang, and though it had never come up, that she was still faithful to him.

It wasn't just that he'd slept with Frannie. Frannie had told him tonight, before and after they'd made love, that she needed, she felt they both needed, more time. He ought to go home.

And he'd wanted to go home. Not to get away from Frannie. Not to figure anything out. Just to be home. What the hell did that mean? That he didn't love Frannie? Or Jane?

The difference with Frannie was that she let him see she needed him. Maybe not for everything, maybe now only for some physical comfort, some familiar warmth, but the door was open. Jane might love him, but he didn't feel like she needed anybody anymore.

So what was it with the Hardy monster? Did he just need to be needed? Well, if there wasn't some need, how real could it be? Okay, but how badly would Frannie just need a father for her baby, not necessarily Dismas Hardy? It would be bad luck to get that part confused.

And when he and Jane had first gotten back together, there had been some serious voltage. Okay, there had always been the attraction—that was still there—but maybe Jane's need at that time was to lay to rest the ghosts of their failed marriage, to prove that it really had been their son Michael's death that had destroyed her man, Dismas, and not some failing in her.

Now, that done, the point made, it was time to coast.

The problem was that until a few months ago, until

he'd gotten back with Jane, Hardy had coasted for the better part of a decade. He was coasted out. Now he was in gear, ready to roll.

He thought about having a third beer, decided what the hell, and filled a plate with the Chicken McHardy. It tasted great.

Frank Batiste had the only real office, with a door, in Homicide. Now he sat at his desk, the door open a crack, and for the first time in what seemed months felt some measure of satisfaction in his position, in the department, in the way things were shaking down. For once, he thought, the good guys might be getting a break.

The word on the dropped charges in the Valenti and Raines investigation had spread through the ranks—guys calling each other at home. Frank had personally called both men to tell them they were re-instated with back pay effective immediately.

At Clarence Raines's suggestion he did something else that was as much the source of his satisfaction as anything else. He'd gone down to Judge Lyons and explained the mutual exclusivity of the Raines/Valenti and Treadwell investigations and requested a warrant right now on Treadwell.

Which he got and served as Treadwell sat flush-faced and shaken in Art Drysdale's office. Treadwell's lawyer had had a shit-fit, which did Batiste's soul some good, and the bare fact was that now, at 9:30 P.M., Fred Treadwell was in the can on his double-murder rap, at least until the morning when bail would proba-bly be set.

Batiste's prompt move on Treadwell had also gotten out to his squad, and they had been returning to the office in dribs and drabs, catching up on things, getting the further notice that Batiste was personally okaying the overtime they needed to serve subpoenas, write their reports, do their work. If he lost his job over that, so be it. You couldn't run this bunch of guys like a kindergarten without the risk of losing them. And if he lost these handpicked pros, then his own numbers, and eventually his job, would also go to hell.

So he sat enjoying the hum of men working—day guys in at night, bullshitting, getting coffee, picking up mail and paperwork. He was soaring on adrenaline—getting the warrant and arresting Treadwell, making some real management decisions—and was taking the opportunity to write it up for Chief Rigby. Sometime in the next week, he was confident the City and County would find some way to clear the money for the overtime. Or they wouldn't find it in the budget and they'd have to borrow from another pot. Batiste thought even the most fuzzy-headed bleeding hearts among the supervisors might realize that taking killers off the street should be a priority item for a police department.

Still, homicide inspector wasn't a punch-in job and it was plain stupid to act like it could be. Of course, the powers that be in this Looney Tune city might still kick his ass over it.

"Fuck it," he said.

"Fuck what?"

Abe Glitsky was back, standing in the doorway, not looking very sick. Batiste had no intention of mentioning it. "Oh, I don't know, take your pick. The supervisors, Rigby and his chicken patrol." He put the tip of his pen in his mouth. "Come to think of it, I ought to mention that. They got money for that, they can pay some overtime."

"Right on," Abe said, pulling a chair out from the wall. "Listen, Frank, I want you to know, I've sent in that application to L.A."

The lieutenant put his pen down. "Don't do that."

Glitsky shifted in the chair. "It's already done."

"Well, I mean don't go. What're you gonna do there in L.A.?"

"What am I doing here?"

"You know what you're doing here. We need you here."

Glitsky smiled, the scar a tight white line through his lips. Batiste held up a hand. "That's not b.s., Abe. I don't spout the line, you know that. And I need you here."

"Thanks, Frank, that's nice to hear. But if you get a call for a reference, give them some kind words, would you?"

He nodded. "Of course I'll do that. But look, why don't you take a few days off, think about it. Maybe you're just having a little burnout. Take a vacation."

"I took today off and thought about it, Frank. I'm not burned out. I still want to be a cop. Worse, I suppose, I am a cop, like it or not. I just want to be able to do my job."

Batiste ran down the day's improvements.

"Yeah, I heard. That's great, but it's like a Band-Aid."

"Come on. It's not all that bad here. It's just bureaucracy, and that's everywhere. You think L.A. will be better? It's so much bigger, it's got to be worse."

"I can't see the chief in L.A. pulling lab time over homicides 'cause some guys do a bullshit prank."

"Chicken shit," Frank corrected him, and Abe had to smile. "There's rot from the top, Frank, and I'm not sure it's just bureaucracy."

"Whatever it is, is over." Batiste got up from behind his desk, went and opened the door. "Forget the past week and look out there. Business as usual."

Abe half turned to look. "It's like your wife has an affair that's ended and you're supposed to pretend it didn't happen?"

"Sometimes, maybe, yeah." He closed the door all

the way. "But you didn't come in here to ask for a reference. I mean, you were already in on something else."

"You ought to be an investigator, Frank. Figuring out shit like that."

Batiste was back in his seat behind the desk. He unwrapped a hard candy from his top drawer and popped it into his mouth. "So you were working." Said with satisfaction.

"Rusty Ingraham." Glitsky grimaced. "I'm sounding like Hardy, but Maxine Weir . . ."

"Yeah? We got the perp on that, don't we?"

"An arrest has been made, right."

"But?"

"Tying things up. Different angles keep popping out."

He told Batiste about his talk with Johnny LaGuardia, the fact that it looked like a professional had done the hit on Maxine, which could include Medina or LaGuardia himself, but seemed to rule out the husband.

"Wait a minute, wait a minute." Batiste raised a hand. "This is all very interesting, but what about the alleged perp, what's his name?"

"Baker."

"Baker. What about Baker? He'd pick up the Armor All trick in the joint, don't you think?"

Glitsky thought on it. "Maybe so. But the problem is also in my guts. The problem is Rusty Ingraham's missing body, the husband's lousy alibi, except why would he know about Armor All? And today—am I wrong—we find our own Hector Medina going pro-active on another violent crime. What's going on?"

Batiste moved the candy around, making a sucking noise. "You want my take, it really sounds to me like you got the right guy. Shit, Abe, there's always some loose ends."

"This is not just loose ends, Frank," Abe said. "This is a hair ball."

Louis Baker wasn't going back in.

They had him now. He'd thought he could pull it off, but then with the shooting, there was no way. That alone, forget the other, the stuff Ingraham and Hardy were talking about, would put him back. He wasn't going.

He wasn't putting up with the game of another trial. Everything stacked against him anyway from day one. And this time, what Hardy had said, going for the gas chamber.

No way.

The hospital room was dark. There was dim light out through the open door into the hallway, where he knew the guard sat.

He was quietly working the sheet back and forth over a jutting bit of metal that protruded from the bars at the side of the bed. A nurse walked by, exchanged a few words with the guard. He saw her silhouette in the doorway and lay still.

Then she was gone. He waited a minute, listening. The chair in the hall creaked, the guard probably settling back.

He got a tear in the top of the sheet and, trying not to move anything but his hands, began ripping a strip down to the bottom.

He only needed three strips. He wanted to get each one started at the top—that was the hardest part, the first tear—so he went back to the little bit of metal, working the old hospital sheet over it again and again, until, again, he got it to tear.

He pulled the new strip down a ways, using only the strength of his hands, showing no movement outside the covers, got maybe ten inches, then started over again at the top.

You only needed three strips to braid.

You braided the three eight-foot strips of sheet into a rope maybe seven feet long. You made a noose in that rope and tied one end to the same metal bar you were using to make the tear. You put the noose around your neck and rolled off the other side of the bed.

He wasn't going back in.

20

Kevin Driscoll was forty-two years old. His marriage to May was going through the readjustment of having two children, ages one and two. He hadn't been laid in three weeks, resented it strongly and this morning had been awakened at 4:45 by Jason's apparently random screaming. Kevin Driscoll had a sore throat. Perpetually, but this morning particularly.

As branch manager, he was out on the floor at Wells Fargo Bank and wondered, taking in the customers and tellers and various assistant vice-presidents (everybody above a teller was an a.v.p.), if the world had always been like this or whether he was only seeing it clearly for the first time. The conventional wisdom was that hardship showed you your true colors—maybe it was true of everything else. When you were having a hard time, you saw everything else in its true colors.

And what he saw depressed him further.

There were seven people waiting in the service line. He would never have thought of it before, but now he wondered how many of them were parents. At least three, maybe four. Had any of them slept in months? No wonder people were crabby at the windows all the time.

And at the windows—only two open. Four more tellers congregated conspicuously at chief teller Marianne's desk catching up on the gossip.

Another man came in. Eight people in the service

line now. Tuesday-morning rush and not one teller even considering heading to a window. Let 'em wait, right. The teller mentality.

Kevin coughed and cleared his throat, hoping Marianne or someone would catch the hint. He hated to have to step into this most basic operations procedure, but getting these people to move sometimes took direct action. The problem was, in his mood he'd likely appear as angry as he was, and that was to be avoided. Bank managers didn't have personalities. They were unflappable.

But he stood up. He'd caught the looks of the customers—rolled eyes or helpless gestures. Shuffling back and forth. Cattle in the pen.

"Hey! Somebody want to open another window? What are you people doing back there?"

Kevin swore to himself. He held a restraining hand up to the security guard who was moving in. He didn't blame the customer who yelled. He felt like yelling himself.

He walked to the bullpen. "Marianne," he said quietly.

She looked up, forever sedentary, endlessly serene, a chief teller for seven years. A hundred and eighty pounds of essence of bovine. But sweet. So fucking sweet he wanted to kill her. She smiled. "Yes, Kevin?"

He gestured to the line, forcing a patient smile that he thought threatened to cramp every muscle in his face.

Sighing, Marianne dispatched one of her minions. One. And the girl didn't hurry. She was carefully counting her drawer when the customer who'd yelled said, "Fuck this!" and turned out of the line.

Another satisfied customer.

"Marianne," he repeated.

She gave him a little wave and mouthed, "They'll wait," then sent another soldier moseying off to the front.

"Are you the manager?"

It was only 10:15. Kevin turned, steeling himself. No matter what, he told himself, don't swing at the customer.

"Yes?" Definitely the smile muscles were cramping up. "How can I help you?"

The man had not bothered waiting in the line. Maybe he wanted to open an account and Kevin could deal him off to one of his employees currently having coffee around the a.v.p. gossip desk. He did not feel like he could trust himself talking to anyone. Perhaps he should say he was sick, check into a motel and sleep about sixteen hours.

The customer was clearly trying to cut a certain type of figure, but Kevin wasn't sure he pulled it off. Was he trying to look like a businessman? Or a pastiche of one with perhaps some artistic statement— mismatched pants and coat, a green tie that was too wide over a pale blue shirt, hiking boots. His longish hair was either heavily moussed or simply greasy. In any event, he was upset, saying something about eighty-five thousand dollars.

The number drove off a little of Kevin's fatigue. He stopped the man in mid-sentence. "Yes, sir. Would you like to sit down, please? Come in where we can talk quietly? Perhaps some coffee?"

The floor had already seen enough vocal disturbance for one day. The thing to do was to get him into one of the conference rooms.

Kevin was walking and the customer had no other option if he wanted to keep talking with him. It also gave Kevin another minute to get himself under control again, to put his own thoughts together.

Of course he remembered Maxine Weir. Who wouldn't remember her? Ignoring even the eighty-five thousand dollars (which, of course, he wasn't likely to do), a man who had not been laid in three weeks did not forget those black tights and high heels. If you'd gotten it in the last five minutes, you'd still perk up at the sight of those nipples peeking out through the holes of the loosely knit skin-colored sweater.

Kevin held the door for the man. It shushed closed behind them. He showed no inclination to sit.

"Now, how can I help you?" he asked.

The privacy of the conference room worked some on the man. He was still upset, but the raving tone was gone. "My name is Ray Weir and my wife and I have—had—an account here . . ."

"You used to have an account here?"

"No. We still do. I mean, I do. My wife"—he paused—"my wife, uh, died last week. Was killed."

Kevin let out a breath. "I'm very sorry, Mr. Weir. And you're settling . . . ?"

"I'm not settling anything. I'm here to find out what happened to a check for eighty-five thousand dollars. An insurance check. The insurance company said my wife signed for it last week, but I called your customer service and there's no record it was deposited. I called the police and asked if they'd found it among her stuff, but so far it hasn't turned up."

"No," Kevin said. "I'm afraid it won't. She cashed it."

"What do you mean, she cashed it?"

Kevin coughed again, stalling for time. His throat was killing him. It was probably turning into strep again.

"She, your wife, came in last week with the check. She brought her attorney with her."

"And you cashed it? Just like that?"

Kevin backed away a step or two. "Not exactly just like that. I suggested she deposit the money and we put a hold on your account until the money cleared, but her attorney made me call the carrier and verify the funds, which wasn't really necessary since it was a cashier's check, after which I couldn't very well refuse could I?"

"So you cashed it?"

There was no denying it. "Yes. We cashed it."

"Right there?"

"Right here. She took a third of it, then, and gave it to her attorney. He had evidently negotiated the settlement, and those are typical fees, I believe. One-third of the recovered amount."

"But in cash?"

Ray Weir had to sit down. All the fight was out of him.

"I recommended to her, privately, that this aspect was very unusual. I had to report the transaction to the police—anything over ten thousand dollars in cash. Drugs, you know. But she'd made up her mind. She wanted the money that day. It was hers. The funds were there to cover it. She was a customer. What could I do?"

"But it was half mine, that money. It was half *mine.*"

"I'm sorry, but the check was made out to her, not to both of you."

"I mean, we were married. Separated but married. Married when she got into the accident."

What could he say? The man kept talking. "It was amicable, the separation. We agreed to split everything. And we hadn't even filed for divorce yet. Maybe we would've worked it out."

Kevin remembered the way this man's wife had clung to her attorney, had almost gleefully handed over nearly $30,000 in cash to her attorney. Except for the moment during which Kevin had spoken with her privately, she'd never lost physical contact with her attorney. Ray Weir and his wife weren't ever going to have worked anything out. She had a new man, her attorney, and she was clinging on.

Kevin felt a wave of nausea and then the fatigue kicked in again. He sat down two chairs away from where Ray Weir slumped.

The customer looked at him. "So what can I do now?" he asked.

The sun, morning bright, reflected into Kevin's eyes off the shiny mahogany conference table. He closed his eyes against the glare, then forced them open to answer Ray Weir. "I can't help you on that," he said.

Hardy had been out jogging and missed Glitsky's call, which first chided him for moving around so much and being so difficult to get hold of, then telling him about Baker's attempted suicide.

He stood in his office, still sweating, in his shorts and sweatshirt. The weather had warmed up again.

Why had Baker tried to kill himself?

Hardy's first take was that it was an admission of guilt, another nail in his coffin. Like Abe, he kept having these ambivalent feelings about old Louis. Since he'd talked to Baker the other day and gotten to know Ray Weir, now that Hector Medina was killing dogs, Hardy had pretty much convinced himself that, whatever else Louis Baker had done, and no doubt it was plenty, he hadn't killed Maxine Weir.

And it wasn't so much that Baker had denied anything. That would have been easy enough to discount. No. What had been compelling was Baker's seemingly genuine ignorance of Maxine's presence on the barge. Even if you were pretty inured to killing people, the least you'd do is notice.

Of course, the fact that he hadn't killed Maxine didn't absolutely necessarily mean he hadn't killed Rusty, but that stretch, in the real world, was too long for Hardy's reach.

And that left the question of why Baker had been at Rusty's in the first place. It was pretty thin. Hardy tried to picture Rusty taking Baker back to the barge. Gun in hand. Not very likely . . .

But why not? After all, how well had he known

Rusty? Rusty had seemed much like himself. An ex-D.A., a guy from Hardy's own club—someone who'd been through some shit and now just wanted to be left alone. That's why he'd come to see Hardy in the first place, wasn't it? He'd been afraid. Or he'd sure seemed afraid, enough to convince Hardy, who had no reason to be skeptical about it. Matter of fact, he'd infected Hardy with the fear bug. So . . . ?

But had Rusty really been so much like him? Okay, there were the externals, which were similar, but there was also the description he'd gotten from Karen Moore of a pretty twisted, driven guy—the compulsive gambler, the user of women.

So it came down to who he believed—Louis Baker or Rusty. Not easy. Not anymore. He didn't believe that Rusty had had a gun—else why would he have stopped at the gun shop and ordered another one that he couldn't pick up for three days? Except Louis's story about the day's events had some kind of ring to them. In a way it was too far-fetched to have been made up. At least completely. Rusty meeting Baker at the bus station to drive him—

Whoa.

What did he drive him in? Rusty had taken the bus to the Shamrock. His own car had been stolen, remember?

Hardy sat on the corner of his desk. The car was a question. The car was maybe key.

How about if Hardy asked Louis and got told that they'd driven in an old model blue Volkswagen Jetta? Well, that would be interesting.

Somehow his darts had found their way into his hands and he was throwing them into the board. One, two, three. Walk in and pull them, go back to the tape line on the floor and do it again. Not aiming, not working on form. Zen and darts.

What if he only knew the color? Or the make?

Okay, Hardy would ask Baker what kind of car

they'd driven in. Color, anything. He'd see where
that led.

He picked up the phone, got the number to County
Hospital and started to push buttons, then stopped
himself. Last time, he'd needed Glitsky to get to
Baker.

But Abe wasn't in at the Hall. Hadn't been in, no
sign he would be in. Hardy wondered where he'd
called him from and what he might be doing, then
talked to Flo and found that he was not working but
avoiding the shop. They were at least still talking
about Los Angeles and Abe wanted to keep some
distance—more than usual—between himself and the
rest of Homicide. Flo said if she heard from him, she'd
ask him to call.

He couldn't get the car out of his mind. After a
shower and a can of sardines he was back in his office,
going over the notes he'd taken at the computer terminal. It wasn't very fertile ground for either analysis
or imagination.

He picked up a pen and started writing down everything he could remember about last Wednesday, when
Rusty had come into the Shamrock. He'd gotten off
the bus. Hardy had remembered his drink—Wild Turkey. He'd told Hardy about Louis Baker getting out,
that he'd called the warden at San Quentin to find out
the time of release. Then he'd made his proposal that
he and Hardy call each other. Finally bringing it
around to maybe looking into buying a gun, and what
type would be suitable.

Was that it?

Hardy got up, walked around his desk and opened
the window in his office. It was after one o'clock and
a light warm breeze freshened the room. He stuck his
head out to smell the roses, only there weren't any
roses around.

Sitting again, he studied what he'd written. Okay, then, impressions. Rusty down and out. Using public transport. Saying he'd called the warden and was told that Louis Baker had cleaned up his act and not buying that. Saying that guns were for "cop types" like Hardy. Then saying he wanted to buy a gun.

Had the idea just occurred to him? The switch in attitude from guns being for cop types to wanting one for himself?

It slowed Hardy down. Rusty had taken a bus out from downtown. Hardy could imagine him devising his phone-call protection idea, finding where Hardy worked from any number of old mutual acquaintances. But none of that was acting scared—it was more like caution. Rusty hadn't really been frightened. He had been planning to go home. Hell, he *had* gone home.

But calling San Quentin to find out exactly when Baker was getting released? That, to Hardy, *was* more than caution. That appeared to be fear. Didn't it?

He stared out the window, back down to his notes. There were two mentions of things he'd found out from the warden at San Quentin—the circumstances surrounding Louis's release and the fact that Louis had been a model prisoner. If Rusty had called out of fear, to find out exactly when he had to start worrying harder, would he have gotten into a discussion at the same time about what kind of guy Louis had become? If you're tied to the tracks and a train is on the way, do you think about whether it's a passenger or a freight?

He must have, or probably might have, called San Quentin two times. So what?

Hardy looked at his silent phone. He wasn't doing anything else.

He spoke to four functionaries, perhaps prisoners, before he got to the warden, Jack Hazenkamp. Hardy had met Hazenkamp a couple of times in his prosecutor days, seen him speak on prison conditions, recidivism rates, the usual. He was a guy who seemed to have spent a lot of time in the military, but during his talks Hardy had found him surprisingly—well, not exactly a liberal, but fairly sympathetic. The cons were his charges, he didn't mollycoddle them, but they were by and large people, not statistics.

Hardy had gotten through to him by telling the various intermediaries that he was an attorney (true enough), and it was about Louis Baker. He sat at his desk, his yellow notepad pulled in front of him.

The warden came on brusquely, hurried. "Hazenkamp."

"Warden, I'd like to ask you a question or two about Louis Baker—"

"Already? What's he done?"

Hardy was planning on explaining it all briefly, up to the suicide attempt, but the warden stopped him as soon as he heard Rusty Ingraham's name.

"Ingraham is dead?"

Hardy went over it a little.

"My God," the warden said. "Talk about a mistake."

"How's that?"

"Ingraham called a couple of times in the past month or so."

"A couple of times?" Hardy repeated.

"Yes, twice I think. He seemed very frightened. It now appears he was justified. I told him he didn't need to worry. Baker wasn't a threat." Hazenkamp swore softly. "I have to tell you that this surprises me, and I don't entertain many illusions in these matters."

"What's that?"

"Well, you know, most of them come back or get killed trying."

Hardy waited.

"But Louis Baker—well, you put your hopes on a few of them, I guess. Have to or go crazy."

"And Baker was one of those?"

"Well, you either believe in rehabilitation or you don't."

"And you do?"

"Not too much. But you get an occasional good feeling. We don't let guys out on minimum time unless we have some confidence they're gonna try to be straight."

"So you knew Baker personally?"

"I know most of them personally. It's not like you don't have time to meet them. I sort of make it a point."

"And Baker . . . ?"

Hardy could hear the man breathing on the other end of the line.

"Baker was tough. Very tough. Had most of the wrong tapes playing in his brain when he got here. But as I said, you like to think you get a feeling for these things when you've been in it as long as I have, and he was one case where I really believed the man had changed. He wasn't a psycho. In his case, and I don't say this too often, I think he grew up tough and mean because he had to survive."

"I knew him back then, Warden. He was a very serious felon." Hardy knew a lot of the things Louis Baker had done. He didn't exactly buy the environmental theory.

"Oh, I'm not denying that. He'll never be, let's say, a Republican. But"—his voice went up in pitch, hope resurfacing—"he wasn't a drug user, his brain wasn't fried out, he got along with other guys, was on the basketball squad, gave boxing lessons—maybe a loner, but the kind who could affect other people. Not a killer. At least I didn't think so . . ."

"Maybe not."

"But I thought you said . . ."

Hardy went on with the story—Maxine Weir, the man in Holly Park, the shootout with the cops, the attempted suicide . . . "So my question," he finished, "is does it make any sense to you? Didn't the parole board give him tests, interviews, that kind of thing?"

"Of course. And recommended on informed opinion—"

"That he get out?"

"That's why he did."

"How often are you wrong?"

As soon as he asked, Hardy regretted it. All the slack—weary or otherwise—left the voice, and he was talking to a drill sergeant again, and a defensive one at that. "Recidivism is, I'm sure you realize, a major problem. But if you're going to let these people out, if you're going to believe anybody can be rehabilitated, then you do it when the evidence—"

"I understand all that. It just seemed, in Baker's case, you might have felt something more. Personally."

There was a longish pause. Hardy looked out his window. Maybe, he thought, Hazenkamp was doing the same thing up in Marin.

"You know, Mr. Hardy, I knew a hell of a lot of guys like Baker in the corps. They come in tough, mean and young and all they want in life is to kick ass, be on top, never show they've got a weakness in them because where they come from, weakness is what you get stomped on for. Black or white, it doesn't matter. Poor seems to be the big thing. No options. So for a while we—both in prison and in the corps—we authority figures get their attention. Bust them all the way down so we can build them up."

"I was a Marine myself, sir," Hardy said.

Another pause, shorter. "Then you remember. The junkyard dogs. Then something happens. At least once in a while. They get on a team, somebody saves their ass or maybe they save somebody's."

Hardy remembered how he had been after his parents' death, joining the Marines, getting his bad self reamed a few times, then getting to Nam and pulling Moses McGuire, still his closest friend, out from under enemy fire at Chi Leng. Hazenkamp was right—it could change you.

"And that happened to Baker?"

"I think so . . . thought so. You know, Mr. Hardy, there are model prisoners, as they call 'em, and then there are the guys that, you'd swear to God, the attitude just seems to go away. They're not just model prisoners—you forget they're prisoners period. That was Baker. Not that he wasn't still tough—you didn't push him—but he didn't need to be anymore. You get what I'm saying? Anyway, it's the same thing I told Ingraham. Just leave it alone and you won't have any trouble."

"Yeah, but Ingraham didn't leave it alone."

"Well, I still feel that Louis Baker could have taken quite a lot of abuse before he felt his options were gone."

"But if there were that much? Abuse, I mean. Pressure."

"Well, then he'd revert. You get cornered, you go back to what you know."

Hardy could understand that. Being tagged for three murders you didn't commit in the first couple of days after a long term in San Quentin would make anyone feel cornered. So then you decide to break out, go after somebody, someone who represents the people who are doing this to you—in Baker's case, Hardy. And then because you're out of practice, you fuck up, and all the good done in nine years is wiped out, all the hope of ever having a life is over, and you try to kill yourself. It could have gone that way . . .

Hardy glanced at his notepad while he still had Hazenkamp on the line. At the top of the page he'd written the number 2 with an exclamation point and circled it.

"One more thing if you've got a second, sir. The two times Ingraham called, were they about the same thing?"

"Yeah. The first time was more general—if he ought to be worried, how Baker was doing, he'd heard about him getting paroled, like that."

"And the other time?"

"Well, that was the one last week, where he wanted to know the specifics—what time he got released, where he was going. I figured it couldn't hurt. He seemed pretty strung out. I tried to calm him down. Told him again—really I didn't think Baker was going to bother him." He sighed. "But he did."

"Warden, by any chance do you keep a phone log? Do you have the date of Ingraham's first call?"

"Why?"

Over the line Hardy heard paper turning. "Just filling in the blanks."

"Okay, here it is. August twenty-sixth. Does that fill one in?"

Hardy moved things around on his desk. Blowfish, paperweight, legal pad. Slips of paper with other notes from other days. A couple of blue jays squawked on a wire outside his window. He looked at the page he'd been studying earlier and put it next to the one he was now writing on.

Ingraham's car had been reported stolen three days after his first call to San Quentin. "It's a possibility," he said.

He thanked Hazenkamp and hung up. So Rusty hears from a parole-officer friend that Louis Baker is getting out of prison. About the same time, he knows he's getting a third of an $85,000 settlement from Maxine Weir. Three days later, his car is stolen. He doesn't rent a car against the settlement from the insurance.

Baker said Rusty picked him up and drove him to his barge the same day Rusty had so clearly for all to see taken a bus out to the Shamrock.

Hardy wondered how many cars got reported stolen that weren't really stolen—that were ditched, hidden, trashed for any number of reasons, the most obvious of which, but certainly not the only one, being insurance. (The other reasons provided some food—hell, a whole Sunday dinner—for thought.)

The telephone, that mute uncooperative toy that had stared silently at Hardy the whole time he'd been home, now jangled shrilly, demanding attention. Hardy, a slave to it, picked it up.

21

Abe Glitsky chewed on ice as he sat at the window at David's on Geary. A banner on the Curran Theater across the street was advertising season tickets for the American Conservatory Theater. Abe was remembering the early years with Flo, when they'd gone to the ACT all the time, "taking advantage" of the City. Now they raised their kids and occasionally went out to dinner. They'd been to maybe three movies in the past year.

Was it them? Or was the Theater really dead? The thought brought a smile. Had the city changed? Would L.A. be any different?

He lifted a hand. Hardy was standing in the entrance to the dining room, then pulling out the chair across from him.

Glitsky had reached Hardy on his second call. He had been working on his own agenda, not interested in going back to the Hall and giving Batiste the satisfaction. Hardy had wanted to know about Baker—was he still alive? He had found out some stuff about Ingraham. This and that, none of it seemingly related, finally mentioning the gambling, which was what LaGuardia had been trying to tell him yesterday.

And Glitsky, hearing that, decided he and Hardy ought to get together and shake a tree or two. Maybe some of these people knew somebody, something else. Hardy jumped at the suggestion and here they were.

"Abraham, *que tal? Como va?*" Hardy in high spirits.

Abe chewed his ice. "I don't know why we're doing this," he now said. Seeing his friend, in his own bleak mood, the idea for the get-together suddenly seemed amateurish, bullshit.

Hardy reached over and took half of Abe's bagel and cream cheese and took a bite. "You done with this?"

"Yeah. Now."

"The situation sucks," Hardy said between bites. "Baker didn't do it." He held up his hand, stopping any rebuttal. "Hey, don't forget, I wanted it to be him, but I just can't see it."

"You really don't think Baker did it?"

"Neither do you or we wouldn't be sitting here this fine afternoon."

Glitsky got his iced tea filled. Hardy ordered a cup of coffee. "Okay, you first," Abe said.

"He was there, right?"

"Abaloolie." Abe grinned. "One of O.J.'s words."

But Hardy was rolling. "If he went to Rusty's to kill him, he would have brought a gun, right? Right. He couldn't possibly have left it to chance that Rusty would have a gun on board that he would somehow conveniently give to him so he could get shot."

"I've still got a problem with Rusty being shot," Abe said.

"Well, hold that. 'Cause I've got a problem with the fact that old Louis had no clue there was a woman on board. Much less a naked one he blasted three times at point blank."

"Yeah," Abe said, "that doesn't exactly fly."

"So?" Hardy asked.

"So what?"

"So what are we left with?"

"Like who else was there?"

"Good, Abe."

"LaGuardia was there."

"Why was he there?"

"To collect Rusty's vig. But he says the girl, at least, was already dead when he got there. And, Diz, look, there is no way Johnny LaGuardia shoots anybody with a twenty-two."

"Ray Weir's gun."

"Right."

"So was Ray there?"

"Would Ray know about Armor All?" Glitsky explained the connection.

"But was he there? We don't know where he was, do we? We just know he wasn't at home, where he says he was."

"How do we know that?" Abe asked.

Hardy described Warren's night, waiting on the steps with a six-pack. Waiting for his friend Ray to get home so they could have a few and get this Maxine melancholia out of the way.

Abe tipped his glass up, flicking at it with his finger until the last of the ice fell into his mouth.

"Is this what we call the break in the case?" he asked.

Ray Weir's eyes in his bathroom mirror were a new shade of red.

It was probably the combination of the crying and the dope, but how could he face anybody this way? Especially the cops.

Out on the steps. Waiting.

He'd told them he'd be a minute. Visine in the eyes. Listerine. He opened the shade to bright afternoon sun. Already afternoon. Threw the window up. Some of the smoke wafted out.

Another knock.

"Come on, Ray, open up."

Suddenly just sitting on the floor. Half the pictures of Maxine torn from the wall, lying scattered around him. "I can't," he said. "I can't."

"What?" Through the door.

"I just can't."

Some mumbling. Another pound. . . . "now or we'll break it down."

"Leave me alone," he yelled, collapsing onto his face, the bright sun going out, arms over his head. "Please, please, leave me alone."

"What's he doing?" Hardy asked.

Glitsky shrugged.

The landing where Warren had allegedly sat with his beer, where Courtenay had hit on Hardy, was windowless. The downstairs entranceway provided some reflected light, and there was a slit under the door like a ribbon of brightness. Carpeted steps led to the hardwood landing, all of it heavy with mustiness and the smell of marijuana.

"Ray, open the door." Glitsky often surprised Hardy, but never more than with his patience. "We're just here to talk." He put a light hand on Hardy's arm and nodded, reassuring.

In twenty seconds they heard another rustling inside, and then a chain being released.

The door opened, and Ray was walking away from them, across the smoke-filled room, to his couch. Hardy and Glitsky followed, stepping over pictures, fallen leaves, of Maxine.

Ray huddled sideways at one end of the couch, legs hugged to his chest. Glitsky motioned for Hardy to sit in one of the director's chairs and sat himself on the couch two feet from Ray, hands folded in front of him, feet flat on the ground.

One of the lamps was knocked over on the floor. This wasn't vu zjahday, but the other one. The scattered pictures, the broken lamps. Did somebody break lamps for a living around here?

"She took it all."

Ray had finally raised his head. Hardy had seen more life in store-window mannequins. His eyes, Jesus!

"Took what, Ray?" Abe, unfazed, gentle.

Ray put his head back down into his knees. Hardy saw the hands tighten around the legs he held close to him. Trying to get collected. Back up. Over to Hardy. There was no look of surprise—he recognized him but couldn't say from where.

"Took what, Ray?" Glitsky prompted.

"Everything," he said. "She took it all."

"The insurance money?" Hardy asked.

Ray shook his head, all inside himself. "I mean, we were splitting that. That was always understood. That was our deal. We'd still be friends."

Hardy and Glitsky exchanged glances.

Abe leaned back into the couch. "What happened to the money, Ray?"

"She cashed it." His eyes went to the wall of pictures, half torn down. "She split it with Ingraham. They just took it."

"Which brings us—" Hardy began, but Glitsky held up his palm again.

"Where did they take it, Ray?" The repetitious first name, like a mantra keeping them close.

"It must have been to Ingraham's." Ray met Abe's eyes. "You guys didn't find it at her apartment."

"At the barge, you mean?"

Ray nodded.

"So was it there, Ray?"

No answer.

"How 'bout it, Ray? Were you there?"

"No. I didn't, I don't even know where it is."

"Maybe they put it in the bank."

Ray turned to Hardy. "No, I went to the bank. They took it in cash."

Glitsky's eyes told Hardy to shut up. "You didn't go to Ingraham's last week at all? The night Maxine was killed?"

"No, I told you. No. I've never been there."

"But your gun was there. Your gun killed Maxine."

"I told you that, too. I gave it to her before. I told you."

Glitsky leaned over, patted Ray's knee. "I know, Ray. I know what you told me. The problem is, you also told me you were here by yourself that night, and we've run across somebody who says you weren't."

"Your friend Warren," Hardy said.

Recognition dawned and Ray glared at Hardy. "You weren't a cop last time. You were with Court the other night."

Glitsky came back in. "That doesn't matter, Ray. What matters is what you were doing that night. If you weren't here."

"I *was* here."

"Maybe we should all go visit Warren, huh?"

"No, we can't do that!"

"Why not, Ray? Is he lying?"

"I don't know, I can't think." He put his head back down on his knees.

"You have to think, Ray." Glitsky closing in. "Is Warren lying? We'll get everybody in one room under oath if you want."

His eyes were wild now, skitting from Hardy to Glitsky, across the room, as though he were giving some thought to running.

"Come on, Ray. Just tell us. You were here or Warren was here. Which one was it?"

"You can't tell him."

"Tell who what, Ray?"

"Warren." He shook his head. "No. I promised I wouldn't tell. We can't."

Suddenly the light went on for Hardy. "You were both here," he said. "You were in bed with Courtenay. You couldn't answer the door for Warren because then he'd find that out."

Ray nodded. "He might not have finished the movie. He would have thought we'd both betrayed him."

"Which you did," Hardy said.

"No! It wasn't like that! Court came by to see how I was doing. She was worried about me being so bummed out about Maxine. Then we had a glass of wine and got a little stoned, and you know . . ." He looked from Glitsky to Hardy. "You're not going to tell Warren, are you?"

"Let's go, Diz." Glitsky was on his feet, Mr. Nice Guy gone with the warm breeze. He was already halfway to the door. Hardy was up behind him.

"I promised Courtenay," Ray whined. "You won't tell Warren, will you?"

Glitsky turned at the door. "Not unless it comes up," he said.

"If he'd done it, forget all the Warren-Courtenay bullshit, he'd have tossed the barge for the money. And there wasn't any sign of that. I believe Ray doesn't have the money."

"So do I." Glitsky didn't take his eyes off the road. They were heading back downtown on Geary.

"So where do you suppose it is, the money?"

"That question has crossed my mind," Abe said. "The money is a new angle."

"People get killed for money all the time, don't they?"

Glitsky stopped at a light. "So I've heard." They sat. The light changed.

"Green means go," Hardy said.

The car moved forward. Hardy told Abe he thought they ought to go talk to Louis in the hospital. Something about a car, but Glitsky's mind was still on the money.

"Baker doesn't have the money," he said. "He never had any money."

"But he might be able to tell us what kind of car Rusty Ingraham was driving."

Abe didn't reply.

"But he might be able to tell us what kind of car—"

"I heard you," Abe said. He hit another light. "Here's the thing, Diz. I'm following the thread of who was there. Baker, okay. But he's on the shelf, for the time being, anyway. For a while there we thought it might have been Ray, but I believe Ray. Rusty was schtupping Maxine. You believe that?"

Hardy nodded.

"Okay. So now we've got Hector Medina and Johnny LaGuardia."

"Hector was on the barge?"

"He says not. He worked a double. But hey, since it seems to be our day to be thorough, and we're going right by there anyway . . ."

The Sir Francis Drake hadn't changed much in the week since Hardy had last been there. A plaque read "Security" on a door on the third floor at the end of a long hall of doors.

Hector was sitting at his desk, reading a newspaper.

He didn't have any outer office, much less a secretary. Glitsky and Hardy pulled up a couple of wooden chairs.

"I don't know if you'd heard," Abe said. "Treadwell's in the can, or was as of this morning."

Hector's hands were crossed over the newspaper. "Yeah, Clarence called with the good news." He looked at Hardy. "I thought you weren't on the force."

"Just spending the day with my buddy Abe."

"The funny thing is," Abe said, ignoring the exchange, "in the course of clearing Clarence and Mario you'll never guess what came up."

Hector looked at his hands.

"He's not guessing," Hardy said.

"You're not here for that? The dog thing." He turned his hands up. "C'mon, you guys. I put a little fear of God in him. And it worked, right? What's the deal?"

"I guess the deal," Abe said, "is that my friend Hardy here and I were talking about Rusty Ingraham and it came up how you treat people you don't like. You didn't like Rusty much, am I right?"

"What are you saying?"

"I'm saying it doesn't seem to go with your personality, with how you do things, that you would call up Rusty and just get cold feet and hang up. It seems more like, if you had a message for him, you'd go see him."

Medina pushed back a ways from his desk. "I never really had a message for him. Not like I did with Treadwell. I realized that when I called him."

"You still say you never saw him?"

"Not in a lot of years. Not to say if I would've I wouldn't have kicked his ass." He got further out from his desk and put his feet up, crossed. It was a good casual posture, maybe even rehearsed. His hands were crossed on his stomach. "If this is about Rusty getting it, I told you I worked a double that night. You can look at the log."

"No, thanks, I'm sure it says that in the log."

"So give me a break. What do you want?"

"You know Johnny LaGuardia, Hector?"

"Sure. Everybody knows Johnny. What's he got to do with this?"

Hardy leaned forward. Abe stood up, cracked his back and asked Hector if he could have a cup of coffee from the pot going by the window. Pouring, he turned to Hardy. "How's this sound, Diz? Hector calls

Rusty to set up some meeting so he can kick his ass. Rusty's on a roll, having just collected some big money on insurance. He rubs that in Hector's face."

"What are you *talking* about? What big money?" Hector's feet were on the floor now.

Abe kept it up. "So Hector calls his good friend Johnny LaGuardia—"

"I didn't say he was my good friend, I just know the guy—"

"—and tells him there's a wad of cash in it for him if he goes over and does Rusty. How's that sound?"

"I like it," Hardy said. "My girlfriend can dance to it. I give it a nine."

Glitsky turned to Medina. "How 'bout you, Hector? That about how it went down?"

Medina had pulled back up to his desk, his hands again crossed over the newspaper. "You got a warrant, Sergeant?"

Abe looked at Hardy. "You got a warrant? I don't have a warrant."

"Tell you what," Medina said. "You come back when you got a warrant. I'll show you the log that says I worked here the whole night. I haven't seen or talked to Johnny LaGuardia in like six months and I didn't send him nowhere." He nodded. "Go find yourselves another patsy. Nice talking to you both."

"I don't think he was sincere," Hardy said.

"About what?"

"About how it was nice talking to us."

Glitsky slammed his car door and put the key in the ignition. "Some guys don't have a sense of humor."

"So where to?"

The late-afternoon traffic was not moving well. They waited, windows rolled down, for a break when the light changed up at the corner behind them.

"You know Johnny LaGuardia?" Abe asked.

"Nope."

"Well, he works for Angelo Tortoni . . ."

"I don't know Angelo either."

Abe pulled out, tires squealing. "LaGuardia might be the man, even if he wouldn't have shot anybody with a twenty-two under normal conditions. Could be Ray Weir's gun was there, he figured what the hell, it would throw somebody like me off the track."

"Somebody like you?"

"You know, a trained investigator with years of experience."

"Oh, that you."

Glitsky drove.

"So where are we going? LaGuardia have an office he works out of?"

"No, but Tortoni does. Though he's probably gone home by now. I think I'll see him tomorrow. No point in going by his home, not without a warrant."

"Everybody wants a warrant."

"We live in a picky world."

They were crossing Market now, going south. Hardy caught a whiff of Chinese food, a glimpse of some rappers putting it out to passersby. The sun was low but still hot, casting long shadows.

"You realize," Abe said, "we're back to the vig."

Hardy squinted at the sun, came back to Glitsky. "Seems like. You think Rusty got caught in the squeeze?"

A nod. "How's this? Rusty had been light on his vig for a while, and maybe Johnny covered for him a few weeks, floated him on his own, knowing this big insurance payment was coming, maybe setting up his own client base. But Johnny gets there and something goes wrong—Maxine doesn't go along, Rusty's already blown it at the track, whatever."

"Or," Hardy said, "Johnny sees the money and an easy way to walk with all of it."

Abe's scar tightened across his mouth. "Okay, and

this is better. Johnny goes, collects his regular vig, and Rusty's bragging about how he's able to pay, he's fat city now. From what you heard about him, that's the way he was, right?"

"Yeah. When he was flying he flaunted it."

"And he was flying. So he tells Johnny all about it. Pays him with cash, of course, and maybe Johnny sees the roll, or figures there's more on board. He goes outside, waits around, figuring he'll toss the place next time Rusty goes out. But instead, Maxine shows up. He gives them a half hour, sees the bedroom lights go on and off and on, maybe looks in and sees them counting money, breaks in the door, blam, blam, grabs the stash, adios."

"And the brace?" Hardy hadn't bought the explanation from the night at Weir's.

"Maybe they were celebrating. Maybe she puts it on one last time while they count the money it brought them." He looked at Hardy. "I said maybe."

"Lots of times," Hardy said.

"Granted."

"And Hector?"

Glitsky shook his head. "That was fishing. Hector's right. Johnny gets around. Everybody does know him."

"And Louis?"

They were pulling into the parking lot at County General. "Louis probably doesn't know what he knows, but another big maybe seems to be he did it." Abe pulled the parking brake, turned toward Hardy. "He was there, he had a motive, and there was a weapon. The trained detective tries to remember these things. Motive, means, opportunity. Detecting One-A."

In the parking lot there was a strong smell of hot tar.

"So what's all this other bullshit we've been doing all day?"

Abe stopped. "This isn't bullshit. This is covering the bases, which is what we do. We nail it down. We find out where everybody was and what they were doing. We eliminate reasonable doubt—"

"So you still think Baker did it?"

"I think he's a real suspect. Would you let him go right now?"

"No."

"Well, there you go."

"But that's because he was coming after me. It doesn't mean he killed Rusty."

"Guess what?"

"What?"

"You want to get technical, Rusty being dead is still an open question."

Louis Baker wondered for a minute if he were dead. If he was, then this certainly be Hell.

Half-open eyes seeing the Man and Hardy standing by the end of the bed, arms crossed, studying. A phlegmy cough rumbled up from somewhere inside him, half smothered, and seemed like to rip his lung— the one already got a bullet through it—seem to rip that lung further apart. His throat burned inside, and the slight movement of the cough made him feel the abrasion on his neck. He went to reach his hand up and found this time that he was strapped to the bed, hands to his sides.

The Man say, "Louis, you hear me?"

He tried to open his eyes further. There was a crust over them that made it seem too much effort.

"I think he's out."

"Louis," the Man repeat. Same quiet voice. What they gonna do to him now ain't been done? He tried his eyes again.

They seemed to have moved closer, Hardy hanging back maybe a step, the Man—mean scar through his mean lips top to bottom, hovering over, the devil himself.

"You want some water?"

The Man held a glass to his lips and tipped it up. "Slow now."

Shit burned. Everything burned down there. Then another hit, getting a little better. He held the water in his mouth, letting it drip back down his throat. Swallowing was where the pain came in.

"Can you talk?"

Some kind of laugh started but it hurt before it got too far. He tried to shake his head.

"But you hear me?"

He opened and closed his eyes. Man want to talk all the time, and Louis don't got nothin' to say. Just want to get out, get back to home turf.

Another sound, he look out again. Woman in white saying he's under heavy sedation now, perhaps they'd like to come back tomorrow.

Maybe she been here all along, other side the bed. He felt something cold on his forehead, good. White woman in white. She got good hands, some kind of towel.

The Man stepping back. "What are his chances?"

"Barring complications, he ought to be okay in a few weeks. Able to talk—much better than now—in a couple of days."

"I guess it'll keep."

Another voice, then, Hardy. "Can he talk at all?" Seeing him over the woman's shoulder, hovering. "I just need a word or two."

Now close up, like before. "Louis," he saying, "you don't like me and I don't much like you either, but I don't think you killed Rusty Ingraham, you hear me?"

Yeah, he hear that. Where that shit come from now? Why he in here they think that? How long they been thinking it?

He opened his eyes as far as he could and looked

at the man. Least he don't look like the devil, like the other one do.

"Wha . . . ," he started to say. Croaking.

"He wants water." The nurse, watching out for him.

But no, man, what he saying is asking "What?" But he takes the water.

Hardy back at him. "You told me about Rusty driving you to his place, you remember that?"

The eyes half close, call it a nod.

"The car you guys drove in—you remember what color it was?"

It come down to this shit? What kind of games these honkies playing?

He opened his eyes again. Everything foggy. His lung hurting, his throat sore. Hardy, though, focused, right in his face.

Louis took in a labored breath. What the hell? Nothing to lose. "Blue," he said.

And it brought on a cough again.

The Man saying, "Come on, let's go."

Then they gone.

It might have been a lucky guess . . .

You could throw darts and reach this Zenlike stage of pure contemplation, or you could sit with a bunch of regulars at the bar of the Shamrock and drink four Irish whiskeys. Poured by Lynne and then Moses, call it the equivalent of six.

When Hardy had come in at six-thirty things hadn't yet picked up. Lynne Leish was still tending, working overtime because of Hardy's vacation, and he'd taken what he hoped was some good-natured abuse about his lifestyle, time off, pursuit of his other interests.

Then Moses McGuire coming on seven to two, taking ten with Hardy in a different vein.

The two guys, best friends, co-owners of the bar, shared a postage-stamp table back over by the dartboards. Hardy was working on his first Irish, Moses as always went with his single malt, The MaCallan.

"So do I have to ask?"

Hardy again remembered pulling Moses, his legs shot up, out from enemy fire, picking up some lead in his own shoulder in the process. Moses hiring him when he'd changed careers after the death of his son.

"I'm not playing any games with her, if that's what you mean."

"If I thought that, your face would already be broken."

Moses had no fear of a fist in the face. You run an Irish bar, even if you're a Ph.D. in philosophy, as Moses was, it comes with the territory. His own nose, he said, liked to get rearranged once a year whether it needed it or not.

"I don't know. Something's happening. I don't think she knows exactly either. She call you?"

"No. I called her. Goes four or five days I don't hear from her and I start to worry."

The Mose had raised his sister from the time she was ten. Hardy knew Moses only cared deeply about ten things in the universe, and eight of them were Frannie.

"So what'd she say?"

"That you were hiding out there a while." Moses leaned forward, elbows on the tiny table. "But I don't know, something about the tone."

Hardy finished his drink, deciding the night wouldn't be one of pure reason, and signaled Lynne to bring over another round. He put his index finger in the new drink, stirring.

"Anyway," Moses said, "it came out."

"What do you want me to say?"

"I don't know, Diz. She's my baby. I still have a hard time thinking of her as all grown up, which I also know she is." The lines deepened around his already sunken eyes. With his black beard shot now with gray,

Moses was Hardy's vision of God before he got real old. He shrugged. "It just worries me. I don't want to get her hurt any more."

"I'm not gonna hurt her, Mose. Whatever comes down, that's not happening."

"I mean, I think she probably wants what she had with Eddie—plans and family stuff. A man comes home every night."

"Maybe she wants that. I don't think she's very sure what she wants."

"She wants the baby. I think she wants a father for the baby."

"Eddie was the father, Mose. Nothing is changing that."

"You know what I mean."

Hardy knew. He sipped some whiskey. "She'll likely let me know when she figures it out."

"And then what?"

"Then I figure it out. And then it moves ahead, or it doesn't, right? Nothing got planned here, Mose. It just happened. It's real good, but Frannie doesn't know where she wants to take it, and I'm not sure either. I don't know where Jane fits in. I'm a mess. What can I tell you?"

Moses tipped his glass up. It was getting on to seven and he knew Lynne wanted to go home. "You can tell me when you're coming back to work," he said. Then, standing, starting for the bar, "I liked you better when you weren't dating . . ."

Now, three hours later, well into a pretty serious right-brain workout, Hardy tapped the bar gently with another empty glass. He sat at the front now, near the window, and Moses would come down and sit on his stool behind the bar whenever there was a lull.

"It probably was just a lucky guess."

"Yeah, I guess there aren't that many colors to choose from."

Moses hit him again, lots of ice, half a shot. Nurse 'em.

"Hardy," he said, leaning over, talking quietly, "you and I know for a fact that there's only three colors anybody ever mentions. Watch this."

Moses walked the length of the bar, maybe a dozen customers on stools, drinking, talking, making the moves. He put a fresh napkin and a pencil in front of each one. "Kind patrons," he said, loud, the gregarious bartender, "listen up a second. Free-drink contest." As always, it got their attention. "Quick, don't think, write down the first color comes to your mind. Quick!" He was already picking up the first napkins.

"Who wins the drink?"

"Hold on, hold on."

He was back down by Hardy. "Okay, you be the impartial judge."

"McGuire, what's the contest? Who gets the drink? Anything we want?"

"Seven blues, four greens, two reds," Hardy said.

Moses held his hands up. "Sorry," he announced, "nobody wins, but thanks for playing."

"That's not a fair contest," one of the women complained. "What were we going for?"

"Anything but blue, red, or green would have gotten the drink," Moses said.

As the mumbling died down, a couple of people saying they were going to pick yellow, Moses told Hardy you occasionally did get a yellow.

"Well, that was sure a good time," Hardy said, "but the point?"

"The point is your man Baker had a good chance of saying blue even if he'd never seen your friend's car."

"But it was blue."

"And if it was . . . ?"

"Then Rusty was lying to me about it being stolen."

Someone called for a drink and Moses went down to pour.

Why would someone you hadn't seen in years appear out of the—pardon the word—blue and tell you a lie? Hardy was getting muscle fatigue of the right brain. He pushed his glass to the back edge of the bar.

Wait a minute, he told himself. What if he somehow got his car that afternoon? He got on the bus across the street from here, then went downtown, stopping to order a handgun he'd have to wait three days for.

The computer said the car was still missing. But then the computer lagged several days behind. If it still had Louis Baker in San Quentin, it wouldn't have the car returned either. Maybe he'd check again tomorrow.

Moses was on the stool in front of him again. Hardy raised his eyes. "I've got an idea," he said.

"Treat it carefully. It's in a strange place."

Hardy pulled his glass up, cradling it between his hands. "Rusty's got a monster vig payment, right?"

Moses nodded.

"Okay, he comes into a lot of this insurance money, he knows Louis Baker is getting out of jail and has threatened to kill him. Maybe he even starts fantasizing maybe it wouldn't be so bad if Louis did kill him— that would at least get him out from under the vig—"

"So he sets himself up to get killed? Get serious."

Hardy shook his head. "He sets himself up to *look* like he's been killed. The whole thing's a scam. He just wants to look dead, get the loan sharks off him."

"Why doesn't he move, disappear?"

"Because you don't move away from mob money. They find you, I don't care where. It's an honor thing. But if you're dead . . ."

"If you're dead they don't look . . ."

"Right. Give me some coffee, would you? And get rid of this."

Hardy watched Moses move, filling a few other drink orders at the bar as he passed, pouring his coffee. Hardy got his darts out from his jacket pocket and opened the leather case on the bar. He rubbed his fingers over the worn velvet inside.

One other thing the Shamrock did right was make great coffee. Ninety percent of it was served in what they called Irish coffee, which made Hardy puke. Three good liquids combined to make one bad drink. But when you wanted a cup of coffee, the straight stuff couldn't be beat.

"I don't know, Diz, there's lots of holes. Why'd he come see you?"

"Because I tie Baker to him. If I'm not in it, who finds out about Baker?"

"Weren't his prints at Rusty's place? That ties him to it."

"I don't know, Mose. It's not as good as me, an ex-D.A., making sure everybody knows Baker had a motive, was fresh out of jail, you name it. Plus, because I'm running now too, I try like hell to get Baker put away, and did it, too, didn't I?"

"He *was* coming after you."

"I'm not saying he wasn't. Look, if Rusty's going to get out from under his vig, he's got to be dead, not MIA. I'm his corroboration. Without the threat, he'd just be a missing person, wouldn't he? Now, with me helping him, he's presumed dead."

"His blood was on the bed, Diz. And why did he buy a gun he was never going to use?"

Hardy leaned over the bar, his elbows almost in the trough. "Rusty was the great American lawyer. Never lost a case. You can bet he's a very thorough guy who wanted his scam to work. And you know what genius is, Mose? It's endless attention to detail."

Moses went to pour a drink.

Hardy fingered his darts, sipped his coffee. Tried to picture Rusty Ingraham at the bottom of the ocean.

Couldn't do it. Not anymore.

22

Lace removed a board from the side of the stoop at the place Samson mostly stayed. The sun wasn't quite up yet, but he hadn't been getting any sleep to speak of anyway, and he wanted some darkness.

Jumpup, he'd gone 'til things chilled out over to his cousins at Hunters Point, but Lace lived here and he wasn't leaving. This be his home turf and, he starting to think, woe betide the man who fucks with it.

Fighting his fear of rats and whatever else might live in there, Lace reached his hand far into the dark hole under the steps. He patted the ground inside, his teeth chattering. He hoping nobody hears it inside.

Nothing.

He sat, arms now tucked into his pits, huddled in the jacket, letting the fear subside.

It wasn't possible. He couldn't be wrong.

The shaking still there, he forced his hand again into the cold and silent space. Retraced what he'd just done, making himself feel the stones, the chunks of rotting wood, a piece of moldy cloth that felt like a dead animal. Reaching back, up, to the front, seeing the yellow rat eyes about to snap at him, take a finger, give him the rabies. He closed his eyes, feeling.

Way in, up in the front, wrapped in the freezing oily animal cloth, he felt the package. The gun felt heavy in his hands.

The strip of light in the east hadn't widened by a hair and he was walking now, the board back over the hole, in place, his pocket heavy, shoelaces trailing around his feet.

Over to the Mama's, around to the front door by the street, away from the view of the cuts. No one around. Nothing moving.

After some knocks he heard somebody moving inside. Then, enormous in a white housecoat, Mama opened the door a crack. Seeing it was Lace, she let him in.

"What time it, child? You all right?"

Lace closed the door behind him and waited for Mama to sit on the couch next to the dim light before he came over and sat at the other end. He noticed that the window over the couch had been covered over again with cardboard. She pulled a knitted cover up over her body, tucking her feet under her giant thighs.

"Now," she said, "what you doing?"

Lace took the gun, still wrapped in an old shirt sleeve, out of his pocket. He started pulling it out from the cloth. "We gotta tell somebody," he said.

The Mama wasn't taking her eyes from the gun.

"This the piece killed Dido, Mama," Lace said. "Ain't no Louis Baker kill him. This Samson's piece."

The Mama nodded. "Who we fixin' to tell about it? You want to put it down?"

Lace had it unwrapped. "It's loaded still," he said. He turned the barrel toward himself.

"Don't!"

He froze. "What?"

"Just put it down! Put it down! Thing go off by itself then what? Put that thing down! On the floor!"

He leaned over and laid it down.

The Mama let out a breath, another one. "They's dangerous, guns. Where you get that one?"

"It's Samson's. It was Samson's."

"You said that."

"And that mean Louis, he didn't kill Dido."

"Child, I knew that. Louis never hurt nobody anymore. He just want to set up house. 'Til they don't
leave him alone."

"But he run."

"You run, too, child, they come after you."

Lace put his back up against the cushions. His red-
rimmed eyes suddenly burned—up all night waiting
for his chance, light enough to see where he's going,
dark enough to get away.

He was safe here with Mama now, and Samson
didn't have the gun. He had it. Seemed that ought to
change the way things felt.

"You know, Mama, runnin'. Don't that make them
think you did it, too?"

Bundled in her blanket, her big head bobbed.
"That's right."

"So Louis ran and he saying he did it?"

"But he don't run and they take him down for it."

"But now he run and they got him anyway."

"That often the way, child." She made a clucking
noise, shifting her bulk, impatient. "This ain't be the
news. You go bad with the law, he keep you bad.
Don't matter what you do, you the first body they
come at."

"But they got Louis for Dido, and he don't kill
Dido. This gun prove that."

"All right," the Mama said. "What?"

"So we let it on to the Man."

She labored to pull herself up. "Here's what happen
then. You listen up now. The Man come here and you
talk about Louis and that gun there. Then he say,
'Interesting, and how come it be you now holding this
piece?' And next you know you down there next to
Louis. You like that?"

"It won't be . . ."

She leaned forward and rested a meaty hand on his
thin leg. "There ain't nobody with Louis more than
me. He don't kill Dido and maybe it come out, but it

don't come out with you going to the Man. He just
resent you interferin'. You got a problem, you best
take care of it yourself."

"And Louis . . . ?"

"Louis take care of hisself, too."

"Seem like I ought to talk to someone. Get some
help. Help Louis out."

She gently tightened her grip on his thigh. "I know
it seem like that," she said, "but that ain't be how
it works."

It wasn't that Abe didn't believe that coincidences occurred. You could be humming a song and have it
turn up on the radio. Somebody's on the phone when
you were just about to call them. That kind of thing.

But when you mentioned, say, a Johnny LaGuardia
to a potential suspect in a murder investigation like,
say, Hector Medina, one day, and the next day you
find yourself at a Dumpster behind the Wax Museum
in Fisherman's Wharf, looking at the holes in Johnny's
head, it made you wonder.

Two holes. One in the back and one at the temple.
Either one would've done the job fine by itself.

Abe wondered if Medina's logbook showed that
he'd worked a double shift all last night. He wondered
if he had some extra money lying around, if he were
at work today.

Maneuvering through the techs, Abe cleared the
morning shade in the alley and stood on the sidewalk
in the bright sun. Knowing that Glitsky had inter-
viewed Johnny recently, Batiste had called Abe at
home as soon as the call with the tentative I.D. came
in. Abe had called Hardy out of courtesy. Hardy had
been groggy, perhaps hungover, but he said he'd be
there.

Now he was walking up wearing corduroys, hiking
boots, a "Members Only" jacket over a turtleneck.

Abe cocked his head back toward the alley and started walking. Hardy fell in beside him. They lifted the yellow tape.

"Johnny LaGuardia?" Hardy said.

"The late great."

They both studied the body, still uncovered, now laid out on a stretcher. One tassled brown loafer was still on. His sport coat hung open revealing a salmon-colored shirt half-tucked into some stylish pleated Italian trousers. His shoulder holster was empty.

"The gun was on him when we got here," Abe said, "in case you were wondering."

"So he knew whoever it was."

Abe nodded. "Safe bet."

Johnny's face, surprisingly to Hardy, showed no sign of exit wounds. "Small caliber, huh?"

"Must have been," Abe said. "Looks like twenty-two or twenty-five."

"Again," Hardy said.

"I noticed. And it didn't go down here either," Abe said. "He was dumped." He motioned to the Dumpster. "Symbolism, yet."

Hardy looked another minute. "You had coffee yet?"

A black Chrysler LeBaron pulled into the mouth of the alley. A chauffeur stepped out and walked around the front of the car. Abe waited, watching.

"Who's that?" Hardy asked.

The Angel sat in the backseat, holding hands with Doreen Biaggi. She had been staying in his upstairs room since Sunday, taking meals with the family. Now she wore sunglasses to cover her black eye. The swelling on her cheek was still visible. Tortoni squeezed her hand. *"Va bene?"*

She nodded. Matteo had come to the door and opened it. He took Doreen's hand and helped her out

f the seat. Tortoni got out his own side and glanced
own at the area surrounded by the police tape. He
ook a thin cigar from his inside pocket and rubbed it
etween his fingers, breathing in the energizing odors
f garbage and crab smell. He lit the cigar, flushed in
he pleasure this perfect morning was giving him. But
e kept his face expressionless. He was supposed to
e in pain here.

He motioned with his head to Matteo, who took
Doreen's elbow and began guiding her forward. The
hree came together at the front of the car.

Here were two men, police, the black one leading
s though he were in charge. Tortoni had seen him
efore. Most blacks looked the same to him, but this
ne—with the scar running through his lips, the
atchet nose, the blue eyes—was distinctive. But he
ouldn't remember the name. The other one he
idn't know.

The black one kept his hands in his pockets. "An-
elo," he said, low key, "how you doing?"

Tortoni saw Matteo tighten his mouth. His son liked
or people to call his father Mr. Tortoni, or Don An-
elo. But Tortoni only lifted his palm—as he might
estrain a well-trained dog—and Matteo settled back.

"I am not so well." Tortoni barely heard himself.
Ie raised the cigar to his lips and inhaled. "Not so
ell if what I hear may be true."

"If you mean Johnny . . ."

He made a show of looking around the officer. His
ands went to his sides and he hung his head. "Do
e know who did this?" he whispered. Doreen was
anding next to him, taking his arm, helping him with
is grief. He raised his eyes. "Johnny was a son to
e."

"We don't know anything yet, Angelo. In fact, it
ossed my mind I might want to talk to you some-
me soon."

"He is here now," Doreen said. "Talk to him now."

Good, Angelo thought, protective already. He pat
ted her arm and said in Italian, "Ignore this buffoon.

"What'd you tell her?" the cop said.

He smiled through his pain. "I told her you wer
only doing your job." He patted her arm again. "She'
upset, too. She and Johnny were very close. You hav
no ideas yet?"

"I have ideas. I don't think he killed himself. H
wasn't hit by a truck. Like that." The cop—Glitsky
that was it—clucked. "No, my idea is somebody di
him your way." He put his index finger to his templ
and cocked his thumb.

Tortoni, the soul of patience, shook his head. "I a
a businessman, Officer. But I am not in the busines
of violence."

"Your man Johnny carried a gun."

Tortoni gestured, a forgiving father. "You kne
Johnny? A baby. He imagines he protects me." /
smile. "Where's the harm? . . . Do you mind, can w
see him?"

They moved back into the alley. Tortoni went t
one knee and crossed himself over the body. He re
mained that way for thirty seconds. A good, clean jol
He leaned over and kissed Johnny's clean jaw.

Doreen had her forehead against Matteo's should
when he stood up. It was all right if she didn't hav
the strength to look, but it was important, he though
that she see firsthand what he could do.

But that was enough. With a tiny move of his hea
he directed Matteo to take Doreen back to the ca
Watching them walk off, he took another puff on h
cigar. *Que bello giornio!*

"Do you have any ideas, Angelo?"

The sun had cleared the lower buildings, so that I
had to squint into Glitsky's face. He shrugged, h
palms out. "Johnny was young, maybe hot-tempere
But a good boy."

"You don't know any enemies he had recently? Maybe protecting you?"

"There has been no trouble," he said. "This I don't understand."

"How about personally? Money troubles? Girls?" Tortoni shook his head.

"Do you have any dealings with a Hector Medina?"

"Who is Hector Medina? I have never heard the name."

Glitsky shrugged. "He knew Johnny, that's all. I wondered how well."

"You think he, this Hector Medina, he did this?"

The white cop, who had been silent all this while, spoke up. "I know who didn't do it."

"Who's that?" Glitsky asked, looking at the other man.

"Louis Baker."

Tortoni stared at both of them. He'd have to check out who these two people were—Hector Medina and Louis Baker.

Glitsky took it up again. To Tortoni, he said, "The thing is, I was talking to Johnny just the other day and he said you were having some problems—you and him."

Tortoni saw no point responding to that.

"This problem—it seemed to involve Rusty Ingraham—something about his vig being short. And Medina's also been mixed up with Ingraham. Sort of coincidence, wouldn't you say?"

Tortoni nodded. "I was you, I'd look into that. But Johnny told me Ingraham was dead."

The two cops exchanged glances. The white guy spoke again. "Johnny told you that? He see him? Dead, I mean?"

Tortoni said that when Johnny told him somebody was dead it usually was the truth. "What, you guys didn't see him?"

"Technically he's a missing person," Glitsky said.
"You lose a lot of money on him?"

"Some. In business you take some risks."

"Did you know that last week he came into, like,
thirty thousand dollars?"

Tortoni made a note to have somebody check out
Johnny's apartment, his mother's flat, his friends. The
son of a bitch. But he only said, "Good for him."

The white cop said, "You wouldn't have seen any
of that, would you?"

Tortoni glanced down the alley. His son had put
Doreen back into the car and waited, arms crossed,
leaning against the hood. He took a step in that direction. "I got an accountant takes care of things like
that. You want to know, make an appointment. I claim
every penny I make." He stopped and pointed to the
body on the ground. "I'm talking to you both so nice
'cause I want to help you find the sumbitch did in my
boy here. You need help, time goes by, I got connections might do some good. Everybody cooperate.
This guy Medina, you talking to him?"

Glitsky nodded. "He works at the Drake. I'll be
going over this afternoon."

"You find anything, I'd consider it a personal favor
you let me know." Tortoni wondered if going back
over to the body would be laying it on too thick and
decided it would be. He straightened himself, bearing
up under the loss. Nodding at the two cops, he started
back to his car.

Hardy was reflecting on the difference between Abe's
professional attitude and his own, why Abe was probably on his way to seeing Hector Medina again, and
Hardy was here eating ice cream at the Gelato just
off Stanyan, waiting for Courtenay Moran to show.

Glitsky had another murder, committed by someone
probably in his jurisdiction, and the killer was walking

the streets. So Abe's job was to follow the threads from that and bring that new person in. If it tied into Maxine's death, all to the good. But the fact that it hadn't been Louis Baker didn't seem to make all that much difference to Abe. Somebody, after all, had killed Johnny, and Abe's job was to find that person. Hardy had to remember that Louis was in as much for the killing at Holly Park as he was for Maxine, and Abe just left it like that.

In fact, the more he thought about it, the theory he'd laid on Moses last night was starting to make more and more sense. He, Hardy, was involved in this whole thing only because Rusty had come to him. Period. And why had he done that?

He had done that, and made it as convincing as possible, because he needed someone with impeccable credentials, with no ax of his own to grind—somebody exactly like Dismas Hardy—to preach the gospel of the dead, not the missing, Rusty Ingraham.

Because the mob didn't look for a dead man.

And setting up Louis Baker? No problem. Guy deserved life in prison anyway. Him getting out after nine years was a mockery of the justice system, wasn't it? Serve him right, after all the crimes he'd gotten away with, to get him for something he didn't do.

And use Hardy to do it.

Putting it together: the call to San Quentin making sure Baker was getting out. Three days later, after you work out the plan, you ditch your car and report it stolen. You go through some inconvenience for a month taking buses to establish some credibility. Then you see your friend Hardy and tell him Baker's getting out and is planning to kill both of you. You do your best to scare the shit out of him, then you order a gun—the picture of a man terrified for his life.

You pick up Louis Baker in the bus station, making your only mistake, which is driving your car. Risks proving you a liar, especially if they ever get to ques-

tioning Baker about it. You want him to leave some—
any—physical evidence that he was on your barge. A
thumbprint would be plenty to police, who were already predisposed—because of Hardy's testimony—to
believe the ex-con did it.

Then what?

You shoot Maxine, administer yourself a flesh
wound, leave a bloody trail to the edge of the barge,
drop the gun overboard, dress the wound, get in your
car—which no one thinks you have anymore—and
head out. But where to?

And the world comes to believe you're dead.
You've got a lot of money, in cash. You're washed up
in San Francisco. Your vig is eating you up. All your
old friends have written you off. Go someplace else.
Start over . . .

"A man in deep thought."

Courtenay, in black and hot-pink Spandex, was six
feet of impressive woman. When she had told Hardy
she would run on down to meet him, she had meant
it literally. Her face was flushed with a light sheen of
sweat, set off by a pink band around her forehead.
The close-cropped blond hair was nearly white in
the daylight.

She pulled up a stool across from him at the window. "You've already had some."

Hardy looked down at his empty dish. "I'll have
another one with you. What do you want?"

He went to the counter and ordered—two chocolate
chocolates. When he got back to her, she said, "I was
mad at you."

"You didn't have to come down here."

"Yes, I did. You never told me you were a cop."

Hardy popped a spoonful of ice cream. "I'm not."

She was still breathing heavily from her run. After
a minute she said, "I came down to ask you please
not to tell Warren. Ray said you—"

He held up a hand.

"Let's leave Ray. Ray's not important."

"He's important if Warren ever finds out."

"I thought you had an open relationship, you and Warren."

"Let's put it this way. We don't ask each other. Maybe one or the other assumes, and it's safer to assume your partner is not faithful because it's probably true. But that's not the same as wanting to be confronted with it, especially if it's one of your best friends."

"And especially if you and your regular partner work together."

"Okay, especially then." She put her spoon down. "Look, I'm not making excuses. Ray and I did what we did. Maybe it helped him a little, made him feel better. I'm sorry about the timing of it being the night Maxine got killed, but remember, we didn't know that at the time."

"So you're not really having an affair with him?"

A slow smile spread into a wide grin. "Why? You interested? I thought you were just being a cop, the other night and now."

Hardy shrugged. "I told you, I'm not really a cop at all. I used to be. Now some things have happened around this whole thing with Maxine and Rusty Ingraham—"

"Like what?"

Hardy took a bite of ice cream, knowing it was going to sound melodramatic. But it was the truth. "People are dying, getting killed. I'm not too happy thinking I might be on the list. If I'm right about some things, it could make me a threat . . ."

"How?"

Hardy ran down most of the events of the past week, but tried to stick to facts only.

She put her hand over his on the counter as he finished. "Since we knew them—Rusty and Max—do you think we're in trouble, too?"

"I don't know. The loop seems to head in a different direction. Rusty was evidently into the mob for a lot of money."

"But why you? You're not in with those people, are you?"

"That's the big question. I got into it the day everything started. I'm part of it." She waited, and he decided to open up some. "Well, if Rusty's still alive, for example, and let's just say he killed Maxine and set up Louis to take the fall, then do you think he's going to let me walk around? I'm the only guy can put this together, which means I'm the only guy who's a threat to him. He may or may not realize it yet, but it's sure to occur to him, and I'd prefer not to wait around for that glorious moment to arrive."

"But Rusty's not alive. You said—"

Hardy held up a hand. "From the beginning, Rusty's body has been missing. I went to a lot of trouble to prove how it could have disappeared because I kept assuming he was dead. It was possible, plausible, even reasonable, but mostly it was what I wanted to believe because of some other preconceptions, courtesy of Rusty, so I believed it."

Slowly, she licked ice cream off her spoon. "So why did you want to see me?" she asked.

"Because maybe you know something and don't know you know it."

"About what?"

"Maxine. Rusty. Both of them."

She licked the spoon again. A bit of ice cream remained on her lower lip. Hardy itched to reach over and wipe it off.

"Well, I didn't know Rusty that well. It was a little tense with Ray around so much, you know? I mean, who are you friends with?"

"But Maxine came around with Rusty?"

"Oh yeah, of course. She was in the movie. She wanted to see how it came out."

"And she came with Rusty?"

"A lot at first. Then it kind of got old. I think Max just lost the dream." She smiled, making a joke. "The vision thing, you know?"

"I don't really know."

She pushed out her beautiful lower lip. "You know, before, the dream had always been making it in films . . ."

Hardy smiled. "As opposed to movies?"

"Stop." She pointed a threatening finger. "Anyway, after she and Rusty got together, it was like they both decided what they were doing wasn't working. I mean, Maxine was like thirty-three or something like that, which is really pretty old for making it as an actress, I mean the kind of actress she was—the looks thing, you know. And Rusty, he just said he wanted to stop being a lawyer, go someplace else, live another life, get away from all the stress, as he called it. I think they fed each other that way."

"Did they say what they wanted to do?"

"Oh, you know, take the money and run. Live on the beach, do nothing, get a tan."

Hardy shook his head. "That doesn't sound like Rusty. He was a pretty driven guy, wasn't he? Type A to the max."

"Well, I guess that's why they picked Acapulco." She scraped the last of the ice cream from the bottom of the bowl, giving it her full attention. "I mean, Rusty could be as Type A as he wanted around his gambling, which he said relaxed him but it really didn't seem to, and Maxine could lie around on the beach and drink margaritas."

"Are there casinos in Acapulco?"

"Yeah, I think so, but that's not it, that kind of gambling. They talked about jai alai. It's like horse racing, except with people. Rusty was going to make their living betting on jai alai."

"This was really their plan? They talked about this? Why didn't you mention this before?"

"What was to mention? As far as I knew they were both dead. Which pretty much means they weren't living in Acapulco, doesn't it? And it wasn't really both of them with that plan anyway. At least not at first. Then it was mostly Maxine. Another big dream of hers that didn't come true."

23

Hardy felt like a horse's ass. What was he really doing here in Acapulco at a cliffside restaurant waiting for the sun to set and the boys holding torches to dive off the cliffs into the oncoming surf?

A mariachi band was serenading an American couple at the next table. Hardy poured his Tecate into a glass and squeezed a lime into the beer. He didn't particularly like Tecate, but he liked Corona less, and those were the options.

Sometimes, he'd told himself, you've just got to do something. And he thought he'd been sure.

Certain enough in any case to risk crossing the border with his .38 Special taped under the fender of his Samurai. He didn't want to think about what would have happened if they had stopped him in Tijuana and searched the car. But he'd driven into Mexico perhaps twenty times before in his life and had never been hassled going in. Coming back, of course, they'd inspected his car three or four times. Hardy had come to the conclusion that if people wanted to bring something—anything—into Mexico, the official word was *bienvenidos.* It was a poor country. They'd take anything you wanted to provide.

For the two and a half nonstop days that it had taken him to get here, sleeping only an hour or two at a time in the car, his hunch had grown more and more into a conviction. Rusty Ingraham was alive—and he was in Acapulco.

Rusty Ingraham, he had been sure, had come to him for no other reason than to have him point the finger at Louis Baker and let nature take its course. And that course ought to lead, with the other clever little games such as buying a gun, presumably for protection against Baker, that he never picked up, to the conclusion that Rusty was dead, killed by Louis Baker.

And that, in turn, gets Rusty off the hook for his crushing vig and puts Louis where he belongs back in the slammer. Or the gas chamber. Either way, Louis Baker was a pawn. Dismas Hardy was a tool. Rusty Ingraham would be free to live out poor Maxine's dream.

The sun kissed the Pacific. Flaming red bougainvillea covered the trellis that bounded the patio where he sat. A warm offshore breeze lulled. He sipped his Tecate.

Across the chasm that divided him from the divers, one of them, still torchless, fell forward. Hardy watched the slow arc as the body cleared the outcropping and fell the long long way down. It was the fourth boy he'd seen go off since arriving here, and he found he couldn't work up a casual touristy feeling about it.

He leaned out over the trellis, making sure the wave below would be there for the boy's arrival. This was not, to him, a relaxing way to unwind.

He left his beer with a tip and went out to the road leading back into town. Half a dozen taxis were lined at the entrance to the place, but he put his hands in his pockets and started walking down the hill.

Palm fronds still littered the roadway. Hurricane Carmine had hit two days before. It hadn't done much damage, but cleanup here did not proceed at the same pace as back home. Especially if you couldn't pay for it. The phone in his hotel still wasn't working, for example, but then again, he wasn't staying at the Princess.

*   *   *

He had arrived the day before and slept through the late afternoon and through the night—seventeen hours. This morning he'd walked down from his hotel, the El Sol (eighteen dollars per night—definitely not the Princess), near the base of the mountains, through the awakening town to the Esplanade. He took an outside table at a place facing the beach and had pineapple juice, some poor coffee and a plate of huevos rancheros, taking it slow, letting the sun get hot, the parasailers floating up around the bay like colored balloons.

Sunday morning. Church bells.

On his way out to the jai alai stadium, still walking, getting the feel of the place, he had stopped at a church and stood in the back, listening to the Mass in Spanish. The ritual appealed to him, but he wished they still said the Mass in Latin. There was nothing universal about this Mass, nothing, he thought, catholic. It made him feel like the foreigner he was here. At communion, he snuck back out.

The sun pounded hot on his head. He bought a hat for a dollar and continued walking.

Hardy loved Mexico. He went every year to fish or dive or soak up sun and either dry himself out or tank up—the place was good for either. He and Jane had taken their honeymoon at Cabo San Lucas long before it was anything but a sleepy fishing village with a thatched-roof airport. Long walks on empty beaches. Huge, nearly free margaritas at the Finis Terra, throwing the glasses down over the cliffs to the water below. Night and afternoons and mornings of lovemaking.

Jane.

Driving down, he had had time to think about her, about Frannie. Part of him recognized that he might have decided to come down here, ostensibly seeking

Rusty Ingraham, because Jane was due home from Hong Kong. It would give him a few more days. Not that it was the whole reason, and not that he was proud of it, but it was there.

He and Jane had both been supposing, in a casual kind of way, that eventually they would drift back into marriage. There would be no future talk of trying for another child—that had already come up and Jane's age, career and the tragedy with Michael had sealed her opinion on that far past the reaches of any discussion. She wanted—and Hardy did not blame her—comfort, respect, lack of hassle. A civilized life. He didn't blame her, but he didn't want the same thing.

She had already hinted more than once that Hardy would probably, eventually, go back to practicing law, buy a few suits, become a professional. She would not force him to do any of that, of course, but it—probably—would come to pass naturally. The problem was, when it came to it, as it seemed to have done now, he knew he was going somewhere, moving toward some definite place after his years of lying low behind the bar of the Shamrock. Something was guiding him, and it wasn't some urge toward passivity and comfort, toward three-piece suits and a better wedge of Brie.

Maybe, four, five months ago, looking into the death of Frannie's husband, he'd come to believe, after years of denying the possibility, that one person—he, Dismas Hardy—could make a difference. And that it even mattered.

Else why was he down here?

Back to old Abe's tragic fallacy. Did he think he was down here to restore order to the cosmos? He had to laugh at that. But if Rusty Ingraham was here, he was going to bust his ass in a bad way. And he was going to get the charges dropped against Baker—the ones he'd influenced.

That was his mission. It was something Frannie might yell at him about. She might even hate him from time to time for being made up like that. But at least Frannie would know where he was coming from. He was, she said, like Eddie that way.

To Jane, the concept would be Greek.

Come on, Diz, was that fair?

Jane would understand it on a theoretical level. She would admit that the world might be better if everybody always did the right thing. Of course. But there were issues everywhere you looked, and you had to decide which ones were yours. And that decision had to be based on some kind of a cost-benefit analysis. Adults understood that. You didn't just go off and crusade your whole life. If you did, you were a professional do-gooder, and everybody knew they didn't get much done, did they?

But he wasn't crusading his whole life. He just wanted to get this one thing straightened out. It had been pushed in his face—it was his issue.

And he could hear Jane's answer to that. Why take the risk? If you did nothing, what would it matter? So what, Louis Baker is in jail—he deserves to be. Didn't he break into my house? Wasn't he trying to kill you? And if Rusty Ingraham is gone, let him go. Who cares? He's gone, it's over.

But Jane, he killed Maxine Weir.

I'm sorry. Police business. Not yours. Let it go . . .

He had come up to the stadium, deserted and empty, and looked at his watch. The first game wouldn't be for a couple of hours. He shook his head—bad timing—and backtracked toward town.

He had sat outside under an awning at a place he had passed coming out. The Tecate had been warm, impossible to swallow even with lime. He had read a Los Angeles *Times,* two days old, cover to cover.

He had still felt hopeful. He was here. He would

find Rusty Ingraham. He would go home and explain
things to Jane. He would tell Frannie he was in love
with her, and what did she want to do about it?

But all that had been before he had gone to the stadium. Now, the afternoon behind him, he kicked palm
fronds and tried to remember why he had thought he
would be able to locate one person here.

The jai alai stadium was nowhere near as big as
Candlestick Park, but Hardy guessed it still held
maybe fifteen thousand people. It was certainly a
good-time place. Hardy was surprised no one he knew
had ever tried to put together a jai alai field trip. Beer
and tequila were everywhere. Outside the gate fifty-
gallon oil drums had been cut in half and set up for
grilling, covered with everything from what looked
like braided coat hangers to corrugated iron, piled
high with shrimp, snapper, chorizo, mounds of green
onions, peppers, mystery meats. Slap it in a tortilla
and pour on salsa, who knew or cared? It was a fantastic, reeking bonanza of smells and smoke, and Hardy,
chewing a shrimp burrito, walked through it, mingling,
taking it in.

Inside, the place was packed. The first disappointment, and it was major, was that there weren't any
windows for betting. Hardy cursed himself for not
doing his homework. He had just assumed . . .

Well, there was no help for it now. The way it
worked in jai alai was that each section had two runners, or bookies, or whatever they were called—one
in a red hat and one in a green hat. They moved up
and down the stands almost like peanut vendors in
the States, calling out the constantly changing odds,
throwing some kind of ball to prospective bettors, who
put their money in a slot in the ball and took out the
chit with the current line.

So Hardy's original idea of waiting by a window for

Rusty to show up looked bleak. He took in the stadium. All through the stands the red and green hats bobbed and zagged. Following any one of them would be a job.

Hardy watched a game or two, hoping against hope that being lucky might make up for not being smart, that Rusty would just pop out of the crowd, maybe bump into him.

He found that he liked the game a lot. Real mano a mano stuff. Handball with no rules about interference or much else. Couple of gladiators playing to the death.

Up at Seguridad he had thought of having Rusty paged when he realized it was a stupid idea . . . If Rusty was here and heard his name he would also know someone didn't think he was dead. He would relocate and it would be all over.

Two more hours, five bottles of orange pop, and thirty-five dollars that he bet on the last couple of games went down the drain. The stadium emptied and Hardy stood by one of the dozen or so gates. A lot of people walked by him. Two of them resembled Moses McGuire. None of them looked like Rusty Ingraham.

Okay, he'd watch the famous Acapulco cliff divers . . .

All right, now he'd done that. Now what?

He found himself back at the Esplanade. A tiny strip of coral sky still clung to the horizon, and already there were a million stars. Well-dressed Americans—mostly couples, or maybe that was only Hardy's vision of it—sat with aperitifs at outside tables. The breeze had changed, blowing out across the town toward the water. The night smelled faintly of oil and urine.

Hardy sat on the beach, facing away from the lights. He could hear the lap of water across the sand. Behind him there was always guitar music, male voices singing, softly, far away.

They had jai alai in Las Vegas, Nevada. There was a stadium in Tijuana about a thousand miles closer to

home and still across the border. Puerto Vallarta,
maybe. Oaxaca? Ixtapa? Who knew how many places?

If Rusty was here, and he was starting to think that
was a pretty big if, and if he was going regularly to
bet on jai alai, then Hardy would still need to have
at least one person at every gate if he wanted some
reasonable chance to get to him.

There was no way. He didn't have that kind of
money and he didn't know anybody. Maybe Abe
could get the local police involved, send down a picture of Rusty . . .

Right, Diz. Count on that one.

He lay back into the sand, crossing his hands under
his head, staring up at the man in the moon.

The El Sol wasn't anywhere near the beach. Beyond
the street-front lobby each ground-floor unit on both
wings of the hotel had sliding glass doors that opened
onto a red-tiled terrace that looked out on the pool.
More bougainvillea climbed the filigreed wrought-iron
to the second-floor walkway. Palms and banana trees,
spared by location from most of the wrath of the hurricane, dotted the inner courtyard.

Hardy sat outside on his terrace with a rare cigar
and a bottle of El Presidente brandy. He wasn't really
drinking—he'd poured an inch into the juice glass
from the bathroom about forty minutes before and
half of it was still there. He'd been in Mexico enough
to know that, all clichés notwithstanding, you really
didn't drink the water. And he was sick of orange pop.

Since one of the advertised features of the El Sol—
in neon over the door of the lobby—was a telephone
in every room, Hardy had a telephone. He also had a
television set. The fact that neither worked didn't surprise him very much. He thought it might be fun
someday to settle down here in Mexico and open a
luxury hotel—Ice machines! Pinball! Cable TV! Magic

fingers! And, of course, telephone. None of them would have to work. The fact that you had them made you special.

He had some luck calling San Francisco earlier from the pay phones near the post office. He got Jane's answering machine and told her where he was, that he might get back in a week. The cryptic and enigmatic Hardy.

Isaac Glitsky, Abe's son, said that Abe and Flo had been down in L.A. since Friday. Interviewing for a new job, Hardy figured, and making a weekend of it. Really doing it? When Hardy decided to head south, he didn't mention it to Abe. He hadn't felt like explaining his somewhat far-fetched reasons, trying to justify taping his .38 up under the fender of his Samurai. Abe would have gone nuts. But now Isaac was supposed to ask him where he was and Hardy told him and said he'd call back the next day.

Frannie hadn't been home.

There was some quiet laughter across the way on another shadowed terrace. Someone had slipped into the pool. He heard a telephone ring faintly up in the lobby. He drew on his cigar and sipped the brandy.

The telephone!

He'd taken it outside to the terrace and periodically lifted the receiver to silence. Now suddenly there was a dial tone. He dialed Frannie's number, waited. Waited some more.

"Hello."

"I don't believe it."

"Dismas?"

"*C'est moi.* No, wait, wrong country, *soy yo.*"

"Are you all right? Abe called here. He didn't know—"

"I know, but you did. I'm here. I'm okay."

The pleasantries, getting used to the distance, the separation. The drive down, the hurricane, the phones being out.

". . . which is why it's taken so long to get through. How are you feeling?"

"Okay."

Not too committal there. "Okay?"

The long-distance wires hummed in the silence.

"I'm okay. I went to the doctor's Friday and heard the heartbeat." The baby's. She took a breath. "It's really there and alive." He could hear her eyes brimming. "I missed Eddie, I missed you, I had a bad night. I think I'm pretty confused about things right now."

Hardy sipped some brandy. "Do you want me back up there?"

"I don't think . . . I don't know what I'd do with you right now. But I know I want you to be careful."

"I'm always careful. I'm using block-out, wearing a hat, not drinking the water, the whole shebang."

"Do you know what you want to do when you get back?"

As though she were sitting in front of him, Hardy shook his head. "No. What I'm trying to do now is figure out what lunacy made me decide I could find Rusty Ingraham down here, if he's alive, if he's here."

"Maybe Abe could somehow get the police down there to help you?"

"Who's going to help a civilian with no hard evidence look for a guy who's considered dead? Abe won't."

"I don't know. When he called"—she paused—"he's your friend, Diz. He really sounded worried, wanted to know where you'd gone, why didn't you tell him, all that."

"It's just not the kind of thing he would understand. That's why he gets paid for what he does."

"Well, he also told me to tell you to come home. The case is closed."

Some parrots screeched in the top of one of the

palms. Hardy's stomach tightened. "They found Rusty's body?"

"No, not that. Just a second, he had me write this all down."

His cigar had gone out. The swimmer's wake lapped the pool's edge. Hardy found he was sweating, gripping the receiver white-knuckled.

"Okay," she said, "are you still there?"

She told him that Glitsky said he had questioned a man named Hector Medina as he'd been planning to. The next day, the day Hardy left for Mexico, Hector evidently jumped from the top of the Sir Francis Drake to one of its lower roofs. They found between two and three thousand dollars in cash on him.

"So Abe thinks he killed this man Johnny LaGuardia. And he says it follows that he paid Johnny to kill Rusty Ingraham."

"What about the girl that was with him?"

"Maybe, he says, it was just bad luck she was there. Anyway, that's what Abe seems to think. That Hector Medina realized he was going to get caught for it and couldn't face it."

"Was there a note? Didn't he have a daughter or something?"

"I don't know. I guess no note. Abe would have said, wouldn't he? I mean, in a message for you."

"And Abe said he really thought that's how it went down?"

"Well, he said it tied everything up pretty well."

Lap of water, screech of parrot, the hum of the long-distance connection.

"Diz?"

"He's in L.A. now, interviewing for a job down there. I wonder if maybe he just wanted to feel like his cases were settled."

"Doesn't it make sense to you?"

"I guess. No. Not really."

"Abe told me you'd made a pretty good case that Rusty was dead."

"I know. I did."

"But now you don't believe it?"

"Well, four days and fifteen hundred miles ago I wasn't sure I believed it. Now, I'm here, I might as well give it a day or two more, but I have to say that after today, even if he's alive, finding him doesn't look very promising."

"And what'll you do if you do find him?"

"I don't know. I guess it depends. Have a party, get drunk, tie him up and ride him back to San Francisco. Maybe go to the police here and try to have him extradited—"

"Would you *please* try to remember he might be dangerous?"

"Okay. I already thought of that."

"I mean it, Dismas."

"I mean it, too, Frannie. What more do you want me to say?"

She waited a beat. "I want you to say you're coming home, that we'll see each other again."

"Okay, I'll say that."

Another beat. "You will?"

"God willin' and the creek don't rise," he said.

24

The eyes opened to darkness. Over by the opening for the window, where the light would eventually start, there was nothing. Gradually as he looked, the one darkness became several different shades of black and gray—the shapes of the desk, a poster, the window, one of the chairs. Stars flickered dimly in the black sky.

Rusty Ingraham sat up on the hard bed. The girl next to him was asleep, her long hair splaying over her pillow. He wearily tapped his good right arm on the mattress, as though asking it to quit being so unfriendly. He got up and went into the bathroom, feeling his way through the still unfamiliar house. Closing the door behind him, he turned on the light and watched the cockroaches scatter.

Outside were no living sounds, not even the birds that herald the coming day hours before the sky began to lighten. So it was very early, perhaps even very late the night before. How long had he slept?

Abruptly, he flipped the light off again, standing still and listening carefully now. Always listening carefully, keeping his eyes open. It was already getting old.

He could just make out the sounds of water in the bay—the slush slap against boat and piling, the gentler wash against sand. The house was north of the city, on the beach.

Something—a lizard? a tree rat?—skittered across the roof. Far off, a motor—a car or a fishing boat—

started up, coughed once, then faded. He turned the light back on. The porcelain toilet didn't have a seat. The mirror over the sink had rust spots through the glass. There was no curtain in the shower area.

Well, what did he expect on the notice he'd given? There would be time, and already money, for something better.

His arm was throbbing slightly and he tried to remember if he'd taken his antibiotics before going to bed with . . . whatever her name was.

Well, whoever she was, she had been just what he liked—pretty, enthusiastic, game for a good time. And going home to Atlanta today. And another one would arrive, or had arrived and was waiting for him. These vacation girls were the way to go. No promises, no pretense. None of the hassles a steady woman could bring you.

He touched the bandage gingerly, trying to see if the throbbing was the onset of infection, which could be trouble, or just the pain of rebuilding tissue. He tried to flex his left arm but thought he was still quite a ways from that.

No, it was a good solid dull pain. He mugged at the mirror, his lady-killer grin. His eyes were clear. No fever, therefore no infection.

He went back to the bed and stretched out next to the girl. The window remained a black hole in deeper blackness. A creaking sound, like a twig breaking, made him jump, and the girl stirred beside him. Then silence.

It was just the house settling.

He drifted back off into sleep.

'

It was only a hunch, but Hardy thought it was better than trying to cover twelve exits at one time.

He thought he would give it two more days and then start the long haul back home. This morning, still pretty fatigued from the drive down, he had slept in, but tomorrow he planned to get in one run at deep-sea fishing, maybe get a nice picture of himself and a sailfish to brag about back at the Shamrock.

He got to the stadium well after the games had started. He heard the loudspeaker and the applause from the edges of the parking lot. There'd been no blue Volkswagen Jettas parked in the street he had taken leading up to the stadium. Tomorrow, if nothing worked today, he would hire a lucky cabdriver and put on some miles covering the streets all around the neighborhood. But today he would start with the parking lot.

There was no concrete. It was a dusty, grassless, potholed couple of square blocks surrounding the stadium, into which people had driven and parked in pretty much random order. If you were near the stadium, Hardy figured it would take at least an hour to let the lot clear enough to make your way out. There wasn't anything resembling a lane where traffic should go, no white lines for parking areas. If your car fit, jam it in there.

Twenty-five minutes of walking in the bright hot sun got pretty depressing. The Volkswagen was a popular car in Mexico. The old Beetle was as common as it had been in the United States in the sixties. But there were also Rabbits and, unfortunately, Jettas. And two of them light blue in his first pass at the outside border of the lot.

Wonderful, he thought. A dozen exits to the stadium. Probably a dozen blue Jettas in the parking lot. He needed twenty guys, a week, and a ton of luck. And even then . . .

He sat on somebody's fender near the entrance to the lot, sucking down an ice-cold Fanta, trying to come up with some plan that might work. The landscape of automobiles shimmered and glared in the heat.

California plates!

Acapulco was a long way from California, and almost no one, except for the lunatic fringe among whom Hardy was beginning to count himself, drove. There wouldn't be more than twenty cars in the lot with California plates, and he guessed the odds of finding more than one blue Jetta with them were significantly on his side.

Whistling, he started walking through the lot.

"Woo, I'm dizzy."

She pressed her body up against his good side.

She was fantastic. Long, leggy, a face for the movies. Hair a deep chestnut, green eyes. She was a secretary from Washington, D.C., and wore a white T-shirt from the Hard Times Cafe that said "I like mine all the way wet." The T-shirt was a little small—her breasts held the front up high enough to show her navel in the slim waist. Maybe she was twenty-two, and with a couple of margaritas already in her. Look out.

"Watch out for the potholes," Rusty said. "Just lean against me."

"Could you believe those bodies?" she said.

"Pretty amazing."

"I mean, I've seen jocks before, but these guys . . ."

He let her go on. Fantasize all you want, he was thinking. And he'd been studying the guys, too. Getting to know them a little now, what to watch for. And getting lucky, hitting two, then three, four in a row, clearing over a thousand U.S. today, more than making up for last week's disaster.

He was glad the hurricane had enforced the time off. He had been starting to press. Just down here and thinking he had to make his mark right away. Wrong. He had time. He kept telling himself he had time. All the time in the world. So he took a few days off, met Atlanta, stayed indoors. It had been good for him.

Now, starting a new week fresh, hitting it right away, this was it.

Most of the cars were out of the lot. He and D.C. were laughing, watching out for potholes. They were going to go down to the Esplanade and have turtle soup and a lobster dinner and blow a wad of this money, then maybe hit a cockfight. Or anyway, something with a cock.

He smiled. Whatever they did, it didn't matter. He was loaded. After being down here ten days, he had more than he had come with. And that's the way it would keep rolling. No more getting behind the eight ball. Study the game. Bet cautiously until you hit your roll. Then, like today, run it.

And he thought he was seeing it already. Some pattern. Some way to make a steady income. It wasn't exactly like the ponies, where there were all these variables. Horses were dumb animals. Jai alai was people, momentum, things you could understand, predict.

It was late afternoon. The green hill had a sepia tone through the dust of the lot. They got to his car and heard footsteps coming up behind them.

"Hey, Rusty! Rusty!" Hardy closed the distance between them. He took off his sunglasses. "It's you, isn't it?"

Rusty was good, Hardy gave him that. Barely a flicker of panic. "Diz!" He reached out his good arm and pulled Hardy into an embrace. "God, it's great to see you."

"Me? It's great to see you. I thought you were dead."

"Dead?" the girl said.

"Oh, hey, excuse me, this is D.C. D.C., an old friend, Dismas Hardy."

She nodded. "What do you mean, dead?"

Rusty laughed. "I'm not dead, thank God."

"Me, neither."

"I can see that. What are you doing down here?"

"Maybe great minds think alike. I'm waiting for your first call and watching the news and I see some girl has been killed on a barge in China Basin, and—"

"What? Who was killed?"

Hardy shrugged. "I don't know. But I knew that's where you lived, so I went down to check it out and it was the slip you'd given me. I didn't want to wait around so Louis Baker could find me. I just went back home, threw some things together and lit out."

"It was Maxine . . ." Rusty leaned up against the fender of his car. He put his hand up, shading his eyes.

"Who's Maxine?" D.C. asked.

"She was a friend, just a friend." His eyes were actually glazing, near tears. "God, Diz, she must have come over to visit and was there when Baker got there."

"That's what I figured. I just split. Especially since you didn't call me, I figured—"

"I know. I just spooked, same as you. When I got home from seeing you I sat around for an hour and realized I just couldn't do it, couldn't just wait there for Baker to come and kill me. What was the point? But I should have called you. I'm sorry."

"What are you guys talking about?"

Rusty was making a point of recovering from the shock of Maxine's death. He told a good story while Hardy and D.C. listened. It sounded romantic, frightening, kind of cool.

"So what happened to this guy Baker?" D.C. asked.

Hardy looked at Rusty and shrugged. "I don't know. I hope he's back in jail by now. He probably left some prints, don't you think, Rusty? Something, anyway." He turned to the girl. "They usually do. I figure I had some vacation, I'd take it and give the cops a month or so to figure it out. If not, time I get back, I can tell them what I think and they'll go get him, but I thought it would be safer to get away first. So I've been bumming in Mexico a couple of weeks."

"It's only my second day," she said.

"Hey, you eaten yet, Diz? We were going to go down and blow some of my winnings. You want to join us?"

"You win at this game?"

Rusty grinned now. He opened the passenger door. "Big time."

They were leaving the lot, bouncing over the dirt. "So what happened to your arm?" Hardy asked.

After he had located the car, Hardy had a good long time to work on the plan. Though it had still been early enough to get back to the El Sol and return with his gun, what good would that have done? He wasn't planning on kidnapping Rusty. It was a long way back home and they'd have to drive—there was no way Hardy could board a plane with the gun.

Hardy couldn't go to the local police, either. Rusty wasn't wanted for anything, here or in the States, and even if he was, Hardy wasn't a lawman. The only way to do it, Hardy realized, was to get Abe involved and somehow make things official.

But first he had wanted to make sure Rusty wouldn't suddenly cop to the whole thing and want, say, to fly home to work it out. Hardy didn't want to have Abe fly down just to have Rusty say, "Sure, guys, I'll go home with you." Figuring he could beat it. He wanted to make sure the guy was denying it, that Abe would be needed.

Any risk he ran in showing himself would be minimized by his own charade. He figured he and Rusty would hang out, Hardy sticking close, for a day or two until Abe could make it down, then they'd nail him.

Rusty had a charming smile. "I'll tell you, my life isn't dull," he was saying. "I got this arm the third day I was here. I was out fishing, sweating like a pig.

Dove in to cool off. So I'm climbing back onto the boat and grab the gaff to come aboard. I slip and the damned thing goes through my arm."

"Both sides, in and out?"

"Yep."

"Ouch!" D.C. said.

Hardy had enjoyed it, watching the show. He tried to see it the way Rusty was telling it, and every little piece fit in just right. If he didn't know the truth, Hardy would have been convinced himself—the flight from vengeful Louis Baker, an insurance settlement that provided some ready cash, the accident with the gaff. Once, in the middle of dinner, another flirtation with tears over Maxine's death.

There was also the mental challenge of holding back, of biting his tongue. He had to remember he hadn't been to the barge, hadn't seen Rusty's blood on the bed, Maxine's body blocking the hallway. He hadn't visited Louis Baker in the hospital, and he'd never heard of Johnny LaGuardia, Ray Weir, any of them.

The girl was gone now, dropped off dead drunk at her hotel after dinner.

Rusty had driven himself and Hardy back up to the cliffside restaurant for a few nightcaps—shots of tequila and wedges of lime. Hardy thought he would get Rusty drunk, drive him home, maybe misplace his keys. Then he'd call Abe and talk him into getting down here.

They walked around to where the boys jumped. The ocean roared far down below them. There was a grotto to the Virgin Mary for the obligatory prayer before going off the cliff. A smell of kerosene—for the torches—overlaid the sea air. The divers had all gone home.

"This is something," Hardy said. The crescent moon

hung over the sea to his right. "I was over at one of the restaurants the other day and couldn't watch it," Hardy said.

"It's Mexico, life's cheap." Rusty was standing next to him. He'd brought a bottle with him.

"Still. It's not done with mirrors."

Rusty lifted the bottle, shrugging. "You lose a few beaners, who's going to notice?"

"Not exactly the words of the burning idealist who used to work for the D.A."

Rusty sounded like he was feeling the drinks. "Diz, let me tell you something. I just wanted to win cases. Same as everybody else."

"I don't know. I like to think I cared about justice a little."

"That why you quit? That passion for justice?" Hardy looked sidelong at Rusty, deciding he wasn't going to have to try to get him drunk. Rusty staggered a few steps further toward the edge of the cliff and Hardy walked behind him.

Rusty's good hand held the bottle down at his side. He turned around, his back to the cliff.

He drank again, tipping the bottle up. He staggered back a few steps. "I guess in a way Baker did me a favor giving me this opportunity to drop out."

Hardy moved up beside him. "Watch out here," he said. "That's a long way down." It was time to start herding him back to the car. "So you're not going back?" All innocence.

Rusty turned again. He seemed to be looking at the moon. "You know how they always tell us don't burn your bridges? Well, that's what I've done. I'm dead, Diz. Nobody in the whole world knows I'm alive. Except you."

"And you like that?"

"It's freedom. You never realize how much you're held back by what you've done before. Your habits. Other people's expectations. I don't know which is worse. But now there's neither of them. It's like being given a second chance, born again."

"A lot of people go look up Jesus, say the same thing."

Rusty laughed. "This isn't forgiveness, Diz. This is a clean slate." He nipped at his bottle. "How about you? Anybody know you're here?"

Hardy decided to keep running with his own game. He shook his head. "Not a soul," he lied. "But I still feel like me. Same baggage."

"Only if you think of it that way."

Rusty walked to the edge of the cliff, bottle in hand. Hardy kept his distance four or five steps behind him, still close enough to the cliff edge to see a phosphorus wave break far below, the sound carrying up like distant thunder.

"Maybe you don't have so many things tying you up," Hardy said.

Rusty chuckled. "You can bet on that one." He turned to look at Hardy. "You think things have got to tie you up? I tell you, Diz, I tried that for about, I don't know, ten years. It sucks."

"I gave it up for about ten years and that sucks too."

Rusty swigged from the bottle. "Well, there you go," he said. He walked to the lip of the cliff and leaned over looking down. Straightening up, he half turned. "I guess I just don't want to think so much anymore. Or try to do anything anymore. My ambition done gone South. Especially since coming down here. I do some betting, keep on top of my game, score a few chicks. You want to know what living is, take my advice and don't go back to San Francisco. Hang out."

"I don't think so."

Rusty shrugged, brought the bottle again to his lips. Then, abruptly, he sat down, hanging his legs over the edge of the precipice. He patted the ground next to him. "Sit down, Diz, have a hit." He held the bottle out.

"I'm good," Hardy said. "What do you say we head back?"

The temptation was getting to Hardy. Rusty had killed Maxine Weir and stolen her money. He had helped undo nine years of Louis Baker's prison rehab. Hardy knew that as long as Rusty was free, he himself would never be safe. Rusty couldn't really let him go back. The word might eventually get back that Rusty was down here—just the "might" was enough. Rusty had already killed for the life he wanted, and Hardy didn't doubt he'd do it again. And now the guy was sitting on the cliff's edge, dangling his feet, half in the bag. A little nudge and Abe's order of the cosmos would be restored.

Hardy looked around the deserted plateau. There was no sign of life except for him and Rusty. He took a breath and did a deep knee bend, scratching at the dirt. "Come on," he said. "I'm ready for the sack." He'd get back to the El Sol, call Abe, put things in gear for tomorrow or the next day, figure how they would get Rusty back to the States.

But Rusty did not move to get up. Instead he pulled at the bottle again, barely tipping his head enough to splash some tequila into his mouth. Hardy wondered how he could function with as much alcohol as he must have had in him. Then he wondered if he was functioning.

He moved up a step. "Rusty?"

Suddenly shaking his head like a wet dog, Rusty put the bottle down on the dirt. He seemed to try to balance himself with his good arm, to push up, but the effort was too great and he settled back heavily, swearing.

Hardy waited.

Rusty lay down flat on his back, staring at the stars,

his legs hanging over the cliff. "I am fubar'd," he said, the words coming out very slurred. "Fucked up beyond all repair."

Hardy, moving no closer, nodded. "So I'll drive," he said. Without looking back, he wheeled and started walking.

It was 12:15 when he got to the car. At 12:30, sitting on the hood with his feet on the fender, he had to decide if he was going to walk home or what. He still didn't know where Rusty lived, and he didn't want to lose track of him. Of course, he could leave him passed out on the cliff, hoping he would walk in his sleep and settle the issue, but that really didn't seem too promising a plan. No, he had to keep Rusty in his sights, keep playing this game as Rusty's friend, get Abe down here, then blindside him.

He crossed the open plateau again. Rusty hadn't moved an inch. The bottle glinted in the moonlight next to him. His good arm was outstretched behind it. He was breathing heavily, noisily, his mouth open.

"Goddammit, Rusty!" Hardy came up behind his head and nudged it with his foot. "Come on, let's shake it."

He didn't stir. For an instant Hardy thought that maybe he was dead, then reminded himself that dead men almost never breathed so loud.

He shook his head, thinking it out. Rusty had one bad arm, in a sling, and was pretty obviously drunk as a skunk. There wasn't much real threat there, was there, Diz?

He could grab the good arm, pull him back away from the cliff like a sack of bricks, get him up and moving somehow. Unless he wanted to sit here all night, or walk home and maybe lose him.

He leaned over and took hold of the good arm around the wrist with both his hands. It was dead.

There was no resistance. He got a better footing and started to pull. Rusty finally made a noise, half-turning. Hardy moved back, letting go. "Come on, get up."

Rusty rolled again onto his back. This was getting old in a hurry. Hardy said fuck it and grabbed him under both armpits, leaning over, off balance for one second, to pull.

Which was when Rusty moved. Both arms came up, grabbed Hardy at the shoulders and pulled him forward, over, covering Rusty's body in a somersault, legs out on no purchase, reaching out, trying to grab on to Rusty—something, anything—but there was only the night air, the cold far moon.

Then there was something under his feet, some small ledge, and one of Rusty's feet, still dangling where it had been, over the cliff's edge, right there, grabbable. But it moved, kicking out, hitting him in the shoulder, pushing him out into the darkness.

25

Rusty liked the idea of bringing the bottle along, because it was much easier to fake that you were drinking a lot. You could just lift the thing to your lips every couple of minutes, start rambling a little in your talking. In any event, it had worked.

He wasn't sure, driving back home, whether Dismas Hardy had been a turn in his luck for the good or the bad. His idea of having him stay in San Francisco, implicate Baker, and get the word out that Rusty was in fact dead hadn't, it seemed, worked too well. He didn't realize Hardy had been such a coward—he thought he remembered a guy a lot more tenacious. He could have sworn Hardy would have gone to the cops, given his two cents.

But no, he'd run . . . Well, you couldn't plan for everything in this world. If gambling had taught him anything it had taught him that. But then Hardy's showing up here, he decided, was pure good fortune, a sign that like today at the games he was on a roll.

Sure, he'd had to give up on D.C., but he knew her hotel and he could pick things up there again if he wanted. Except since she'd been with him and Hardy, maybe that wouldn't be too smart. The less they could be put together the better.

He got out to the road, running along the bay and turned north. It was too bad. D.C. really was his kind of woman—young, enthusiastic, beautiful, not too deep. Here for a party, and intended to have one. Couldn't hold her liquor worth a damn, though.

He pulled up off the road, looking at his watch. Nearly one A.M. He and Hardy had half carried D.C. back to her room at the Las Brisas around 9:30.

He was pumped up. Things were going perfectly, and that's when you took your flyers. The losers were the guys who didn't run with it when they felt the roll kick in, and he wasn't a loser, not anymore. He was invincible.

Now he took a real shot out of the bottle, U-turning back toward town, toward D.C. and what he felt like doing right now.

Tomorrow he'd find out about the body at the base of the cliffs. He'd go to the restaurant where they'd started tonight, ask if anyone had seen his friend. Of course, the first divers would find him—if the tide didn't take him out.

He thought about Hardy. At first, he hadn't really planned on doing anything about him, but as the night had worn on, it became inevitable. Hardy would eventually go back to San Francisco. He would tell someone he'd seen Rusty—hell, the guy was a bartender and it was a great story. Next thing you know, the word somehow gets back to Tortoni or even—which might be worse now—to the police.

He kept forgetting he had killed Maxine.

Imagine forgetting something like that. It was interesting, he thought, and like with Hardy tonight, it had been a spur-of-the-moment thing, going with the vibe.

Maxine showing up after he'd already scared the pee out of Louis Baker. Baker gone. He, Rusty, screwing up his courage with the gun. Even with brass-jacketed .22s, he knew it was going to hurt like hell. He had his own cash in his briefcase—twenty-some thousand would have been enough had the other sixty not just jumped up in his face.

No. Maxine had been getting too serious anyway. He'd been planning that he would just die—to her as to everyone else. But then the fool woman comes over the day before they had planned to go, with all her money in her duffel bag . . .

He parked at the Las Brisas—individual spots for each guest in front of D.C.'s cabin. He took another hit of tequila, thinking back. It was strange he hadn't gone over it so carefully before. He thought well on his feet, he had to give it to himself on that. That's why he had been such a pistol of a trial lawyer . . .

That Wednesday night, Maxine had come in, unexpected. Unaware. Happy. Finally getting out of San Francisco and those dead dreams. Wasn't it wonderful, Rusty?

Sure, wonderful.

But, goddammit, Johnny LaGuardia would be coming over in about two hours for his vig and Rusty had to be dead by then, blood tracking to the rail, body floating out to the bay.

She'd been excited, sexed up, geared for her new life. She'd started giving him her patented head, and okay, doing it wouldn't hurt easing up some of his tension either. Didn't take long.

Then her shower, him waiting now on the bed. The water turning off and then Maxine coming out, dancing, posing with the neck brace on—the thing that had made them all their money, that had made it all possible. She'd looked at him questioningly. What was he doing with Ray's gun? Why . . . ?

He opened the car door. If D.C. was still drunk it'd be easy. He and Hardy had left her on the bed, closing the door behind them. It might still be unlocked, and he'd just let himself in. Or, even if she'd gotten up and put the chain on, which was unlikely, he bet he could sweet-talk her back between the sheets in two minutes. He was good on his feet.

*   *   *

Later, Hardy would say the fall lasted twenty-six minutes by his best count.

He had had parachute training in the Marines, though it had been a long time. What saved him was that as he lost his balance, thinking he was dead, he still had pushed out, jumping, in some control.

He had noticed the boys diving—how the first part of the dive cleared the outcropping of rock. It was not far out. The length of the fall after that was what made it so impressive.

So he hadn't spun or flipped, but dropped, in black panic, but with an eye on the phosphorus field forming under him, moving toward shore under him.

Hitting, feeling the impact through his shoes up to his shoulders, immediately ground into the bottom sand by the incoming wave, he struggled for what he hoped was the surface. There was no telling up from down and he hadn't timed anything like when to take a breath.

Seawater. Lungs filling up. Slamming against rock. Under again.

And then he was on the sand throwing up. The stuff dripping down his right arm felt warm and looked black in the dun moonlight. The same moon was up there. He couldn't see the top of the cliffs from the beach. The arm was starting to throb. He'd lost his right shoe. He reached down and there was more blood. He tried to stand and another wave came, knocking him down again.

He struggled to his feet, still gagging. He pulled off the other sand-filled shoe. His arm was killing him now. He was afraid to look at it. He sat into another wave and rubbed the blood away with the salt water.

His eyes gradually adjusted enough to make out depressions in the rocky face of the cliff. Footsteps. Only about five hundred of them, he thought. He put one

foot in the first depression. Another in the next. The
right foot was at least sprained, but he put weight on
it and it held, through the pain made him catch at his
breath. His teeth were starting to chatter. He tried
another step.

"Okay, Rusty," he said, "you want to play dirty."

It was 3:15 A.M. by his watch when Hardy got to the
El Sol. The office was a small room with rattan furniture and a bamboo desk with a glass top, under which
were featured brochures of all Acapulco had to offer.
Hardy leaned up against the bamboo and rang the
bell. He was looking at a man standing next to a
seven-foot sailfish. He moved the bell to reveal a platter of seafood. He rang it again.

He closed his eyes, suddenly dizzy. The cuts on his
arm were more painful and bloody than deep, and
they had clotted pretty well. Still, a few drops of blood
had splattered to the floor. He figured his foot was
beyond pain, that he would walk with a limp the rest
of his whole life.

He banged on the bell again, gave up and got
around behind the back of the desk. There was an old
green metal box with a red cross on it and he picked
it up and limped out on his bare and bloody feet,
through the bananas and bougainvillea, back to his
room.

"Who was that?" Flo Glitsky sat up in bed. "What
time is it?"

Abe was pulling on his pants.

"Where are you going?"

Normally Flo didn't ask, didn't stir in the middle of
the night when Abe got up to, say, question a suspect.
But they had only gotten back from Los Angeles that
day, and her husband had seemed maybe interested

in the job they were offering—a gang task force of some kind, community interaction, counseling. He said he felt that his live cases here had been wrapped up. So where was he going in the middle of the night?

"Hardy," he said.

"What about Hardy? Where is he?"

"He's in Acapulco. Rusty Ingraham just tried to kill him."

As he threw things in a bag, he filled her in. She draped an afghan over her and sat straight up cross-legged.

"So what does he want you to do?"

"He wants me to come down there."

"And do what?"

Abe sat on the bed and started tying a shoe. "Pick Rusty up."

"Pick Rusty up," Flo repeated. "In Acapulco? How are you going to do that?" Then, as though remembering something. "Is Dismas all right?"

"He seemed fine." He turned to his wife. "You want to call the airport and see when the next plane leaves?"

He went into the bathroom to shave. Halfway through, Flo came to the doorway. "Mexicana, seven-twenty."

"Well, I've got some time. How about a little breakfast?"

"You still haven't told me how you intend to pick Rusty up."

Abe had to be careful shaving around the scar that ran through his lips. He made funny faces into the mirror, scraping away.

"That's perceptive," he said finally. He threw some water in his face, reaching blindly for a towel. Flo picked it from the rack and put it into his hands. "And the reason is, I don't know. It will take some finesse, though."

He was back in the bedroom, taking a long-sleeved

purple T-shirt from a dresser drawer. "Hardy knows me pretty well," he said. "Rusty's my collar."

"But you don't have jurisdiction down there. Why don't you just get a warrant, have him extradited?"

"On what?"

"How about murder?"

"Murder's good," Abe agreed, "except he's not wanted for murder. We could say we'd like to question him about a murder, but they wouldn't extradite for that, to say nothing of the fact that extradition takes a year on a good day. We have any chub? Cream cheese and chub on a bagel sounds good. I might even have some caffeinated tea."

"Abe."

He patted the bed next to him. When Flo sat down, he put an arm around her. "He's my collar. He's alive and tried to kill Diz—it points strongly to him killing Maxine Weir. You just said as much yourself . . . If he hadn't tried to kill Diz I'd say it wasn't definite. But since he did . . ." He shrugged. "At least, for my own peace of mind I've got to talk to him."

"Are you going to take your gun?"

"Hardy's already got one."

"In Mexico? How'd he . . . ?"

Abe patted her shoulder. "He's a resourceful guy, our Diz. And his having one saves me the trouble of hassling with the airlines, going through the locals for permissions, all that."

"Except that if you use it, how do you explain it?"

Abe stood up. "We're full of good questions today."

"Well?"

"Well, we'll have to think of something."

It was still dark, but Hardy heard a rooster crowing far off. He was trying to pull a sock onto his right foot and it was a tight squeeze over the bandage. The cut on the side of that foot, from ankle to little toe, was deeper, longer and uglier than anything on his arm. From the walk, the soles of both feet were raw.

He felt a little bad about his omission to Abe that he didn't have a real idea of where Rusty might be. At dinner, Rusty had bragged about his beachfront place five miles north of the city. So Hardy thought he'd drive on up the road looking for that telltale Volkswagen. Of course, he knew it could be in a carport, a garage, off the road, whatever. Well, then he would go back to the jai alai stadium. If Rusty thought he was dead, he'd probably just go back to his habits. If . . .

One sock on, he stopped.

He considered calling Abe back. Never mind. I'll go to the Mexican police and report my attempted murder. File charges. Let them look. Fuck it.

But, he realized, if he thought things had been personal before, Rusty had upped the ante by about a thousand. He wanted to take him, wanted to get him for what had started this whole thing, not just for the legalities. Abe deserved his chance, too, what with running around after Ray Weir and Johnny LaGuardia and Hector Medina and Louis Baker. Let's get the posse together, saddle up and kick some ass. He had told Abe to come to the El Sol when he got in. If he had left Abe with the impression that he'd have Rusty here, trussed up and ready to roast, he figured his friend would forgive him.

He was wearing dry jeans, a pair of suddenly too small tennis shoes, an Armani long-sleeved shirt Jane had given him, probably ruined forever now with the blood seeping through the bandage he'd wrapped around his arm. Well, too bad. He smiled at himself in the cracked brownish mirror—the Miami Vice look. Very nice. He grabbed a light tan Windbreaker on the way out.

His Samurai was where he'd left it, around the corner from the El Sol's office, halfway up the hill. It was

a long way up the silent, dark street. He felt under
the driver's side fender. Still there.

He sat in the driver's seat, feeding the bullets he
had taped under the bottom of the glove compartment
into the chambers. He didn't think he was going to
shoot Rusty on sight, but . . . Playing it as though the
man was just screwed up, a once-nice guy gone a little
bad had nearly cost him his life tonight and he wasn't
about to let it happen again.

The sky behind him was starting to get light. He
heard something drop onto the canvas roof of the car.
A large dark shape appeared at the top of the windshield. Hardy knocked at it with his hand and the
lizard skitted down and off the hood into the leaves
on the side of the road. Hardy shivered. Get moving,
he said, even if you don't know where you're going.

The ignition caught right away. Hardy slipped the
Samurai into gear. Sitting still, even for a moment,
sapped his energy. He thought he had probably lost a
fair amount of blood, but not enough to weaken him.
The fatigue must be from the hour—he'd been awake
now for nearly a day, one filled with more than the
usual ups and downs. But once a month or so at the
Shamrock he'd pull an all-nighter talking to Moses, so
he felt in shape that way.

He hoped.

At the corner he stopped, suddenly remembering
that there was one other person in Acapulco who
might know where Rusty lived. And he knew where
to find her, though she might be a little tough to
wake up.

Make that knocking go away.

There was dim light at the corners of the curtains.
Dull gray light of very early morning. But he could
see everything in the room. He didn't feel like he'd
slept more than two hours. D.C., who definitely had

been worth the stop, lay turned away from him on her side, naked and uncovered. Absently, he ran his hand along her flank. She made a sleepy, purring noise.

More knocking. He listened. Somebody was already up playing tennis—Rusty heard the rhythmic *thok* of the ball being hit. That must be it.

No, it was the door. Someone knocking on the door. Jesus, what time was it?

"Si?"

"Servicio, señor."

D.C. stirred. "What's that?" she asked.

"Room service."

She mumbled that they had the wrong room. Rusty tried to say "wrong room" in Spanish but it didn't seem to take. The guy knocked again.

D.C. moaned and rolled out of the sack. "I'll just tell him." Rusty watched her walk across the room. He wondered how breasts so big could ride that high. He liked how she looked as she reached up for the chain, undoing it, opening the door a crack to tell the guy . . .

Stepping back away, her hands to her mouth. And before Rusty could react, Dismas Hardy was inside, the door closed behind him, pointing a gun at his head.

"Remember that thirty-eight Special I recommended you buy," he said. "I thought you'd like to see what one looked like."

26

"You can't shoot me."

"I can't?"

"Please God don't shoot us!" D.C said.

Hardy grabbed the sheet that covered Rusty and threw it toward D.C. "Wrap yourself up and sit down," he said. He motioned to a chair with his head and leveled the gun at Rusty, now back up against the headboard, naked, covering himself. "I'm sorry, where were we?"

"You'll never explain the gun."

"This gun? The one you stole from me in San Francisco?"

"What's he saying?"

Both men ignored her. Hardy continued. "You mean the gun we fought over and it went off by accident? This gun?"

"They'd never believe that."

"I think they might if a San Francisco cop came down and said you were already a murderer."

"Rusty, what's he saying?"

Hardy glanced at the girl, shivering and huddled in the chair. "About four hours ago your friend Rusty here pushed me off a very high cliff."

She looked at Hardy as though he were a madman. "No. He was here all night. I remember, you both were driving in the car with me and—"

"Wrong," Hardy said. "You passed out. We went for a nightcap and Rusty tried to kill me."

She looked at Rusty. "What's he saying?"

Rusty shrugged. "Diz, give it up. What are you gonna do?"

Hardy drew it out one word at a time. "I am going to bust your ass." He cocked the gun. "I hate to be so melodramatic, but get some clothes on, Russ."

"You can't do this," D.C. said. "This is kidnapping or something. He was here. I know he was here."

Hardy kept the gun on Rusty. He moved closer and kicked the bunch of clothes that were next to the bed into the middle of the room. "You gonna need help, with your bad arm and all?"

Rusty flexed his bandaged arm, grimacing. "I'll need the sling."

"Pants first," Hardy said. He felt the pockets, checking for a weapon, then threw them onto the bed.

Ingraham was silent.

"Remember that woman—Maxine—I mentioned earlier? Last night. The friend of Rusty's, just a friend?"

She nodded.

"Rusty here killed her. He shot her three times. Close-up. With a small-caliber gun. She crawled about twenty feet before she died. I bet that was a long twenty feet."

It was D.C.'s turn to be silent.

Hardy threw Rusty his shirt. "And that horrible gaff wound in his arm? You ever been on a real fishing boat, Rusty? There's no mate in the universe will use a gaff to help a human being pull up. Good basic idea, though, given short notice to come up with it. Creative." Hardy was back at D.C. "He needed something to explain the wound through his arm, since what he in fact did was shoot himself to make it look like someone had killed him. His blood all over the place. A trail of it leading to the edge of his barge, where it disappeared into the foaming brine."

"You've got it all figured, don't you?" Ingraham said.

"Yep." Hardy was curt. "Shoes," he said. He thought of his own aching feet. "Better yet, no shoes. Get up."

"Is this all true?" D.C. had pulled her feet up under her on the chair, tucking the sheet in all around.

"This is the gospel," Hardy said. "Let's go, Russ." He threw him the sling and Rusty draped it around his neck. Then he leaned over and reached for one of his shoes. Hardy took quick but careful aim and fired. In the room the shot was a bomb blast. The pair of shoes exploded. There was a gash in the floor and plaster fell from the wall where the bullet had ricocheted up and through. Hardy smelled the cordite. D.C. screamed, then settled into a quiet sobbing.

"Jesus, Hardy. You're crazy."

"No, but I am a little pissed off. No shoes."

He went to the door, opening it, pointing the gun at Rusty. "We'd better move. I imagine that woke up some of the neighbors." He clucked, looking at D.C. "Horrible the way these Mexican kids will just go shooting off barrel bombs at all hours. Right? You understand?"

The girl, terrified, nodded. Hardy said he hoped so.

Rusty was at the door. Hardy looked back in at D.C. "This is really happening," he said. "And what I want you to do now is sit in that chair until you've counted very slow to three hundred. Don't open the door for anybody. Don't make any noise. Don't do anything. Do you understand?"

She nodded again and Hardy closed the door. Other doors around the complex were opening. Hardy kept the gun out of sight under his Windbreaker. He was grinning.

"This is fun, isn't it? Now we're going to walk briskly to that car next to yours, looks like a Jeep, and get in and drive away into the sunrise. Is the plan clear? Because if it's not, a mistake could happen."

"Look, Diz, I've got a lot of money, maybe we can—"

"Maybe, but let's talk later. Perhaps we'll do lunch."

The thing about running around is sometimes you didn't take the time to think.

Abe Glitsky wasn't running now. He had had three hours alone on the plane, three hours to sort facts without interruption. Now, beginning their descent into Acapulco, he was drinking a glass of papaya juice over ice and wondering how he had let himself slip so far in the past couple of weeks.

He imagined it had been a function of all the b.s. at the Hall, the pissing and moaning about the bureaucratic aspects of the job. Wondering whether Lanier's cases intersected with his, wanting to close the book on investigations just because he didn't want them outstanding when he left.

If he left.

He was thinking now, with Ingraham alive, what that did to his neat little package regarding Maxine Weir's death. After Hector Medina's suicide, or apparent suicide, it had all seemed clear. He hadn't given that case a thought during his four days in Los Angeles, he was so satisfied with what must have happened.

He had chosen to accept that Medina's grudge against Ingraham had been reawakened by his involvement with the Raines/Valenti investigation. He had hired Johnny LaGuardia to go kill Rusty. LaGuardia had somehow—ah, how easily that "somehow" slid down when you wanted to get around something— gotten hold of Ray Weir's gun and used it to shoot Rusty and Maxine, whose presence there was just bad luck for her. Finally, since LaGuardia was the only thing tying Medina to the crime, Medina aces Johnny. But once Abe Glitsky shows up, already suspecting Medina, he sees that he's about to be accused again, there'll be another murder investigation—his job will go, his reputation, the same thing that happened before—and he can't take it anymore so he jumps from the roof of the Sir Francis Drake.

All plausible, but now, with Ingraham not dead, with Ingraham trying to kill Hardy, a good possibility that none of it was true.

Which left the reality of Johnny LaGuardia with a bullet in his brain. And Medina? Maybe still a suicide, but maybe not. He crunched some ice as the plane descended.

He was the one who had given Hector Medina's name to Angelo Tortoni. Smart, Abe, he thought disgustedly, real smart. So what he'd really done was to provide a Mafioso with a way to apparently cover for the execution of his own lieutenant. He had told Tortoni he suspected Medina. So how about this, Abe? Tortoni has one of his sons go and push Medina off a roof. Case closed, courtesy of your local SFPD.

And Glitsky had somehow—again, that word—chosen to ignore or forget what he realized was a major psychological truth about Hector Medina. As the sole support of a semi-retarded daughter, he wasn't ever going to kill himself. Medina would tough it out no matter what. He hadn't liked Medina—he was a bad cop—but he was no quitter. He wouldn't run from another investigation. He'd fight it the way he'd gone back for Raines and Valenti. He might fight dirty. He might lie, cheat, steal, do violence, but Medina wouldn't run, wouldn't cop out—wouldn't kill himself.

But Abe had swallowed that he had done just that—because it was convenient, because it closed his caseload—like it was sweet sweet candy.

San Francisco cases again.

His city. His turf.

He knew why he was down here. He was a San
Francisco cop, and Rusty Ingraham was, as he had
told Flo, his collar. His. Personally.

"How much money?" Hardy asked.

Rusty Ingraham's feet were belted to the leg of Hardy's bed at the El Sol. Hardy sat in the reading chair,
the shades drawn, gun in hand, trying to keep awake.

His own foot was throbbing and he felt the unmis-
takable onset of fever. He didn't want to, but if Abe
didn't show up in about an hour he was going to have
to try and figure some way to get the Mexican police
involved and avoid getting himself arrested for having
a gun. Because if he didn't have the gun on Rusty,
even for a minute, Rusty would be gone.

What made it worse was that Rusty had slept for over
two hours after they'd gotten here. With his feet on the
ground, belted hard to the bedpost, he had simply put
his back on the bed and was snoring in five minutes.

Hardy had ordered a pot of coffee from the lobby
and opened the door a crack to take it in. Rusty
hadn't stirred.

Now Rusty half reclined on his good elbow, eyes
sharp, alert. "Close to fifty thousand."

It amazed Hardy. This guy would lie to his dying
mother. "What happened to the other thirty-five?"
he asked.

It took Rusty a minute. "Jesus, you do know everything."

Hardy nodded. "I know Maxine's check was for
eighty-five grand and her husband didn't see any of
it." Hardy took a few minutes telling him the other
things he knew, what he'd really done since Rusty had
turned up missing.

"I'm impressed. You really floated out the canal,
checking the current?"

"I wasted a lot of time. Not just that."

Rusty didn't seem nervous anymore, even seemed to be enjoying himself, reminiscing. "I probably should have just left you out of the plan, but I needed somebody who was out of the loop and still had access to it. I mean, we—you and I—weren't exactly buddies anymore. They'd believe you."

"I think they were coming around to it."

"So why didn't you just let it go?"

Hardy couldn't think of what to say. It was like trying to explain red to someone who was color-blind. He could just hear himself saying, "Because it wasn't true, because I almost shot my best friend, because you had me scared to death for a week, because of Frannie and Jane . . ." He poured the last of the coffee, bitter and tepid. And then Rusty would say, "So what?"

"The one thing I don't understand," Hardy said instead, "was how come you didn't just pay off. You had the money. I mean, even before Maxine came over, you had—what?—twenty-five grand? So give the five or six to Johnny LaGuardia, you're out of the hole, forget about it."

Rusty didn't even have to ponder. "You don't forget about it, Diz. You don't ever get out. You know how much I paid fucking Angelo Tortoni over the past five, six years? How about five hundred to a thousand a week for like two hundred and fifty weeks? That's the vig alone, like a quarter million bucks. And his people seeing everything, so every case I settle, every horse I hit, Johnny's there with his hand out. You know what that's like? Three grand, four grand a month down the drain?" He shook his head. "There's no way I give him another dime. Then Maxine comes around, there's that much more. Girl always did have lousy timing."

"So she was just an afterthought? Killing her?"

Rusty shrugged. "Hey, no way I take her with me

Number one, she can't keep her mouth shut—she tells one of her friends, her husband, somebody, and next thing you know Johnny's down here putting me in a blender. Plus, Diz, you know."

"I know what?"

"Women. You know, you get to a certain point . . ."

"You kill them?"

Rusty laughed. "Hey, the thing is, we're here. I've got the money. You get maybe twenty-five—"

"I get maybe whatever I want. I might take it all. Where is it?"

"No, no, no. See? Then I lose my leverage."

Hardy cocked the gun. The guy had colossal balls. "Your leverage position is weak at the moment, Russ. Where's the money?"

He just shook his head. "Nope. You shoot me, you don't get it anyway. You take me back for trial and I'll need all of it for my defense."

"What defense? Tortoni finds out you're alive and you're meat anyway."

"I'm thinking the best thing to do, if it comes to it, is to turn state's evidence against Tortoni, cop a plea, turn the thing around."

Hardy uncocked the gun. "You're an impressive piece of work, Rusty. You got a lock murder-one with Maxine. You also tried to kill me and I'm not inclined to let it go."

"Why not, Diz? No, I mean it. It wasn't personal. I like you. So I pay for your inconvenience, I disappear someplace else and we forget the whole thing."

"We forget you tried to kill me?"

"Right."

"We forget you set up Louis Baker, using me to do it, fucked up the rest of his life?"

Rusty Ingraham rolled his eyes. "Oh, please."

"He's just a dirtbag nigger ex-con anyway, right?"

"At best." He sat up, leaning forward on the bed. "Come on, Diz. What'd I do to the guy he didn't deserve anyway? He should have done his thirteen for what we put him down for. They let him out after nine, that's their problem. Fuck Louis Baker. Even thirteen years wasn't enough. They should have thrown away the key."

"I think they will with you, Rusty. How's that grab you?"

Rusty shook his head, smiling. "I think it's unlikely. Listen, Diz. Who knows but me and you what really happened? I guarantee you Baker was there. So he shot Maxine and me. I'm hit but I get away. It still all works. I give you half the money."

"And the white man walks?"

Rusty raised his good hand, gesturing, still smiling, conspiratorial. "It's not black or white," he said. "It's who I am and who Baker is."

Hardy emptied his coffee cup in a long slow swallow. "That's right, Russ. That's exactly what it is."

After he'd shown up at Hardy's room at the El Sol, Abe had gone out and bought a length of rope, a pair of cheap sandals for Rusty and some over-the-counter tetracycline. Mexico was different that way.

Hardy had said he couldn't do anything until he'd gotten a little sleep, so Abe had moved Ingraham, over his polite objections, tying him elbows and knees to a chair while Hardy took his pills and crashed on the bed. Ingraham had spoken little, pretty beat himself. He showed no inclination to deny killing Maxine Weir. And eventually dozed off.

So Abe had spent the afternoon on the terrace, reading Loren Estleman's *Bloody Season* and wondering how Wyatt Earp had ever acquired such a good reputation. Every ten minutes he checked through the double doors.

At a little after three he had finished his book and awakened Hardy. He had a fever but he was okay.

He had taken some more pills. They sat across from each other on the terrace.

"Okay," Abe said. "Now what?"

"I was hoping you'd tell me."

Abe sat back and sucked some air through his front teeth. "You want to drive him back, all of us?"

"Three days, small car. I don't know how I'd be," Hardy said. "I have felt better." He thought a minute. "Isn't there any way they can hold him here?"

Abe shook his head. "I don't know. I'm not here officially. I can't arrest him."

"But they can arrest him down here, can't they?"

Abe's scar tightened through his lips. "There is a rumor that anybody can be arrested here for anything. A humble and cooperative California police officer, such as myself, for example, could probably speak to the locals and arrange something." Abe stood up, yawning, and glanced back inside. "He's tied up good, Diz. Let's go down by the pool."

The reason they had never taken him was they weren't too smart.

Okay, they had the gun, but a weapon doesn't do you any good if you can't use it. Hardy taking that shot this morning had rattled him a little, made him forget where they were for a while. It was possible that maybe Hardy was crazy enough to shoot him and the consequences be damned.

But now, with Glitsky here, it wasn't going to happen. Glitsky was a good cop and he was going to try to arrest him and have him held until they could get the extradition together. At least, that's what they'd said, with the door open, thinking he was still sleeping. Not too smart.

It was surprisingly comfortable with the pillow and the blanket. Rusty reviewed his options.

When they untied him they'd probably manhandle

him away into Hardy's car and, even if it was a long trip, that would be their only choice. Well, he didn't want to spend three or four days tied up, heading back to the border.

On the other hand, he could pretend to cooperate, be docile, let them bring him to the Mexican police, and then gently point out that Messrs. Glitsky and Hardy here were the ones that had kidnapped him. And see? Look at this! They are illegally armed!

Don't you Mexican authorities look with extreme displeasure upon civilians with guns, especially foreign civilians, most especially big-shot United States policemen, coming down here doing their extralegal we-don't-need-no-stinking-badges extradition bullshit without okaying it up front? Any good macho *jefe* would likely be outraged at the imperialistic arrogance of it all.

No question. They'd take it up with Hardy and Glitsky first.

It was a far better chance than the drive.

They wouldn't hold him on Glitsky's say-so after that. There wasn't even a warrant for him in the States. Did they forget he knew this stuff? I'm a lawyer, fellas, this is what I do.

He smiled under the blanket.

Hardy and Glitsky were coming back into the room, Hardy saying, "It's still risky."

Glitsky prodded him with his shoe, pulled the blanket off him.

Rusty moaned, stirred, made a good show of it. "That was a good rest," he said. "What time is it?"

They sat alfresco in the late afternoon, three American tourists at a table on the Esplanade, looking out at the bay, the bodies in swimsuits, the beggars. Hardy carried his gun, loaded, tucked into his belt under his Windbreaker.

They were all eating shrimp cocktails and drinking

draft Heineken. Rusty said he'd pay for it from his winnings the day before. He was well rested, in apparent high spirits.

Hardy excused himself to go to the bathroom.

"I appreciate the last meal," Rusty said.

Abe nodded, noncommittal. "Your nickel."

"I've heard stories about Mexican jails, you know. Where it's just like a hotel. I mean, you buy your food, have women sent in, same as a hotel. Just depends on how much money you have."

Abe sucked the meat from the tail of a shrimp. "That's nice," he said. "And you've got money, right?" He drank some beer. "Though I don't think you'll be there too long."

"Yeah, well, you gotta make the best of the cards you're dealt."

Glitsky didn't pay much attention. He ate as though he was hungry. Hardy came back up to the table.

"You got him?" Abe asked.

Hardy nodded and Abe got up. "Later," he said.

"Personable guy," Rusty said, looking after him. "Very personable."

Hardy picked up his fork. "I don't think he likes you."

With two shrimp cocktails, two beers and a cup of coffee inside him, Rusty felt good, but Hardy wasn't being much company. Abe had been gone about a half hour. Rusty moved his chair back into the shade of the umbrella over their table. It was still hot, but the sun was moving lower.

"What's taking him so long?"

"Think about it. You in a hurry?"

Rusty smiled. "No, I guess not. But he could've just taken me straight in."

"Not really. He had a little explaining." He looked up the street. "Here they come."

A couple of *guardia* with their green uniforms and submachine guns were following a few steps behind Glitsky. Next to him walked a very tall, skinny man in a black suit, white shirt, electric-blue tie.

"A regular party," Rusty said.

The *guardia* stood on the sidewalk. Glitsky and the tall man pulled up chairs. "This is Lieutenant Mantrillo," Abe said. He turned to Hardy. "We've been having a nice talk."

Up close, Mantrillo's face was sallow and pocked. He pulled a pair of handcuffs from his pocket and threw them onto the table. Several other patrons looked over.

"Do you speak English?" Rusty asked.

Mantrillo nodded. "Pretty good."

He smiled and pointed a finger at Hardy. "This guy's got a gun on him. Right now. Under that jacket."

Mantrillo's black eyes flared in his sad face. Good, Rusty thought, it was the reaction he had hoped for. Mantrillo turned to Hardy, back to Glitsky, who shook his head wearily.

"He came with us voluntarily," Abe said, "like I told you."

Rusty was getting into the performance. He shook his head back and forth. "No! Check him! I came with them because I thought it was my only chance to get away from them. They've had a gun on me all day!" Rusty met Mantrillo's eyes. "Lieutenant, they've got the gun. *They're* breaking your laws, not me."

Damn! he was thinking, I am good. Just like in court. He looked again at Hardy. "Please, check him."

Mantrillo didn't have to move. Hardy stood up, unsnapped a few buttons, and lifted his jacket away from his body. He turned all the way around. "Lieutenant, I don't know what he's talking about," Hardy said. He looked down at Rusty. "Too many beers, buddy. Ain't no gun here."

Mantrillo was pushing up, reaching for the handcuffs. "Let's go," he said. "We will get the . . ."

But it was impossible! Hardy had the gun. He had been with him the whole time except . . .

"The bathroom!" he cried out. "He left it in the bathroom!"

Hardy smiled at him. Rusty whirled, or tried to whirl, to run back and check for himself—Hardy had stashed the gun to set him up for this—but Mantrillo grabbed him by his good wrist.

He heard Glitsky say, "The poor boy's deluded."

Mantrillo was starting to pull him around, get the other wrist. "Let's go." Roughly now.

He pulled back, came free. "No! No, you can't do this—"

He backed up into another table. The customer turned around. "Hey, watch it!"

Hardy was coming around the side of him, cutting him off. He stepped forward and grabbed a knife from the table with his good hand. He tipped the table up, spilling everything, shoving it at Glitsky and Mantrillo. He swung the knife at Hardy. The *guardia* had come up into the eating area, behind Mantrillo. There was only one way out through the other tables, and Rusty broke for it, vaulting the low fence, sprinting up the sidewalk.

With the confusion around the tables, Rusty got a good start. Mantrillo blew on his whistle. The two *guardia* were pounding down the pavement after him, blowing their own whistles, blocking the crowd aside. Several people were on the ground.

Hardy, his foot killing him, was trying to keep up behind Mantrillo and Glitsky. More *guardia* had appeared from the narrow streets leading back into the city.

It was too crowded. There was a sound like firecrackers and screaming ahead, people lying down now, getting off the sidewalk onto the sand. Far ahead of him a sea of bodies still was visible, parting to let the runners through.

Now Hardy saw Rusty, maybe a hundred yards ahead, suddenly appear on the beach. The crowd on the sidewalk must have pushed him out into the open. Either that, or Rusty thought they were slowing him down. Breaking his stride, slogging through the sand, Rusty threw a glance over his shoulder, around the sunbathers and vendors.

Glitsky and Mantrillo were twenty yards in front of him, now crossing the sand themselves. Hardy took the short fall off the pavement. A dozen *guardia* were crossing the beach.

Rusty got to the hard sand near the water and turned, backtracking, up toward Hardy. But that area had pretty much cleared with everybody coming up to see what all the excitement was about. Rusty ran along, silhouetted against an orange evening sky on the nearly deserted stretch of the beach.

More firecrackers seemed to be going off everywhere, and Rusty cut into the water, back up, running with his legs high.

Another burst cut a line in the sand coming up to him, and he stopped, abruptly. He started to raise his hand up, his other hand, the one in the sling. He half turned, and a string of cherry bombs went off fifty yards up the beach to Hardy's right.

Rusty Ingraham lay in a heap. When Hardy got to him, Mantrillo and Glitsky were kneeling on the sand. The lieutenant had turned him onto his back, and the wash of a wave was retreating from him in a pink foam.

"The dumb shit," Glitsky said.

Hardy took the weight off his hurt foot and went down to one knee.

Rusty opened his eyes. He stared at the sky, gradually focused on Hardy. "Hey, Diz," he said, "don't let 'em tell you gamblers always die broke." He tried his courtroom smile. "I'm loaded."

"Where is it, Rusty?" Hardy asked. "The money?"

He closed his eyes, opened them. "I tell you, I lose the leverage," he said. He started to laugh, then coughed once. His face froze in that rictus, and then his eyes, still open, weren't seeing anything.

EPILOGUE

Marcel Lanier put a leg over the corner of Abe Glitsky's desk. "You'll be happy about this," he said.

"What's that?"

"Louis Baker."

Abe put his pencil down. "Louis is back at Quentin."

"Yes, he is."

"That makes me happy?"

"No. What'll make you happy is you know how the D.A. didn't go on the Holly Park thing—no evidence he killed Dido?"

Abe suppressed a small smile. "Yeah, justice prevailed."

"And you don't think he did it anyway?"

Abe shrugged. "Evidence talks, shit walks. Not that I'm burning a candle for Louis Baker, but he looked better for Maxine Weir than he ever did for Dido."

Lanier got a little defensive. "He looked okay for Dido."

"Well, hey, Marcel, this is America. Let's pretend if you can't prove it, he didn't do it, huh?"

"Well, he didn't, is the point."

Abe leaned back in his chair. "No shit."

" 'Nother guy, street name of Samson, took over Dido's cut and seems he stepped on a runner—this kid called Lace. Where these people get their names, Abe?"

"They make 'em up, Marcel. So what happened?"

"So Lace evidently got this guy's gun, Samson's, and being aced out of the cut, had no place to go, so he shoots Samson. No mystery, does it in front of about forty people, two of whom remember seeing something about it. But two's okay. I can live with two."

"And?"

"Ballistics matches the gun with the one did Dido. So how do you like that?"

"Lace—the kid—killed Dido?"

"No. Samson did. It was his gun. He did it to take over the territory. Timed it slick, figured we'd lay it on Baker."

"Which we did."

"But didn't nail him for it, did we? Score one for the good guys."

Abe looked out the window at the October fog. It was late in the day. He tapped his pencil on his desk. "If you say so, Marcel. If you say so."

The trees across the street, at the border to Golden Gate Park, bent in the freshening wind. Hardy pulled a Bass Ale for a customer and limped up to the front of the bar where he'd put his stool, where Frannie sat with a club soda.

She looked at her watch. "Ten minutes. Where's my brother?"

Hardy reached over and took her hand. "He'll be here. He's always here."

Hardy had been back three weeks. He had told Jane. Jane had met someone in Hong Kong and was going to tell him. They had laughed about it. They had also gone to bed, cried about it, put it to rest. Friends. No doubt forever. Maybe.

He squeezed Frannie's hand. She was showing now. Still radiant, blooming. Sometimes, lately, Hardy hadn't known at all what to do with it. "How are you feeling?" he asked.

"Okay. Nervous. Do you think he knows?"

He squeezed her hand again. "I think he suspects."

"Do you think it's too soon?"

"No. Do you?"

"Nope."

"I'm glad you're sure. I kind of need you to be sure."

Hardy watched the wind bend the trees some more. The fog was swirling ten feet away outside the picture window in the near dusk. The Traveling Wilburys were on the jukebox, singing 'bout last night. Hardy thought of last night at Frannie's just kind of wondering if she would like to be married to him.

Remembering how she had answered him, he slid off the stool and stood on his good foot and leaned over the bar, kissing her. "I'm sure," he said.

Read on for a preview
of John Lescroart's
riveting novel

The Hunt Club

Available from Signet
in January 2007

Although he was now considered an official hero, Inspector Devin Juhle was coming off a very bad time. Six months ago, he and his partner, Shane Manning, were on their way to talk to a witness in one of their investigations at two in the afternoon, when they'd picked up an emergency call from dispatch—a report that somebody was shooting up a homeless encampment under the Cesar Chavez Street freeway overpass. As it happened, they were six blocks away and were the first cops on the scene.

Manning was driving, and no sooner than he had pulled their unmarked city-issue Plymouth into the no-man's-land beneath the overpass, a man stepped out from behind a concrete pillar about sixty feet away and leveled a shotgun at the car.

"Down! Down!" Juhle had screamed as Manning was jamming into park, slamming on the brakes. One hand was unsnapping his holster and the other already on the door's handle, and Juhle ducked and hurled his body against the door, swinging it open and getting below the dash just as he heard the blast of the scattergun and the simultaneous explosion of the windshield above him, which covered him with pebbles of safety glass. Another shotgun blast, and then Juhle was out of the car on the asphalt, rolling, trying to get behind a tire for shelter.

"Shane!" he yelled for his partner. "Shane!"

Nothing.

Peering under the car's chassis—he remembered all of it as one picture, though the images were in different directions, so it couldn't have been—he saw two bodies down on the ground by a cardboard structure and behind them a half dozen or so people crouched in the lee of one of the concrete buttresses that supported the overpass, penned in so they couldn't escape. At the same time, the man with the gun had retreated behind the pillar again. To the extent that Juhle was thinking at all and not just reacting, he thought the killer was reloading. But it was his only chance to get an angle and save himself and maybe these other people as well.

He bolted for the low stump of a tree that sat in the middle of the asphalt. It shouldn't have been there—Caltrans should have uprooted the thing before they poured, but they hadn't. Now there it was and he'd reach it if he could. Running low, then diving and rolling, he got to it in two or three seconds, enough time for the shooter, who had come out in the open again, to fire his next round, which pocked into the stump in front of him and sprayed him with wood chips and pulp.

Juhle, on his stomach and with the side of his face and body pressed flat to the ground, knew that the stump didn't give him six inches of clearance and that the man was advancing now, sensing his advantage. He was still probably sixty or seventy feet away—and coming on fast. Once he got to forty feet or so, the shooter's height would give him the angle he needed. The next shotgun blast and Juhle would be history.

There wasn't any time for thought. Juhle rolled a full rotation, extended his gun gripped in both hands out in front of him, drew a bead, and squeezed off two shots. The man stumbled, crumbled, dropped like a bag of cement, and did not move.

Juhle called out for his partner again and again got no reply. Still in a daze, his adrenaline surging, he eventually got to his feet, his gun never leaving the downed man. In half steps, he warily crab-walked sideways toward him, with his gun extended across his body in a two-handed stance. When he got to his target, he saw that he had made the luckiest shot of his life. One bullet had hit the man between the eyes.

Which should have been the end of it. After all, Juhle had six witnesses to everything. Manning was dead, killed by the first blast. The car was a shot-up mess. It was clearly self-defense at the very least and heroism by any standard.

But not necessarily.

Not in San Francisco, where every police shooting is suspect. One of the homeless in the encampment, a highly intoxicated diagnosed schizophrenic, insisted that police had run up to the deceased and executed him for no reason. The fact that he claimed there had been five such officers and that he maintained that the man had not had a shotgun—in spite of Manning's death by shotgun blast—didn't even slow down the right-minded public nuisances of the antipolice crowd.

Beyond that, Juhle's shot was so perfect that it led Byron Diehl, one of the city's supervisors, to opine that perhaps the killing had, in fact, been an overreaction by an overzealous and enraged cop. Perhaps it had, in point of fact, been an execution. Nobody could hit a moving man with a pistol between the eyes at fifty or sixty feet. That just wasn't a possible shot. The man with the gun might have already surrendered, laid his gun down, and Juhle—out of control because of the murder of his partner—had walked up and shot him point-blank.

The other witnesses? Please. Most of them wanted the shooter dead, anyway. Plus, they were naturally afraid of the police. If Juhle told them they'd better back up his story or else, they'd say anything he wanted. They were simply unreliable and their testimonies worthless. Except for the schizophrenic, of course, who was struggling with his substance abuse issues. The idiocy was so palpable that it may have been fun to watch but not to be part of.

So Juhle spent the next three months on administrative leave, under the shadow of a murder charge. He testified four times before different city and police commissions, not including a formal session defending his actions and confronting Diehl in the chamber of the board of supervisors. He was asked to demonstrate his prowess with a handgun on various police ranges in San Francisco, Alameda, and San Mateo counties, where they had pop-up targets that demanded speed as well as accuracy.

Finally, a couple of months ago, he'd been cleared of any wrongdoing. Returning to his place in homicide, though—Manning was of course gone forever—he found himself newly partnered with an obviously political hire, Gumqui Shiu, whose ten-year career didn't seem to have included much real police work. He'd been an instructor at the Academy, worked in the photo lab, and been assigned to various other details, where his progress had been rapid but unmarked by any real accomplishment. He clearly had juice somewhere, but nobody seemed to know where it came from.

This morning, Juhle was at his desk. Insult to injury, he still had his right arm in the sling from arthroscopic rotator cuff surgery—three little holes. His doctor had told him it was an in-and-out-in-the-same-day procedure, little more than an office visit. He'd be pitching Little League practice again in no time.

Not.

Like he ever wanted to do that again, anyway. Little League was pretty much the reason he'd thrown out the damn arm in the first place, letting his macho devils con him into a little mano a mano with Doug

Malinoff—perfect baseball name—the manager of Devin's son Eric's team, the Hornets. Doug was a good guy, really, if maybe slightly more competitive than your typical major-leaguer during the playoffs, talking Assistant Coach Devin into playing a game of "burnout" for the enjoyment of the kids. Give them a taste of what it's like to *really* want to win.

Burnout's a simple game for simple adults and pre-adolescent boys: You throw a baseball as hard as you can starting from, say, sixty feet. You use regular gloves, no extrapadded catcher's mitts allowed, and you move a step closer after each round. First one to give up loses. Devin was no slouch as an athlete, having played baseball through college. He still had a pretty good gun of an arm. Nevertheless, he gave up, conceding defeat, after seven rounds, his opponent nearly knocking him down on his last throw from thirty-five feet. Malinoff had played shortstop in minor-league ball, made it to double-A. He could throw a baseball through a plywood fence.

Juhle caught the sixth toss not in the webbing but in the palm of the mitt. He never mentioned to a living soul and never would that on top of ruining his shoulder through his own stupidity on that cold and misty March day, he also allowed Malinoff's major-league fastball to break two bones in his *catching hand.*

Since then, Juhle had been having confidence issues. He found it hard to convince himself that he was among the most brilliant homicide inspectors on the planet when at the same time he considered himself a certified idiot for going at it with Malinoff.

It was Tuesday morning, May 31, nine fifteen. June, just a day away, is synonymous with fog in San Francisco, and today Juhle couldn't see the elevated free-way sixty yards to his left out the window. Awaiting the arrival of his partner, he was at his desk in the crowded, cramped, and yet wide-open room without interior walls that was the homicide detail on the fourth floor of San Francisco's Hall of Justice. He was sipping his third cup of coffee this morning, his right arm and still untreated opposite hand—damned if he was going to let anybody know—both throbbing in spite of six hundred milligrams of Motrin every four hours for the past ten days. He turned to the second page of the transcription of a witness's testimony in one of his cases that he was checking against the tape and suddenly took off his headphones, stood up, and made his way past the shoulder-high, battered green-and-gray metal files that served as room dividers, and stopped at the door of his lieutenant, Marcel Lanier, who looked up from his own paperwork.

"What's up, Dev?"

"We gotta do something about the quality of people they hire, Marcel."

Lanier, only fifty-some and yet still a hundred years with the department, scratched around his mouth. "That's a song I've been singing for years. What kind of people this time?"

For an answer, Juhle handed him the printout he'd been reading. "You'll see it," he said.

Five seconds into his reading, Lanier barked out a one-note toneless laugh, then read aloud. " 'And what is your relationship with Ms. Dorset?' "

Juhle nodded. "That's it. You don't see a relationship like that every day."

"He was her power mower?"

"Must have been, since it's right there in black and white."

"Her power mower?"

"Yeah, except maybe instead of *power mower,* what he actually said was that he was her 'paramour.' " Juhle leaned against the doorpost. "And this is, like, mistake ten on one page, Marcel, not counting the big chunks that she has marked 'unintelligible' on the transcript, but that *I* can hear perfectly on the tape.

Do they give an IQ test before we start paying these people? Of course, I've got to correct the transcript, anyway, but now it's going to take me two days instead of an hour. It'd be quicker to write the whole goddamn thing out in longhand."

Shiu floated up behind Juhle into the space left in the doorway. "What's going to take two days?"

Lanier ignored both the arrival and the question. His phone rang and he picked it up. "Homicide, Lanier." Frowning, suddenly all serious, he pulled over his yellow pad and started jotting. "Okay, got it. We're moving." Looking up at his two inspectors, he said into the phone, "Juhle and Shiu." When he hung up, there was no sign that he'd ever laughed or thought anything in the world had been funny ever. "Either of you already signed out on a car?"

The inspectors shared a glance. "No, sir. Paperwork day," Juhle said.

"Not anymore it isn't. Grab a ride in a black-and-white downstairs," he said, "and have 'em light it up out to Clay at"—he shot a quick look at his notes—"Lyon. Don't pass go, guys. I'll get word to the techs. I want a presence there yesterday. Somebody just killed a federal judge."

Available in January 2007 in Hardcover

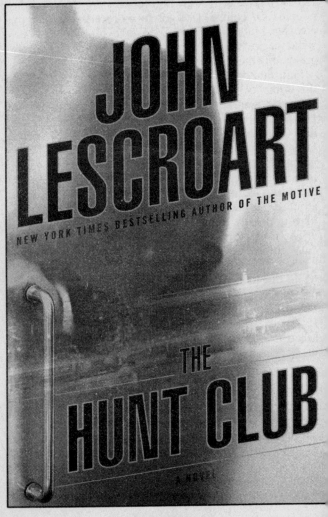

JOHN LESCROART

NEW YORK TIMES BESTSELLING AUTHOR OF THE MOTIVE

THE
HUNT CLUB

A NOVEL

DUTTON

New York Times bestseller
John Lescroart

Nothing but the Truth   0-451-20285-6

San Francisco attorney Dismas Hardy wants to know why his wife is willing to go to jail to protect another man. He's looking for the truth—but not quite sure he wants to find it...

The Hearing   0-451-20489-1

Hardy's best friend, Lieutenant Abe Glitsky, has been keeping a secret. Hardy never knew that Abe had a daughter—until she was shot dead. But there is more to this murder—much more. And as both Hardy and Glitsky risk their lives to uncover the truth, others are working hard to stop them.

Hard Evidence   0-451-20646-0

When the bullet-ridden body of a Silicon Valley billionaire washes up on shore, Hardy finds himself the prosecutor in San Francisco's murder trial of the century...

Available wherever books are sold or at penguin.com

B165

New York Times besteller
John Lescroart
The Oath
0-451-20764-5

When HMO executive Tim Markham is hit by a car during a morning jog through his exclusive San Francisco neighborhood, he has the bad luck to be transported to one of his own hospitals . . . and winds up dead in his ICU bed. But in spite of the rumors about his company's substandard care, this death appears to be a case of malice, not of malpractice—especially after Markham's entire family is gunned down in their home.

The First Law
0-451-21022-0

Stunned within the corridors of power while trying to defend a local bar owner, Lt. Abe Glitsky and Dismas Hardy must protect themselves as they step cautiously into a world where the only law is survival.

The Second Chair
0-451-21141-3

In this novel featuring Dismas Hardy, John Lescroart skillfully and subtly weaves together a story of a privileged youth on trial for murder, and an entire city on the brink of panic, taking this popular series to new heights of stylish suspense.

Available wherever books are sold or at penguin.com

Penguin Group (USA) Online

What will you be reading tomorrow?

Tom Clancy, Patricia Cornwell, W.E.B. Griffin,
Nora Roberts, William Gibson, Robin Cook,
Brian Jacques, Catherine Coulter, Stephen King,
Dean Koontz, Ken Follett, Clive Cussler,
Eric Jerome Dickey, John Sandford,
Terry McMillan, Sue Monk Kidd, Amy Tan,
John Berendt…

You'll find them all at
penguin.com

Read excerpts and newsletters,
find tour schedules and reading group guides,
and enter contests.

Subscribe to Penguin Group (USA) newsletters
and get an exclusive inside look
at exciting new titles and the authors you love
long before everyone else does.

PENGUIN GROUP (USA)
us.penguingroup.com